IVAN FRANKO

BORYSLAV IN FLAMES

UKRAINIAN BOOK INSTITUTE

This book has been published with the support
of the Translate Ukraine Translation Program

BORYSLAV IN FLAMES

by Ivan Franko

First published in Ukrainian as *Борислав сміється* in 1922

Translated from the Ukrainian by Yuri Tkacz

**This book has been published with the support
of the Translate Ukraine Translation Program**

Introduction © Marko Pavlyshyn, 2023

Proofreading by Stephen Dalziel

Cover image © Max Mendor, 2023

English translation © 2023, Glagoslav Publications

Book cover and interior book design by Max Mendor

© 2023, Glagoslav Publications

www.glagoslav.com

ISBN: 978-1-80484-110-5
ISBN: 978-1-80484-111-2

First published in English by Glagoslav Publications in November 2023

A catalogue record for this book is available from the British Library.

IVAN FRANKO

BORYSLAV IN FLAMES

TRANSLATED FROM THE UKRAINIAN BY YURI TKACZ

GLAGOSLAV PUBLICATIONS

IVAN FRANKO

(1856 – 1916)

CONTENTS

INTRODUCTION

In January 1881 the first issue of *Svit* (*The World*, but also *Light*), a journal of literature, politics and scholarship published in Lviv and dedicated to the propagation of socialist ideas, contained the first instalment of a novel about labour and capital. Its setting was the oil mining town of Boryslav, one of the few industrial sites of the province of Galicia in the Austro-Hungarian Empire. The novel, *Boryslav in Flames* as it is called in Yuri Tkacz's translation (its Ukrainian title was *Boryslav smiiet'sia – Boryslav is Laughing*), appeared serially in *Svit* until the journal ceased publication in September 1882; the novel was never completed. Its author, Ivan Franko (1856–1916), not 25 years of age when publication of the novel began, already had a substantial body of literary work to his name: a novel in the Gothic manner, short prose works on peasant life and its hardships, the realist early stories of his Boryslav cycle, and numerous as yet unpublished poems. Franko was also notorious as a political firebrand, the translator of a chapter of Marx's *Capital* and the author of numerous political essays with such titles as "Solidarity," "Workers and Employees" and "A Catechism of Economic Socialism." He had twice been arrested by the Austrian authorities for his political views and activities (two more arrests would follow later).

In the course of Franko's life material hardship proved no barrier to his prodigious industriousness in an extraordinarily broad array of fields: poetry, prose and drama; literary scholarship and criticism; philology and folklore studies;

translation and editorship; as well as party politics, political organisation and political journalism. His political convictions evolved with time. Always dedicated to the ideal of human liberation from injustice and oppression, Franko came to the conviction that the precondition for the achievement of an individual's social rights and political freedoms was the liberation from foreign dominion of the nation within whose compass alone those rights and freedoms could be secured. In the twentieth century Franko came to be viewed as one of the triad of Ukraine's pre-eminent cultural nation-builders, alongside the poet Taras Shevchenko (1814–1861) and the dramatist and poet Lesia Ukrainka (1871–1913).

In Franko's lifetime the territory inhabited by Ukrainians was divided between the Russian Empire, home to more than 80% of Ukrainians, and the empire of the Habsburgs, where more than 6 million Ukrainians lived, mainly in eastern Galicia and northern Bukovina. In the Russian Empire tsarist edicts of 1863 and 1876 placed onerous restrictions on Ukrainian-language publication and cultural activity. One of the consequences was that Lviv, the capital of Galicia, became the main cultural and intellectual centre for the whole of Ukraine, just as it was a significant hub of Polish and Jewish culture and politics.

Franko was born in the village of Nahuievychi, less than fifteen kilometres from Boryslav. His father was the village blacksmith, while his mother was one of the large number of persons in Galicia who were of aristocratic descent, but so impoverished that their material conditions differed little from those of peasants. Franko identified himself with society's lower estates, famously referring to himself as a "peasant's son." He attended school in the nearby city of Drohobych, the business centre for the Boryslav oilfields. As a child he was exposed to stories about the Boryslav mines: "I listened to those stories as if to fantastic tales of distant enchanted lands. Boryslav with its horrors and its wild anecdotes and wild leaps of fortune, its strange industries, strange way of life and strange people fuelled my imagination."[1] Franko had occasion to visit Boryslav during his school years and to observe the way of life of workers there. The experience was undoubtedly vivid in his memory as, during his university years in Lviv, he became active in the socialist movement and read works by such socialist thinkers as Ferdinand Lassalle and Friedrich Lange and his Ukrainian compatriots in the Russian Empire Mykhailo Drahomanov (1841–1895) and Serhii Podolyns'kyi (1850–1891).

The economy of Galicia was overwhelmingly agricultural. Peasants, emancipated from serfdom after the revolution of 1848, remained in a state of poverty so dire that many could not support their families by working their small tracts of land. From the 1880s onward, many emigrated. Boryslav was one of the few places in Galicia where peasants could augment their income by taking seasonal work in industry.

Oil mining commenced in Boryslav in the 1850s. The region also proved to have major deposits of ozokerite, or mineral wax. Prior to the advent of the internal combustion engine the refined end products were used mainly for lighting. As historian Yaroslav Hrytsak shows, an industrial boom ensued, in the course of which Boryslav's population exploded from 759 in 1850 to 12,439 in 1900. Workers came from the surrounding Ukrainian rural areas and nearby Jewish shtetls, but also from ethnically Polish western Galicia; there were also a small number of professionally experienced miners from the Czech lands and Prussia. About half of the workforce was Ukrainian, one quarter Polish and one quarter Jewish – an obstacle, as Hrytsak points out, to the evolu-

----

[1]   Ivan Franko, "U kuzni (iz moikh spomyniv)" [In the Blacksmith's Shop (From my Memoirs)], *Zibrannia tvoriv u piatdesiaty tomakh* [*Collected Works in Fifty Volumes*], Vol. 21 (Kyiv: Naukova dumka, 1979), p. 164.

tion of a sentiment of worker solidarity. As for the industrialists, in Boryslav they were mainly Jewish, in contrast to some other Galician oil-mining sites, where Polish capital prevailed. The Boryslav enterprises, of which there were some hundreds, were generally small until the 1890s, when laws imposing minimum safety standards and mandating the use of modern equipment put many out of business. By the early twentieth century the industry was dominated by large foreign firms.[2] In the 1880s Boryslav saw practically no labour unionisation and little worker unrest. It was not until the consolidation of the industry into larger enterprises and the increase in the permanent (as distinct from seasonal) workforce that significant worker activism led by Polish, Ukrainian and Jewish social democrats emerged, culminating in a major strike in 1904.[3]

Readers of *Boryslav in Flames* will readily notice that the social phenomena which Franko describes as prevailing at the time of his writing would come into being only two decades later. In 1879, writing to Ol'ha Roshkevych, he acknowledged the anticipatory quality of the book he was planning:

> This will be a novel somewhat larger in scope than my previous ones. Along with the life of Boryslav workers it will also show "new people" [proletarians with a developed class and ethical consciousness] at work – in other words, it will show not what is [at present] the case but, as it were, the full embodiment of what now exists only

....

[2] Yaroslav Hrytsak, *Ivan Franko and his Community*, trans. Marta Olynyk ([Edmonton]: Canadian Institute of Ukrainian Studies Press; [Cambridge, MA]: Harvard Ukrainian Research Institute; Brookline, MA: Academic Studies Press, 2018), pp. 246-49. Hrytsak's study, first published in Ukrainian in 2006, is to be recommended as an invaluable guide to Franko's life and the social and political context in which *Boryslav in Flames* was written and received.

[3] Hrytsak, p. 251.

embryonically. [...] The main idea is to show what in reality does not [yet] exist in the context of what *does* exist and in the colours of what exists.[4]

What is it, then, that does not yet exist, but is projected in the novel as desirable? It is the set of values espoused by the bricklayer and workers' organiser Benedio, the hero of one of the novel's two interwoven plot lines (the other concerns the family lives of two industrialists), as well as the organisational principles and resistance strategies that Benedio introduces. Benedio's objectives are fair pay for miners, scaled to take account of the difficulty and danger of different kinds of work, and decent working conditions: insurance for workers in the event of injury or disablement; financial support for the families of workers killed or incapacitated at the workplace; the establishment of a fund providing for the subsistence of workers during strikes; and respectful treatment of miners by their employers. At the same time Benedio strives, successfully, to establish a high degree of worker organisation, solidarity and discipline, resolute picketing against strike-breakers and a clear focus among miners on practical measures that bring advantage to all workers in the industry. What Benedio explicitly does *not* wish for, and what energises Andrus Basarab, another member of the workers' leadership group, is resistance in the form of revenge: violent action with no goal beyond punishing employers. It is clear that the "author" – the structuring intelligence responsible for the construction of the work and the arguments that it implies – sides with Benedio, however egregious the abuses committed by the employers and their lackeys might be, and however understandable the outrage and pain of Andrus and the great majority like him.

....

[4] Ivan Franko, letter to O. M. Roshkvych, c. 14 March 1879, *Zibrannia tvoriv*, Vol. 48 (1986), pp. 205-06.

To make these points, and to sharpen the focus on the conflict in the Boryslav oil industry as a class conflict, Franko represents the social and economic situation in his fictionalised Boryslav as somewhat simpler than the state of affairs in the real Boryslav of the early 1880s. In order to render plausible the rapid development of worker solidarity and the swift dissemination of information among them, the novel depicts workers as a culturally homogeneous group. No ethnic descriptors are applied to them, though their real-world counterparts belonged, as pointed out above, to several groups. Employers and overseers, on the other hand, are consistently identified as Jews and as members of a single ethno-cultural community. The confrontation between labour and capital is presented as a conflict, not between a multiethnic workforce and employers mainly of Jewish background, but between workers and Jews. The workers' adversaries – the "Jews" – are represented in almost wholly negative terms, whether drawn as a collective or revealed through detailed portraiture, as in the case of the two capitalists Hermann Goldkrämer and Leon Hammerschlag. Their motivations are never good; personal profit is their only value, deceit their chief method, compassion for workers non-existent. In instances where characters of Jewish ethnicity are not directly involved in exploitative economic activity, they are represented as deviant in other ways. Goldkrämer's wife Rifka suffers from what readers are guided to recognise as hysteria, which is explained as the result of this simple and uneducated working woman's transition into a life of leisure, luxury and boredom. The Goldkrämers' son Gottlieb, poorly endowed with intelligence but spoilt by his adoring mother, grows up lazy, talentless except when exercising emotional blackmail, verbally and physically violent, and obsessive in his fixation on objects of desire. The sole exception is Hammerschlag's daughter Fanny, an embodiment of the literary stereotype of the beautiful and virtuous Jewess who shines by contrast to her environment.

Boryslav in Flames thus appears to replicate without objection, indeed to share, the prejudicial view of Jews characteristic of much of European, and especially central and east European, society of its time. This is difficult to reconcile with Franko's quite different attitude to Jews attested in his life practice and some, though not all, of his other literary and journalistic works. He was involved in the endeavours of a socialist committee associated with the journal *Praca* (*Labour*) to establish a Ukrainian-Polish-Jewish political party for workers and peasants, and his fluency in Yiddish qualified him to interact with the party's potential Jewish constituency. In the aftermath of pogroms in the Russian Empire in 1881 he wrote a cycle of poems, "Ievreis'ki melodii" (Jewish Melodies), based on Jewish folklore that he had recorded, expressing sympathy with the victims. Jewish characters are represented with warmth in such novellas as "Poluika" (The Barrel, 1899) and "Gava" (Crow, 1888). Philosemitic and antisemitic elements stand side by side in Franko's work. As Hrytsak puts it,

> Franko's socialist views led him to defend the weak and the downtrodden, and where the Jewish community was concerned, his sympathies lay with poor Jews who were exploited by wealthy Jews. But the need to defend the poor non-Jewish population forced him into a confrontation with the entire Jewish community which, in his view, demonstrated a high level of internal solidarity on the question of the exploitation of Ukrainian and Polish workers and peasants.[5]

Franko's depiction of miners gaining the upper hand in their struggle against capital is one factor that distances the content of *Boryslav in Flames* from the reality of the 1880s attested by historical sources. Other features of the novel that

....

[5] Hrytsak, pp 312-20; quotation p. 320.

stretch plausibility are the heavy reliance of its plot on coincidence, the impossibly short timeframes in which complex transformations of collective habits of thought and practice are supposed to take place, and the hyperbole that accompanies the description of the behaviour of characters intended to be perceived as eccentric or disturbed.

Imperfect correlation with what is generally perceived as "reality," however, by no means disqualifies a work from being classified as "Realist," as *Boryslav in Flames* generally has been in Ukrainian literary history. Realism is the conventional designation of a period and a style in the literature and other arts; features generally shared by works regarded as Realist which are readily found in *Boryslav in Flames* include attentive description of social relations, emphasis on the underlying (genetic or environmental) causes of human behaviours, nuanced description of psychological states, and a critical authorial stance toward prevailing forms of human oppression. The erudite Franko was familiar with the contemporary Realist canon, including Balzac, Flaubert, Dickens, Eliza Orzeszkowa and Ivan Turgenev. He was alert to the Positivist thought of Auguste Comte and the idea that society was subject to general laws and knowable through science as the physical world is knowable. He held in high esteem the work of Émile Zola and Zola's advocacy of a literature scientistic and objective in its analysis of the laws that determine human behaviour. He did not, however, find satisfaction in the cool detachment of what Zola termed "Naturalism," proposing in his essay "Literature, its Tasks and its Most Important Features" (1878) a literature that would not merely offer an accurate image of society, but seek to change society for the better. This would be a literature of "scientific realism":

> Like contemporary science, literature must labour on the field of human progress. Its tendency and method must be scientific. It collects and describes the facts of everyday life, caring only for truth, not for aesthetic rules, and

at the same time it analyses these facts and draws conclusions from them. *That is its scientific realism.* By these means it shows forth the flaws in the social order where science may not always be capable of penetrating (in everyday life, in the psychological development of drives and human passions), and strives to ignite in its readers the will and the power to combat such flaws. That is its *progressive tendency* (emphases in the original).[6]

Objective description, analysis, the drawing of conclusions and the correction of social faults: such were the tasks that Franko in his essay set for modern literature, and such, evidently, were the goals that he set himself when writing *Boryslav in Flames*. His success in achieving them, as the preceding discussion has sought to show, was mixed.

How should readers in the third decade of the twenty-first century assess this unfinished, from our contemporary perspective ideologically awkward, late nineteenth-century novel? One way of valuing it is to see it as a document of an historical period. The novel is a vehicle for understanding, not so much Boryslav and the intersection of social, cultural, economic and political forces that it embodied – the novel is too partisan and too one-sided in its vision for that – but one contemporary perspective upon that reality. It is a perspective energised by a powerful drive to defend justice and humanity, yet limited by its own ethical blind spots. It is also possible to apprehend *Boryslav in Flames* as an important document of one station along the complex creative path of a remarkable and gifted individual. Franko was one of the giant intellectual figures of Europe at the end of the nineteenth and the beginning of the twentieth centuries, unjustly invisible to much of the world because the country and the culture from which

....

[6] Franko, "Literatura, ii zavdannia i naivazhnishi tsikhy," *Zibrannia tvoriv*, Vol. 26 (1980), p. 13.

he came and which he did much to shape were themselves scarcely visible to the world, occluded by the shadows of two imperialisms. Finally, however, it is possible to appreciate *Boryslav in Flames* as the literary scholar Tamara Hundorova has done: "The veracity and vividness with which characters familiar from earlier works of the Boryslav cycle are depicted, the picturesqueness of descriptions and the plasticity of mass scenes, the attention paid to the inner world of individuals, the introduction of the parallel plot line from the life of the Galician bourgeoisie [...] secure the intrinsic worth of this literary text."[7] We value *Boryslav in Flames* not for what it documents, but for what, when all is said and done, it is: a story well told.

Marko Pavlyshyn

7   Tamara Hundorova, *Franko ne kameniar / Franko i kameniar* [*Franko: Not a Stonecutter / Franko: Also a Stonecutter*] (Kyiv: Krytyka, 2006), p. 63.

BORYSLAV IN FLAMES

I

The sun indicated that it was nearing midday. The town hall clock struck eleven hastily and dolefully. A building supervisor left the small group of cheerful, well-dressed gentlemen from Drohobych who were strolling along the alleys near the Catholic church in the shade of blossoming horse chestnut trees. Waving his polished cane about, he crossed the street to join the workers at a new construction site.

"Well, Master Mason," he called out, "are you ready?"

"Everything is ready, sir."

"Well, time to sound the end of the workday then!"

"Yessir!" replied the Master Mason and, turning to his assistant, who was standing by his side and putting the finishing touches to a huge foundation stone cut from sandstone in nearby Popeli, said: "Come there, Benedio, you dimwit! Didn't you hear the building supervisor say we need to sound the end of the workday? Shake a leg there!"

Benedio Synytsia set aside his masonry hammer and hastened to fulfill the Master Mason's order. Dodging among the scattered rocks littering the ground, he sprinted as fast as his thin, wiry legs would carry him, panting and turning blue from the effort. He made his way to a tall fence, where a board hung suspended by two ropes. Alongside it, hanging from similar ropes, were two wooden mallets used to strike the board, a device employed to signal the start or end of work. Running up to the fence, Benedio grabbed the mallets with both hands and began pounding them against the board with all his might.

Clatter! Clatter! Clatter! The joyous, loud barking of the 'wooden bitch' sounded across the building site. This was how the masons had dubbed the device.

Clatter! Clatter! Clatter! Benedio thundered incessantly, smiling at the board he was torturing so mercilessly. And all the masons who were busy working on the large site, some carving stones for the foundations and some slaking lime inside two deep containers, all the men who were digging trenches for the foundations, the carpenters behind them who were chipping away like woodpeckers at the hefty fir logs and oak beams, the sawyers who were cutting planks with hand saws, the bricklayers who were stacking the newly-delivered bricks – all these workmen who were scurrying about like ants on a parade ground, moving things, chipping away, staggering, moaning, rubbing hands, joking and laughing – everyone stopped working like a huge, hundred-armed machine, whose frantic movements were terminated by pressing a single button.

Clatter! Clatter! Clatter! Benedio refused to stop, although everyone had long since heard the barking of the 'wooden bitch.' The masons, had been hunched over the boulders, clanging loudly against the hard sandstone surface, causing sparks to fly from time to time from under their masonry hammers. Now, having dropped their instruments, they straightened their backs and spread their arms wide to fill their lungs to capacity with air. Some, who preferred to kneel while working, slowly rose to their feet. Lime hissed and gurgled in the lime-pit, as if it were furious that it had been earlier thrown into the fire and was now tossed back into the water. The sawyers left their saw suspended in the timber beam; it hung there, its upper handle resting against the beam, while the wind played with the free end. The diggers pressed their spades into the soft clay, and jumped out of the deep trenches being readied for the foundations. Meanwhile, Benedio had stopped his clattering, and all the workmen, covered in crumbs of brick and clay, with wood shavings and stone chips on their clothes, hands and faces, began to assemble at the front corner of the new building, where the Master Mason and the building supervisor were standing.

"And how, if you please sir, should we lower this stone into place?" the Master Mason asked the building supervisor, resting his coarse strong hand on the hewn foundation stone, which, although it lay flat on small wooden rollers, almost reached up to the Master Mason's waist.

"How should we lower it?" repeated the building supervisor in a drawl, as he cast a glance at the stone through his monocle. "Well, on sticks, of course."

"Won't that be a little too dangerous, if you please, sir?" added the Master Mason.

"Dangerous? Who for?"

"Well, obviously, not for the stone, but for the people," the Master Mason replied with a smile.

"A-hah! Come on! Dangerous! Don't be afraid, nothing will happen to anyone! We'll lower it into place!"

And the building supervisor wrinkled his forehead gravely and pursed his lips tightly together, as if he himself was already straining and lowering the foundation stone into its appointed place.

"We'll lower it safely!" he repeated once more, this time with utter certainty, as if he was convinced that his strength alone would be enough for the undertaking. The Master Mason shook his head in disbelief, but said nothing.

Meanwhile, the people who had been strolling in small groups along the 'alleys' around the Catholic church, began to slowly drift toward the construction site. Leading the way was the owner of the new building, Leon Hammerschlag, a tall and stately man with a round-trimmed beard, a straight nose and lips like red raspberries. He was very cheerful on this day, talkative and witty, sharing jokes with those around him and, apparently, entertained everyone following him, for they all gathered and huddled around him. Nearby, in another throng, was Hermann Goldkrämer, the most respectable (in other words, the wealthiest) of the town's inhabitants. He was more reserved, quiet, and even somewhat unhappy, although he tried hard not to show it. Then came the other businessmen, rich people from Drohobych and Boryslav, some government officials and one outlying landowner, a great friend of Hammerschlag, possibly because his entire estate was in Hammerschlag's pocket.

All these men dressed in fashionable black frock coats, in overcoats made of expensive fabric, in shiny black top hats, wearing gloves, with canes in their hands and rings on their fingers. They were in stark contrast to the grey mass of workers, whose adornments included sprays of red brick dust or white streaks of lime. The cheerful chatter of both groups seemed to bring them closer together.

The whole parade ground at the corner of Panska and Zelena streets was filled with people, wood, stones, bricks, wooden cladding and piles of clay, and resembled a large ruin. Only the wooden shed standing in the remains of the orchard, looked lively and alluring. It was decorated with green spruce at the entrance and hung with carpets inside. Servants were rushing about inside and around it, shouts and curses filled the air... They were preparing food to celebrate the laying of the foundation stone for Hammerschlag's new home. And another unusual guest looked on with great surprise at this crowd of assembled people and objects. It was a tiny individual, and everyone observed it with curiosity and wonder.

"Benedio," asked a worker smeared with clay, "why have they hung that goldfinch there?"

"They must be thinking of doing something with it," Benedio replied.

All the workers whispered among themselves and looked at the goldfinch flitting about in the wire cage hung on a long shaft above the trench, but no one knew what it was for.

Even the Master Mason had no idea, although he pretended to be in the know and answered the workers' questions with the words:

"Oh, you'd like to know everything, wouldn't you! Thou shalt grow old when thou knowest all things!"

Having recovered from its initial fright due to the sudden influx of the crowd of people, the goldfinch was hopping about on the perches of its cage, picking at hemp seeds with its beak. Occasionally, standing on the top perch, it fluttered its red and yellow wings and chirped thinly: "Ti-kili-tlin! Chirrup, chirrup! Kool-kool-kool!"

Leon Hammerschlag's head appeared above the murmuring crowd. He jumped onto the foundation stone and loudly addressed those present:

"Ladies and gentlemen, neighbours and benefactors!"

"Quiet! Quiet! Shoosh!" a voice rang out and the crowd grew quiet.

Leon continued:

"Thank you very, very much for being so kind as to honour me with your presence on this occasion, which is so important for me today…"

"Oh, the pleasure is all ours!" several voices, both coarse and high-pitched, responded.

"Ah, here come our ladies! Gentlemen, first, let's congratulate the ladies!" And Hammerschlag disappeared again into the crowd, while several of the younger gentlemen went out to the street where several carriages with ladies had just arrived. The gentlemen helped them out of the carriages and escorted them to the square, where a place had been prepared for them beside the huge block of stone.

The ladies were, for the most part, old and unattractive Jewish women who tried to hide their lack of youth and beauty with a lavish and ostentatious display of wealth. Silks, satins, sparkling jewels and gold shone on them. They constantly checked their dresses, taking care not to bring them in contact with the chips of red brick and stone, or the equally dirty workers. Only Fanny, Hammerschlag's daughter, stood out among the ladies precisely because of what the others lacked – youth and beauty. In their midst she appeared like a blooming peony alongside withered thistles. The younger men from among those assembled, flocked around her, and a lively, vocal conversation soon ensued among them, while the other ladies, after their initial customary exclamations of astonishment and shrill, rehearsed good wishes to the property owner, became somewhat reticent and began looking around, as if waiting for some performance to begin. Their anticipation quickly spread to the others. The cheerful chatter died away. It was evident that with the arrival of the ladies, an air of boredom and forced restraint had descended upon those gathered, which seemed of no benefit to anyone.

Hammerschlag was flustered. He seemed to have forgotten that he had started a speech a moment earlier and wandered about, initiating conversations about unrelated topics with various people, but nothing seemed to flow well. Suddenly, he found himself in front of Hermann, who stood silently, leaning against a pile of wood and surveying the building site, as if he were considering buying it.

"And why is your wife not present, dear neighbour?" Leon said, smiling.

"Forgive me," Hermann replied, "she must be feeling unwell."

"Ah, I'm sorry to hear that! And I had hoped…"

"It's alright," Hermann tried to appease him, "she's no bigwig! I'm sure we can do without her!"

"No, my dear neighbour! Please don't say such things… How can you? My Fanny, poor child, how happy she would be if she were to have such a mother!"

The insincerity of these words was evident in Leon's face and eyes, but his mouth, obeying his determined will, spoke them, and his mind tried to justify them, as required by self-interest.

Suddenly, from the direction of the meadow where a tall whitewashed synagogue was visible, there came a loud exclamation and commotion. All the guests and workers turned their eyes in that direction. After a short while, what appeared to be a black storm cloud appeared in the street – it was a Jewish qahal surrounding the rabbi, who would be performing the consecration of the foundations to the new house.

Soon, the entire square was flooded with Jews, who, as was their custom, spoke all at once, loudly and quickly, moving around like ants in a disturbed anthill, examining everything and appraising everything with their eyes. They sighed and shook their heads, as if marvelling at Leon's wealth and regretting that it was not in their hands. The few Christian gentlemen who were present fell silent and moved to one side, feeling out of place here. The local squire frowned and bit his lip in anger, finding himself amid a crowd which paid him no respect. Surely, deep inside, he was cursing his 'dear friend Leon' vehemently, but he did not leave, choosing to stay until the end of the ceremony, after which refreshments were to be served.

The general clamour in the square not only persisted, but grew louder. The goldfinch, startled by the sudden influx of this noisy crowd dressed in black, began to flutter in its cage and crash into the wires. Two attendants led the rabbi, an old grey-haired man with a long beard, by the arms and brought him right up to the foundation stone. A tight circle of people pressed around him, as if everyone wanted to be beside the rabbi, even though there was hardly enough room for everyone. Because of the shouts of the crowd, and the pushing and shoving, it was impossible to hear what the rabbi was reciting over the foundation stone. But whenever the attendants responded to his prayers with a shout of 'umayn,' meaning 'amen,' the rest of the crowd repeated 'umayn' after them.

In the bell tower next to the church, right opposite the building site, a huge bell began to toll, signalling noon. Following this, all the other bells in Drohobych's churches joined in. It seemed as if the air above Drohobych was moaning with sorrowful voices, among which the chaotic, many-voiced 'umayn' sounded even more mournful and sad. Upon hearing the bells, the workers removed their hats and began to make the sign of the cross. One of the attendants approached Leon and bowing before him, began to whisper:

"May God bless you and the work you have begun here. We have finished." Then, leaning even closer to Leon, he said more softly: "You see, the Lord God has sent you a sign that everything will augur well for you, whatever you intend to do."

"A good sign? What do you mean?" Leon asked.

"Can't you hear that the Christian bells are doing you a good service and invoking the blessing of the Christian God? It means that all Christians will willingly serve you. They will help you achieve whatever you set out to do. These bells are a good omen!"

Had Leon heard such words from someone else, he probably would have laughed in their face. He liked to present himself as a freethinker in front of others, but deep down, like all ignorant and self-centred people, he was superstitious. So now, knowing that no one had overheard the attendant's conversation, he gladly accepted the good omen and placed a tenner into the attendant's outstretched hand.

"This is for you and the synagogue," Leon whispered, "and may the Lord be praised for the good sign!"

Delighted, the attendant resumed his place beside the rabbi, and immediately began to whisper to the other attendant, who was apparently asking how much Leon had given them.

Meanwhile, the building supervisor began to direct the workers.

"Alright, lads, grab your poles!" he shouted. "Benedio, you hopeless dimwit, where's your pole?"

The commotion in the square grew even louder. The rabbi was led aside, the Jews made way for the workers who were about to move the huge foundation stone and lower it into its designated place in the deep trench. The ladies pressed forward curiously, panting. They were keen to see how the enormous rock would be moved. The goldfinch continued to chirp merrily in its cage and with its broad blinding face the sun smiled down from the deep-blue cloudless sky.

The building supervisor's orders were quickly carried out. Across the small path, where the foundation stone needed to be moved, four logs were placed, each as thick as the ones the stone was currently resting on. Two similar logs were placed across the trench where the stone was to be lowered. Workers surrounded the foundation stone with their poles in hand, to start it moving and break its obstinate stillness. Some joked and laughed, calling the foundation stone a 'grey cow' that so many people were trying to herd into a barn.

"Move along, giddy up!" one fellow teased, nudging the stone along.

But then the building supervisor's command sounded, and everyone went quiet. In the crowded square, the only sounds that could be heard were the breathing of the people and the chirping of the goldfinch in its cage.

"Alright, let's go! One, two, three!" the building supervisor shouted. And ten wooden poles, like ten huge fingers, lifted the stone from both sides, and it slowly rolled along the tracks, crunching loudly on the gravel underneath.

"Hurrah! Hey! Keep pushing it, so that it doesn't stop moving!" the workers shouted cheerfully.

"Keep it moving!" the building supervisor called out at the top of his voice.

The workers strained again. The gravel crunched once more, the rollers creaked under the weight of the foundation stone and, like a huge tortoise, it crawled slowly forward. There was joy on the faces of the assembled guests, the ladies were smiling, and Leon whispered to one of his 'neighbours':

"Just you look at that! Say what you will, but man is indeed the true master of nature! There is no force he cannot overcome. Here is this mighty stone, this heavy burden, and it moves at his behest."

"Exactly," added the 'neighbour,' "the power there is in a community of people! United effort works wonders! Would one person ever be able to achieve something like this?"

"Yes, yes, united effort, that's quite a powerful phrase!" Leon replied.

"Hurrah, altogether now! Come on!" cheered the workers. The stone was already above the trench, resting on two crossbeams, which under its weight became deeply embedded in the ground on both sides of the trench. But now came the most challenging part – to lower the stone properly into the trench.

"Come on, lads, move a leg there!" commanded the building supervisor. The workers scattered in an instant to both sides of the trench and placed five pairs of thick poles under the stone.

"Right under its ribs we go! Let's make its heart jump," the workers joked.

"Now lift it! And as soon as the crossbeams are moved to one side, when I shout: 'Now!', all of you are to pull out your poles together and scramble away from the trench! Understood?"

"Understood!"

"But all at once! Anyone who is late will be in trouble!"

"Alright, alright!" shouted the workers and pressed down on the poles to raise the foundation stone. Slowly, almost reluctantly, it detached itself from the crossbeams on which it lay, and rose a few inches. All hearts involuntarily trembled. The workers, red with exertion, held the stone on the poles above the trench, waiting for the crossbeams to be removed and the building supervisor to give the signal to remove the poles from under the stone.

"Now!" barked the building supervisor amid the prevailing silence, and nine of the workers, together with their poles, scattered in opposite directions. And the tenth? Along with the muffled thud of the foundation stone dropping into its designated position, the assembled crowd heard a dull, piercing moan.

"What was that? What's happened?" people began to murmur. Everyone began pushing closer to the trench, trying to see what had happened.

A simple thing had occurred. Nine workers had simultaneously pulled their poles out from under the stone, but the tenth, a mason's assistant named Benedio Synytsia, had been a split second too late and that moment could have cost him his life. With all its weight the stone had jerked the pole out of his hands. It struck Benedio across his body and luckily had missed his head. Benedio let out a moan and fell lifelessly to the ground.

The sand splashed upward in a cloud where his pole had fallen. The workers rushed up to Benedio in mortal alarm.

"What's wrong? What's happened?" the guests clamoured. "What's going on?"

"One of the poles has struck a worker."

"Is he dead? Oh, my God!" the ladies began to murmur.

"No, he's alive!" one of the workers called out.

"He's alive! Ah!" Leon exhaled, for his heart had clenched after he heard Benedio's cry.

"Is he badly injured?"

"No, not really!" boomed the building supervisor's voice, whose knees had begun to tremble for no apparent reason.

The crowd murmured and pressed around the injured man. The ladies gasped and squealed, their mouths becoming contorted, as they demonstrated their sensitivity and soft-heartedness. Leon felt a vague buzzing in his head, and was unable to string his words together. Even the goldfinch in its cage chirruped mournfully and fluttered into the corners, as if it too couldn't bear to witness human suffering. Benedio still lay in the same place, pale as chalk, unconscious, with clenched teeth. The pole had knocked the wind out of him, catching him on the side with its sharp edge, and tearing through his shirt and skin. It had gouged a wound from which blood was now flowing.

"Water! Water!" the workers shouted, as they tried to revive Benedio and bandage his wound. Water was brought, the wound was bandaged, and the bleeding was stopped, but they were having a hard time to revive him. The blow had been very strong and in a dangerous place. A cloud of uncertainty once again settled over the assembled crowd.

"Take him out there into the street!" Leon eventually called out. "Or better still, take him home and summon a doctor!"

"Lively, there!" the building supervisor urged them on.

While two workers grabbed Benedio by the hands and feet and carried him through the crowd to the street, the Master Mason approached the building supervisor from behind and tapped him on the shoulder. The building supervisor gave a start and turned sharply, as if he had been stung by nettles.

"See there, sir, I was right…"

"What are you talking about? What did you say?"

"I told you," the Master Mason whispered calmly, "not to lower the foundation stone with poles, because it's too dangerous."

"Eh, you fool! It's only because that idiot was probably drunk and didn't jump back in time, it's his own fault!" the building supervisor responded angrily and turned away. The Master Mason shrugged his shoulders and grew silent. But the building supervisor felt a sharp pain deep inside and was fairly seething with anger.

Meanwhile, it was time to conclude the foundation stone laying ceremony. The attendants led the rabbi to a small yet sturdy ladder, and he climbed down to the bottom of the trench, where the foundation stone lay in its required position. A deep rectangular hole had been carved into the upper surface of the stone, and around it were fresh splotches of blood from Benedio's wound. The rabbi muttered another prayer, and then threw a small silver coin into the carved hole in the stone. The rabbi's attendants did the same, and then the other guests began to climb down into the trench and toss coins, some larger and some smaller, onto the foundation stone. The ladies shrieked and swayed on the steps, supported by the men, except for Leon's daughter Fanny, who proudly and boldly descended into the trench and threw in a ducat. After this, the other ladies and gentlemen began to climb down into the trench one by one. A descendant of Polish nobility who was right behind Hermann, shot a sideways glance at the wealthy capitalist when he threw a shiny golden ducat with a clink onto the stone. The nobleman only had a silver rinsky[1] in his pocket, and so as not to lose face, he swiftly unclipped one of his gold cufflinks and tossed it into the hole.

The line of guests stretched for quite some time, the gold and silver coins clinked for a long while, filling the depression in the stone with a lustrous wave. Waiting for the Master Mason's instructions, the workers stood beside the trench and looked on enviously at the whole ceremony. Finally, the last coin was tossed in, leaving the depression almost full. Leon, who was standing by the steps and amicably shaking the hands of everyone coming out of the trench (he even exchanged kisses with Hermann and the old nobleman out of sheer joy), now stepped forward and ordered that the slab and the cement be brought to seal the foundation stone. The

[1] A Rhenish gulden, a monetary unit in circulation in Galicia and in the part of Poland, which after the division of the Polish-Lithuanian Commonwealth in 1772 went to Austria; the name derives from the Rhine River. A rinsky equalled 100 Austrian cents (kreutzers).

workers rushed to fulfill his orders, while he came up to the cage with the goldfinch.

"Tweet-tweet! Chirrup, chirrup! Kool-kool-kool!" chirped the bird, suspecting nothing, as Leon approached. Its delicate, clear song resonated in the still air like glass. Everyone fell silent, curiously watching the conclusion of this solemn foundation laying ceremony. Leon took the cage with the bird from the post, held it aloft, and said:

"My fellow neighbours, my dear guests! This is a big day for me, a very big day. A man who wandered for forty years through desolate deserts and sailed turbulent seas, has today for the first time spied the calm of a peaceful harbour. Here, in the happy town of Drohobych, I have decided to weave a nest for myself, which will become a part of the beauty and glory of this city…"

"Bravo, bravo!" the guests shouted, interrupting his speech.

Leon bowed, smiling, and continued:

"Our parents taught us that if you want to start a venture fortuitously, if you want to complete it fortuitously, and if you want to enjoy its fruits fortuitously, you must first bring together the spirits of a place. Do you believe in spirits, ladies and gentlemen? Maybe there are those among you who don't. I must confess, I believe in them. Strong, mysterious spirits dwell here in this soil, in these blocks of stone, in this sizzling lime, in these human hands and heads. Only with their help will my house become my stronghold. They will bring good fortune and defend it. And to unite these spirits, we are making a sacrifice here today, a sacrifice in blood, which is the aim of today's solemn ceremony. So that wealth and prosperity – not only for me, but for the whole city – blossom in this house, you threw a golden seed into the furrow in the stone with your kind hands. So that health, joy and beauty – not only for me, but for the whole city – may dwell in this house, I sacrifice to the spirits of this place a lively, healthy, cheerful and beautiful songbird!"

With these words Leon thrust his hand into the cage. "Pee-pee-pee!" the small bird squeaked, fluttering about and hiding in the corners, but Leon deftly caught it and brought it out of the cage. The goldfinch fell silent in his hand, looking about with frightened eyes. Its red-feathered chest looked like a large bloodstain in Leon's hand. Leon took out a red silk thread and tied the goldfinch's wings and legs with it, and then went down the steps into the trench. Everyone was silent. The workers brought in a large slab of stone and placed cement around the edges of the hole in the foundation stone, so that it could be sealed straight away. After whispering a few more words, Leon took off the golden ring from his finger and threw it among the other treasures in the depression, placing the goldfinch on top. The bird lay calmly on its cold death bed of gold and silver, and only its small head was turned upward, toward the sky, toward its bright, spacious abode. And then a large cold slab covered the living creature from above, this living burial affirming the future happiness of the house of Hammerschlag…

At that moment Leon looked to one side and saw traces of another sacrifice on the foundation stone – human blood, the blood of the mason's assistant, Benedio. The blood, already congealed on the stone, shook him to the core. He saw that perhaps the 'local spirits' were making fun of his words and were accepting a sacrifice that was not at all as innocent as his own. It appeared to him that this second, terrible, human sacrifice would hardly benefit him. The drops of blood adhering to the stone in the dark trench looked like the black heads of iron nails, which were drilling into the foundations of his magnificent building, making holes in it and eating away at it. He suddenly felt cold and confined in the trench, and scrambled out as fast as he could.

Guests pressed around him, wishing him well. Hermann shook his hand and announced loudly for all to hear:

"May that small treasure, sown with friendly hands in the foundation stone of your house, grow and multiply a thousand times. May it become the foundation stone of the glory and wealth of your line!"

"Just as your house is now founded on a foundation of solid stone and gold," another nobleman added loudly from the other side, "may the happiness and prosperity of your family now be based on sincere friendship and the goodwill of all people!"

Leon eagerly shook the hands of his guests, cheerfully thanked them for their friendship and service, promised to work in the future only with the people and for the people – and yet his heart was filled with a cold twilight, through which he could see large black menacing drops of blood, like living iron nails, piercing and hollowing out the foundations of his happiness. He sensed a certain coldness in the words of his guests, for it was obvious that envy lurked deep in their hearts.

Meanwhile, under the guidance of the building supervisor, the workers began to lay bricks on all sides of the foundation stone and quickly raised a wall inside the trench. The clocktower struck one o'clock.

"Well, that's enough work for now, good people!" Leon called out. "You need to enjoy yourselves as well. There are not too many days like this in my life, so let it be a festive day for you as well. They'll bring you beer and snacks presently, and you, Master Mason, please keep order among the workers!"

"Thank you, sir!"

"And I ask you, my dear guests, to follow me. Fanny, my child, be a darling and look after the ladies! Come, please!"

Chatting merrily, the guests walked among the piles of bricks, stones and timber to a wooden hut decorated with wreaths and colorful bunting, for refreshments. Only the rabbi and his attendants, together with a few other Hasidim left, not wishing to sit at the same table with those eating non-kosher food.

While the gentlefolk were enjoying themselves in the wooden hut, the workers sat in a wide circle in the open air on the rocks. Two assistants poured beer, another two distributed slices of bread and dried fish. However, the workers were somehow very taciturn. The incident with Benedio had affected everyone deeply, and they didn't approve of the strange Jewish rite behind the laying of the foundation stone. Why brick in a live bird? As if this would bring happiness? But who knows, maybe that was the case... After all, someone had invented the saying: 'For gentlemen to wine and dine, chickens must die.'

The workers who had taken Benedio home, finally returned and began to recount how Benedio's old mother was frightened and wept profusely, seeing her only son passed out and covered in blood. At first, the poor woman thought that he had died, but when they managed to bring him around, she was comforted like a child, rushing up to him and kissing him tearfully, sobbing uncontrollably.

"You know what, lads," said the Master Mason, "we should do something to help the poor fellow, because if he's poorly and unable to work, then I don't know how the two of them will manage. After all, the old woman won't be able to feed them both!"

"That's true, so true!" shouted the workers from all sides. "After we are paid, we can donate five kreutzers[2] each. It's nothing for us, but a great help for them."

"And what about the building supervisor," said one of the masons, "won't he be donating anything? After all, this whole misfortune occurred because of him!"

"Just as well it finished at that," said another. "The foundation stone could have just as easily crushed the lot of us!"

....

[2] A kreutzer was an Austrian cent.

"He has to be told that he too needs to chip in to help the poor injured fellow."

"But I'll leave it to you to tell him," said the Master Mason. "I refuse to."

"Alright, then, all of us will tell him!" the men said in unison.

At that moment the building supervisor emerged from the hut to look in on the workers. His face was flushed a deep red from the wine he had consumed, and his glistening cane flew very deftly from one hand to the other.

"How are things, my children!" he exclaimed as he approached the men.

"All's well, sir," replied the Master Mason.

"Well, make sure it stays that way!" he retorted and turned to go back inside.

"We would like to make a request of you, sir," said a voice from among the workers. The building supervisor turned around:

"Of me?"

"Yes," everyone buzzed.

"Well, what is it?"

"That you, sir, would be so kind as to join us in helping out the assistant who was injured today."

The building supervisor stood there without saying a word, his face turning a deeper shade of crimson, a sign that the request of the workers had upset him terribly.

"Me?" he said finally. "And why come to me with such a request? Was it my fault or what?"

"Well, sir, we are not to blame either, but it seems to us that it is appropriate to help the poor fellow. He is weak, he won't be able to work for some time, and he and his old mother need something to survive on."

"If you like, go ahead and help him, but it's nothing to do with me! Why do I need to help some useless ragamuffin! Really!" The building supervisor turned away angrily and began to walk back, but then one of the workers, outraged by the conversation, said loudly:

"Eh, just look at this 'gentleman,' will you! He's the one most to blame for Benedio being injured! If it had been him who was struck down, I surely would have spared even ten kreutzers, not just five, to help the wretch!"

"What?" the building supervisor suddenly roared with all his might and rushed up to the seated workers. "Who said that?"

There was silence.

"Who dared say that? Hah?"

No one made a sound.

"Master Mason, you were sitting here: who said that? Speak up, or I'll fire you instead of that good-for-nothing!"

The Master Mason surveyed the workers and said calmly: "I don't know."

"Don't you just? Then I don't know you either. Off you go!"

"It was me who spoke," said one of the workers, getting up. "I said, and I'll say it again, that you're an utter wretch if you don't want to donate toward that poor worker. And you can shove your work…!"

The building supervisor was livid, he was so enraged that he couldn't utter a single word. Meanwhile, the worker picked up his mason's square, trowel and measure and, bidding his comrades farewell, calmly made his way toward the market-place. The other workers were silent.

"Ah, you rascals and slackers!" boomed the building supervisor. "He's a useless worker! All he does is lie about on his stomach like a dead pig in the mud. Just wait, I'll teach you all some order! I'll show you how to work! You useless good-for-nothings!" And, still shaking with anger and cursing all the rabble in this world, the building supervisor returned to join the gentlefolk.

In the meantime, everyone was enjoying themselves in the hut. After refreshments, the servants collected the empty bowls and plates, and in their place set out glasses and bottles of wine. The glasses were quickly filled and the wine untangled people's tongues, giving rise to gaiety and clamour. Fragrant smoke from expensive cigars wafted toward the wooden ceiling, drifting outside in a thin wisp through an open window. Leon's servants circulated among the guests, serving them whatever they desired. Some of the guests sat in groups, while others stood or walked about, chatting, joking or engaged in business dealings.

Leon did not leave Hermann's side. Today, for the first time, he had come to know this great Boryslav tycoon and felt a strange affinity toward him. Until now, they had regarded each other as adversaries. Leon had arrived in Boryslav two years earlier, already with considerable capital. He was more educated than Hermann, was well-versed in commerce, and had read books on mining, and thought that it was enough for him to simply appear in Boryslav, and things would fall at his feet. He would become an absolute nobleman. He had plans to buy up extensive and very suitable tracts of land for mining, to acquire machines for faster and cheaper extraction of the earth's treasures, to improve the prestige of the entire oil industry, be able to raise and lower market prices at will. But things turned out to be completely different.

Boryslav already had its established powers, and Leon found it challenging to compete with them, with Hermann being the most formidable figure among them. Leon had initially been infuriated by the apparent reluctance of the old Boryslav businessmen to accept him, particularly Hermann, whom he regarded as a simple, uneducated peasant. Leon had attempted various strategies to retaliate, never missing an opportunity to demonstrate his superiority over Hermann. Despite Hermann's indifference to Leon's provocations, he made it difficult for him to conduct business, intercepting shares that Leon wanted to buy, luring across his best workers, all the time pretending that he knew nothing about such matters. This was too much for Leon, who saw that he could get nowhere this way. True, he had been lucky in Boryslav: he had found several rich veins of wax, and the oil flowed well from many of his shafts; but Leon justly feared that fortune would not always be in his favour, that it might in the future spurn him, and in that case, it was better to have firm friends rather than firm enemies. And it also transpired that after the death of his wife, with time Leon decided to establish himself here, to settle down in peace and put down roots in the locality, and in his old age enjoy the fruits of his restless, passionate life, providing a good life for his only daughter. The ultimate thing here was to have a circle of friends, rather than enemies.

Furthermore, Leon had learned that Hermann had an only son in Lviv, apprenticed to a merchant, and his thoughts dwelled on the fact that Hermann's son and his Fanny would make a fine couple; instead of fighting and undermining each other, the two biggest powerhouses in terms of capital, could come together, bound by close family ties. And in his imagination Leon was already building golden castles on these uncertain foundations.

"You see, dear neighbour," he said to Hermann, "I don't quite know myself what it is that makes me long to have my own calm, quiet and happy place. For up until now I have been like a migratory bird: now here, now there. But now it's time to settle down!"

"I agree," said Hermann, who seemed to be very interested in the course of the conversation.

"God did not give me a son like you, that's true, but I have a daughter, a kind child. To see her happy, with a loving husband, surrounded by children – oh, that is my only wish in life."

"God willing, your wish will come true."

"I would really like that… Oh, and a circle of good friends like you, my dear neighbour, and I wouldn't ask for anything more…"

"As for me," Hermann said, smiling, "I won't run away from Drohobych anytime soon, so you can always count on me being at your service."

"Oh, I know," said Leon and firmly squeezed Hermann's hand. "I know that you are a sincere, good man! You won't believe how long I've wanted to get to know you better… And how about your son? True, I haven't had the honour of getting to know him personally, but he already seems such a sweet and dear person, like my own child."

Hermann grimaced a little at the memory of his son. It was as if he had suddenly bitten into a peppercorn in a honey cake.

"My son…" he said reluctantly. "Thank you for your kind words! He works as best he can."

"Please, don't say such things!" Leon exclaimed. "I myself know that the son of such a father would probably not sit around idle for too long! Ah, my dear neighbour, how happy I would be, if we could both come closer together, become closer in everything so that…" He broke off and looked at Hermann, who looked back at him, unsure what he was hinting at.

"You know," Leon began again, "today is such a great and happy day for me…" In the middle of the conversation both men rose to their feet and moved over to the window, as the hut was becoming a little stuffy. Hermann looked outside. He had barely stepped back from the window, when suddenly a chunk of brick flew through the window like an arrow, right past where he had been standing. And just as Leon was talking about the great happiness he was experiencing now, the brick fell onto the table in front of him into a tray of glasses. There was a painful crash and shattered glass flew everywhere, while the brick continued on its way and struck the opposite wall, falling to the ground. Everyone jumped to their feet, while Hermann turned pale as a piece of canvas: he guessed that the brick was meant for him.

"What's this? What's this? Who did this?" anxious cries were heard. Leon, Hermann and some of the other guests dashed outside. People were also shouting outside.

"Catch him, that ragamuffin!" shouted the Master Mason at the top of his voice.

"Who's this throwing bricks here?" Leon shouted.

"Over there, if you please, sir, it was some ragamuffin, a young coalman. He was loitering in the street, looking here and there, and then, when he saw that gentleman there (he pointed at Hermann) in the window, he grabbed a brick, turfed it and ran off! Catch him, catch him, and take him to the police!" the Master Mason turned around again and shouted at the two workers who were chasing a fellow fleeing down Zelena Street in a shirt black as pitch and an equally black apron.

"Oh no, the beast is getting away! Might as well stop chasing him!" yelled the Master Mason.

The workers who had been chasing the lad also seemed to be of the same opinion, and stopped running, short of breath. But one of them bent down and picked up a stone, hurling it at the fleeing fellow, who had already reached a bend in the street. The stone hit the young coalman on the heel and he yelled like a madman from the pain, before disappearing around the corner. The cry took Hermann by surprise.

"Who was this fellow?" he asked.

No one knew the young coalman. But Leon looked at Hermann and grew scared.

"Good God, what's wrong?"

"Nothing, it's nothing," replied Hermann. "It must be all that stale air. I felt a tightness in my chest. But that voice, that voice… it seemed quite strange…"

Leon could not understand why the voice sounded strange. It seemed rather ordinary to him. And Hermann could not explain what it was about the voice – he thought that he had heard it somewhere before, but he could not say where. He only knew that by some secret, inscrutable force, that voice had aroused in him some terrible, long-forgotten feelings, stirring up a storm, the effects of which had not yet been smoothed over in his heart. But why he felt this way, and how was it connected to that young coalman's wild, painful cry, Hermann could not explain.

Meanwhile Leon took him by the arm and led him into the orchard, under the shady trees and onto the fragrant tall grass. The cold, fresh air immediately calmed Hermann, and Leon spoke again about his aspirations and hopes:

"Ah, how eagerly I have been expecting a day like today! How I wished that it would give birth to a new, calm, happy era in my life! So that happy knots could be tied in every direction! And so this day has come, my hopes have been realized, the knots have been tied, except for that last and most important one… Ah, and you, my dear neighbour and friend, you would make me the happiest man in the world, if you could help me to tie that last, most important knot!"

"Me?" asked Hermann, surprised. "And what kind of knot could that be?"

"What is there to talk about here," said Leon and grabbed both of Hermann's hands in his. "My deepest, heartfelt wish is for our children, my Fanny and your Gottlieb, to become a couple!"

Hermann was silent. The idea wasn't unexpected, but he was still slightly taken aback to hear such a proposal coming from Leon first.

"What do you think?" asked Leon.

"Hm, I don't know how to…" said Hermann hesitantly.

"Are you unsure? There's no need for that, my dear neighbour! Can't you see the benefits that will come from such a union? Just consider this: both of us, dare I say, are the top two forces in Boryslav, and when we come together as one, bound through marriage, who can compete against us? Everyone will follow our lead, and those who don't will bite the dust, if we so desire! Think about it: we become the lords of the oil trade, we determine the prices, we buy up the surrounding villages, forests, quarries and mines. We have the entire region in our hands. Controlling not only commerce and industry, but also the political affairs of the region. All elections go the way we want, ambassadors and representatives say what we dictate to them and defend our interests, lords and counts seek our favour! Do you understand? We become a force, and as long as we stay united, no one can stand against us!"

Energized by his own words, Leon rushed to embrace Hermann.

"Are you in agreement, my dear friend, brother of mine?" exclaimed Leon.

"I agree," said Hermann, "but I'm not too sure about my wife."

"Why, does your honourable and wise wife not want happiness for her son and my child? No, that can't be! Let's go, let's talk to her. I must first settle this matter at hand today, but once the guests leave, we can go to her together, introduce ourselves, and discuss this…"

"She loves her son very much, that's true. But it seems to me that she won't find a better match for him than your Fanny," said Hermann.

"Ah, my dear friend!" shouted Leon with delight. "What happiness has befallen me today! My God, what happiness! Let's go, let's go!"

II

Hand in hand, the two friends walked along Boryslav Road to Hermann's residence. Leon did most of the talking. He was a very impressionable man and was deeply moved by every thought. He tirelessly painted Hermann new pictures of their future greatness and power. Everything pouring forth from his mouth seemed sweetened with honey, all difficulties melted away, like snow in the sun. Practical and cold, Hermann was initially not very swayed by these golden mountains of promises, but the more Leon spoke, the more he managed to convince Hermann of his vision, and in Hermann's sceptical mind, the question slowly began to materialize: 'Really, why can't this become reality?'

He had long ago had countless disagreements and problems with his son Gottlieb, so much so that he had never even considered that anything worthwhile might ever become of him. Just recently, the merchant with whom Gottlieb had been interning for two years, wrote to him, maybe for the hundredth time, complaining that Gottlieb was performing poorly, neglecting his duties, squandering money sent from home as if he were going insane, squabbling with others at work and getting up to various other nonsense.

'With regret, I must admit,' the merchant wrote further, 'that his two-year stint in my establishment has brought him almost no benefit. His knowledge of commerce is now the same as it was the day he arrived here…' All this involuntarily came to Hermann's mind now, as Leon painted his tempting picture of the future of their 'houses' through the union of

Gottlieb and Fanny. 'As long as I am alive,' Hermann thought, 'perhaps he will manage somehow, but what will happen after that?' For Gotlieb to change and improve, it would take a miracle, something which Hermann could not hope for. All the same, he listened to Leon's words, slowly succumbing to their enchanting influence, as if he was sailing in a light boat on a gentle undulating sea gilded with an evening glow. He began to feel so light and dreamy, as if indeed his wildest hopes were already coming true. 'Why not? Why can't this become reality?' he thought, and a firm conviction began to take hold of him, as if all of this could not only be possible, but was indeed about to happen, had to happen.

By this time, the two friends had already walked down from the marketplace to the bridge, from where the street began to ascend again between two rows of tall ash trees, ending at the top of the rise, where a shining gold cross glimmered in the sunshine. Just beyond the bridge on the right there was an extensive garden, enclosed by a high wall. Where the wall ended, there was a fence made of oak pickets set in masonry posts topped with shiny black caps made of fired clay. There was no longer a garden behind these fences, but rather neglected flowerbeds surrounding an old-fashioned, rambling, single-storey wooden-clad house. A wide entrance gate led to it from the street, and beside it was a small side gate for visitors on foot. This was Hermann's residence. He had been living here for several years, although he still owned several other houses in different parts of town and three stone buildings in the marketplace. He rented out all these other buildings, and himself had no desire to move from this old-fashioned, comfortable nest. He had bought this house, along with the large orchard, vegetable patch, courtyard, stables, and all the necessary facilities from the widow of a Polish nobleman of grand lineage. That nobleman once owned large estates and several nearby villages. But much of that estate was used to support the unfortunate uprising in 1831[3] and what remained was spent in lengthy legal disputes over some inheritance. After the abolition of serfdom, the old landowner found himself on thin ice and could call nothing his own except this one house with a garden and a pair of horses. Here he lived out his days in peace, and after his death, his wife sold this last vestige of former grandeur and left these parts. And so the old Polish landlord was replaced by a new master – Hermann, who was just beginning to feather his nest at the time. The purchase of this house was the first step toward his later wealth, which was probably why he grew to like this old residence so much.

However, Hermann wasn't too concerned with the interior arrangement of the house – and he was even less interested in the orchard, where the former owner used to spend entire summers and where, people said, even now during moonlit nights, one could still see his tall figure, with a long moustache and milky-white hair, wandering among the tall grass. They saw him examining each tree, as if it were an old friend, and sometimes he would wring his hands or sigh heavily. Hermann had heard those rumours and although he laughed at them, he nevertheless was not drawn toward the orchard. He contented himself with counting the trees every spring and then leasing the orchard to a gardener, hardly ever venturing among the trees.

Inside the house itself, Hermann made only a few changes. The antique furniture was reupholstered with new fabric, new tiled stoves replaced the old Polish ones, large mirrors were hung between the windows, and that was basically it. On the walls, alongside some new paintings, hung the blackened portraits of old Polish magnates with bushy eyebrows, stern moustaches and shaved foreheads. This eclectic mix of

....

[3]   The November Uprising in the Kingdom of Poland and Lithuania lasted almost a year – from November 1830 to October 1831.

antiques and clumsy random attempts at modernity looked strange, but Hermann didn't much care; he was occupied with other, more important matters. His goal was to accumulate, not to enjoy; and accumulate he did, collecting, multiplying, adding with a kind of feverish haste, without caring who would enjoy his wealth.

"This is my nest!" Hermann declared, opening the side gate and letting Leon pass. It was the first time that Leon was entering the property.

"Ah, what a nice place, how spacious it is!" exclaimed Leon with polite enthusiasm, as he surveyed the yard. It was paved with stone slabs. In the middle there was a well under a small roof, with a large hand wheel and two buckets. Further to one side was a stable, and next to it – the entrance to the orchard.

"Spacious it may be," replied Hermann, "but if the truth be known, it feels rather empty. You see, for a man of my years, this is not enough. I would be happy to find myself surrounded by a whole bunch of small, cheerful…"

"Oh, yes, yes," Leon interrupted him, "that's exactly what I was thinking. Really, to live here with a brood of young offspring would be heaven, true paradise!"

"But what do we have now?" Hermann continued. "Our son is in Lviv… Well, alright, a young man needs to learn something in his youth…"

"Quite, quite!"

"And it's just my wife and me, the two of us, and she's also poorly… one must admit that it sometimes makes a man feel miserable."

They entered the house.

"Right?" Hermann said. "It's as quiet as a grave… We don't keep many servants: a coachman, a cook, and a maid – we don't need more than that. And it's like this all day long. Of course, I'm rarely at home, there's always business to attend to."

"Oh yes, yes," said Leon, "our life is so hard. They say: what could possibly trouble a capitalist, the loafer lives comfortably and simply rakes in the money. But if they could only see, spend a few days like us, then they would probably want to have nothing to do with this capital and this lifestyle."

"Oh, definitely, I'll vouch for that!" Hermann confirmed. Although at that instant a mischievous thought flashed through his mind: despite all this hardship, despite all the inconveniences of this lifestyle, not a single capitalist had ever voluntarily given up his property or exchanged it for a beggar's staff and sack.

Hermann had already passed through three rooms with his guest. It was quiet and empty everywhere. He was looking for his wife, but couldn't find her anywhere. They crossed into a fourth room, which was as vast as a manège. Hermann looked around – there was no one here either.

"How strange, where could she be?" Hermann said in a low voice, but then he heard something resembling loud sobbing coming from an adjacent room, his wife's bedroom.

"What can this be?" he said, straining his ears.

"Could it be someone crying?" asked Leon, pricking up his ears as well.

"Please make yourself comfortable, my dear neighbour, sit down and rest a while. Here, look through this album from my friends, maybe you'll find some familiar faces there… And excuse me, I must step out for a moment and see what is the matter…"

"By all means," answered Leon, sitting in the chair beside a round table. He picked up the album, but had no desire to look through it. He sat motionless for a while, his mind a blank. His flight of fantasy had suddenly petered out, grounded by this silence, this almost tomb-like coolness that reigned in this house. He was unsure why this silence made him feel uneasy.

'Ugh, damn it, it's like being in some bandit's tavern, it really gives me the creeps!' he thought. 'It feels like someone is about to jump out from behind a door and grab me by the throat. And these portraits, these stupid faces! Ugh, I wouldn't be able to stand this even for a moment. But what about him? He lives here, like a mouse in a burrow, and doesn't give a damn about any of this…'

Leon strained his ears, attempting to discern the sounds coming from the adjacent room, where Hermann had gone. At first, all he could make out were the same mournful sobs he had heard earlier.

"Not a promising start…" he muttered under his breath. "I came here with such expectations, only to find some woman on her death bed… It must be the lady of the house. I've heard she's a real mess… But what choice do I have? Sometimes one must engage with such people for the sake of business!"

He listened again. There were voices. It was Hermann speaking, but it was unclear what he was saying. There was a rustling sound. Then silence. Again voices and more sobbing. Suddenly there was a loud thump, as if something heavy had struck the floor, followed by a shrill female scream:

"You thief! You bloodsucker! Get out of my sight! Get out, may I never lay eyes on you again!"

Leon leaned back into the armchair. What was this? He continued to listen, but now he could not make out any words because of the squealing and banging. He imagined that terrible curses, insults and accusations were being hurled at Hermann, but he could not tell for what reason.

Neither could Hermann! On entering his wife's bedroom, he saw her lying on the sofa, dishevelled and unkempt, sobbing and looking as if she were dying. Tears flowed from her eyes and there was already a damp patch on the sofa. Hermann was astonished and did not know what to think. His wife, it seemed, had not noticed his entrance, she did not move, only her chest rose and fell sharply, as if she were in great distress. Hermann was afraid to approach her, knowing her bad temper, but then he mustered his courage.

"Rifka, Rifka!" he said softly, drawing near.

"What do you want?" she asked, abruptly turning her head.

"What's the matter? Why are you crying"

"What do you want?" she repeated sharply. "Who have you brought home with you?"

"No one. Really, there's no one."

"Don't lie to me! I heard two of you enter. Who is it?"

"Leon Hammerschlag."

"And what does he want?"

"You know that he had the laying of his foundation stone today, so he asked me..."

"But what brings him here?"

"Listen, Rifka," Hermann began, seeing that she seemed to have calmed down a little. "Leon is a rich man, a good man, with a great head on his shoulders..."

"Are you telling me why he's here or not?" Rifka interrupted him, clenching her fists.

"Will you hear me out. Just listen. Leon, I said, is a rich man. And he has no wife, only a daughter. Do you hear, Rifka, do you know his daughter Fanny? She's a fine girl, no?"

"So?"

"You know what Leon told me? 'My neighbour,' he said, 'I have a daughter and you have a son'..."

Hermann did not finish. At the mention of her son, Rifka turned blue, her whole body began to shake, and then, kicking the chair away from under her feet, she straightened up and screamed:

"You thief! You bloodsucker! Get away from me! Get out of my sight!"

Hermann was stunned. He didn't know what had happened to Rifka, and only kept stammering:

"But, Rifka, what's wrong? What are you doing, Rifka?"

"Get out of my sight, you monster!" Rifka shrieked. "May God strike you down and punish you! May the ground beneath you give way! Get away from me! You… you are talking to me about my son! Did you ever have a son? Did you ever have a heart?"

"But, Rifka, what's wrong? Listen!"

"I don't want to hear anything you have to say, you executioner! May God not hear your words on Judgement Day! And did you ever listen to me when I told you not to torture our child with schooling, and that there was no need to push our child into that damned practice… Oh, but you never listened! And now you've achieved your goal!"

"What's happened, Rifka? I don't know anything!"

"You don't know? Hah, you wouldn't know what day it is, you heartless bastard. Take a look! Here!"

And she threw a piece of paper at him. With trembling hands Hermann took the crumpled, tear-stained letter. Meanwhile Rifka fell back on the sofa as if she were exhausted, breathing heavily, covering her face with her hands and sobbed bitterly.

The letter was from Lviv, from the merchant to whom Gottlieb was apprenticed. Hermann read under his breath: 'Honourable sir! I don't know where to begin and how to explain what has happened here. Your son, Gottlieb, disappeared three days ago, and all attempts at finding him have been in vain. So far, the police have been able to find his clothes rolled into a ball in the undergrowth on Pelchynsky Hill.[4] But there is still no sign of him. There was a growing suspicion that he might have drowned in the pond, but so far, no body has been found. Please come as soon as possible, perhaps we will be able to find out what has happened to him. However, if we receive any news before this letter reaches you, I will inform you telegraphically!'

....

[4] Named after the former owners of the land, the burgher family Pelky. Now within the Lviv city limits.

Hermann glanced at the date on the letter: it was the day before yesterday! And there had been no telegram – so there was no additional news! For a long moment he stood stock still, not knowing what was happening to him. Rifka's loud sobbing brought him to his senses.

"See," she cried, "what you have done to your child! My little son has drowned, my poor Gottlieb has drowned! Why couldn't you have been swallowed up by crude oil in one of your damned Boryslav pits!"

"My God," said Hermann, "have some sense, woman, am I to blame for this?"

"If you're not to blame, then who is? Maybe me? Leave, you monster, and don't say a word. Go off to Lviv, maybe there's still some way to save him or at least to find his body! Good God, why do you punish me with a husband who has driven his own child to the grave! And he has no other children! Gottlieb was the only one, and now even he is gone! Oh-oh-oh, my head, is bursting!"

"Calm down, Rifka, maybe things aren't as bad as it says in the letter. After all, they only found his clothes! So? He could have simply taken them off..."

"What a pity you can't shed your callous skin, you wretch! You're still arguing with me, cutting me to the quick, you bastard! Oh, I know that it barely matters to you that fish might be nibbling away at your son somewhere in the water! What do you care! But as for me, my heart is bursting, I feel that all is lost, my golden little son is no more!"

Hermann saw that it was futile to continue talking with his wife, as it seemed utterly impossible to reason with her. He rushed off to order the coachman to harness the horses and prepare to leave. Back then there was no railway to Drohobych. Thus to reach Lviv, one had to go by coach to Stryj, and from there catch the train to Lviv.

As he passed through the spacious guest room, Hermann noticed Leon was still sitting in the armchair, as if on pins and needles. He had heard snatches of the conversation, punctuated by sudden bursts of crying and sobbing, but still had no idea what the problem was. Only now did Hermann remember that he had left Leon here, having completely forgotten about him because of his wife's hysterics and their misfortune.

"Ah, my dear neighbour," he said, approaching Leon, "forgive me, but misfortune has struck..."

"My God, what has happened?" Leon exclaimed. "You are as pale as a sheet, you are trembling and your wife is sobbing. What's the matter?"

"Oh, don't ask," Hermann said quietly, "misfortune has struck our house like a thunderbolt from the blue, and it was so unexpected that I still don't know whether it's all a bad dream or cruel reality."

"But tell me, for heaven's sake, is there really no hope?"

"What hope can there be! Who can bring the dead back to life! Gone is my happiness, my hope!"

"Dead?"

"Yes! My son, my Gottlieb, is no longer alive!"

"Gottlieb? What are you saying? Can it be true?"

"His principal has written from Lviv that he has disappeared. For several days it has not been possible to find any trace of him. But now the police have found his clothes in the undergrowth on Pelchynsky Hill."

"And the body?"

"No, no body has been found."

"Maybe he's still alive then!"

"It's difficult, my dear neighbour! I thought as much myself at first. But after taking into consideration his character and everything... I have lost hope! No, I won't ever see him again, never!"

Only now that Hermann had unburdened his heart, did tears flow from his eyes. Although he knew that his son had been spoiled and was half-crazy, he also knew that he was his only son, the heir to his estate. And just today, Leon had lulled his heart with such sweet hopes. He had already begun to think that even if Gottlieb did not change, perhaps a good, sensible woman like Fanny might be able to restrain his whims and gradually accustom him to a calm, reasonable life. But now, suddenly, everything had vanished, like a bubble bursting upon water. The last threads of paternal love and the strong threads of self-love ached terribly in his heart – and he wept.

Leon rushed to comfort him:

"Oh, my dear neighbour, please don't cry!" he said. "I'm certain that your Gottlieb is alive, that you will still enjoy his company. Just don't let yourself be consumed by grief. Summon your courage! We stalwart individuals, we capitalists who stand at the forefront of our time, must always be strong and resolute!"

Hermann shook his head at these words.

"What's it to me?" he answered sadly. "What is the use of my power and capital, when there is no one to pass it on to. And I am already too old!"

"No, don't lose hope, don't lose hope!" insisted Leon. "Hurry off to Lviv. I assure you that you'll find him there."

"Oh, if only God would let it be so, if only He would let it be so!" Hermann exclaimed. "You're right, I'll go, I must find him, dead or alive!"

"No, not dead, but alive," Leon interjected. "And don't leave him there with that merchant, bring him back here, for the comfort and joy of us all! Yes, my dear neighbour, yes!"

At that moment the door from the bedroom was flung open and Rifka burst into the room, still teary-eyed and red-faced. Her broad face flared with anger when she saw Leon. Leon felt very uneasy when he saw Hermann's wife – tall, plump, and formidable, the living embodiment of divine vengeance. Hiding his confusion, he approached her with exaggerated politeness, bowed, contorted his face to express compassion, and had already opened his mouth to speak, when Rifka, scornfully eyeing him from head to toe, asked brusquely:

"And what do you want here, you scum?" she yelled.

Leon was taken aback by such a greeting. A cold, forced smile appeared on his face, and, bowing once more, he began:

"Indeed, gracious lady, I am very sorry that I have come at such an inappropriate time…"

"But I asked you, what are you doing here?" Rifka shouted and looked at him with such anger and disdain that Leon was frightened and involuntarily staggered back.

"I apologize," he said, still not losing courage, "your husband and I were making plans, oh, such fine plans, about our future, and I firmly believe that the Lord will help us see them realized!"

"You? God will help you? You are deceitful monsters, hypocrites!" Rifka grumbled, and then, as if coming to her senses, she raised her clenched fists and lunged at the terrified Leon.

"Leave this house, you murderer!" she screamed. "You dare to tear my heart apart with your nonsense, when my son has disappeared from this world because of you and your damned money! Get out of this house! Out! And if you dare show your face here again, I'll gouge out those shameless, vile eyes of yours! Understand?"

Leon turned white as a sheet, grimaced under the hail of these words, and, without taking his eyes off her menacing expression, backed away toward the door.

"But, Rifka," Hermann interjected, "what's come over you? Why are you insulting our good neighbour? Maybe, just maybe, it's not as bad as it seems, perhaps our Gottlieb is still alive, and everything we have been discussing can come true?"

Hermann had hoped to comfort Rifka with these words, but they seemed only to fuel her anger toward poor Leon.

"Even if that were the case," she cried, "I'd rather see him dead ten times over than to have this scoundrel as an in-law! No, never, as long as I live that will never happen!"

Both men were stunned for a moment, not knowing what had happened to Rifka and what had spawned such intense anger toward Leon. As Rifka continued screaming, lashing out and chasing Leon out of her home, he hunched over and, holding onto his hat, darted from the inhospitable rooms into the yard and out into the street. Without looking back, trembling all over from this unexpected turn of events, he hurried off toward the town.

"My God, that woman really is insane!" he grumbled. "And she was meant to become my Fanny's mother-in-law? That wretched, quarrelsome creature would have devoured her in a single day! How lucky I am that it happened this way, that they have lost their son somewhere! Ugh, I want nothing more to do with them!"

Leon shook his head and kept spitting on the road. Only now did he understand why the other wealthy men avoided Hermann and reluctantly visited his home. Apart from business and financial dealings, they wanted nothing to do with him. All the same, Leon was saddened by what had happened: he longed for those bright hopes and plans he had until recently nurtured to come true. His head was always fertile ground for such plans, and when a plan was torn to shreds, he did not worry too much, but quickly seized on another. Now that he had swiftly abandoned his recent dreams, he tried to grow used to the idea that he would no longer be 'working' in partnership with Hermann, but on his own, either without Hermann or in competition with him.

'I'll need to compete with him!' he thought. 'In all likelihood, Hermann himself will probably try even harder to make things difficult for me.'

Leon couldn't quite pinpoint why it seemed inevitable for Hermann to become his adversary. He wouldn't openly admit, not even to himself, that he was projecting his own emotions onto Hermann. Deep within, there simmered a fierce hostility toward Hermann, fuelled by the insult he had just endured and the shattering of his grand plans. Leon couldn't bring himself to acknowledge his burning desire to harm Hermann in some way, 'to teach him a lesson.' Instead, he fixated on the impending struggle, strategizing its countless contingencies, approaches, and potential setbacks. He aimed to create as many hurdles as possible for Hermann. As his pace slowed, he immersed himself further in these thoughts, wishing ever more severe setbacks and losses on Hermann, seeking to subdue the seemingly invincible, affluent man and sow anxiety within him. In the end, just before reaching his own house, he had successfully brought Hermann to his knees, even driving him and his erratic wife out of their home.

"Serves you right!" he whispered, as if rejoicing at their downfall. "If only you knew, you witch, how much I would love to claw your eyes out!"

At the same time as Leon, engrossed in his dreams, was rejoicing at the downfall of the Goldkrämer family and was starting to calculate the benefits that would befall him from this great victory, Hermann himself was rushing through the streets of Drohobych in a carriage toward the Stryj highway. His face was still completely pale, and from time to time he felt a chill pass down his spine and a slight tremor course through his body. His thoughts were swirling and turning, like water in a mill wheel. The unexpected misfortune which had befallen him, a misfortune so strange and unverifiable, made him finally decide not to think about anything and to wait patiently to see what would come of it all. He resolved to spend a few days in Lviv and use all possible means at his disposal to try and find his son, as well as clarifying why and where he had disappeared. In a few days, he needed to be in Vienna, where a business acquaintance had summoned him via telegram to settle an important matter concerning his venture in Boryslav. If in those few days he was unable to achieve his goal in Lviv, he decided to leave the matter in the hands of the local police and to proceed to Vienna all the same.

True, his wife had told him not to return without their son, alive or dead, and she didn't even want to hear about his going to Vienna on 'oil' business, but what did a woman understand! She must have known that even though Hermann would be in Lviv, he might not find Gottlieb. But if there was anything left to find there, his money would take care of things. Meanwhile it was imperative for him to be in Vienna, otherwise the business deal might fall through. This played on Hermann's mind, as he rushed in the carriage along the highway to Stryj. The undulating foothills moved past him, making no impression on him. He waited impatiently for the towers of Stryj to appear and was bored by the endless rows of birches and rowan trees growing on both sides of the highway. Slowly he began to calm down, swaying from side to side in the carriage, and eventually, leaning against a pillow, he fell asleep.

After Hermann had left, Rifka returned to her sofa, sobbing and dabbing at her tears, and several times she glanced at the unsettling letter from Lviv. Each time tears once again gushed from her eyes. The tears soothed her pain, dispersing her thoughts and washing them away. Lost in her sorrow, she forgot all about Gottlieb, about the letter, about her grief and sensed only the relief brought on by her tears.

Where had those times gone when Rifka was a poor working girl? What had become of that Rifka of yesteryear, who was agile, industrious, playful and satisfied with what she had? Those times and that Rifka had vanished without a trace, faded away even in the clouded memory of the Rifka of today!

Twenty years had passed since she, a healthy, strong, hard-working girl, had one fine evening accidentally run into a poor slob named Hermann Goldkrämer. They talked and got to know one another. Hermann was then embarking, rather uncertainly, on his journey to wealth; he had obligations to supply to the imperial depot, and he was close to losing everything because he did not have the money to complete what he had committed himself to. Hearing that Rifka had put aside some money for a dowry, he hastily married her, and used that dowry to salvage his business and achieve substantial profits. Good fortune smiled on him, and from then on, it never left him. Wealth flowed into his hands, and the more he accumulated, the fewer were his losses, the more secure his profits. Hermann devoted himself entirely to the pursuit of wealth. Rifka had now become a fifth wheel to him; he was rarely at home, and when he did appear, he avoided her. And not without reason. Rifka had changed greatly over these past years, and not for the better, although probably not through any fault of her own. It could be said that Hermann's wealth had consumed her, eroded her moral being. Naturally strong and healthy, she needed movement and work, and errands to engage her mind and hands. So long as she lived in poverty, there was enough of such work. She had served in wealthier Jewish households, earning her way in various capacities to support herself and her aunt, her only relative who had survived the cholera epidemic. As was common among impoverished Jews, she had no education, not even a basic traditional education. A hard life and hard work, naturally monotonous and mechanical, had made her strong in body, but had not influenced her mind. She grew up in profound ignorance and spiritual darkness, lacking even the natural ability and 'agility' that one usually associates with village girls. She could only comprehend and deal with the material things that were directly around her; beyond that, she understood nothing. Hermann accepted her for who she was.

There was no love between them. Initially, their youthful and vibrant natures drew them together – their immature emotions and desires sought nothing more than basic physical gratification. But even then, they usually did not see each other throughout the day – which made their meetings in the evening even more pleasant. A daughter was born to them, although she died soon after – apparently, due to the carelessness of her mother at night. Back then, the Goldkrämers were still considered poor: Hermann spent whole days running around town or the surrounding villages, and Rifka kept house, cooking, washing, chopping wood, sewing and cleaning – in short, she lived like a worker, just as she had been living before. And this was still the happiest time of her married life. The first child, a healthy and beautiful girl, delighted her greatly and took up a lot of her time. The more Rifka worked and the busier she was, the healthier and happier she became. True, she never quite realized that it was precisely because of all this work that she was happy. She often complained to her husband that she never had a moment's rest, that her health was suffering, echoing more the common conversations of other women than speaking her own mind.

Unfortunately, her wishes were fulfilled all too quickly. Hermann grew rich, bought a comfortable and expansive house on the Boryslav highway, hired servants whom Rifka despised – and she suddenly felt relieved. She walked through the rooms, which she had recently only dared to peek at from the street, and looked at the paintings, furniture, mirrors, and wallpapers. She managed the kitchen, poked her nose into the pantry, but quickly realized that all this was unnecessary. Hermann gave the servants everything they needed according to a strict budget, and threatened to dismiss them for the slightest mistake – and given the small size of their household, there was no need to fear that the servants might steal things. The hired cook knew far more about cooking than the lady of the house, and he accepted her advice and orders with a polite smile. Moving the furniture about and rearranging the paintings quickly bored her – and now began a new, terrible period in her life. She had never known what boredom was, but now it seeped into every pore of her body. She sometimes drifted through the spacious rooms like a cursed soul, sat in the kitchen chatting with the servants, lay for hours on the sofa, or went out into the street and soon returned home, unable to find anything to occupy herself with, anything at all to keep her nerves and mind from atrophying. The servants kept to themselves, knowing she might explode at the slightest provocation. She rarely visited other people's homes, for everywhere she was treated coldly. Besides, she found it a torment to pay visits on people. Among the new circle of people into which her husband's new-found wealth had so strenuously introduced her, she felt completely out of place. She didn't know how to behave, what to say, didn't understand people's compliments or their biting remarks. And her coarse jokes and simplistic talk provoked only laughter. She quickly realized that she was becoming a laughingstock to all these people and stopped attending social gatherings or receiving strangers in her own home, except for a few older women. But before long even these ladies stopped coming because of her irritability and her rude, unrestrained outbursts. Left on her own, Rifka was tormented and struggled like a wild animal locked in a cage, unable to understand what had happened to her. Her underdeveloped mind could neither fathom why she felt this way nor find a way out. Nor was there any activity to occupy her healthy, strong nature, which, left with no work to do, with no vital interest in life, was consuming itself, making her explode with excessive anger at the slightest provocation. As Rifka became increasingly detached from work, chores became increasingly hateful and burdensome: she could not bring herself to read a single book, although her aunt had taught her to read a few years earlier. Boredom veiled everything with a grey, unbearable curtain, and she became increasingly lonely, sinking ever deeper into the abyss that her husband's wealth had created around her, and which neither she nor her husband knew how to fill with either heartfelt love or meaningful spiritual work.

At this time in her life, Rifka gave birth to a son, Gottlieb. From the outset, the doctors did not promise that he would live. The child was sickly, cried and screamed continuously, and the servants in the kitchen whispered among themselves that he was 'possessed.' But Gottlieb survived, although he did not seem to get much better. However, he brought a ray of light into his mother's world at least for a while. She rushed about and fussed over the child all day long, and suddenly felt healthier and less irritable. The boredom had disappeared. Concurrent with her own recovery, the weaker and more troublesome her son was, the more she loved him. Sleepless nights, constant care and attention – all this made Gottlieb more precious and dearer to her. With time, the boy seemed to recover his health a little, but it was immediately apparent that his mental abilities would not be brilliant. He barely started walking in his second year, and even in his third year, he babbled like a six-month-old baby. But to his mother's joy, he began to eat well, as if he had suddenly become very hungry. His belly was always full and bloated like a balloon, and as soon as he felt slightly hungry, he began to scream at the top of his voice.

However, the older Gottlieb became, the worse was his behaviour. He needed to annoy everyone, destroy everything he lay his hands on, and went around the rooms like a little demon, constantly looking for something nasty to do. His mother loved him unconditionally, doted on him and satisfied his every whim. Because of her underdeveloped mind and long-suppressed feelings she couldn't find any other way to express her maternal love; she never even considered raising her child sensibly, caring only to satisfy his every whim. The servants feared little Gottlieb like the devil, because he liked to attach himself to one of them and either tear at their clothes, slapping, scratching and biting them, or he would start screaming at the top of his lungs. His mother would come rushing over, and the poor person he had attached himself to would then fare even worse. Arguments and punches were the least of the punishments. It was rumoured that a maid was fired on the spot because of him.

Hermann, on the other hand, did not love his son at all, if only because even on the rare days that he was at home, he never had any peace because of him. Little Gottlieb was at first afraid of his father, but when his mother resolutely stood up to his father on his behalf several times and his father relented, the boy realized with his childish instinct that he could do as he pleased here too, because his mother would always defend him. And he began to oppose his father ever more boldly. This infuriated Hermann, but since his wife indulged their son in everything and was ready to sacrifice even her own eye for him, Hermann could do nothing, which further fuelled his resentment toward both his wife and his son.

The discord in the family increased further when it was time to send little Gottlieb to school. For several days before enrolment day, Rifka wept over her son, as though he were being led off to the gallows. She spoke to him as if she were saying goodbye forever, told him how severe the people were there, how bad the teachers were, and threatened to deal with them if any dared touch her golden little son. She instructed him that as soon as someone at school offended or wronged him in any way, he should immediately let her know, and she would tell the teachers how they needed to treat him. In short, even before Gottlieb had started school, he already had such an aversion to it, as if it were some kind of hell invented by evil people to deliberately torture such 'golden sons' like himself.

On the other hand, Hermann took a different approach. He went to the rector of the Basilian fathers, who at that time ran the only main school in Drohobych, and asked him to keep an eye on Gottlieb, to ensure that he studied and became accustomed to discipline. He explained that the boy had been spoiled by his mother, and asked the rector to be strict, not sparing threats or even punishment, and to pay no attention to what his wife might say or do. He even added that, if necessary, he would find separate lodging for Gottlieb outside of home to remove him from the harmful influence of his mother.

The rector was quite surprised by Hermann's words, but soon saw for himself that Hermann was telling the truth. Not only was Gottlieb not inclined to learn anything, but his initial upbringing at home was so bad that the reverend teachers surely never had as much trouble with any of the other pupils. Gottlieb's classmates and peers came to complain about him all the time: he tore one boy's exercise book, gave another a black eye, threw another's hat out of the window into the monastery yard. If anyone was making the most noise and commotion in the corridors and in the classrooms, it was most certainly Gottlieb. And if anyone talked during lessons or knocked on the desk, it was most often him. If anyone in the class dared to argue with the teacher, leave the classroom, and even slam the door behind him, it was also Gottlieb.

At first the teachers weren't sure how to deal with him; they complained to the rector day in and day out. The rector wrote to his father, and his father merely replied: 'Punish him.' From then on, punishments and beatings rained down on Gottlieb, which seemed to calm his wild temper somewhat and break his defiant spirit, but they made him become secretive and filled with a deep-seated malice, thus completely corrupting his moral character.

In barely seven or eight years, Gottlieb finally completed the four-grade school, and, morally destroyed, spiritually underdeveloped, with an intense aversion to learning and malice toward people, especially his father, he entered the gymnasium.[5] But after three years here he still hadn't completed the second grade, when a terrible and dark incident permanently interrupted his school education.[6]

But who knows whether those years of unhappy school education took a heavier and more miserable toll on Rifka than on Gottlieb himself. One thing was certain – the school separated her from her son for most of the day, thereby plunging her once more into a bottomless abyss of idleness and boredom. And then, Gottlieb's constant complaints further infuriated and irritated her. Like a wounded lioness she would run to the Basilian fathers every day, complaining about the unfairness and incompetence of the teachers, shouting and cursing, until the rector reprimanded her and forbade her to come. After this she had thought of insisting on taking Gottlieb away from the Basilians and sending him to another school, but she quickly realized that there was no other school in Drohobych, and to send Gottlieb off to another city, among strangers – she could not even think about such a thing without growing anxious. She struggled with her desperation for a long time, beating about like a fish in a sack, and more than once spent entire days sitting on the sofa, crying and thinking that perhaps, at this very moment, they were dragging her son off somewhere, beating him, laying him on a bench, and caning him. She loudly cursed the school, his education, and her executioner of a husband who had deliberately invented such torture for both her son and herself. These emotional outbursts became ever more frequent and eventually she began to hate all people,

....

[5] Secondary school.

[6] That incident was the subject of Ivan Franko's story "Boa Constrictor," published in 1878.

consumed by incessant irritation, ready to explode into wild curses for no good reason. Now Rifka wouldn't even think of joining a social circle or doing something to allay her boredom. She wandered about the house as if cursed, and none of the servants dared to appear before her eyes. This state of hers reached its peak after Hermann sent Gottlieb off to Lviv for two years and apprenticed him to a merchant. At first, Rifka went out of her mind, tore at her hair, dashed about the rooms and screamed, demanding to see her son. Later she calmed down a little and for months on end remained silent, like a wild beast in a cage. The loneliness and emptiness around her and within her became ever more terrifying – even her husband was afraid to approach her and tried to stay away from home all day long. Amid all this darkness, there was only one thing that kept Rifka going – an insane, almost beastly love for Gottlieb. And now capricious fate dared to take even this last vestige of sanity from her, to erase this last sign of humanity from her heart. It was a terrible blow to Rifka, and the only reason she did not go insane was because she could not fathom the misfortune that had befallen her.

After Hermann's departure, she just lay back down on her sofa. No thoughts stirred in her head and only tears flowed. Her world had vanished, the light had dimmed, people had disappeared – all she felt was a relentless, incessant pain in her heart.

Suddenly, she jumped to her feet, trembling all over. What was this? What was this noise, this knocking, this talk that had reached her ears? She held her breath and listened. There was talking at the main entrance. She heard the voice of the maid, who seemed to be arguing with someone, not letting them into the house. There was another voice, terse and angry, then came a thud as if someone had been knocked to the ground. A door slammed shut, steps resounded through the rooms, drawing closer and closer…

"Ah, it must be him, my son, my Gottlieb!" Rifka cried out and rushed to the door. At that moment, the door burst open, pushed by a forceful hand, and there stood a young coalman dressed in ragged black clothes, his face smeared with coal dust.

Rifka involuntarily screamed and took a step back. The young coalman surveyed her with large, angry eyes filled with fury and hatred.

"Don't you recognize me?" he said tersely, and in that moment Rifka rushed up to him, as if insane, and began to squeeze and kiss his face, eyes, and hands, crying and laughing.

"So it is really you? So I was not mistaken! God, you're alive, you're healthy, and I almost died with worry! Oh, my son! My love, you are alive!"

There was no end to her cries. Rifka pulled the young coalman onto the sofa and did not let go of him until he finally managed to break free. Hearing the approaching footsteps of the maid, he closed the door and, turning to his mother, said:

"Tell that cursed monkey to go to hell, otherwise I'll smash her empty skull, if she doesn't leave us alone right now!"

Through the closed door Rifka obediently ordered the maid to go to the kitchen and not to come out until she was summoned. After that, she began to hug and caress her son again, never taking her eyes off his puffy blackened face.

"Gottlieb," she began, "what's happened to you? What have you done?"

And she began to look at him with an expression of endless sorrow, as if his ragged clothes were a mortal wound on his body.

"Aha, and you thought that I would endure that damned merchant until the day I died!" Gottlieb shouted, stamping his feet angrily and breaking free of his mother's embrace. "You thought that I wouldn't dare do as I pleased! Hah?"

"But, my darling, who would have thought that!" Rifka exclaimed. "Only your brute of a father thought so!"

"And you didn't?"

"Me? Good Lord! I would have given my own blood for you, my dearest. I told him as much…"

"Where did he go?" Gottlieb interrupted her.

"To Lviv, of course, to search for you."

"Oh, I see," said Gottlieb with a satisfied smile," then let him keep searching!"

"But how did you get here, my love?"

"How? Can't you see? With the coalmen returning from Lviv."

"My poor baby!" exclaimed Rifka. "And you travelled the whole way with them! Good Lord, it must have been terrible! Quickly, remove this filth. I'll call for some water so you can wash yourself and change into fresh clothes! I won't let you go, I won't let that brute take you back there, no way! Take that filth off right now, my darling, and I'll go and find some clean clothes for you. And you must be hungry… Wait, I'll call the maid…"

And she stood up to ring the bell, but Gottlieb stopped her.

"Don't worry, there's no need," he said curtly.

"But why, my son? You certainly can't go about looking like that…"

"Aha, you thought," said Gottlieb, standing before her, "that I escaped from Lviv in these rags and trudged for fifteen miles with the coalmen, just so that I could surrender myself to your will again, to be locked into some cage and have to listen to your crying and your preaching? Oh, that won't happen!"

"But, my son," exclaimed Rifka, pale and trembling with anxiety, "what will you do? Don't be afraid, I'll stand by you here at home, no one can harm you!"

"I don't need you to defend me, I can stand up for myself!"

"But what are you going to do?"

"I'll live as I please, without your protection!"

"Good God, I'm not stopping you from living at home as you please!"

"Oh, please, don't defend yourself! At least I'll be able to go out somewhere and have fun now without being asked countless questions, listening to your crying and the devil knows what else! I don't need this. And when he returns, oh, that will be my victory!"

Something gripped Rifka's heart at these words. She felt that her son no longer loved her, could not bear her caresses, and this filled her with terror, as if she was losing her son for a second time, this time forever. She sat motionless on the sofa, her eyes fixed on him, unable to utter a word.

"Let me have some money, so I can live on my own," said Gottlieb, paying no heed to her feelings.

"But where will you go?"

"That's none of your business. I know what you'll say to him when he returns, and he will have the gendarmes bring me back."

"But I swear to God, I won't tell him!"

"Well, I won't tell you either. Why do you need to know? Let me have some money!"

Rifka got up and pulled open a drawer in the desk, but found only fifty Rhenish guilders there and silently handed the money to Gottlieb.

"What's this!" he said, twirling the bills about in his hands. "Is this what you give to the beggars who come knocking?"

"I don't have anymore, see for yourself."

He rummaged about in the desk, and finding no more money, said:

"Fine, that's the way it is then. Try to find some more in a few days."

"Will you be back?" his mother asked happily.

"I'll see. If he's not here, then I'll come back, otherwise I'll send someone else. When the fellow shows you a sign from me, you can give him the money in a sealed envelope. But remember," and here Gottlieb shook his fists menacingly in her face, "not a word to anyone about me!"

"To anyone?"

"No one! And that's an order! Not to him, not to the servants, not to anyone! No one in Drohobych knows that I'm here. I want to be left in peace. And if you tell someone, just you watch out!"

"But the maid saw you."

"That monkey? Say that I was delivering a message from someone! Say whatever you want, but not a word about me. And if he finds out that I'm alive or if someone tries to follow me, remember this: I will make your lives so miserable that you will wish you were never born. I want to live my own life, and that's that!"

"Oh my God!" Rifka exclaimed, wringing her hands. "How long will you live like this?"

"As long as I please!"

And with these words Gottlieb walked over to the window, opened it as if wanting to look outside, and in an instant jumped out of the window. Rifka screamed and ran over to the window, but Gottlieb was nowhere to be seen. Only the tall burdocks in the garden were swaying, as if whispering something quietly among themselves.

At that moment, pale and frightened, the maid ran into the room next to the bedroom and began to shout:

"Ma'am, ma'am!"

Rifka quickly came to her senses and opened the door.

"Ma'am, what's happened? I heard you calling!"

"Me? Call you? When?" Rifka asked, turning red as a beet.

"Just now. I'm sure I heard you yelling."

"That was just something yelling in your stupid head, you silly monkey! Off to the kitchen! Didn't I tell you not to come unless I called for you?"

"But I thought I heard you calling me," the maid replied timidly.

"Off you go to the kitchen, when I tell you," Rifka shouted. "And next time don't assume anything, understand?"

III

Three weeks had passed since the laying of the foundation stone. Leon's house was quickly rising upwards: the foundations had already been laid, and the front wall of hewn stone was standing almost two feet above the ground. The building supervisor oversaw the work, and in those first days Leon himself hung around for days on end, poking his nose into every corner and urging everyone to hurry. But this did not last long. Leon was forced to rush off to Vienna on urgent business, and although the work did not slow down in his absence, the workers nevertheless breathed a little easier, not having to constantly endure his relentless scrutiny.

Just before six one morning, several of the workers were sitting on planks and rocks before the start of work. They chatted about this and that, waiting for the rest of the workers to arrive. After a short while the building supervisor appeared, looked around and shouted tersely:

"Is everyone here then?"

"They're all here," answered the Master Mason.

"Let's start work then!"

One worker got to his feet. Everyone at the construction site began to stir. The masons spat into their hands and picked up their trowels, levels, and hammers; the boys and girls hired to carry the bricks, groaned as they bent their shoulders and strapped on the wooden devices for carrying bricks, inserting two long poles resembling a yoke on both sides of their necks. The carpenters swung their shiny axes, stonecutters climbed onto the scaffolding and the massive machinery of human labour began to move with sounds of creaking, groaning, and sighing.

Meanwhile, a fellow made his way down the street from the marketplace, looking haggard, sickly and destitute, and entered the construction site.

"God bless you, may you have a nice day!" he said in a weak voice, standing close to the Master Mason. The Master Mason looked at him, together with the other masons.

"Is that you, Benedio? Have you recovered then?"

"I'm healthy enough," replied Benedio. "There's no time to lie around, my mother is old and frail, she can't take care of me!"

"But can you work, man?" asked the Master Mason. "You look like a corpse there, are you sure you can work?"

"Depends," answered Benedio. "I'll do whatever I can. And once I get into the swing of things, I might even recover my strength. Is there a place for me here then?"

"There should be... of course there is. We need all the hands we can get, because the owner is in a hurry to finish the place. Report to the building supervisor and you can start work."

Benedio put his bag of bread and masonry tools to one side and went over to inform the building supervisor that he had turned up to work.

The building supervisor was chastising a carpenter for not trimming a plank properly, when Benedio approached him, hat in hand.

"And what are you doing, dragging your feet there?" the building supervisor snapped at Benedio, not recognizing him immediately and thinking that he was one of the day masons coming to him with some query.

"I wanted to start work, and the Master Mason sent me to let you know that I've recovered and am ready to work. I wanted to know where you want me to start."

"Recovered? Ah, so this is your first time here?"

"No, please, sir, I've already worked here before, but I was injured during the laying of the foundation stone."

"Oh, it's you!" the building supervisor exclaimed. "You caused us all so much trouble then, and now you're coming back?"

"What trouble, sir?"

"Shut up, you fool, when I'm speaking! You were drunk, you didn't move away on time, and I was blamed for everything! No matter what happens, the building supervisor gets the blame. They say he's at fault, he doesn't care about human life, he doesn't know how to lower a foundation stone! No, enough of that, I don't need such workers here!"

"I was drunk?" Benedio exclaimed in surprise. "Sir, I've never been drunk in my life... Who told you that?"

"Oh, so if I was to believe you, you'd swear that you don't even know what vodka looks like. No, forget it, I don't need you here!"

"But sir, have a heart! What did I do to you? I lost my health here, barely managed to recover, and if you drive me away now, where will I earn a living? Who will hire me?"

"Whoever wants to hire you is free to do so! What's it to me! It's entirely up to me to hire whoever I please!"

"But I've already been accepted here. And if I've been absent for three weeks, it wasn't through any fault of my own. I'm saying nothing about the pain that I endured, nor am I demanding any money to help support me during that time. If it wasn't for some kind people who helped me out, I would have died of hunger along with my mother. But I'm entitled to work here!"

"Ha-ha-ha! Entitled, are we? What makes you think that? Do you know, you stupid fool, that every day and every hour that you work here, you do so at my mercy? If I decide that you must go, then you leave! Take me to court, for all I care!"

At this, Benedio was lost for words. He hung his head and remained silent, but the building supervisor's words cut him to the quick. True, he had heard such words before, but they had never made such an impact on him, never had they evoked such a strong feeling of injustice in his heart. 'Can this really be true?' he thought. 'Does a worker always toil at someone else's mercy? And if the worker makes ends meet, then, it seems, it was also only thanks to some person's mercy? And so whose mercy left me crippled? And if he's always so kind to the workers, then whose mercy is now forcing me out of work, leaving me to starve to death? No, something isn't right here! I don't know whether the mercy of the building supervisor has kept me alive until now, but I do know, that by his 'grace' I was left injured, weak and unable to work!'

"Well, what is it?" the builder interrupted his thoughts. "Why are you still standing there? Get out of here!"

"I'm not in your way, sir, but I'll go. It just seemed to me that things shouldn't be as they are."

"What? Are you trying to lecture me? Well, well, well, tell me, then, how should things be?"

"You must know, sir, that you are just as much a servant as I am. If they didn't hire you to do this job, like they hired me, you would also die of hunger."

"Ha-ha-ha! You must have acquired all that wisdom while lying in bed! Alright, continue… How should things be then?"

The building supervisor stood in front of Benedio, his hands on his hips, and laughed. And yet his face was flushed red, indicating that he was seething with anger, ready to explode at any moment despite the forced laughter. But Benedio paid no attention to his laughter nor his anger. The injustice he had just experienced emboldened him.

"And what's more, sir," he said firmly, "you shouldn't go offending poor workers or deriding them for being sick in bed, because who knows, what fate has in store for you."

And then, without waiting for the fellow's response, Benedio turned around, grabbed his sack, and called out to the other workers: "Stay well, brothers!" and left the building site.

Where to now? Poor Benedio had pinned all his hopes on this job. He knew that others wouldn't hire someone as weak as himself. But now, with this last hope shattered, he stood in the street like a man defeated, not knowing where to turn. Should he return home to his old mother, who was awaiting his earnings? Or search for work? But where? Hope seemed nowhere in sight. And then it occurred to approach someone higher than the building supervisor – in fact to seek out Leon himself.

While he was pondering this, standing in the street near the construction site, a messenger ran up and loudly called for the building supervisor to come and see Leon. The building supervisor was surprised and asked if Mr. Leon had already returned from Vienna.

"He arrived last night and asks that you come promptly to see him."

Followed by Benedio, the building supervisor went off to Leon's home. Leon was walking around the yard, and when he noticed the two men approaching, and made his way toward them.

"I have a small matter to discuss with you," he said, greeting the building supervisor. And then, turning to Benedio, he asked: "And what brings you here?"

"I'm after work, sir," said Benedio.

"That's not my department, ask the building supervisor."

"I already have, but he refuses…"

"Of course, I don't want to," the building supervisor interjected. "This is the same fellow," he said, turning to Leon, "who was injured during the laying of the foundation stone because of his own negligence. What use is such a worker to me? Moreover, he's still weak, and I already have enough workers."

"Ah, that one!" Leon recalled. "Hmm, it would seem appropriate though to do something for him, anything at all."

And he added, turning to Benedio: "Well, well, wait here until I call you. You can sit on the porch and rest awhile."

Leon and the building supervisor talked for a long time inside the house. Meanwhile, Benedio sat on the porch, basking in the sun.

The building supervisor emerged after a while, sour-faced, and marched off without paying any attention to Benedio. A few moments later Leon came out as well.

"Are you after work?" he asked Benedio.

"Indeed, sir. A man lives by work, for him work is equivalent to life itself."

"Well, as you can see, the building supervisor doesn't want to employ you here in Drohobych. But don't worry, I'm starting to build a new steam mill in Boryslav, so there'll be plenty of work for you there."

"In Boryslav? A steam mill?" wondered Benedio out loud, and then bit his lip, not daring to engage in conversation with such a gentleman.

"What's so surprising about that?" asked Leon with a smile. "A mill is a mill, it should be all the same to a mason."

"As I was thinking to myself, sir, it's your business to give orders, and ours to follow them. A mill is a mill."

"The only thing is," Leon continued, "I'd like the building to be simple, just so, the walls two bricks thick, without a second floor, only a little wider than usual. It won't be your ordinary steam mill, like others are building. I found a man who came up with the idea, drew up the plans, and he'll be overseeing the construction. The building supervisor turned up his nose at the work when he saw the design. Do you understand how to work off a plan?"

"Sure! If you have a drawing and a ruler, it's no big deal."

"Exactly, sure, it's no big deal," Leon repeated. "Unfortunately, I won't always be able to oversee the work there in Boryslav, and the building supervisor argued so much with me that I'm sure he's ready to build something quite different to what is in the plans. I will ask you to let me know as soon as possible, if you agree to take on the work."

Benedio stood there and wondered what kind of mill this could be, that the building supervisor turned up his nose at it and that Leon was afraid that he might not build it according to the plans? And why had Leon approached him to supervise the construction? Benedio couldn't find an answer to any of the questions and stood before Leon, as if hesitating.

"Don't worry, just be frank with me, and you surely won't regret it. Since the mill is being built in Boryslav, you will have to work there, and you'll be paid as a mason rather than an assistant. And after that – we'll see."

This surprised Benedio even more. Why suddenly this generosity from Leon? And yet, who knows, what his reasons were. Maybe he genuinely needed it built this way, so he was willing to pay. But why was it such a big deal? However, for a poor mason's assistant, this was a significant act of kindness. After reflecting on this, Benedio decided to agree to Leon's terms and thanked him for his generosity.

"Come, don't thank me," answered Leon. "I don't need your gratitude, only loyal service: if you do well, I certainly won't forget you. Now go and make your way to Boryslav as quickly as you can, so that tomorrow you can be on site there, on the outskirts of Boryslav, by the river."

And with these words Leon gave Benedio a few rinskys as an advance and went back inside the house. Benedio had not expected such a lucky twist of fate that day. Comforted, he returned home and told his old mother everything that had transpired that day.

"I have no choice, mother!" he finished his story. "I need to accept work where it is offered. I must go to Boryslav."

"I'm not stopping you, my son, just make sure that you act honestly and never lend your hand to wrongdoing. Because something seems not quite right with that mill. God knows what that cunning gentleman is up to, but you should take care of your soul."

"Yes, I too felt there was something strange about the way he spoke. And I didn't particularly like the idea of having to oversee the construction. It's true that the builder is a deceitful fraud, but who am I, a simple worker, to oversee the work of masons? Well, if I really see that something is wrong, I'll let him know and take no money from him. We'll see what happens."

But when Benedio was about to leave and was saying goodbye to his mother, the old woman suddenly burst into tears. Embracing her son, she wouldn't let go of him for a long time.

"Oh, come, mother, we'll see each other soon enough!" Benedio tried to comfort her.

"Yes, yes, it's easy for you to say!" replied his mother, tears streaming down her face. "Can't you see how old I am? I have so little time left. And when I see you walking away, it seems to me I will never see you again."

"God forbid, mother! Don't say such things!"

"I'm saying what's in my heart. And I get the feeling that you are entering some sort of trap by going to Boryslav, and that it would be better if you returned that advance to Mr. Leon and remained here."

"But, mother dear, how can I stay here when there is no work? I promise you, as soon as I see any mischief, no matter how much that man pays me, I'll stop working for him right there and then."

"Well, if that's your wish, then go. May God bless you!"

With tears in her eyes, the old mother saw her son off on the road to Boryslav. When she returned to their modest home, she stood for a long time, her hands folded, and then burst into sobs:

"My dear Benedio! May God bless you on your journey! I may never see you again!"

IV

Benedio began his journey on a Sunday. As he passed by the Holy Trinity Church, he heard the deacons singing their praises to the Lord in deep voices. On the opposite side of the road from the church, a group of oil workers, wearing oil-smeared shirts and tattered jackets, sat along a brick wall on the uneven cobblestone pavement. They were waiting for the church service to conclude so they could continue their journey to Boryslav. Some of them crossed themselves and quietly recited the Lord's Prayer, while others dozed in the scorching sun. A few of them nibbled on inexpensive loaves of bread, which they helped down with onions.

Benedio didn't linger around the church. Although the distance from Drohobych to Boryslav wasn't far and, unlike most of the oil workers, he didn't need to search for work once he arrived there, he had heard that it was difficult to find lodgings in Boryslav. He preferred to live somewhere close to the factory site where he would be working. After sustaining injuries while laying the foundation stone, his legs were still weak, and he knew that he wouldn't be able to cover any great distance through Boryslav's notorious mud which supposedly never dried up. Thus, Benedio was in a hurry to reach Boryslav to secure lodgings before the influx of workers had occupied every available nook and cranny. He needed to rent a room for an extended period, by the month. Such rooms were harder to come by because most of the rat holes in Boryslav were rented out on a nightly basis to transient individuals, as this earned the landlords greater profits.

On leaving town, Benedio was amazed to see that as far as the eye could see there were groups of oil workers slowly plodding along the highway, raising clouds of dust. They had not waited for the church service to end, but had hurried on to find any type of work. Each one carried bread in his soiled cloth bag; in some cases, onion greens also poked out of them. At first, Benedio overtook these groups of men and walked by himself. But with time he grew weary and bored walking alone. The sun was parching the earth, which was already baked dry and cracking. Although it was almost the end of spring, the crops in the fields gave no indication of it. The oats, having come up already, were withered for lack of rain and hugged the earth. The winter wheat had pushed its stalks out of the earth a little and then remained that way, refusing to set ears, although this was the time for it. Vegetables and potatoes had not even sprouted; the soil, bone dry and with a crust several inches deep, delivered no moisture to the sown seeds. Sadness gripped the hearts of the people when they looked at their fields, for there were only nettles and mustard weed, which had sprung up early and sunk their spindly roots deep into the ground, flourishing and spreading. Meanwhile, the sun kept beating down and parching the earth. Almost as if to tease the wretched tillers of the soil, clouds would gather in the sky toward evening and then, without shedding a single drop of rain, disperse at nightfall.

In the villages through which the oil workers passed, they came across people who were long-faced and black as the earth. The usual Sunday laughter and banter was not to be heard. The older farmers would look up at the sun and then down at the earth as though with reproach, and hung their heads in despair. Bathed in sweat and covered in dust, with brooding thoughts weighing down on his spirits, Benedio tramped morosely through these villages that were already starving even before the harvest, waiting for more terrible times to come.

The heartfelt prayers of the villagers reached Benedio's ears from nearly every household. "Show us Christian folk your tender mercies, oh Lord," they entreated. But the heavens appeared unmoved, the sun continued to relentlessly scorch the earth, as if trying to surpass itself. The thin, whitish and translucent clouds drifted lazily in from the west.

Benedio felt uncomfortable walking alone amid this misery, so he joined a small group of oil workers.

"Where is the good Lord taking you?" they asked Benedio, after the customary greetings.

"To the same place as yourselves," Benedio replied.

"Oh, but you're not heading for the oil pits, are you?"

"No, I'm a mason."

"So maybe there's something new being built somewhere?"

"Sure, I've already been hired. Hammerschlag is building a new…" Benedio stammered. He hadn't believed the talk about Leon's new steam mill before, and now, after talking with the oil workers, he sensed that it would be unwise to mention the steam mill to them. "…a new oil refinery," he concluded.

"Well, thank God, at least there'll be some new work," one of the oil workers said. "Maybe one can find a berth there somehow."

"Isn't there work in the oil pits?" Benedio asked.

"Well, there is," replied the oil worker, waving his hand dismissively. "But what's the point when the pay is so meagre that you can barely make ends meet? Look at the hordes of people flocking there, and mind you, what you see here is only a small part of those looking for work! This year the time before the harvest is particularly harsh, and to add to our woes, just look at God's wrath! It's only May, yet the heat is as intense as during harvest time, and there's no rain. You think there won't be a famine? And what can the people do? Those who still have a glimmer of strength in them come here in the hope of earning something. It's a boon for the Jewish pit owners. The more workers that arrive, the lower they push the wages. And you either accept what they offer, or find yourself replaced by one of the ten men waiting eagerly in line to take your job. And don't assume that they aren't there! Step out into the streets of a morning and the unemployed are as numerous as weeds, they're everywhere. About half of them find work, while the rest either return home empty-handed or scrounge work here and there, fetching water or chopping wood and the like in exchange for a piece of bread or a bowl of gruel. That is the misery of our Boryslav!"

The oil workers in the group all began talking at once, sharing their own experiences of suffering in Boryslav. Their comrade's account of the misery in the town had deeply affected them. Each worker found something to add, and Benedio was confronted with a horrifying picture of human suffering and oppression. While he had heard that the work in Boryslav could be dangerous but was well paid, seeing the wretched appearance of the droves of oil workers who sat around the Drohobych church on Sundays made him question the truth of those claims. But he had never had the opportunity to learn firsthand how bad things really were. The accounts of the oil workers opened his eyes to the truth. The terrible, desperate situation of so many people moved him profoundly and as he walked, he was unable to think of anything else.

'Can this really be true?' he asked himself. Throughout his life he had witnessed enough misery and suffering – poverty, hunger, oppression, arbitrary actions, and unemployment. However, nothing he had experienced could compare to the depths of despair and humiliation described by these oil workers. They recounted horrifying tales of death from starvation, suicide and robbery. What struck Benedio most was something he hadn't encountered before: a lack of solidarity among the workers in dire need. Instead of extending a helping hand, they left each other to the whims of fate. The oil workers recounted how their sick comrades had died, abandoned and covered in maggots, with their lifeless bodies discovered days later in remote corners. These stories deeply affected Benedio.

He had grown up and been raised in Drohobych. His father had also been a mason's assistant, so from an early age Benedio had experienced firsthand the traditional ways of tradesmen. While the guild system was poorly organized during Benedio's time and there had been somewhat weak attempts at mutual aid, he still recalled the strong sense of fraternity among those who worked in the same trade.

True, back then the guild structure among the masons of Drohobych was at an all-time low. The Master Masons had long since cleaned out the guild treasury, into which both they and their assistants had for a long time paid their dues, but which had been managed by the Master Masons alone, with no supervision or accountability. The guild hall, where the guild council assembled on appointed days and once a gathering place for apprentices seeking work, had fallen into disrepair due to the lack of funds. The Master Masons had ceased to be involved in guild affairs and now cared only about whose turn it was to carry the old guild banner on ceremonial occasions.

During Benedio's time, a nascent form of solidarity had begun to emerge among the masons of Drohobych, albeit in a somewhat undefined and fragmented manner. When one of their own fell ill, the other masons and assistants voluntarily contributed to provide a weekly benefit to support the afflicted person or their family while they were ailing. Similarly, a modest benefit was extended to those who found themselves out of work, with concerted efforts made to help them secure employment within the trade or in other fields. While these initial efforts at mutual aid were still in their infancy, they persisted and gained strength over time. It was hoped that, eventually, in times of need, not just some, but all the tradespeople would wholeheartedly contribute their pledged share.

Benedio had grown up in a town where these guild relations were a way of life. After finishing his apprenticeship, he worked first as a labourer and later as a mason's assistant, becoming actively engaged in the emergence of labour solidarity. Poor and in fragile health, Benedio felt the importance of unity and mutual support more keenly than others. Right from the beginning of his apprenticeship, he never ceased to encourage his fellow workers to fulfill their commitments and make only promises they could keep. Once a promise was made, he urged them to stand by their word, so that people could trust a worker's word. While these principles weren't new in theory, they were seldom put into practice. They demanded strong self-discipline of one's will and desires. Alongside a few dedicated apprentices who shared his passion, Benedio spent many years tirelessly working to teach people greater precision and restraint in their actions.

The Drohobych masons acted in relative isolation, so to speak. They had little to no contact with workers from the larger cities, apart from their counterparts in Stryj and Sambir, who were equally uninformed. The Drohobych masons remained oblivious to the rising tide of worker solidarity and unity in other countries. They were unaware that workers worldwide were coming together, preparing for a monumental battle against entrenched wealth and societal injustices. These workers were advocating for improved wages, the security of their families, financial stability in their old age, and assistance for widows and orphans. The Drohobych masons were also ignorant of the surge in worker ideals in Western Europe. Yet despite their lack of knowledge, similar circumstances led to the gradual emergence of these very same ideals and struggles within their own midst.

In difficult moments Benedio had frequently contemplated the plight of the common worker. Born with a delicate constitution, he possessed a keen sensitivity to suffering, whether it was his own or that of others, and he abhorred any form of injustice. When a Master Mason unjustly scolded an apprentice, when a paymaster shortchanged a labourer, when a contractor terminated a man's employment without valid reason or for something he had uttered – Benedio felt as if a dagger was being driven into his heart. He would turn pale, bend over double, his face, already gaunt, would become even more drawn out, and he would quietly resume his work, though his inner turmoil was evident. At such times Benedio asked why it was that anyone was free to mistreat workers with no redress. For instance, a building supervisor could push a worker off a wall, hurl the vilest insults at him, and even physically assault the man, even dismiss him. However, if the worker were to retaliate with a single well-placed punch, he would find himself dragged off to a police station, facing court, and likely ending up behind bars. Benedio recognized that these injustices stemmed from the social disparities among men. And although he often repeated, as millions of others did, that 'things shouldn't be this way,' these words failed to provide him with answers to the enigma of the root causes of such inequality and whether it could ever be eradicated.

That was how things stood at present. Benedio walked in silence, absorbing the accounts of the oil workers about their harsh life in Boryslav. He couldn't help but wonder how it was that thousands endured such gruelling toil day after day, while thousands more eagerly sought to partake of this bitter feast? They seemed to be doing themselves harm in the process. It was true, life was even harsher in the villages, for even if no one subjected the people there to such cruelty or exploited them so harshly, they still had to grapple with hunger. Oh, Lord, how can such a multitude of people be helped? There was no way!

"And what about you," Benedio suddenly asked the oil workers, "have you ever thought of a way of helping one another?"

"What way can there possibly be?" an oil worker asked frankly. "There's no way at all."

Benedio lowered his head. The oil worker had stated with unwavering determination and with the greatest conviction what he himself had concluded. It seemed things were destined to remain as they were. But maybe there was another way, one they were either oblivious to or too reluctant to pursue, or else they should have stumbled upon it by now.

"Well, have you tried taking up collections among yourselves to help those who are sick or in need?" Benedio asked.

The oil workers burst out laughing.

"How many contributions would it take to help all the needy men! Everyone's needy these days."

"Yes, but some are worse off than others. Surely the more needy ones, the sick and the unemployed, can be given a helping hand. That's what the masons do back home."

"Eh, it's one thing there, and another thing here. The people here are from all over the place."

"It's no different back home."

"All the same, what might work for you, won't ever work for us here."

It seemed to Benedio that the oil workers were unaware of their own potential and had no faith in it. He fell silent, reflecting on their words. 'Ah,' he mused, 'even from this, it's evident that there must be a way out of their misery. Some may be blind and will never discover it, while others are simply too apathetic to search for it!'

Meanwhile, the group had turned off the Tustanovychi Highway and set off along a path across a creek and over a hill that led to Boryslav. After wading across the creek and making their way up a steep high bank through dense undergrowth and hazelnut thickets, they now stood on the crest of a hill. Boryslav lay before them, as if on a platter. Squat, wooden-cladded houses shone in the sun like silver. Here and there above the buildings rose the thin, tall, red chimneys of the oil refineries, looking like scarlet ribbons rising into the sky. On a hill far away, on the other side of Boryslav, stood a little old church surrounded by linden trees, and around it huddled the remains of a former village.

Although Benedio had visited Boryslav briefly in the past, he was not familiar with the town. Therefore, he told the oil workers where he would be working and asked for their help in finding the place. The oil workers directed Benedio to an extensive open area on the outskirts of Boryslav, not too far from where they were standing. As there were not many houses nearby, Benedio bid them farewell and decided to go door to door in search of lodgings. But the Jewish owners of the first houses he entered refused to rent him a room for a protracted period. These houses were spacious, with many nooks and crannies under their low roofs to accommodate oil workers. They were conveniently located on the outskirts of Boryslav, which allowed them to cater to both new and late arrivals.

Benedio inquired at five or six houses without any success. Then he found himself standing before a tiny old house, unsure whether he should go in and ask for a room, or to give the shanty a miss and continue on his way. The roof, like all the others, was made of wood, but this had started to rot and was covered in green moss. Two tiny windows faced the street, located barely above ground level. Mud from the high embankment of the street seeped down into the yard, staining the walls and almost reaching the window frames.

The front yard of this house was bare, much like the surroundings – no garden or grass, as one might find in other places. After a brief pause, Benedio finally made up his mind to step inside.

The door squeaked and Benedio entered: first there was a narrow, dark anteroom, and then a whitewashed living room. To his surprise, he came across an old oil worker and a young woman, aged thirty or so, dressed in a white blouse with red buttons. She was sitting on a bench beside the window, resting her head on her elbow, weeping. The old oil worker sat in the middle of the room on a low stool, a pipe between his teeth, and appeared to be comforting her. When Benedio entered the room, the young woman quickly wiped away her tears, and the old man began to cough and poke about in his pipe. Benedio greeted them and asked whether they might consider taking him in as a regular boarder. The oil worker and the woman exchanged glances and remained silent for a moment. Finally, the man spoke:

"How should I know? Ask the woman here – it's her house, she can decide."

"Really!" the woman exclaimed sharply. "How can I decide! I haven't been living here for a whole year now, and God knows if I'll ever live here again," and with her sleeve she wiped away her tears. "Stop making out that I'm in charge here. You live here and the decision is all yours. Do whatever pleases you, I have no say in the matter!"

The old oil worker was somewhat taken aback and began to poke about more assiduously in his clay pipe, although there was no tobacco in it. Benedio remained standing in the doorway, his sack over his shoulder.

"The house is small, as you can see," the woman began again, "and maybe you wouldn't be comfortable here. I can see you're a townsman, and you may not be accustomed to the way things are here…"

The woman had made this remark because she noticed the furrowed brows of the oil worker and thought that he wanted to turn Benedio down.

"So what if I'm a townsman?" replied Benedio. "Don't worry, I'm accustomed to all kinds of privation. Like any man who must work for a living. But, you see, here's my problem – I have some weakness in my legs due to a work accident. These sorts of mishaps are not uncommon with us masons. The work I've secured here is close by. They're building a new factory. So, you see, I'd like to find living quarters in the area, just a place to sleep, for I'll be at work all day long. I'm not in any shape to walk great distances through your Boryslav mud. In the rooming houses they refused to take me on as a steady boarder, and anyway, I would prefer lodging with working folk like myself. But if you…"

The old oil worker interrupted him at this point. He cast his pipe aside, rose from his stool, and rushed toward Benedio. With one hand, he wrested the sack from Benedio's back, and with the other he gently urged him to sit down on a bench.

"Oh, for God's sake, man," the old man shouted with feigned anger, "don't dawdle there! Take a seat and may good fortune enter our house together with you. Why didn't you say from the very start what it was you wanted? Now I'm liable to think that I'm worse than other people!"

Benedio stared at the queer old chap, as though he didn't understand his words, and then asked:

"So what does that mean? Are you taking me in?"

"Can't you hear that I am?" the old man said. "Only you'll have to behave yourself, of course. If you don't, out you go the very next day."

"I guess we'll get along then," Benedio said.

"Well, if we get along, you'll be like a son to me, though to tell you the truth, I haven't had much luck with those sons."

The woman wiped away her tears once more.

"What will you charge me?"

"Have you any family?"

"I have a mother."

"Is she old?"

"Yes."

"Well, then you'll pay me a shistka[7] each month."

....

[7] Unit of currency – one shistka equalled ten Austrian cents (kreutzers).

Benedio stared incredulously at the old man again.

"You probably meant 'each week'?"

"I know best what I meant to say," the old man snapped back. "My word stands and that's that."

Benedio couldn't shake off his astonishment. In the meantime, the old fellow sat down on his stool again and, frowning, began to pack his pipe with tobacco.

"Should I fetch some vodka to seal the bargain?" Benedio spoke up.

The old man looked at him askance.

"Don't start coming around here with any of that brew, young fellow, don't even let me see any in the house, or I'll turf you out together with your bottle!" he snapped angrily.

"Forgive me," Benedio apologized. "I don't drink myself, and I wouldn't care if there never was any alcohol. But I've heard that everyone who works on the oilfields in Boryslav likes to drink, which is why…"

"Yeah, the person who told you that was right, but you know how it is, truth can be a bit tricky sometimes. Anyway, enough chitchat – why don't you take off your coat and rest for a bit? You've had a long journey, and you don't seem to be in too good a shape."

At this point the woman rose to her feet.

"May the Lord grant you happiness and a good wage," she said to Benedio. "Goodbye, it's time I went."

She stepped outside, followed by the old man, who returned a minute later.

"She works in Tustanovychi, so she needs to hurry off to work. And she has a small child…" he muttered under his breath and sat down once more to fill his clay pipe.

"Your daughter?" Benedio asked.

"As good as, but not by blood."

"Stepdaughter?"

"No, young man. She's a local, and I'm not. But it's a long story, maybe you'll hear it one day. For now you should rest!"

The woman was Mrs. Pivtorak, the widow of Ivan Pivtorak, who had died in the Boryslav pits, and the oil worker was old Matiy.

Benedio removed his overcoat, spread it on a bench beneath the window, and lay down to rest. He was extremely tired, his legs ached from the long arduous journey. But for some reason sleep eluded him. His thoughts flitted about, akin to a restless swallow in flight. Initially, he couldn't help but worry about his elderly mother back in Drohobych and the uncertainties of his new life in Boryslav. The stories shared by the oil workers during his journey here replayed in his mind as vivid images. Here was a sick helpless oil worker, abandoned by everyone, dying alone in a den in some godforsaken corner and crying out in vain for food and drink, and there was no one to bring him any! And there was a boss firing a worker after underpaying him, abusing and insulting him, with no one to stand up for the worker in his time of need. 'No one cares about anything, except themselves,' Benedio thought, 'which is why they are all suffering. If they could only band together… But what could they achieve then?' Benedio had no answer. Nor did he know how they could all be brought together. "Lord Almighty," he sighed at last with the despair of the common folk, "bestow upon me some useful thoughts!"

At that moment his thoughts were interrupted. Several oil workers entered the house and, after greeting old Matiy, sat down on a bench. Benedio sat up and began to examine the newcomers. Two of the young men would immediately have attracted anyone's attention. Tall and strong like two oak trees, they had broad, red, slightly puffy faces and small grey eyes. In the wee house they looked like giants. They were so much alike in build, hair and eyes that you needed to watch and listen closely to tell them apart. One of them sat on the bench by the window, his broad shoulders shutting out the light streaming into the room from the setting sun.

The other settled down on the small stool by the door and, without a word to anyone, calmly began to fill his pipe, as though the place beside the door belonged to him and had been his for ages.

Apart from these two giants, Benedio's attention was drawn to a short man who was no longer young and who was extremely talkative and lively. He hadn't stopped darting from corner to corner since he entered the house, as though he was looking for something or trying to find a comfortable spot to sit. He had looked Benedio over several times, exchanged glances with Matiy, who followed his movements with a smile, and had even whispered something in the ear of one of the giants, the one on the stool by the door. The giant only shook his head, and then got up, opened the iron door of the oven and shoved his pipe into the embers to light it. Meanwhile, the lively fellow made the rounds of all the corners of the room once more, patted down his hair, which was bristly as a brush, adjusted his belt, and finally began to wave his arms about.

In the dim twilight, aside from these three men, Benedio made out the figure of another old man with a long grey beard, but youthful and robust in appearance. Seated next to him was a young lad with a round face and rosy cheeks, but he appeared despondent and gloomy, as though he had been sentenced to death. Further in the corner, shrouded in darkness, sat several others whose faces Benedio was unable to make out. Soon after, a few more oil workers entered the room, creating a commotion.

"And who's this? A bailiff come to take your furniture away for not paying taxes?" boomed the giant sitting by the window in a deep voice that sounded like a foghorn.

"No, thank God," Matiy answered, "this is an honest man, I've learnt, a worker, a Master Mason. He arrived today from Drohobych to work on the new factory they're building down on the meadow."

"Is that so?" drawled the giant. "Well, it's alright by me. Whose factory is it going to be?" he asked, turning to Benedio.

"Leon Hammerschlag's, the one, you know, who came here from Vienna two years ago."

"Oho, that one! Oh, we have enough notches against him to last a while. Isn't that so, brother Derkach?"

The lively man was at the giant's side in a flash, dancing around him on tiptoe.

"That's true, that's true, we have more than enough notches against his name," he laughed, "but it wouldn't hurt to cut him a few more!"

"Of course it wouldn't," the giant confirmed. "But can we conduct our business here today, brother Matiy, or do you want us to find another place to meet, since you've got yourself a new lodger?"

The giant looked at Matiy sternly, and the words were evidently meant as a rebuke. Matiy sensed this and became a little confused. But then he rose from his stool, removed the pipe from his mouth and said:

"God forbid, I would never chase you out! My dear brethren, once I've joined your ranks, I won't ever forsake you, you can count on that. My home is always open to all of you. As for the new lodger… it's true, I was wrong to take him in without first consulting you, but as you can see, a man appears who is weary and ailing, no one wants to offer him a roof over his head. You can tell from his face – and I have experience in that department – that he's a good man, so what could I do? However, I'll leave it up to you? If he can't be part of our group, I'll send him on his merry way. Yet, it seems to me he could be a valuable addition. He claims not to drink, which is one good thing in his favour. Moreover, he'll be working on the new factory, so he can keep us informed of the situation there from time to time."

"You say he doesn't drink vodka?" asked the giant.

"I myself heard him say so, but there he is, you can ask him yourself."

A heavy silence filled the room. Benedio sat in a corner on his coat, growing increasingly puzzled by the reason for this gathering. Why were these people assembled here, and what did they expect from him? He found it astonishing to hear Matiy apologizing to them, despite having claimed that the house was his own. Yet, the most bewildering aspect was the commanding demeanour of the husky-voiced giant, who acted as if he were in charge, summoning one man after another and whispering into their ears, without budging from his seat. Finally the fellow turned his attention to Benedio, interrogating him with a stern tone, sounding like a judge in court, while all present rested their eyes on him.

"What are you then, an apprentice?"

"No, I'm an assistant, but while I'm working on the factory here, I don't know who I have to thank for it, but I'm being employed as a Master Mason."

The giant nodded.

"Hm, a Master Mason? How d'you earn that favour? I suppose you're good at snitching on your fellow-workers?"

Benedio became incensed. For a moment he hesitated whether to answer the giant or to spit in his face, pack his things and leave this house and these strange people. But then he restrained himself.

"You're talking nonsense," he said sharply. "Maybe your father's son knows how to inform on others, but where I come from, we don't go in for that sort of thing. And as for earning the favour of my boss, I never asked for it. Maybe it's because I was nearly killed when we were laying the foundation stone for his new house!"

"Aha," the giant drawled gruffly and his voice grew milder.

"Brother Derkach," he suddenly turned to the small, lively man, "don't forget to cut a notch against Leon Hammerschlag for what this man has just told us!"

"Naturally, I won't forget. Although it took place in Drohobych, and we're responsible only for Boryslav, but that won't hurt. It won't make matters any easier for that gentleman."

"Well, and how about you," the giant continued to question Benedio. "Now that you're a Master Mason here, are you going to be ruthless, exploiting workers and dismissing them at the first sign of protest? Like all the others, I bet! All Master Masons are cut from the same cloth!"

Benedio's patience was wearing thin. He stood up, grabbed his coat, and turned to Matiy:

"When you offered me lodging in your home," he said in a trembling voice, "you mentioned that if I behaved, I would become like a son to you. But please tell me, how can I be kind and proper, when people march into your house and start insulting and harassing me for no reason at all? If this was why you took me in, it would have been better had you turned me away, for by now I would have found a more peaceful place to stay. Now, I'll have to venture out into the twilight. But at least I'll know what kind of people the workers of Boryslav are! Goodbye!"

With these words he put on his coat and, hoisting his bundle onto his shoulders, turned toward the door. Everyone was silent, only Matiy winked to the giant by the window. Meanwhile the other giant sat like a mountain in front of the door, blocking the way out. Although Benedio said to him angrily: "Let me pass!" the fellow didn't move a muscle, as though he hadn't heard a thing, and only kept puffing on his pipe.

"Lord Almighty!" Matiy suddenly exclaimed with comically exaggerated zeal. "Hold on a moment, my good man! Where are you rushing off to? Can't you take a joke? Exercise some patience and you'll soon understand what all this is about!"

"Why should I stay!" Benedio replied angrily. "Perhaps you want me to accept more of the same insults from this man? I can't figure out where he heard that I'm cruel to people and treat them harshly?"

"So you feel that my words have shamed you?" the giant inquired, a blend of meekness and sternness in his voice.

"Naturally."

"Well, then, I beg your pardon."

"There's no need to beg my pardon, rather you could be more polite and stop insulting people, instead of begging their pardon afterwards. I'm a common man, a poor workman, but is that any reason why anyone who comes along should treat me this way? Or maybe you're hoping that because you are strong, you can bully me without fear of retaliation? Well, then let me pass, I don't want to hear any more of your talk!" And he turned to face the door again.

"Well, well, well," Matiy interjected, "these folks might end up having a real quarrel here, not even realizing why themselves! Just hold on there, my friend, you're getting all worked up without understanding what this is all about."

"What do you mean? Don't worry, I'm not such a dimwit," Benedio replied in a huff.

"Of course, you're not. You took this man's words for an insult, but he was merely testing you!"

"Testing me? About what?"

"To see what's in your head and your heart. Do you understand now?"

"And why does he need to know?"

"You'll find that out later. For the moment, take off your coat and sit down. And there's no need to be angry, my good man. If we went about getting huffy about every little thing that ruffled our feathers, we wouldn't have the strength to last the day. The way I see it, a man must suffer small injuries to avoid major ones. Although with people it's usually the other way around: they grumble about small misfortunes, but stay quiet when it comes to the big ones."

Benedio stood in the middle of the room in his coat, his sack slung over his shoulder, and surveyed those present. In the meantime Matiy lit a candle made of yellow Boryslav wax and in its light the faces of the assembled oil workers appeared yellow and glum, like the faces of corpses. Matiy grabbed Benedio's sack and helped him off with the overcoat, and then, grasping him by the shoulder, he led him over to the giant sitting by the window, grim and threatening.

"Come, let's bury the hatchet once and for all, lads," Matiy said. "I have a feeling this man will prove to be a fine comrade for us."

Benedio and the giant shook hands.

"What should we call you?" the giant asked.

"Benedio Synytsia."

"I'm Andrus Basarab, and this here is my brother Sen. That over there is our 'notcher,' Derkach, and this old fellow is brother Stasiura. The young lad is Pryidevolia and those folks over there are our brethren as well. And of course this here is your landlord..."

"You must all be from same village, since you call one another brothers," said Benedio, intrigued that both the young and the old men had formed this fraternity. For it was more common in villages for people of the same age to join such fraternal associations.

"No, we're not from the same village," Basarab replied, "and we are brethren for another reason altogether. Sit down and you'll see for yourself what we are about. And if you wish, you can join our fraternity."

The explanation astonished Benedio even more. He sat down without a word and waited to see what would happen.

"Brother Derkach," said Andrus Basarab to the 'notcher,' "it's time to get down to business. Where are your sticks?"

"They'll be here presently," Derkach answered and ran into the anteroom, returning with an armload of thin sticks, tied tightly together. Each stick had bigger or smaller notches cut into it, like the ones boys made when tending geese in the fields, allowing them to keep track of their flock.

"Let's add a notch for Leon based on what Synytsia told us," added Basarab. A deep hush settled on the house as everyone found a seat and focused their attention on Derkach. He settled down near the front of the oven, placed the sticks beside him, took a knife from his belt and, selecting one of the sticks, added another notch to the large number already carved into it.

"Done," said Derkach upon finishing the task, and returned the stick to the bundle.

"And now, my dear brethren," said Andrus, "tell us in turn what each of you experienced this past week, and whether you saw or heard of any instances of cruelty or injustice. Who performed it, to whom, and why – tell us everything, so that when the cup of our suffering runneth over, when our time and our judgment day comes, everyone will receive their just deserts!"

There was a minute of silence following this appeal, and then old Stasiura began to speak:

"You say that our time and our judgment day will come… You know, I probably won't live to see that day, but at least you younger ones might… So, to make sure that each one gets what is coming to them, listen to what I saw and heard this week. Yoska Bergman, the overseer at the workers' barracks where I work, once again beat up four labourers this week. He went as far as knocking out two teeth of a Boyko worker who had been hired to carry away the clay extracted during the sinking of a new pit. And why, you may ask? Simply because the poor fellow, who was hungry and cold, lacked the strength to carry a full basket of earth on his shoulders!"

"Notch that one, Derkach!" said Andrus in a calm and even voice, but his eyes were gleaming with a strange fire.

"That young Boyko," Stasiura continued, "is an upstanding fellow and I would have brought him with me, only he must have fallen ill, because he didn't show up for work yesterday."

"Bring him with you next time," Andrus interrupted. "The greater our numbers, the stronger our collective power. Nothing forges bonds among people like shared suffering and shared injustice. And when we have amassed sufficient strength, our day of reckoning will be at hand. Do you understand, old fellow?"

The old man nodded and continued speaking:

"And Motia Krum, the paymaster, again shortchanged the men in our barracks by five shistkas this week, and even threatened to fire us all if we complained. Word has it that he was buying a well in Mraznytsia[8] and fell short by 59 rinskys for the purchase price, so he deducted it from the workers' wages."

The old man remained silent, while Derkach found Motia Krum's stick and cut a new notch into it. Then he continued:

"And yesterday I was walking past Moshko Fink's tavern. Suddenly I heard yelling. Two of Fink's sons had cornered a middle-aged man and were beating him so ruthlessly, punching him in the ribs, that the man could barely groan any more. When they finally let him go, he couldn't walk without assistance, and started spitting blood… I took him by the arm and helped him along, asking what the trouble had been and why they had beaten him so cruelly. 'It's my bad luck,' the man replied and wept. 'Last week I ran up a bit of debt at that damned tavern, thinking I'd get the money to pay him back. Well, payday came and the paymaster must have forgotten about me or something, because he didn't read my name out. I stood there, waiting, until all the others were paid, and still he hadn't called my name. When I walked up to him to ask what had happened, he quickly shut the door in my face. I knocked, and I banged, and I shouted, but it didn't

....

[8]   Back then Mraznytsia was a village 3 km. southwest from the centre of Boryslav. Today it is a suburb of Boryslav.

help. His servants ran out and beat me and called me a drunk, saying I was trying to start a riot. So I went away. Later I met the paymaster on the street and I asked him why he hadn't given me my wages. He glared at me and then shouted: 'You sod, how dare you accost me in the street! Where were you when the pay was being handed out? I don't know you. Go and get your pay where everyone else gets theirs!' But the pay-office was closed today. I was hungry and went to Moshko's to get a meal on credit until I received my pay, when those two bears walked up to me, shouting: 'Cough up what you owe!' No matter how much I begged them, and tried to explain what had happened, it was no use! They pushed me into a corner and nearly beat the living daylights out of me!'"

"Cut another notch, Derkach, another one!" said Basarab in a firm, stern voice, having listened to the story with clenched teeth. "Our oppressors are becoming more and more brazen, a sign that their punishment is nigh. Cut a notch there, brother, cut it quickly."

"That's just how it is," Stasiura continued, "our oppressors have pulled out all the stops, bullying working people, and meanwhile they are becoming filthy rich! The more you look around and listen, the more poverty and injustice you find among regular folks, and the more big shots you see living the high life. Right now lots of folks are pouring into Boryslav because the villages have been hit hard by hunger, drought and disease. But is it any better here? Every day I see sick, hungry, jobless folks in the back alleys. They're lying there, groaning, and waiting for death to come, because they have given up hope of receiving any kindness from their fellow man. And they've cut our wages again and keep reducing them each week, until there won't be enough to live on! The price of bread keeps growing, and if there is no crop this year, we'll all starve to death. That's the injustice that affects each and every one of us, cutting deep to our core, but I don't know into whose stick we should cut a notch for this!"

The old man delivered his speech in a more animated voice than usual and his lips trembled with emotion. Once he had finished, he looked around at everyone before resting his gaze on Andrus Basarab's sombre expression.

"Yes, yes, you're right, brother Stasiura," all those present cried, "that's the injustice we all share: poverty, desperation and hunger!"

"But who deserves a notch for this?" the old man asked again. "Or should we bear it patiently, this biggest injustice of them all, the one we all suffer, and notch only the small, inconsequential injustices which together equal this big one?"

Andrus Basarab eyed Stasiura and the other brethren, initially with a dismal and seemingly indifferent air. However, gradually something began to gleam in his eyes, as though a concealed joy was welling up from the depths of his heart. He stood up, his towering figure nearly brushing against the low ceiling of the small house.

"No, we won't stand for that big injustice either. We won't take it lying down like sheep. No injustice must go unpunished, every injury must be avenged right here on this earth, for we never know what God's judgment will be like in the afterlife! And don't think that while we are notching all these petty wrongs that we have forgotten about the big one? No! Why, every single wrong, even the smallest one suffered by a working man, is part of that general mistreatment of people which penetrates deep into the bones of each of us. When judgment day rolls around and it's time for payback, you think we won't make them pay for all those injustices as well?"

Stasiura shook his head with a hint of sadness, as if harbouring doubts about the sincerity of Basarab's promise.

"Hey there, brother Andrus," he began, "you talk about seeking revenge, but who even knows when that might happen… And secondly, how does it help us in our current situation to know there will be revenge sometime in the distant future? Even if we do get our revenge, do you truly believe that things will improve afterwards?"

"What's wrong, old man?" Andrus asked, his tone firm, his eyes intense. "Why are you upset for no reason? Yes, it's tough for us all, no doubt about that. I've been through it, and so have the rest of you. But can anyone really change things so that we don't need to suffer anymore? The truth is, no one can, not ever! So we've got to endure until the end, and that's that. Whether it's hard or not, does it really matter? Endure it silently, don't let anyone see that it's getting to you. Keep persevering, and if you can't escape poverty, find a way to ease your suffering, even if it's through exacting vengeance to ease your pain a little. And I think you'll all agree, right?"

"Yes," the brethren responded in unison, though their voices carried a hint of despondency, as if accepting that the truth was a bitter pill to swallow.

"Well, if that's so," Andrus continued, "then there's no need to delay. Let's hear what other injustices have come to your notice."

He sat down. Silence filled the room. Then Matiy began to speak. In his neighbourhood a workman had died in a dark 'closet.' No one knew how long the man had been lying there sick, and the house owners refused to tell anyone. There were rumours that the worker had some savings, and when he fell ill, the house owners had taken his money and kept him locked up until he died. The corpse was frightfully thin, un-washed and bluish in appearance. And just two days earlier a woman had spent the night at a nearby rooming house. During the night she gave birth. Because she had no money, she was promptly expelled from the house with her newborn infant. An oil worker, who knew the woman, said she took the child to the priest to have it baptized, but he refused un-less she disclosed the identity of the father. In desperation, the woman threw the baby into a pit and rushed off to the municipal authorities, crying out for them to hang her there and then because she no longer wanted to live. Matiy had no idea what happened after that.

One story followed another, each marked by grave injustice and a deafening sense of despair. After each story, the speaker would pause, waiting for the recorder, Derkach, to notch a mark on a stick so that 'each received their just deserts.' Some of the brethren spoke with a calm, measured tone, their expressions revealing a stoic acceptance of the pervasive injustice and oppression in society. Others grew passionate as they spoke, cursing those who oppressed them and demanding swift justice.

The most poignant moment for everyone in the room came when it was young Pryidevolia's turn to speak. Being the youngest, he was the last to share his story. Overwhelmed by emotions that he had suppressed for so long, he burst into uncontrollable sobs. With his powerful fists clenched tightly, he strode into the centre of the room.

"Before the good Lord and before you, my brethren, I will reveal my sorrow! The grievous injustice done to me! I've been orphaned for the rest of my life… The very last thing that I had was taken from me and trampled underfoot merely for amusement! Oh, Lord, how can You witness all this and still bear it? Well, you might be able to bear it, but I can't any longer, I refuse to! Brothers, my dear friends, tell me how I should seek revenge! I'll do anything, I'm ready to try anything, just don't tell me to wait, for god's sake, don't tell me to keep bearing this pain!"

He fell silent, sobbing like a small child. After a moment, he continued in a calmer voice:

"You all know I'm a complete orphan, you know the hardships and misery I've endured in my youth, until hard times brought me here to this damned hell. But all that hardship, all that misery were nothing, as long as I had just one person who could comfort me, console me, hold me close, someone who was ready to give their life for me… Someone who loved me! And my enemies envied me that one small glimmer of happiness! Listen to what they did. You know she left behind her home and her old mother to come here to Boryslav to be with me. We lived together for half a year. She worked at the store of that rich fellow Goldkrämer. Unfortunately, she caught the eye of all the hounds who saw her there. Among them were the young Jewish paymaster Shmuel Blutegel, the overseer, also a young Jew, and some other wretches, damn them! They began to pester her, giving her no peace. A few times she rebuffed them tactfully, but later, when Blutegel caught her alone in the store's portico and, emboldened, tried to get too familiar with her, she swung her hand around without thinking and whacked him so hard between the ears that blood spurted from his mouth and nose, and he went rolling among the barrels like a log. How we laughed at the impertinent fellow that evening when she told me the whole story.

"But our laughter was premature. The fellow became enraged and conspired with the others to take revenge on her. The day before yesterday was payback; I came home in the evening, and my Varka was still not at home. I sat by the window, waiting and looking out for her, but my heart felt heavy, as if a snake had curled up around it. It grew dark, and still Varka had not returned. I threw on my coat and went out into the street to search for Varka. But she was nowhere to be found. I asked the female workers who were with her when they were paid, and they said they had left without her, that she was probably one of the last ones to be paid. I felt something clench at my heart and ran to the office. It was locked, but lights shone in the windows. I knocked, but no one answered. Then I thought to myself: 'Why am I knocking, perhaps she isn't here? Perhaps, she's already at home waiting for me...' I rushed back home, but she wasn't there. I ran through the streets again, dropping in on all her acquaintances, visited all the taverns where we sometimes popped in for a bite to eat after work or to buy some herring – but she was nowhere to be found. I asked everyone if they'd seen Varka – and no one had. She had vanished, like a stone into water. I headed back to the office, drawn there for some unknown reason. On my way, I thought: 'I'll break the door down, I have to find out what happened to her, where she is.' But once I got there, the courage left me. I stood looking at the lights in the windows, but the curtains were drawn, and I could see nothing except for fleeting shadows. I thought to myself that she must be there, where else could she be? And yet, I couldn't quite believe it, because what would she be doing in there? The incident with the Jewish fellow Blutegel crossed my mind and I shuddered all over, feeling paralysed. No matter how much I tried to convince myself that it was all a funny story, a bit of a joke, something kept me there, under the window of that damned office. I'll remain here, I said to myself, I'll wait until the lights go out – no, I'll wait until the morning. I sat on a barrel by the window, and began to shiver, as if I was caught in a cold draft. Listening intently, I could hear drunks singing songs in raspy voices in a tavern nearby, dogs were barking in the distance, and from the church came the watchman's call: 'Take care with fire!' Then I heard laughter coming from the office, mocking male voices. I recognised Blutegel's voice and that of the overseer. Then there was a sound as if something had crashed against the walls. This was followed by more laughter, more mocking voices – and then there was silence. Lord, every sound pierced my heart like a sharp dagger… I sat there, my ear pressed to the wall.

"Suddenly, just before dawn, a horrific scream came from the office. It was momentary, but it struck me like thunder, it stung me like a serpent's bite. I instantly jumped to my feet – it had been my Varka's scream. And just as I was thinking what I should do, the door burst open and out flew Varka, like a cannonball. But she wasn't screaming anymore… I recognised her only by her clothes, because in the dim light I couldn't make out her face at first. She didn't see me either, and after rushing out, she kept running straight ahead, over mounds of earth, between enclosures and pits. I followed her. 'Varka,' I yelled, 'Varka, what happened, what's wrong? For God's sake, stop, turn around!' She paused for a moment, looked back, and that's when I saw that her entire head was black as coal, smeared with oil, and her long hair had been shaved. 'Oh Lord, Varka,' I cried out, drawing closer, 'what's happened to you?' But the moment she recognised me, she immediately turned away and, raced blindly ahead, colliding with posts that marked the pits. With every ounce of strength I had left I chased her, until suddenly there was a terrifying scream, and right before my eyes in one fleeting moment Varka disappeared like some ghost – she had plunged into an open pit!

"I rushed up and stood still, hearing only muffled sounds as her body struck the sides of the shaft, eventually plunging into water. And that was that. What happened to me afterward, I can't recall. I only regained my senses today at noon, and when I inquired about Varka, I was told that they had pulled her out of the pit after hearing my screams and had already buried her. So, everything is lost! And no one will say what they did to her on that dreadful night. Those monsters devoured my poor Varka alive, they destroyed my happiness! My dear brethren, before the Lord and yourselves, I lament my misfortune and seek your advice: tell me what I should do, just don't tell me to wait!"

Pryidevolia's account moved everyone deeply, even though they had all heard the vague rumours of the tragedy that had befallen their comrade. Throughout his narrative, every face in the room mirrored the range of emotions he conveyed – from unease to utter distress and despair. Meanwhile these same emotions played out vividly on Pryidevolia's face. When he fell silent and stood in the middle of the room, wringing his hands like some mute witness to a great sin, everyone remained silent, as if dumbstruck, each putting himself in his comrade's position, trying hard to comprehend the depth of his sorrow and pain. But to give him advice – what advice could they give him regarding a matter where there was no advice to be given. There was no way out, apart from death! How could they advise him which path to take?

Derkach was the first to regain his senses and grabbed his sticks to notch the case.

"Stop, brother Derkach," Andrus Basarab commanded, "there's no need to notch this one!"

Derkach looked at him, puzzled.

"There's no need," Andrus said brusquely, and then addressed the brethren. "Has anyone else anything to report?"

No one spoke.

"That means our business is done for today! Leave one by one, please!"

Despite this command, no one made a move. They exchanged peculiar glances, leaving Andrus puzzled as he looked sternly at them, uncertain of what was happening. Then Stasiura, the eldest among the brethren, stood up.

"Listen, brother Basarab," he spoke calmly, "to what we've been discussing among ourselves these past few days. I speak not just for myself, but for all of us. Remember when we joined forces to gather all the wrongs inflicted upon the people and to mete out workers' justice to those who couldn't be brought to trial in the noblemen's courts? You promised us back then that once enough of people's suffering had been accumulated, we would assess it to see whose cup was overflowing. Is that not so?"

"Yes," Andrus replied somewhat reluctantly.

"Well, for almost a year now we've been accumulating those notches denoting inflicted wrongs. Brother Derkach has notched a whole pile of sticks. And we ask you, when will the time for action arrive?"

"It's not time yet, but it is drawing near," said Andrus.

"You keep saying that! You know, the morning dew will burn our eyes out before the sun rises! You can see for yourself that as our oppressors grow richer through our toil, they also become more arrogant. It's time they received some sort of warning!"

"There will be a warning," said Andrus, firmly and calmly.

"When?" questions echoed from all directions

"That's my concern. You'll hear about it when the moment arrives. There's no need to discuss it beforehand," Andrus replied. "And the final reckoning isn't far off either. The oak sapling must reach up to the clouds before lightning can strike it. Just wait a little longer… And for now, goodnight!"

Knowing Andrus Basarab's strong and decisive nature, and having confidence in his word, the brethren prepared to leave without further discussion.

"Brother Pryidevolia, stay behind, I have something to discuss with you," Andrus said, and there appeared a glimmer of joy on the face of the poor young man, a hope that he might be able to shake off his terrible agony.

The brethren departed slowly, one by one. Only old Matiy remained seated in a corner, leaning against the wall. His long-extinguished pipe had slipped from his teeth and lay on the floor. Andrus and Benedio also remained in their places, each lost in their own thoughts.

Meanwhile Pryidevolia stood by the door with a deathly pale face and wrung his hands, appearing the embodiment of pain. He did not take his eyes off Andrus Basarab, as if he was expecting some kind of relief.

Matiy was the first to approach the young fellow.

"Have you thought what you might do?" he asked in a soft, sympathetic voice. Pryidevolia looked at him uncertainly.

"How on earth would I know what to do?" he replied hoarsely. "I'll do myself in, if I can't take revenge on my enemies!"

"Take them to court, let the darned thieves do time behind bars!" advised Matiy.

"Take them to court?" Andrus responded gloomily. "Sounds like good advice! Take them to court! But even if they are convicted, so what? They'll serve a couple of months and be released. And then they'll seek revenge with renewed energy. But will they even be convicted? And what will he accuse them of in court, when he himself doesn't know what they did to the young lass? Even if he was dead sure what happened, where are the witnesses, how can he prove it? Maybe the young girl killed herself of her own free will, or maybe, God knows, maybe there was some other reason? Matiy, Matiy, you and your court case! This requires a different kind of court, another type of justice!"

At these words, Matiy, hung his head and sighed heavily, as if he was forced against his own will to admit that they were right. Pryidevolia looked even more intently at Andrus and said in a barely audible voice:

"Yes, brother, they were my thoughts too... There were no witnesses! I mean, had she not died – oh Lord, if only she were still alive! But you know how proud and unbending she was, unable to endure any disgrace or insult! So, what can I possibly do now?"

Andrus grabbed him by the shoulder and led him over to a far corner of the room, winking to Matiy to move away, and began to whisper something into his ear. Andrus' words must have made a big impression on the young fellow, because he turned deathly pale, then his face flushed, and in the end, trembling all over, as if in a cold sweat, he burst into loud sobs. Grabbing firm hold of Andrus' arm, he exclaimed:

"Yes, you're right, brother, there is no other way! That's what I'll do, and may the Lord deal with me as He pleases!"

"Just relax, be courageous and confident, there's nothing to fear! Each of us lives in the shadow of God's judgment, which is fair and impartial for all. Human judgement alone is not just! You'll see, you'll feel better after this! Off you go now, good night!"

Pryidevolia bowed silently and left.

Andrus paced restlessly about the room, trying hard to regain his composure, though it was clear that he was deeply agitated. Eventually, he approached Benedio and stood tall, his imposing figure accentuating his presence.

"Well, did you see us at work?"

"Yes, I did," Benedio replied.

"And what do you think?"

Benedio lowered his head, as if gathering his scattered thoughts.

"I can see you are preparing for something great and formidable, although I can't quite understand where you draw such ideas from."

"From where? Oh, that's a long story, and it's not particularly relevant right now."

"And afterwards, do you believe you will have enough strength to see your plans through?"

"We sow the seeds, but we can never be certain whether they will yield threefold or tenfold!"

"One more thing..." Benedio hesitated. "Have you given much thought to..."

"To what?"

"To what is of utmost importance..."

"Meaning?" Andrus prompted him.

"What good will result from your efforts and who will benefit?" Benedio asked earnestly

Andrus fixed his gaze intently on Benedio before letting out a bitter laugh:

"Ha-ha-ha, benefit! And why does there need to be any benefit?"

"Well, as I see it," Benedio replied calmly, "when something is done deliberately, you must also consider if it will benefit anyone, no?"

"Hm, you can think that, if you like! But here's what I think: the enemy is encroaching on me from all sides. There is no escape, so what can I do? I load my gun. And it's all the same to me, whether I kill the enemy or myself."

"No, no, no," Benedio remonstrated, "that's just blind, hopeless despair talking, not reason. Has it really come to this, that there's no other way out? And even if it were so, do you believe it's all the same, whether you kill your enemy or yourself? If you take your own life, it only makes things easier for your enemy!"

Now it was Andrus' turn to lower his heavy head and gather his thoughts.

"You're right!" he admitted to Benedio at last. "This demands careful consideration. Would you like to join our brotherhood and help us?"

"I'd like to join, but I don't want to be a mindless instrument of your will! I want everyone to be free to think as they wish and to share their thoughts with others."

"We already have that freedom. You heard tonight…"

"Yes, but I want to have it made clear once more, for my sake and everyone else's."

"Very well!"

"In that case, I'll join the brotherhood and together we can explore whether there might be an alternative solution to the great injustices that are heaped on people!"

Andrus, followed by Matiy, warmly embraced Benedio like a brother.

The brethren were so engrossed in their conversation that they failed to hear the knocking on the front door. It opened with a slight creak and someone entered the anteroom. They only noticed him when the door to the room squeaked open and the visitor stood in the doorway. It was a tall, ruddy Jewish man with sidelocks, with a bad-intentioned look in his grey eyes, his freckled face slightly beaming with an expression of malevolent joy.

"God bless!" grunted the Jewish fellow, raising the tip of his hat just a fraction.

"God bless!" replied Matiy, who felt bad at the sight of this new visitor. For this was his mortal enemy, Mortko, the overseer in Hermann Goldkrämer's workers barracks. Matiy was rather surprised what Mortko might want now, so late in the day. However, the customary respect that Ukrainian people showed to anyone entering their home made Matiy conceal his loathing deep within his soul, together with the painful memories which surfaced at the sight of Mortko. He greeted the man with a cold courteous voice:

"Have a seat, Mortko!"

Mortko nodded and sat down.

"What news is there, that brings you to our house so late at night?"

"What else could it be? It's all good news!" replied Mortko with a gloating grin, and a moment later added: "Did the court bailiff pay you a visit today?"

Matiy shuddered at the mention of the word 'court,' as if someone had stabbed him.

"No," he could barely utter, sensing bad tidings.

"Then he'll probably come around tomorrow. He visited me today."

"Well, and what news is there?" Matiy asked, his whole body trembling.

"Our case has been closed."

"Closed?"

"Yes! And closed in the way that I told you. You shouldn't have gone meddling in something which did not concern you!"

"That did not concern me?" Matiy exclaimed painfully. "Please, don't say such things, because even though you may find yourself in my home, people aren't saints, you know!"

"Come on," Mortko replied, "there's nothing to get angry about. That's not what I meant to say. I mean, there was no use casting suspicion on me since, God is my witness, I have nothing at all to do with this case! The prosecutor in Sambir has confirmed this and said that there is no evidence against me, so that he can't charge me with the offence that you are accusing me of. Pivtorak got drunk, fell into a pit, and what fault is that of mine?"

At these words Matiy dropped his head, as if stunned by a heavy blow, unable to utter a single word. 'You've lost!' the words hissed inside his head. 'A man's died, his trail's gone cold, and this fellow...'

Just then Andrus Basarab, who until now had been silently listening to the conversation, addressed the visitor directly:

"What's this case about, Mortko? What business have you got with Matiy?"

"What's it to you?" Mortko replied, piqued.

"Don't you go asking me, why I need to know," replied Andrus. "So, what's the problem, why can't you tell me?"

"Th-there's no problem, but..."

The fellow looked intently at Andrus, as if he was afraid of making a new enemy.

"Speak up then, if it's no problem!" said Andrus and stood over Mortko, like a devil towering over a sinful soul.

"There's nothing to tell, really – it's all empty business, *püste Geschäft*, nothing more! It's been two years since a man's bones were retrieved from a pit. By the ring on his finger they identified him as Ivan Pivtorak, the husband of that Mrs. Pivtorak, whose house this is. He had disappeared a year or so before that. Well, Matiy here got it into his head that I'm to blame that he fell into the pit, and decided to take me to court. He thought they would grab me straight away and hang me... But courts don't work that way: if you accuse someone, you first need proof! And how can you prove anything here? But, thank God, the case is closed now! Listen, Matiy, I'm telling you one more time, why did you need to get involved in all this and spend money on the court case?

Now that you've lost the case, let's forget about everything and be good friends again, like we were before this! Come on, shake on it, old man!"

Mortko offered his hand to Matiy.

"What?" exclaimed Matiy. "Shake the hand that drove my dear Ivan from this world? No, never!"

"Well, see," said Mortko. And turning around to face Andrus, he said: "He keeps harping on it. Listen, Matiy, take a rest from those conversations of yours, because now that the court has declared that I'm not guilty, no one dares accuse me of anything. Now I can take you to court for defamation!"

"Go ahead and do that!" yelled Matiy. "Let them hang me, instead of you. No matter what ten courts declare, I will stick to my guns: no one else but you pushed Ivan into that pit! That's enough. Now leave my house, because if I run out of patience, I can't vouch for what I will do to you!"

Mortko shrugged his shoulders and left. But in the doorway, he turned around once more, looked contemptuously at Matiy and said: "You stupid *goy*! You thought that you could harm me with your court case, but you needed to get out of bed much earlier to do anything to me!"

And with these words Mortko left. Matiy remained sitting on the oven hearth, pale, crestfallen, trembling, his mind blank and his body motionless, and inside his head one dark, empty, cold phrase rattled around and around like a millwheel: All is lost! All is lost! All is lost!

Andrus Basarab stepped up to him and rested his strong hand on his shoulder.

"Brother Matiy!"

Matiy looked up and the look in his eyes was that of a drowning man.

"What was this court case about? What was it all about? Why have we never heard about it?"

"Eh, all is lost, it's all lost!" Matiy replied. "What's the point of even talking about it now!"

"No, please, tell me, you'll feel better after you've told me!"

"How can I feel better?" Matiy asked. "The case is lost, and that's that!"

"Who knows, if it's lost," Benedio interjected. "After all, it's possible to revisit a lost court case a second time and win! And here, as that Mortko said, things aren't all that cut and dried. After all, your case never even made it into court, and only the prosecutor has found that there is no evidence to be able to charge him. Which means that if there was evidence, he can still be charged."

Matiy's face brightened a little upon hearing these words.

"Is that so?" he asked, straightening up. But some heavy thought once more weighed down on him, and he bent over.

"No, no, no, there's no point in talking," he said. "One way or another, all is lost. Three years have passed, where can I find that evidence now? Forget it, it's not even worth thinking about it!"

He covered his face with his hands, and hot tears, the result of long-suffered pain, flowed from his eyes, streaming between his fingers and falling onto the ground. Benedio and Andrus understood that it was futile to talk to him now. The blow had been far too severe and unexpected, shattering his determination. So, without a word, Andrus shook Benedio's hand, donned his hat, and left. Benedio, too, undressed in silence and lay down on the bench, resting on his coat.

Matiy remained sitting on the hearth, as if carved from stone. The oil lamp burned low and became ever paler as it stood shimmering on the fireplace. Twilight hugged the corners of the room, as if waiting for the lamp to become extinguished, to be able to rush forward and to crush and ensnare everything from top to bottom. Benedio fell into a deep sleep as soon as he lay down, exhausted by the numerous emotions he had experienced that day. The lamp became extinguished only after midnight, but Matiy remained seated on the hearth, his face buried in his hands, without moving, without uttering a word, without a thought in his head, sensing only a great pain in his heart, a great emptiness, and a fresh wound caused by the thought that a poor worker like him could find no justice in the courts. Only toward morning did sleep take hold of his exhausted body and he slid down onto the bare hearth. Matiy fell asleep for an hour, until he was woken by the early morning clatter and ringing, summoning labourers to work.

V

On Monday morning the brilliant sun emerged from behind the small pink clouds, only to scorch and further bake the parched hillside throughout the day. Leon Hammerschlag was travelling from Drohobych to Boryslav in a shiny, light carriage pulled by a pair of swift dappled-grey horses. His spirits were high, lifted by bright hopes of a rosy future, which was growing, filling out, taking on flesh and blood. The gentle rocking of the carriage lulled him, and his own thoughts and ideas gilded the world around him. He had worked hard these past three weeks, dashed about, endured unrest and anxiety, dealt with various people, until he had finally achieved his goal and amid that hustle and bustle had grasped the golden thread which would lead him to a great ball of wealth!

His stay in Vienna had, to put it mildly, resulted in one of the boldest and most lucrative of his speculative ventures! It was like catching the golden fish[9] in that fairy tale! And, indeed, this fishing expedition turned out so well for him that one couldn't have hoped for better! Leon was pondering all the details of his heroic catch, calculating the time and money required to ensure everything in his planned scheme went smoothly, like clockwork. The venture which occupied his thoughts concerned the following.

....

[9] In a Russian fairy tale good fortune comes to the person who catches the golden fish.

The Belgian chemist Van Hecht, resident in Vienna, had for several years been working on an analysis of earth wax, and after long experiments, had discovered a way of purifying this wax to such an extent that it lost its characteristic unpleasant oily smell. A small admixture of beeswax gave it a pleasant smell, and another chemical admixture – left it the colour of ordinary beeswax. He called this new product ceresin and obtained a patent for the exclusive use of his discovery. Van Hecht sent samples of the wax to, among others, the church synod in Russia, asking if a use might be found for such wax in Orthodox churches there. He also declared that, if need be, he could deliver large shipments of the wax at a price much lower than the cost of beeswax. The synod wrote back after a while, that the proffered wax had been tested, that it had turned out to be no worse than beeswax and that candles from the wax were free to burn without any restriction in praise of the Lord in every Orthodox church in Russia. If he, Van Hecht, were able to supply large quantities of the wax at a cheap price, the synod assured him of a vast market in Russia.

Armed with this important letter and a seven-year patent for the ownership of his invention, Van Hecht had decided to become rich. Until now he had been a poor technician, and with great difficulty had saved up enough money to set up a small chemical laboratory of his own in Vienna in which he worked alone, helped only by an assistant, a German called Scheffel. Small wonder, that now he had decided to sell the fruits of his labours to the highest bidder. To this end he announced his invention in Viennese trade and stock exchange magazines, inviting 'P.T.[10] entrepreneurs, manufacturers and capitalists, who would be interested in entering into an advantageous speculative investment in cooperation with the

....

[10]   Abbreviation of *Pleno titulo*, a Latin expression for "by full title(s)."

inventor, to contact Van Hecht, either personally or through agents.'

The announcement immediately created quite a sensation among the Viennese capitalists, especially the Galician Jews, who had long been lining their pockets by extracting oil and wax in Boryslav. Various agents began to surreptitiously drop by Van Hecht's impoverished laboratory in his rented damp basement apartment. Each one avoided the other, and none of them directly addressed the issue at hand, preferring instead to beat about the bush. Van Hecht saw all this, and though at first he was a little impatient to obtain his dreamed-of millions, on the other hand he was pleased, knowing that in the capitalist world it was accepted practice that people first sniffed around where some more serious enterprise was concerned, and that no one trusted anyone, everyone feared everyone, and although each person was happy to outrun his competitors in the race for profit, and along the way to knock a few of them to the ground, on the other hand, everyone tried not to reveal anything to his competitors, even though they might be consumed with fever on the inside. Van Hecht knew this only too well and tried not to show any emotion. He continued to work with his assistant as before in the laboratory, occasionally visiting the stock exchange, but steered clear of the limelight. All the same he noticed that his short, stocky, slightly scruffy figure had begun to attract the attention of people in this world of capitalist tycoons.

And small wonder, for this was taking place in the late 1860s, during the era of great industrial expansion in Austria, a time of great speculative fever, a great *Aufschwindl*.[11] At the very same time that Van Hecht's advertisement appeared in the newspapers, the foundations were being laid for the

....

[11] Upsurge, expansion (German).

world-famous Rotunda, the main building of the Vienna World Fair of 1873! In these feverish times no one realized that the seeds of the Viennese 'crash' of 1873 were already being sown, and this certainly did not concern Van Hecht in the least.

But certainly no one was moved more by Van Hecht's advertisement than the two Boryslav bigwigs, Hermann Goldkrämer and Leon Hammerschlag. They had long been searching everywhere for a better and more secure market for Boryslav wax than the present one. The very nature of their pits had pressured them into the realization that the time had come to rely principally on the extraction of wax, which was becoming the foundation of wealth in Boryslav, as oil was steadily becoming much less profitable.

One should remember that initially in Boryslav, it had been the exact opposite. Oil had constituted the main source of income, while wax, when people came across veins of it in those first shallow pits, was either avoided and left in the earth, or if it was extracted, then only on a small scale. Itinerant workers would harvest it, and travelling salesmen visiting Boryslav would often take large slabs of it back home. The Jewish businessmen cared little about wax, especially the small pit owners, those with just one or two pits.

But now things had changed. Most of the pits had run out of oil; the sources which the Jewish businessmen thought would flow forever, had begun to dry up. And then those darned Americans had begun shipping their oil to Europe and, to top it all off, their oil proved to be better refined and cheaper than the oil from Boryslav! Small wonder then, that Boryslav businessmen were forced to migrate from oil to wax production.

They rushed to uncover the shallow pits and followed the veins that were left from long ago; from the main vertical shafts they began to dig side tunnels, simple and steep, as dictated by need. They also began to dig down further;

whereas before the deepest pits were 200 to 350 feet, now they went down to 550 to 700 feet; the deeper they went, the more prominent the veins of wax became. The only thing that thwarted the Boryslav bigwigs was the expense of refining this wax; its distillation when treated with sulphuric acid and other processes to produce white paraffin wax from the yellow earthy mass was expensive. The price of paraffin, although quite high, was unable to bring the manufacturers large and quick profits. And then, like an angel from heaven, there appeared this ingenious Belgian with his invention! 'The cost of producing ceresin,' he wrote in his advertisement, 'will be cheaper than the production of paraffin. And ceresin has an assured market in Russia. What's more, the inventor was a Belgian national! And Belgians, of course, were hard-working stately people, who could be relied upon, quite unlike those scatterbrained Frenchmen or those German charlatans! Thus, profits would be both quick and large – and assured!'

Having read Van Hecht's advertisement, both Hermann and Leon immediately wrote to their agents to become acquainted with the case, and to learn of the conditions, promising in the event of agreeable terms to come to Vienna and close the deal. Hermann's agent was a decent German businessman, who even though he charged Hermann big money, kept his business affairs in Vienna in very good order. Having received Hermann's request, he went directly to Van Hecht, quizzed him about the conditions, bargained with him a little, and, having asked him to keep their preliminary agreement secret, promised him that in one week, two at the latest, the businessman himself would appear in Vienna to conclude the agreement. The agent assured Van Hecht that Hermann was a thoroughly decent fellow and in signing a contract with him, he could be assured of a good commission. Of course, at the outset the agent tried to dismiss Van Hecht's dreams about making millions, but all the same he assured him, that he could expect to earn at least half a million and that the person the agent represented could make that dream come true far better than anyone else. Van Hecht agreed to everything, albeit with regret in his heart: even if it was half a million, it still meant he could acquire a beautiful estate, something he couldn't have dreamt of doing in the past. The agent once again insisted that Van Hecht keep the deal secret, and the Belgian, not guessing the reason for this, agreed to this as well. After this the agent quickly telegraphed Hermann to explain how things stood, and asked him to come to Vienna as soon as possible to conclude the deal with Van Hecht. We have already seen Hermann's state of mind and the circumstances he found himself in when that telegram arrived.

But meanwhile Leon Hammerschlag's agent wasn't sleeping either. He was an expeditious, cunning Viennese Jew, known to Leon from way back. For a small retainer he served as his agent. Like so many so-called German-Jewish liberals, Leon liked to play the knight in shining armour in public, but in private, he could never shake the inherent cunning of the merchant. So he preferred to have a lousy agent, just to pay him less. True, the wily agent had always managed to slyly manage Leon's business interests. Leon was doing well 'behind his back,' and had already sent him bonuses on several occasions as a sign of his appreciation.

Once again, the agent successfully completed this crucial task, much to Leon's delight. True to his style though, he did not address the issue directly, unlike the German, but instead navigated through back channels, discreetly gathering information. Subsequently, a rumour surfaced that Van Hecht had exceedingly high expectations. The German himself, Hermann's representative, informed his circle of business associates that he had approached the Belgian (without revealing on whose behalf) and that the fellow had stipulated the following terms: he would agree to run the ceresin factory if the owner assured him seven years of continuous employment, a weekly salary of 5,000 rinskys, and a five percent share of the net profits from the ceresin produced during the final two years. Such demanding conditions undoubtedly deterred everyone, leading Leon's agent to lose any remaining interest he might have had in meeting with Van Hecht.

However, he sniffed out another path into the vegetable patch. Just a few days earlier, as agreed with the German agent, Van Hecht had closed his laboratory and was trying to sell it. He also sent away his assistant, Scheffel, who now, unemployed and without a steady income, was living in one of the narrow alleys of Vienna's Vorstadt. It was to Scheffel that Leon's agent made his way, beginning to question and probe him. He discovered that Scheffel knew in detail the secret of manufacturing ceresin, would be able to arrange the necessary boilers and equipment, and in short, could run a ceresin factory.

Indeed, Scheffel was a man of modest means, timid and conscientious, and would likely have turned down anyone directly offering him a job to produce ceresin. But the astute agent did not put forth this proposition straight away. Instead, after his conversation with Scheffel, he penned a letter to Leon, urging him to come. He mentioned that although Van Hecht was setting high demands, the matter could be approached from another perspective, and would be much more profitable and easier to handle.

Meanwhile, the agent began to manipulate Scheffel to serve his own agenda. He befriended him over a few rounds of beer, visited his home on several occasions, and observed the frugality and hardship of his life. Scheffel lamented his poverty, his lack of resources, and in contrast, the agent painted vivid, glowing pictures of profit, wealth, and prosperity, hinting more and more clearly that the gates to this golden paradise were not entirely closed to him. Poor Scheffel could only sigh and pour out his woes once again. To secure Scheffel's loyalty, the agent tactfully lent him small amounts of money now and then. He promised to find him a job, and not just any job, but one that would prove so advantageous that Scheffel would be eternally grateful to him. Scheffel looked on with disbelief, but the agent was so persistent in his narrative that slowly, like a man being enveloped in fog, Scheffel allowed himself to be swept away by the agent's rosy promises. Needless to say, by the time Leon made his appearance, Scheffel was almost fully primed to embrace the role the agent had envisaged for him.

Leon arrived in Vienna, unaware of how his agent was considering to settle the matter. When he heard the agent's plan, he was taken aback, but after a more extended discussion with the agent, he consented to the whole scheme and instructed him to bring Scheffel to his hotel. After a brief verbal altercation, pressed by the direness of his current situation and lured by Leon's glowing offers, Scheffel capitulated. He promised Leon that he would accompany him to Boryslav and oversee a clandestine ceresin factory for a modest salary. To disguise the construction and operation of the new factory, and divert public attention, Scheffel, ignorant of the situation in Galicia, proposed that Leon publicly claim he was erecting a small steam mill. This was precisely what Leon did, without fully contemplating the potential repercussions of such advice.

After settling the matter with Scheffel, Leon had no time to rest. He immediately embarked on seeking markets for his ceresin production. With the help of his agent, he managed to find several Russian-Jewish capitalists who were passing through Vienna. They were more than happy to act as intermediaries in the supply of ceresin wax, and indeed, within three weeks, Leon had already signed a contract with the newly-incorporated Wax Association in Russia. The agreement was to supply 200,000 hundredweight of ceresin over six months. The terms regarding price and transportation were so favourable that Leon could readily estimate a net profit of 100,000 rinskys from this single deal.

After this, with the golden goose Scheffel onside, he made haste to Galicia to set the plan in motion. He already had stockpiles of wax amounting to 10,000 hundredweight in his Boryslav warehouses. He hoped that for the initial phase, he could purchase two or even four times that amount locally, using his own funds and benefiting from the lower prices offered by the small pit owners. Later, his contract partners would send their representatives to Boryslav. Their task would be to personally verify the quantity and quality of the manufactured wax. And once that confirmation was obtained, Leon expected to receive part of the sum as agreed in the contract. With that money, he hoped to provide the rest of the product. Thus, any remaining funds would translate into sheer profit, minus perhaps his payments to Scheffel and the expenses of building the factory.

Meanwhile, Scheffel was not sitting on his hands either. Eager to make a good impression on his new benefactor, he drew a detailed plan for the new factory. Along with the agent, he placed orders for boilers, pipes, and other essential equipment from Viennese manufacturers, emphasizing the urgency of their request. During his three-week stay in Vienna Leon unquestionably exerted himself in laying the foundations of his future wealth and prosperity. He was constantly on the move, as if consumed by fever. He did not socialize or entertain, avoided friends, and even failed to acknowledge Hermann Goldkrämer, despite spotting him on several occasions amid the throngs on the streets. Leon was entirely consumed by the speculative fever that gripped the people of that era. The world around him had become transformed, and within this new reality of gold, riches and glitter, Leon no longer had time for friends or family, and failed to differentiate right from wrong.

The fever did not subside upon his return to Drohobych. On the very day that he arrived from Vienna, he summoned the building supervisor and Benedio. And with the start of the week on the Monday, he set off for Boryslav to personally supervise the construction of the new factory. He appeared to be driven by some invisible force which propelled him to expedite the project. Hence, upon his return from Vienna, he decided, albeit reluctantly, to temporarily halt the construction of his lavish home. This move would allow him to allocate more funds and energy toward the swift completion of his new lucrative venture. 'After all, my house, my joy, my strength, will still be built and will rise to the skies! But it is the successful culmination of this enterprise that will serve as one of the main pillars of my home!'

Such recollections and thoughts flitted through Leon's mind during his swift journey to Boryslav. The sturdy jostling of the carriage lulled him into a comfortable state, and his personal reflections tinged the world around him with a golden hue.

He had passed Hubychi and was on the approach to Boryslav, when he asked the coachman to stop on the flats by the river. He got out of the coach and made his way across the meadow to the river, where it was planned to build the factory. But even before he reached the spot, he heard a commotion coming from there. On approaching, he was surprised to see a large crowd assembled on the site, talking loudly and curiously looking about. Most of them were Jews, owners of the Boryslav oil pits, although there were also plenty of unemployed miners, Jewish women with children, and lots of other riffraff. 'What's going on?' Leon thought to himself. 'What could have happened to draw such a crowd here?'

It all proved to be quite straightforward. As soon as the crowd saw him, the Jewish pit owners immediately moved toward him and bombarded him with questions: What? How? Was it true that he was building a steam mill? Where did such an idea spring from? Why was he risking inevitable losses, for a steam mill in Boryslav surely would bring him no profit?

Leon was quite taken aback by these questions. Only now did he realize that by announcing he was building a steam mill, he wasn't diverting people's attention from his enterprise but, on the contrary, was only intensifying their curiosity. So, in response to the questions of his business acquaintances, he forced a smile, unsure of how to answer them. Soon he was surrounded by Jewish women and all the poor people, some asking for work, while others were thanking him for his great benefaction to the poor of Boryslav, who would now find it easier to bake their sacred bread. Leon felt even more disoriented, realizing there was no escaping the people's attention.

"But, my good people," he began, collecting himself, "who told you that I was building a steam mill here?"

"The building supervisor himself, who came by this morning looking for workers for the new project!"

"Ah, the building supervisor merely played a joke on you!" said Leon. "It's not a steam mill at all, just a plain old oil refinery that's being built! I've no need of steam mills!"

"Ah!" exclaimed everyone present in a collective gasp of surprise and disappointment. The poorer folks immediately began to disperse, while the Jewish pit owners began speaking more freely with Leon, probing him why he was building a new refinery. Would he need more oil and wax? What kind of business was he planning to conduct here? Some of the more curious ones even asked if he had signed any contracts with anyone.

"We've heard," said some of the pit owners, "that over in Vienna a big new Erdwachs Exploitations-Compagnie is being set up. Are you in negotiations with them?"

"In Vienna? An Association for the Extraction...?" Leon feigned surprise. "No, I've never heard of such an association nor am I involved with them!"

"Really?" the pit owners expressed their astonishment. "But you were in Vienna. How could you not even have heard about the formation of such a significant association?"

"Oh, come on!" Leon tried to defend himself. "I was in Vienna on personal business. I had no time to visit the stock exchange!"

Leon barely managed to free himself from the pit own-ers. True, he promised to talk to some of them later that day about the purchase of earth wax from them, which he would need for his new refinery. Having gotten rid of his unwanted curious guests, he went out to the building site, where hired workers were already levelling the ground, removing stones and bricks, and where the building supervisor and Benedio were measuring up the plan and pegging out where the foun-dations were to be dug. The building was to be finished in a month – exactly the time that the manufacturers in Vienna had promised to send the equipment ordered by Scheffel.

The building supervisor was very morose and constantly muttered something under his breath. Benedio only occa-sionally caught snatches of words such as 'stupid Jew,' 'char-latan,' 'wants to deceive, but has no idea how.' When Leon approached and greeted the workers with a 'good-day' and a 'God bless you,' Benedio was the first to approach him.

"Sir," he said, "isn't it true that you were joking when you said that this was meant to be a steam mill?"

"Why are you asking?"

"Because we couldn't agree with the building supervisor regarding the plan. I've already worked on a steam mill in Przemyśl and know how it should be set up. And as soon as I looked at the plan, I immediately recognized that this is going to be an oil refinery, rather than a mill. I had already suspected it before, because why would you build a mill in this dry wasteland? But the building supervisor was adamant that the plans needed to be changed, saying that there was probably a mistake, that we should wait until he himself had drawn up plans for a steam mill..."

"Of course I was joking!" Leon declared in a loud voice, trying to mask his confusion with laughter. "I'm not that stu-pid to go and build a steam mill in Boryslav!"

Having heard these words, the building supervisor came up to Leon, who was surveying the site with a smile.

"Mr. Hammerschlag," the building supervisor said in an unpleasant, terse voice, "so which one of us will be the liar now?"

"Liar?" Leon repeated and took a step back, sizing up the building supervisor with a defiant look. Although beneath his defiance there was still confusion, and Leon would have given anything for the building supervisor to calm down. But the building supervisor had no intention of calming down.

"Yes, a downright liar," he said. "Didn't you tell me earlier that you wanted to build a steam mill here?"

"I was joking."

"You were joking? Well, I've never seen anyone joke so seriously before! I admit, I didn't understand your joke. And now, because of your joke, I've assembled all these workers and caused an uproar in the whole of Boryslav…"

"That's not good!" said Leon.

"Of course it's not good, because now all these people are calling me a liar."

"But that's your problem, not mine!"

"My problem? But they were your words!"

"I gave you the plans! How good a building supervisor are you, if you can't tell whether the plans are for a steam mill or a refinery?"

The words deeply piqued the building supervisor.

"Ah, those stupid plans of yours! I never even looked at them!"

"That's your fault, then!" Leon snapped back. "What do I pay you for then?"

The altercation was conducted in raised voices and grew increasingly louder. Leon turned red as a lobster, while the building supervisor's full face was flushed with crimson. Meanwhile, hearing the argument between the two 'gentlemen,' some workers and bystanders gathered to watch the spectacle.

"Sir," yelled the enraged building supervisor, "I didn't come here to listen to your impertinent remarks."

"Nor I to listen to your nonsense!"

"Sir, you are insulting me!"

"It's not such a big offence!"

"You have harmed my reputation!"

"And you have harmed my business interests!"

"Is that so? Then please pay me for my work, and I will make my way back to Drohobych this very day."

"Oh, certainly! Please present me with a bill, and not only for the work done here, but also the building works in Drohobych! We'll try to manage without such a genius of a building supervisor!" And Leon haughtily turned away, indicating that the conversation was finished. Meanwhile, boiling over with anger, the building supervisor threw down what he was holding, pulled his hat over his ears, spat onto the ground and set off for Boryslav to the loud laughter of the workers who had heard the altercation.

The work continued as usual. Leon walked around the site for a long while, looking around, breathing heavily, until his agitation settled. Only after some time did he come up to Benedio:

"Well, so what are we to do now? There's no building supervisor."

"If you'll allow me, I can supervise the construction myself according to the plans."

"You?"

"And why not? It's no big deal. Everything will be ready within a month."

"As you wish then! I can see that you are a good and honest fellow. Go ahead, build the factory! And I don't need any caution money from you, I'll keep an eye on things myself. And don't worry about the pay, I'll look after you!"

If the truth be known, Benedio was somewhat glad to be rid of the haughty building supervisor. And then there was Hammerschlag's unexpected generosity, allowing Benedio to oversee the construction without paying any caution money, and the hope of even higher wages – all this seemed to brighten his world, awakening many new thoughts. He began to rush around and immerse himself in the work, as if it were his own building, even though the other workers looked at him askance, and some might have even considered him a sycophant. But what did he care! His mind was preoccupied with the project, which, surely, was worth enduring a bit of human envy.

VI

June was drawing to an end. Haymaking had begun. The wide wet meadows in the foothills were lush and boasted a vibrant and colorful array of grasses and herbs. Like vast lakes between rocky grey shores, they rippled with fragrant greenery and fresh life. But all around them everything was grey, dead, and gloomy! Ploughed hillocks were covered in dry scorched clods of bare earth; the thin stems of rye curled and yellowed in the sun, unable to set seed. There was no hope for the oats either: they had barely grown a few inches before they started to turn yellow, and drooped, as if seared by fire. The potatoes were turning yellow as well, even before they could flower. Everything seemed to be conspiring to snatch the last crumb of hope from the poor farmer. The warm weather, which had come unusually early this year, was now dragging on far too long – the Feast of Saints Peter and Paul[12] had passed, yet there were no raspberries, berries, or cherries to be found in the woods. There was an endless lament in the villages. People blacker than black earth[13] made their way along roads and field paths, collecting wild mustard, pigweed, sheep's sorrel and various herbs, digging out couch grass. These they dried, ground into dust and mixed with bran and flour obtained with their last pennies, baking

....

[12]   A liturgical feast observed on 12 July (29 June according to the Julian calendar).

[13]   "Blacker than black earth" – quote from Taras Shevchenko's poem "I Grew up in a Foreign Land…" (*I vyris ia na chuzhyni…*).

bread out of this mixture. Every Sunday one could see church processions pass down roadways; with tears in their eyes people pressed their faces to the ground and begged the Lord for rain. But the sky seemed as if it were sealed, and the sun, with its broad, shamelessly bright face, seemed to mock the tears and prayers of the poor.

Diseases began to spread among the people: infectious fevers, typhus, and dysentery. Peasant children, swollen from hunger, bare and blue, roamed the commons and hayfields in droves, searching for sheep's sorrel; not finding any, they grazed on the grass like calves, picked leaves from cherry and apple trees, chewed on them, collapsed on the ground and died by the dozens. Villages that once echoed with the clamour and songs of children on a fair summer's day, now stood silent and gloomy, as if a plague had passed down their dusty streets. This unusual, deathly silence weighed heavily even on strangers. You walked through a village, and there was not a living soul in the streets, save for the emaciated, starved livestock that wandered freely, grazing along fences. Here and there, a man, gaunt and hunched over, traipsed along as if in a trance. In the evenings, the houses were dark: there were no fires in the ovens, for there was nothing to cook or bake – everyone scurried off to their corner, hoping not to hear the moans or see the suffering of others throughout the night. This terrifying, deathly silence in the villages around the foothills was a sign that the people were beginning to lose hope, falling into a state of sheer apathy, when a person ceases to feel pain and dies quietly and mercilessly, just as the wilted grass quietly withered away under the scorching sun.

And the haymaking, that most lively and poetic of field work, did not bring any life or poetry to the general lifeless appearance of the dwellings in the foothills. Slowly, as if after a funeral, emaciated young fellows and grown men trudged off to the haymaking: they could barely hold up the scythes on their frail shoulders. And it was deeply heartbreaking to watch them work: their movements were so strained, painful, and laboured. There were none of the usual songs, no loud laughter, no jokes, or banter to be heard. Some would mow a swath or slightly more, drop their scythe to the ground, sigh heavily, and then lie down on the damp, cold grass to refresh, rest, and draw strength from the earth into their weakened bodies. It was heartbreaking to watch and seemed more like agony than work.

Through these villages, fields, and meadows, a light carriage pulled by a pair of sleek horses travelled along the Sambir highway to Drohobych. The horses were well-fed and healthy, the driver was robust and well-dressed, the carriage was new and shiny black, and the very appearance of the gentleman – a stout, portly man in his prime, with a ruddy face, bushy black beard, and in an expensive stylish outfit, all were in stark contrast to the impoverished appearance of the surrounding region and its people. However, the appearance of this gentleman and his carriage was no more in stark contrast to the sight of the exhausted, famine-stricken foothill region, as were his thoughts and intentions in contrast to the dejected thoughts lingering in the air above these destitute villages.

All around there was despair, a feeling of inevitable doom, a semi-conscious desire to merely prolong this impoverished, tormented life for at least a few more days, and meanwhile, inside the carriage… What thoughts and intentions were buzzing and flitting about inside the head of the gentleman? Anyone could easily guess, once they learned that the gentleman was none other than our old acquaintance, Hermann Goldkrämer. After a long stay in Vienna and Lviv, he was now returning to Drohobych. The sight of immense poverty and suffering around him filled him with a contented, satiated tranquillity, almost a sense of joy. 'All this is happening for my benefit,' he thought. 'The sun is my faithful friend. Drying those fields, sucking all the living juices from the soil, it works to benefit me, it will drive cheap and submissive workers to my oil pits and my factories!' Right now Hermann needed this submissive and cheap labour more than ever, because he had embarked on a new, brilliant, and grand venture, which would elevate him even further up the ladder of wealth.

But to truly understand and gauge Hermann's emotions and thoughts upon his return to Drohobych, it is essential to chronicle his recent experiences and tribulations from the moment we last saw him at the laying of the foundation stone for Leon Hammerschlag's new house and until he unexpectedly received the terrifying and shocking news of the disappearance of his son Gottlieb.

Deeply shaken and spiritually broken, Hermann had journeyed to Lviv, seeking answers about his son. He was caught in a whirlwind of emotions: at times clinging to hope that Gottlieb was alive, and at other moments piecing together evidence that suggested his son's demise. This internal battle exhausted him, muddling his thoughts until they became faint shadows and fragments in his head. He attempted to find solace in the rhythmic motions of the carriage, hoping for sleep, but it eluded him. The weight of his thoughts and the raw edge of anxiety drove him into an almost feverish state.

As the journey dragged on, the endless, sombre marshlands along the Dniester River seemed to have a numbing effect on Hermann's frayed nerves. Desperate to stop thinking about his son, Hermann pulled out the telegram he had received from his Viennese agent just before leaving home. He painstakingly dissected each word of the message, which hinted at the beginnings of an unfolding grand tapestry. Each word, each potential plan, began to soothe his restless mind, offering a respite from his torment.

Upon reaching Lviv, Hermann immediately made his way to the police station. There were no leads, no news. He offered a reward of a hundred rinskys to anyone who could provide concrete information about his son. He probably handed out five times that figure to various policemen and spent a considerable amount on entertaining commissioners to ensure they put in their utmost effort to find his son. His offer of a reward was published in the newspapers, and Hermann stayed in Lviv for another two weeks, each day hoping for a messenger from the police to arrive and summon him to the director. But no messenger ever arrived.

Hermann regularly visited the police station, but in vain. Apart from the clothes found beside the pond, there were no other clues. After two weeks, the policemen and commissioners unanimously declared that Gottlieb had not met his end in the vicinity of Lviv. But could Hermann find solace in that? If not here, could he have perished elsewhere? And even if he had not died, where could he possibly be? All these thoughts intensified Hermann's torment. He requested the police to issue a search warrant for Gottlieb, while he himself headed to Vienna to attend to his business interests.

In Vienna, Hermann's agent was eagerly waiting for him, and by the next day, he had introduced him to Van Hecht. Negotiations followed for the next two to three days. Hermann bargained hard, applying his business acumen with precision. Van Hecht, initially buoyed by high expectations and hope, found himself pressured by Hermann's shrewd and distinctly Jewish business sense and was reluctantly forced to relent. He began to reduce his asking price, and eventually the two struck a deal. They agreed on a weekly wage of 500 rinskys over the course of seven years, on the condition that Van Hecht would manage the factory during this time. Additionally, there was an agreement for a five percent dividend from the net profit made from the sale of ceresin produced in the last two years of the contract.

Understandably, Hermann wasn't entirely pleased with committing to such a sum, which was unprecedented in Boryslav. However, he consoled himself with the thought that he would find a way to outmanoeuvre Van Hecht in Galicia, aiming to extract maximum benefits from him while paying him the bare minimum. And, as events would unfold, Hermann did manage to achieve his goal.[14]

The production of ceresin was to begin in the new year. Van Hecht was to arrive in Drohobych in the fall, to oversee the construction of the factory. Up until then Hermann promised to pay him a small monthly wage of 100 rinskys, since the contractual obligations only came into force in the new year.

However, apart from this primary concern, Hermann addressed another matter of even greater significance while in Vienna. Mixing with many familiar speculators and capitalists at the stock exchange, he frequently engaged in discussions about the Boryslav mines, their productivity, the purification of wax, the costs, the output of paraffin, and so on. He was initially puzzled as to why he was being so diligently questioned about all these finer details by individuals who, up until recently, had shown little interest in them. His surprise deepened when he realized how much some of these people already knew about Boryslav, the extraction processes employed there, the wealth of its underground treasures, and all the practices involved in refining and producing ceresin.

Only later did he discover that in Viennese 'capitalist circles' there was a budding idea to establish a major Association for the Extraction of Earth Wax. At first, this idea did not appeal to him. He feared that the Association might encroach on his interests, clash with his plans, and potentially impact on his wealth.

But after giving it some thought, Hermann laughed off his initial fears. Viennese capitalists setting up an Association

....

[14] Since the novel was never completed, the promise to reveal this remained unfulfilled.

in Boryslav? This was a laughable proposition. Who would manage the affairs of such an Association in Boryslav? If it were to be some Viennese, or broadly speaking, European individual, rather than a Galician Jew, then the downfall of the Association would be inevitable, and in a very short time. For business in Boryslav did not operate in a way that would have allowed any European entrepreneur with a more or less straightforward approach and more or less compatible manufacturing ideas, free from underhanded tactics, scams, counterfeiting, or deception, to survive in Boryslav. He was of the firm belief that to survive in Boryslav one needed a different set of skills and strategies.

True, even European manufacturers and entrepreneurs weren't entirely free of those shrewd and unscrupulous traits often associated with Jewish businessmen. While they may have also not operated entirely conscientiously, they usually didn't stoop to the level of shameless exploitation common in Boryslav, although no longer legal in the West. Moreover, in Europe there was a stronger inclination toward order, systematic approaches, and meticulous bookkeeping. In contrast, these habits were still not commonplace in Boryslav.

Most entrepreneurs in Boryslav conducted their affairs almost deceitfully, without much order. Their main goal was to extract as much as possible from the worker, to cheat him of his wages, and if possible, even swindle him out of the payments he was due. Given such a business environment, it was understandable why European entrepreneurs, especially the methodical and punctual Germans, would be unable to survive in Boryslav.

Hermann hastily considered these matters and sought to gather more information about the key players behind this Association and on what basis it was being established. Everything he learned about the venture further reassured him. Many renowned capitalists had joined the Association, and its core funds would be substantial, nearing almost a million. 'There are significant profits to be made here,' was a persistent thought developing in Hermann's head.

Before finalising the Association, these capitalists had sent a competent Viennese engineer to Boryslav and the neighbouring oilfields to meticulously inspect the mines and factories, determine the worth of the pits, the cost of raw wax, and gather all the necessary information for laying down the future action plan of the Association. The engineer had returned after a two-month stay in Galicia, and his reports satisfied the capitalists. Moreover, they corroborated what Hermann had conveyed, which reassured the consortium establishing the Association for the Extraction of Earth Wax.

Hermann found himself in a quandary. Having concluded his dealings with Van Hecht, he sat in Vienna, idle, restless, and exhausted, waiting and hoping for something. Primarily, he was waiting for news from the Lviv police and what would become of the Association. Then, one fine day, he received an invitation to a gathering of the Association's founders. Some of those present asked him to join the Association and assume responsibility for its operations.

Hermann hesitated, weighing up the advantages and disadvantages in his mind. Managing the Association's affairs would mean neglecting his own ventures. Would profits from the Association compensate him for this? Furthermore, as a member, he would need to make a substantial financial contribution to the operating fund. Meanwhile the future of the Association's shares was uncertain and the immediate benefits seemed limited. Moreover, if the Association were to go bankrupt, which Hermann considered a real possibility, he could find himself embroiled in potential legal troubles or significant financial losses.

Clearly a savvy businessman, Hermann decided to play it safe. By opting not to formally join the Association or take on any leadership roles within it, he ensured that he was not directly tied to its potential successes or failures. Instead, he found a way to benefit without binding himself too closely. By striking a deal to supply raw wax to the Association, he was able to maintain a business relationship, while keeping a safe distance. The terms of the contract seemed favourable to Hermann. The Association was responsible for transportation and quality checks, reducing potential headaches for him. The size of the order, a significant 100,000 hundredweight to be delivered by November, promised a hefty profit. By then, and at the very latest before the new year, a refinery for purifying the wax would be established. After this initial deal, there was the promise of a future contract. Besides this, Hermann had promised to mediate between the Association and other Boryslav entrepreneurs for the supply of wax and even the purchase of pits.

Having settled his business dealings, Hermann hurried back to Lviv. There was still no news of Gottlieb. A chill passed through his heart. How would he face his wife? What would he tell her? He already imagined her terrible screams and curses. He waited another week, but there was no news, so he decided to return home, especially since he had business to attend to in Boryslav. Along the way to Drohobych, on the well-travelled road through the foothills, he grappled with his thoughts, shifting from feelings of self-contentment and satisfaction to the suppressed joy of a businessman at the sight of the immense poverty and despair about him, testifying to an increasing number of 'cheap and submissive workers.'

As Drohobych drew near, the image of his distraught and tearful wife loomed larger and more menacing in Hermann's mind, casting a heavy pall of unease over his heart. But upon arriving home, he was perplexed by his wife's unexpected demeanour. Instead of the anticipated tears, curses, and fiery outbursts, Rifka radiated an unsettling sense of smug satisfaction. Like a magpie intrigued by some shiny trinket, she scrutinized his face, noting every new wrinkle born from worry and uncertainty.

While she did inquire about Gottlieb, even gasping at Hermann's inability to provide any news, her underlying demeanour seemed more playful than genuinely concerned. Her rosy cheeks, the sparkle in her grey eyes, her spirited movements, the spring in her step, and the crispness of her voice – all indicated anything but grief. It was as if the time Hermann had found so unbearable while he was away, had been devoid of any sorrow for Rifka. This unexpected reception left Hermann entirely disoriented.

"Hm," he said to his wife, when after lunch (Rifka had lunch with him and ate heartily and with a healthy appetite, which Hermann hadn't seen in a long time) they sat down next to one another on the soft sofa, and Rifka, barely forcing a smile, once again began to question him about Gottlieb. "Hm," said Hermann, "and you, I see, have cheered up in my absence. You seem as happy as if you'd married off a daughter!"

"Me? Lord Almighty! I've cried my eyes out, but now, since you are back after all this time..."

"That might be the case," Hermann said sceptically, "but I find it hard to believe that such great joy and this change in you is all because of me. Come on, tell me, what's the reason?"

He smiled, looking into her face. She laughed too.

"The reason? Have you gone mad? What reason could there be?"

"Has Gottlieb appeared?"

"Oh, oh, oh, as if you care? Gottlieb? My poor Gottlieb!" and she contorted her face as if she was about to cry. "If he had returned, I wouldn't be feeling like this!"

"So, what's gotten into you? Your eyes are filled with joy, and there's not a trace of tears on your face. Tell me, whatever it is, there must be a reason for it."

"Go on, get out of here, you silly fool, you're just imagining things!" Rifka playfully scolded him, giving his shoulder a light tap with her fan. She then retired to her bedroom with a smile on her face, locking the door behind her.

Hermann remained seated for a while, contemplating the enigma of his wife's behaviour. Eventually, he let out a resigned sigh and mumbled, "Women!" With that, he rose from his seat, paced around the living room for a while, and then headed off to attend to his affairs in Boryslav.

Rifka also paced back and forth a few times in her bedroom, opened a window, and took a deep breath, as if a heavy load had shifted from her shoulders. Her heart was beating briskly, and an even livelier flush appeared on her face when she pulled a small, carelessly folded and sealed letter from under her corset. Just before Hermann's arrival, she had received it through a messenger – a young chimney sweep who had ostensibly come to inquire if their chimneys needed cleaning. The fellow had discreetly slipped the soot-covered letter into her hand. She hadn't had time to read it yet, but the fact that the letter was from Gottlieb – the chimney sweep being his usual messenger – filled her with joy. Her eagerness to find out what Gottlieb had written had been simmering within her as she sat and conversed with Hermann.

'Phew, at last I got rid of him! My misfortune is that I can't conceal anything, my nature is so transparent. Now that old rascal has likely pieced everything together. But I'll see you in hell before you learn the truth from me!' She sat down on the sofa, opened the letter and began to read slowly, one syllable at a time, deciphering the carelessly written letters.

Ever since Hermann's departure for Lviv, Rifka's life had taken a dramatic turn. The unexpected return of her son, in such an unusual manner, had electrified her like a surge of electricity. She moved with joyous abandon, as if possessed, darting around rooms after Gottlieb's arrival, rearranging furniture without rhyme or reason, pressing kisses upon his portrait from his school days, and only managing to settle down with great effort. Though outwardly composed, a tempest of emotions roiled inside her. Her blood coursed faster, and her imagination soared like a summer swallow, attempting to fathom where her son might be at that moment, what he might be doing, and when their next meeting might take place.

She fretted about how to secure more money for Gottlieb, rejoicing when he occasionally visited her in his coalman attire. She inquired about his life and endeavours, but Gottlieb offered only terse replies, cautioning his mother to keep mum about him in front of his father and everyone else, and to concentrate on finding funds for him. In this perpetual state of tension and restlessness, Rifka discovered something she had long yearned for – purpose. She had found an unending subject for her thoughts, and it invigorated her, making her appear rejuvenated and more vibrant.

Gottlieb often sent letters instead of coming personally. Although short and simple, these letters, became a new source of preoccupation and contemplation for Rifka. They were all the more precious because the written words remained on paper, coming alive before her each time she read them. She could read and reread Gottlieb's letters a thousand times, always finding something to admire in them. She selected and read these letters with a trembling excitement, akin to the way young girls read love letters.

The need for love and strong emotions, unfulfilled in her youth and only developing into nervous fervour in her later years of prosperity and idleness, now gushed like a long-contained stream that had finally burst its banks.

"What has my turtledove written this time?" Rifka whispered as she opened the letter. Filled with eager anticipation, she began to read in a hushed voice, pausing and struggling to decipher the words:

'Mama! I still haven't enough money, I need more in a week. But this is not what I wanted to write about today. I heard that father is meant to return soon. Remember, don't let slip anything, otherwise I'll create a lot of trouble. But that is not what I wanted to write about today. I want to tell you something interesting. I have enough free time now, I go where I please along streets and through fields. You know, during one of my walks I spied a young girl. I have never seen anyone like her in all my life. And yet I do not know who she is. I followed her secretly, trembling the whole time, as if consumed by fever. And then she suddenly disappeared around a corner – there were several large lavish houses there, but I have no idea into which one she disappeared. And ever since then I know not what is happening to me. I'm not my usual self, I feel like I'm hallucinating, both in my dreams and in real life. I have firmly decided that the moment I see her again, I will approach her directly and ask who she is. But so far, I have not been able to see her again. I wander along the street where she disappeared, staring into all the windows, but in vain. If I at least knew which house she lived in, I could ask the caretaker or someone. But I won't relent, I must find out who she is, because that first time when I saw her, I realised that I can't live without her. Yes, Mama, she must become mine, no matter what! I will write to you as soon as I find out.'

This letter had a profound impact on Rifka, one that couldn't be expressed in words or penned on paper. She trembled all over, as if in a fever. For the first time in her life, she was holding a letter that conveyed a truly tangible feeling – love. It was expressed in a rough form, perhaps a bit too laconically and coarsely, but undeniably the feelings were deep, vivid, and maybe even far too romantic, yet they were undeniably strong. Such love must have appealed strongly to Rifka, a woman with little education, nervous and passionate, who had never experienced love herself.

How delighted she would be now to see her Gottlieb, to hold him close to her heart, to follow his every step, to live through his thoughts, and to burn with his emotions. After all, he was in love, and he had shared the innermost secret of his heart with her! Once she knew this, Rifka loved Gottlieb even more, precisely because of his ability to love. It was true that if the girl whom he loved had been here, living nearby, and if the girl had loved him back, Rifka would have surely detested her and poisoned her life out of jealousy!

The days passed in feverish anticipation for Rifka. She struggled mightily not to reveal this burning secret to Hermann. Fortunately, Hermann soon left for Boryslav, where he expected to stay for a few days. Left alone at home, Rifka felt a restrictive, stifling air in the house. Her blood seemed to boil in her veins. She left her bedroom on that hot summer's day. The spacious orchard behind the house was alluring with its luxurious coolness, dark greenery, vibrant scents, and the soft, mysterious rustle of leaves. She involuntarily made her way there.

The gardeners were in the process of picking cherries and large ripe gooseberries. Two boys with baskets stood on the thin cherry branches, using one hand to hold onto the rungs and the other to pluck the ripe cherries. An elderly gardener was collecting gooseberries into a larger basket, squatting in front of the spreading bush and lifting branch after branch. The boys in the trees were laughing, making jokes, and chatting while the old man hummed a tune. When he noticed the lady of the house, he approached her, bowed, and complained that the cherries were scarce this year but on the other hand the gooseberries were abundant, and they fetched a good price. He then gathered several handfuls of the ripest gooseberries, as big as damsons, and offered them to Rifka. She placed them into a handkerchief.

Meanwhile the boys had climbed down from the cherry tree with full baskets. The ripe, full berries glistened in the sun like jewels. The sun filtered through their thin, translucent skin, transforming and shimmering into a reddish wine-like fluid, as if the cherries were filled with blood. The boys also plucked some dark-green cherry leaves, lining the bottom of a small tub with them and carefully began to tip the cherries inside. Rifka stood there and watched, absorbing the sweet coolness and luxurious dampness into every pore of her body, delighting in the freshness of the orchard and the intoxicating scent of the freshly-picked cherries. She felt contented, as never before, and stood there without uttering a word.

However, Rifka turned around when she heard the soft, almost stealthy creak of the gate leading from the yard into the orchard. A small, soot-covered chimney sweep stood holding the gate open, and with his gaze, he gestured for her to come closer. She practically ran toward him.

"Madam, there's a small letter for you here!" whispered the chimney sweep. Trembling more than usual, Rifka eagerly took the crumpled, unsealed letter. The chimney sweep prepared to dash off.

"Wait, wait," Rifka called out, and when he turned around, she emptied the gooseberries she had received from the gardener into his hat. Delighted, the chimney sweep rushed off, munching on the gooseberries and savouring their juicy flesh. Rifka returned to her bedroom, trembling all over, her heart pounding madly. She locked the door, settled on her sofa, let out a deep sigh to calm herself, and began to read:

'I've seen her! Lord Almighty, what beauty, what a face she has, and her eyes! I was drawn to her, I couldn't stop myself. She was riding in a carriage somewhere in the direction of Zadvirne when I unexpectedly chanced upon her. And I immediately went crazy, just like that, completely crazy. I rushed in front of the horses, I don't even know why. I must have wanted to stop the carriage to ask her who she was. But the horses took fright and veered to one side. She screamed, looked at me, and turned pale. And I grabbed hold of the steps of the carriage, and was dragged along over the stones. I didn't feel any pain in my legs; I just kept looking at her. 'I love you! Who are you?' I called out to her. But the coachman turned around and hit me on the head with the whip handle so hard that I let go of the carriage and rolled into the middle of the road. The carriage rumbled on. She screamed again, looked back, and then I couldn't understand a thing anymore. I did manage to get to my feet, intending to run after her, but after two steps, I fell again. My legs were battered against the stones, they were bleeding, my head ached and was swollen – I nearly fainted. An old woman came up to me, gave me some water, and bandaged my legs. I slowly made my way back home. I'm in bed now, writing to you. Settle things for tomorrow and pass a little money on to me through the chimney sweep. Ten rinskys, do you hear? Now there are strangers around me, they might put two and two together...'

Without finishing the letter, Rifka fainted and collapsed onto the sofa.

VII

It was evening. Matiy and Benedio had returned from work and sat in silence in the small room, illuminated by the flickering light of candle made of unpurified Boryslav wax. Benedio stared at the plan spread out before him, while Matiy, sitting on his stool, repaired his boots. Since the evening when Mortko had declared that 'their business was finished,' Matiy had been as quiet as a nail driven into wood. Though not entirely sure about the nature of their business, Benedio felt very sorry for Matiy and was willing to assist him. However, he dared not broach the subject with him to avoid reopening old wounds.

The door creaked and Andrus Basarab entered the house.

"May God grant us good times!" he said.

"May He grant us good health!" replied Matiy, not moving from his spot and grabbing some waxed thread.

Andrus sat down on the bench by the window and remained silent, looking about the house. It was obvious he wasn't sure how to begin the conversation. Then he addressed Benedio:

"Any news, brother?"

"Well, yes," replied Benedio.

"Luck seems to be on your side in our Boryslav," Andrus said somewhat bitterly. "I've heard you're making big money in that factory of yours!"

"Three rinsky a day. Not that much for a Master Mason, but for a poor assistant, it's obviously enough. I need to send some money to my mother, and as for the rest – well, we can talk about the rest later, when everyone arrives. I've been doing a bit of thinking about our plight."

"And what have you come up with?" asked Andrus.

"We'll talk about it at the meeting. But for now, let's try to cheer up brother Matiy – look how downcast he is! I wanted to have a talk with him myself, but I don't know him well enough yet…"

"That's actually why I'm here," said Andrus. "Brother Matiy, it's high time you told us what business you had with Mortko and why you feel so bad about it?"

"Eh, what can I say?" Matiy replied reluctantly. "What's the use of talking, when the matter is finished? It's no use talking now, you can't turn back time!"

"But who knows, who knows, maybe it's not finished," said Benedio. "Just tell us. Three heads can sometimes come up with more than one. Perhaps there's still a way out. And if indeed all is lost, it will at least be easier for you after you share your burden with us."

"Aye, aye, my thoughts exactly," confirmed Andrus. "One fellow is a fool when he confronts a crowd."

"How true, brother Andrus," Matiy replied sadly, putting aside his finished work and lighting a pipe. "You're right, that a man is a fool: he befriends another fellow, and then he not only has to grapple with his own problems, but with those of the other fellow, and a third one as well! And I'll tell you the truth, it is harder to grapple with another person's problems than one's own. That was the case with me. Alright then, I'll tell you what happened to me and the business I had with Mortko.

"It's been almost fourteen years now. Exactly five years after my arrival in this cursed Boryslav. Back then, things were different here. The oil pits were just starting up – it was still more like a village, even though the Jews were already swarming about here. Back then it was sheer hell here, and it's sad to even think about it. The Jews were buzzing around every house, flattering the people, dragging them off to taverns, or even treating them to food in their own homes, defrauding them of their land. I saw things back then that made my heart ache! And as soon as that damned scum defrauded a man and squeezed all they could out of him, they would turn on him! Accuse him of being a drunkard, a scoundrel, a worthless son of a bitch, and they would kick him out of their taverns and drive him out of his own home. They inflicted terrible suffering on the people!

"So one day, I'm on my way to work early in the morning, and I see the whole street packed with people, yelling about something. Shouts and cries rose from the middle of the crowd. And to one side, the Jews had already entered a small straw-thatched hut, acting as if they were in their own house, and were throwing everything out from inside: plates, pots, shelves, a chest… 'What's going on?' I asked. 'What do you think,' one fellow replied. 'They've pushed poor Maksym to the edge. He was a well-off farmer, and a kind-hearted soul too…' 'So what's happened to him?' 'Can't you see?' answered the fellow. 'They've squeezed every last bit out of him. They defrauded him of his land, pilfered his livestock, and now they've come to throw him out of his own home, saying that its theirs now. He tried to stop them, but the Jews didn't ask questions. He got into a fight, and they all came flying, like a flock of rooks, and started beating him up! There was a commotion, our people began to gather too, and they barely managed to free Maksym. All beaten up, looking terrible, he started yelling:

"'Good people, do you see what's happening here? Why are you just standing there? Do you think this is only happening to me? The same will happen to you soon! Go, take whatever you have in your homes – axes, chains, scythes – come and drive these wretches out of our village. If you don't, they'll tear you apart just like they've torn me apart!'

"'The people stared at him, standing and talking among themselves… Just then one of the Jews, who was looking out of the window, tossed a rock which struck Maksym on the head. He collapsed on the spot, and only managed to utter: Kind people, please don't let my child die as well!'

"I didn't finish listening to the story and waded into the crowd. In the middle of the street lay a man, probably forty years old, in a torn blood-soaked shirt, starting to turn blue. Blood was still dripping from his head. Next to him was a small girl, crying and sobbing. I felt a chill run down my spine when I looked at him, and the people had formed a wall around him, murmuring, but not moving from their spots. Meanwhile, the Jews had surrounded Maksym's house, and everything seemed to turn black around them – the wailing and shouting were so intense that I couldn't even hear myself think.

"I stood there, stunned, looking about, not knowing what to do. Suddenly, I saw the Jew who had killed Maksym lean out of the window. He seemed to have gained courage and started shouting:

"'Serves him right, the drunkard! Serves him right! And why are you standing around there, you swine? Trot off home, every last one of you!'

"My blood boiled over.

"'Good people,' I roared in a voice that was not my own, 'are you dumbstruck? Have you lost your minds? Can't you see they've killed a man before your eyes and they're still laughing? And you're standing there doing nothing? May God's wrath strike you down! Give those thieving Jews a hiding!'

"'Beat them up!' people roared from all sides, making the ground quiver. 'Beat the thieves, beat the bloodsuckers!'

"It was like a spark falling into a bundle of straw. In an instant, the whole world turned upside down. Before I even had a chance to look around, a hail of stones was flying at the Jews. I saw the fellow peering from the window suddenly leap up and grab hold of his head with both hands. He fell to the ground, writhing in agony. I saw nothing more, heard nothing more. The cries and hubbub were like Judgment Day. People roared without restraint, surged forward, ripped apart whatever they could lay their hands on: fence posts, branches, poles, logs, and rocks – hurling everything at the Jews. There was a loud screeching and wailing, as if all of Boryslav was being sucked into the ground. Some of the Jews scattered like gunpowder, but several barricaded themselves inside Maksym's house. Through the window, we could see they had axes, hoes, and pitchforks – they grabbed whatever they could. But upon realizing that the crowd had surrounded the house like a roaring flood, they stopped shouting, petrified with fear. The people rushed to the door, the windows, and the walls. Boards creaked, windows shattered, doors splintered – there was a cacophony of noise and chaos, and then a thunderous crash, a cloud of dust… People tore apart the walls, the roof collapsed on the people inside, and the dust enveloped that dreadful scene…

"But meanwhile, I had something else on my mind. Seeing how fiercely the crowd was attacking the Jews, I scooped up the small girl, Maksym's orphan, in my arms and quietly began to make my way through the throng. I had barely managed to break free of the crowd when there was an almighty crash as the house collapsed. I hurried along the back roads, taking a shortcut home, fearing that the Jews might intercept me on the main road. Once I reached home, I bolted the door and laid the unconscious child on the couch, then started to tend to her. For a while I was unable to revive her and even thought that she might have been hit by a stone as well. But, by the grace of God, she eventually came to, and I was so relieved, as if my own child had come back to life before my eyes."

Matiy paused for a moment. The pipe in his mouth had gone out, and his face, which had been animated and impassioned while he was talking, now gradually became shrouded in a long-forgotten, sombre, and desperate expression. A moment later, he resumed his account:

"While pottering about the house and tending to the child, I had completely forgotten about the fracas. It was only later that I learned it had amounted to nothing. After ransacking Maksym's house, the people appeared to have become frightened by the result of their actions and scattered in all directions. Equally alarmed, the Jewish residents remained barricaded in their homes, and only toward evening did some of the more adventurous ones dare to come out to assess the situation. They approached Maksym's house and heard something squealing from within the wreckage. As they cleared away the debris, they discovered that three Jews had died, and five others were injured. It was a tragedy. True, an investigative team arrived and detained a few individuals on suspicion, but they were released shortly thereafter.

"Meanwhile, Marta stayed with me. The decent residents of Boryslav had their own share of troubles and didn't interfere in the plight of the poor orphan. Occasionally, a few of the women from town would bring her food, wash her clothes, mend them, and that was the extent of their help. She was twelve years old at the time. Although not particularly attractive, she was an intelligent child with a kind heart. Initially, she mourned her father, but she soon realized there was nothing she could do about it and resigned herself to the situation. She became attached to me, as if I were her own father. I, too, I must admit, cherished her as if she were my own child, and we became very close. The other oil workers would tease me, asking when the wedding would be, or if there might be a christening first, but I paid no attention to them. Let them talk!

"The little girl grew up with me, God bless her, peacefully and gracefully. Though I may be a rugged oil worker and a community shepherd from way back, life's trials taught me many things as I aged. And I thought to myself, perhaps, God willing, she'll have a better life than mine. I treated her with respect – I didn't make her work hard, never uttered a harsh word to her… She learned how to sew, I have no idea where and how, but it was a marvel. Women would supply her with material, and she would sit indoors for days, diligently sewing. She was not only an amazing seamstress, she could easily engage people in conversation, crack a joke, and offer sensible advice – she was so easy to get on with…

"She got to know a young fellow, a local lad from Boryslav, an unfortunate orphan like her. He was an oil worker, a labourer – Ivan Pivtorak was his name. You knew him well, Andrus… He began to visit her. I could see that the girl was smitten by him, so I started inquiring about Ivan. They said that he was poor, yes, but he was an honest, hard-working, and intelligent lad. One Sunday, he came to our place, thinking Marta was at home, but she was out somewhere. He wanted to leave, but I asked him to stay because I had something to discuss with him. He stood there, hesitated a bit, but then sat down.

"'Well, what did you want to talk about? I'm all ears!' he says.

"I sat there a while, silently observing him. I wasn't sure how to initiate the conversation, so as not to offend the young man.

"'What do you think, Ivan?' I finally asked. 'Do you think our Marta is a good girl?'

"'Why should you care what I think?' he replied sharply, his face flushing crimson.

"I realized that one needed to tread carefully with this one.

"'Well,' I said, 'I don't have much to do with it, but I can see that you have feelings for her, right? You know she has no father, so I'm both a father and a guardian to her, as well as a matchmaker and a brother. You follow me? As soon as I see something I don't like, something that's not quite right… so consider there's no messing around with me!'

"Ivan was visibly shaken by our conversation.

"'May the Lord protect you,' he said, 'threatening me for no reason at all! Has someone told you lies about me? That I have bad intentions toward her? Don't worry, Matiy,' he continued in a respectful tone, 'even though I may be young, I understand a little about how things should be in life. We were planning to discuss with Marta today what we were thinking of doing and when, and then intended to approach you, as her guardian, for your advice and blessing.'

"I told him he'd better watch out, but as I spoke, I felt a strange dizziness in my head, and tears streamed down my cheeks... Silly old fool that I am!

"Anyway, we reached an agreement and they were married. By a stroke of good luck, Ivan had inherited this piece of land here from his father. Not only did he build the house that spring, but it was as if we'd both built it. So the two of them started living here. Of course, you couldn't make any money from this bare piece of land, so Marta continued with her sewing and spinning. Later, when work became scarce, she, too had to go to work in the wax pits. What could I do? I moved out, but when I could, I helped them out – of course, you get used to such things, you adapt...

"And then a few months later I bumped into Ivan and he says to me:

"'Do you know what Marta and I have been thinking about? I'm curious to hear what you think.' 'Well, out with it,' I said. 'It's like this. We want to start setting aside some of the money we're earning. You know, summer is coming, and they'll pay a bit better. So we thought that we could save a little money by tightening our belts, as they say... And, well, there's this fellow in Tustanovychi who is prepared to sell us a plot of land with a house – I've already talked to him about it. He wants 250 rinskys for it. The land is good, and we could probably bargain it down to 200. And I could probably sell my kennel and scrap of land for 50 rinskys. What do you think?'

"I told them that if it was what they wanted, then they should do it. I wished them success. It was certainly not a bad idea, and would allow them to leave that accursed pit.

"'That's not the end of it,' Ivan said. He thought it would be difficult for the two of them to save up the 200 rinskys by autumn, that it might take them two years. 'But what if there were three of us? What do you think?'

"I looked at him.

"'Well,' he said, 'why are you looking at me like that? It's a simple matter: join us as well. Come and live with us, you won't need to pay rent, and our food will cost less. We'll work together and be able to save more.' I saw that the lad was making sense. Coupled with my own desire to leave that forsaken hellhole, and driven even more by a wish to help them, I agreed to move in with them.

"We began to work. Things were going well for us, and we were happy that in no time at all we would be able to move into our own place. Ivan was rushing about here and there like an ant, wishing he could fly away from Boryslav like a bird. The work was good that year, and we managed to save up a decent amount of money. We had enough to buy the land and there would be something left over for farm implements. 'Oh, Lord!' Ivan used to say in the evenings. 'When will the day finally come?' But who knows whether he was destined ever to live to see that day or if wicked people had stopped him.

"We made one foolish decision. We worked together and didn't take our earnings from the Jewish pit owner. We thought the money would be safer in his safe box than under our shirts. Besides, it was recorded under our names in his ledger, so not even the devil could snatch it away. So that's what we did, taking only a few bills from time to time, just enough to get by on.

"Summer slipped by, then fall, and winter arrived, the festive season began, and we were meant to leave Boryslav right after that. On Palm Sunday Ivan left for Tustanovychi to complete the agreement – he was meant to give the fellow there a deposit, and once we moved to Tustanovychi, he would hand him the rest of the money. And so my Ivan left. It began to grow dark – Ivan was nowhere to be found. We assumed he was held up there with celebratory drinks. But Marta was restless all day for some reason, fretting, unable to explain why. The night passed, and still there was no sign of Ivan. We turned up at work, but he hadn't appeared. The overseer, Mortko, asked me where he was. I told him everything, and the fellow began yelling: 'The lazy good-for-nothing is drunk and sleeping it off somewhere, not coming to work!'

"I kept thinking where Ivan might be. In the evening I returned home and he still hadn't appeared. I decided to visit all the taverns, and ask if anyone had seen him. I entered the main tavern – it was full of oil workers. I spied Mortko among them too, but can't recall if there was anyone there that I knew. Four strangers, who seemed to be drunk, were standing in the middle of the room singing: one sang carols, a second – Passions, a third – a dancing song, and a fourth – a melancholy folk *dumka*. They even asked me if they sounded good all together.

"'Go to the devil!' I barked back. 'They'll appreciate your singing there!'

"They set upon me. One grabbed my arm, another grabbed hold of my coat, and they yelled for some vodka to be brought. Reluctantly I gulped down a mug in one breath. They began to roar with laughter and ordered another. God help me to be rid of them! And then I noticed that Mortko was winking at them, meaning, don't let him out of your grasp! I emptied a second mug. My head started to buzz, and the room and everyone in it began to spin about. I vaguely remember that two familiar oil workers entered. I exchanged greetings with them and we had a few drinks, but for the life of me I can't recall who they were."

"Why is it so important for you to know?" Andrus interrupted him.

"It's extremely important! I think that I lost the case merely because of this!"

"What? Because of that? How do you mean?"

"Oh, listen! It's only now, after all this time, that I started to recall everything down to the tiniest detail, how it all happened back then. Only now have I realized that it was two people I knew, but for the life of me I can't remember who they were. Otherwise, they might be witnesses now."

"Witnesses? What for? What do you mean?"

"Just listen to me! I was drinking there in the tavern when I heard a glass crash to the floor in the side room. In a flash Mortko raced off there. I heard voices coming from there: Mortko spoke in hushed tones, but another fellow was raising his voice. I was sure I recognised the voice, it sounded just like Ivan's! You could tell he was drunk, slurring his words, but the voice was definitely his. I rushed up to the door of the side room and accidentally bumped into one of the fellows who had plied me with drink. The fellow crashed to the floor. His companions raced up to me.

"'Hey, there!' they roared. 'What are you doing throwing people to the floor? Hah?'

"'It was an accident!' I replied.

"'Yeah, an accident!' one of them bellowed. 'We know your sort!'

"At that moment the door to the side room opened, and in the doorway I saw – I'd swear to it right now – my Ivan, holding onto the doorjamb. Mortko was standing behind him, holding him up under his arms. Once again, I dashed toward them. But at that moment Ivan disappeared, the door slammed shut, and one of the oil workers grabbed me by the shirt.

"'What if I were to accidentally punch you between the eyes, my friend!' exclaimed one of them and struck me hard in the face, so that a hundred thousand candles lit up before my eyes and I became completely disoriented. All I remember is that I grabbed one of them by the hair, and that the others pounced on me like wolves and bowled me over. It was obvious that they had been put up to it, because I didn't know them from a bar of soap, and never did anything to them. What happened to me after that, what happened to Ivan, and who those two oil workers were whom I knew – I have no recollection of that at all. Everything has become blurred in my mind.

"I woke up at home on my bed. Marta was sitting beside me, crying.

"'What's wrong? Where's Ivan?' was my first question.

"'Disappeared.'

"'Hasn't he returned home?'

"'No.'

"I looked at her, she was utterly worn out and distressed. What could have happened, I thought?

"'But I saw him last night,' I said.

"She smiled through her tears and shook her head.

"'No,' she said, 'you couldn't have seen him last night. Because last night you were lying here unconscious.'

"'Why, isn't it Tuesday today?' I asked.

"'No, it's Friday today. You've been lying here, dead to the world, racked by fever and delirium, ever since Monday night.'

"'And Ivan hasn't appeared since then?'

"'No. I've been everywhere, asked everyone – no one knows where he is or what's happened to him.'

"'But I saw him in the tavern on Monday.'

"Marta said nothing in reply, only shrugging her shoulders, and burst into tears. The poor thing probably thought that in my drunken state I had imagined it.

"'But I swear to God that I saw him with my own eyes!'

"'Well, had he been in Boryslav, he would have returned home by now,' said Marta.

"'That's what I find strange. Was he in Tustanovychi, do you know?'

"'Yes. I quizzed some lads from there. They said he was there, organized the sale of the house and the fields, and in the evening drank to seal the deal and partied until way after midnight. They said he spent the night there, and left on Monday before noon, to pick up his money from the paymaster in Boryslav. That's all that I was able to find out.'

"I felt as if someone had driven a wedge into my head. But no matter how frail I was, I felt I needed to get up and to find out what had happened. But what would it help?

"'Do you know if he left a deposit for the land in Tustanovychi?' I asked Marta.

"'No, I don't.'

"'So, we need to see the paymaster and find out if Ivan withdrew his money. It's payday today, anyway. If he took the money, then maybe he returned with it to Tustanovychi or Drohobych.'

"The two of us went to Hermann Goldkrämer's office, where we both worked. We asked there. They checked the books and said: 'Your Ivan Pivtorak took the money.' 'When?' 'Monday night.' Well, there you go! I made my way to Tustanovychi and asked: no, Ivan hadn't left a deposit, he hadn't been there since Monday, although he had promised to return on the Tuesday afternoon at the latest. They were surprised that he never returned. What had happened? Had he changed his mind, or what? I told them that he had taken the money from the paymaster, and that both the money and Ivan had disappeared. No one knew a thing.

"I went off to Drohobych and asked among my friends: no one had seen Ivan. The fellow had disappeared into thin air. Not a sign of him anywhere. I asked Mortko, where Ivan had gone from the tavern and what he had been doing there. He said that it was a lie, that he hadn't even seen Ivan there. He said that I had been drunk, and that when I had been fighting my own grandma must have appeared before my eyes, and that I had mistaken her for Ivan. I began to ask around, who else had been in the tavern that night, who were the guys who beat me up, but the devil take them, there was nothing to go on! And that was that.

"Well, there's no need to tell you what our Easter was like. Poor Marta cried her eyes out! All hope was lost. A month passed, then another – no news at all about Ivan. Then we heard that some of the oil workers had begun to joke: 'Smart fellow, that Pivtorak: grabbed the money, left his old lady, and took off!' At first it was all said in jest, and then people began saying that it had been true. Once more I asked around: who had heard this? Who saw this? No one knew. One fellow would say: 'Nykola saw him,' and Nykola would say: 'Prots told me,' and Prots would say: 'Someone said Simon heard it somewhere' and Simon couldn't remember where he had heard it, but as far as he could recall, he'd heard it from the overseer Mortko. And Mortko denied everything and spat in everyone's face.

"And then finally, two years later – last year in spring – some bones were pulled out of one of the old pits. From the ring found on a finger and the belt we realized it was Ivan. His money belt was empty, slit open with a knife. A thought became firmly entrenched in my mind at that time, and I still can't shake it. A bad thought, very sinful, if unjustified. Having weighed everything up, I said to myself: Mortko must have gotten Ivan drunk, paid off some guys to get me blind drunk and beat me up, and then robbed Ivan, the poor fellow, and pushed him into the pit.

"I started asking around again, and when a commission finally came to inspect the bones two days later, I couldn't stop myself and repeated everything that was on my mind, as if I was in a confessional. The gentlemen heard me out, wrote everything down in their report, summoned everyone: Mortko, Ivan's wife, and the tavern keeper. They wrote more reports, and then went and arrested… me. I had no idea what they intended to do with me, why they were dragging me off to Drohobych – but then I thought: who knows, maybe this is the way things need to be. I took pleasure in my misery, silly fool that I am. They held me there for a month or so, called me out twice to finish their report, and then they let me go. I came back here and asked if there was any news? Nothing. They had summoned Mortko one more time, Ivan's wife, and three or so guys from Tustanovychi. People said they sent their reports to Sambir, to a higher court.

"Well, now that court case has been dragging on for over a year, and there's still no end in sight. The number of various gentlemen's offices I've visited in that time! I was in Sambir twice, and the number of times I was in Drohobych! I paid the lawyer fifteen rinskys. 'Listen,' he said to me, 'it's quite possible that Mortko did away with Ivan somewhere and took his money. But in court you need to have conclusive proof, and everything that you have told me is not enough. But,' he said, 'you need to keep trying. If some clever judge takes up the case, perhaps he can uncover more facts than you have been able to assemble.' Well, obviously the judge found nothing! Oh, that Sambir judge seemed so useless and incapable! He kept asking all sorts of random questions, it was clear he didn't know where to begin, but then again, who knows, maybe he simply didn't want to!

"In Boryslav, everything grew quiet, as if a lid had been placed on the case. At first, Mortko was terribly frightened, he went about white as a sheet and kept his distance from me. But with time, he grew more sure of himself, started teasing and ridiculing me so badly that I had to leave Goldkrämer's pits and moved here to work for Hammerschlag. Although both are equally bad! So Mortko got off scot-free. You see, Goldkrämer himself was protecting him. He's filthy rich, and so how can a poor oil worker find justice there! We are nothing compared to him! Ivan's wife has a child to take care of and needs to work, and I'm stuck in this hellhole what seems like for the rest of my life. But it's not me I'm concerned about! I mean, I'm nothing! But what pains me is that a man has died, and all in vain. Meanwhile that thief Mortko has gotten away with it – wandering about town now and laughing! That's what irks me most, is that a poor worker can find no justice in this world!"

Matiy grew silent and, sighing deeply, lowered his head. Andrus and Benedio were silent too, overwhelmed by his simple, yet profoundly painful account.

"You know what, brother Matiy?" Andrus said after a while in an almost irritated tone.

"What?"

"You're a stupid fool, that's what!"

Matiy and Benedio stared at him.

"Why haven't you told me this before?"

"Why?" Matiy repeated reluctantly. "What was the point of telling anyone?"

"Phew, to hell with your stupid way of thinking!" Andrus grew angry. "You took that Jewish fellow to court, and if you had won, the trial would have served as a great encouragement to other poor oil workers. It would have shown them that workers cannot be treated unjustly. But winning such a court case requires witnesses, and you sat there quietly, not speaking up, just silently clenching your fists in the corner. Well, tell me, is that smart?"

Matiy became lost in thought and grew melancholy.

"Hey, hey, two witnesses!" he said. "I'm telling you, Andrus, that only now I remembered about those two witnesses, just now, a short while ago. But who can find those witnesses now…"

"I can!" Andrus interrupted him angrily.

"You?" Matiy and Benedio exclaimed.

"Yes, me! Because I and old Stasiura saw you that time in the tavern."

"You? And Stasiura? That was you two?" exclaimed Matiy.

"Yes, it was us."

"And you saw Ivan?"

"How could we not see him, of course we saw him."

"And he was drunk?"

"That he was."

"And he was with Mortko?"

"Yes, with Mortko. When the fight started, we joined in to help you, but then one guy punched old Stasiura so hard, that he lost consciousness. I couldn't help you, because I had to drag the old fellow into the side room, where I saw Mortko with Ivan. I finally revived the old man, and meanwhile Mortko kept prancing around Ivan, plying him with vodka and beer, engaging him in conversation so that he wouldn't talk to anyone else, and then he dragged him off somewhere. I never saw Ivan after that. And when Stasiura came to, you were already lying unconscious on the platform, covered in blood. I couldn't carry you home, and had to ask two oil workers to take you. I told them where you lived, and helped Stasiura home. That's all I know. But how in the hell could I have known that this would be important evidence in your court case?"

"Lord Almighty," Matiy exclaimed, "does this mean that I can now win the case?"

"Who knows," replied Andrus, "but at least you have a greater chance now. You know, it would be a good idea to find the fellows who attacked you back then! You say that you saw Mortko egging them on?"

"I can vouch for that!"

"That would be a great help. You could find out from them, whether Mortko had put them up to it. And to what end?"

On hearing this, Matiy's face brightened for a while, but then this new train of thought unsettled him again.

"But how can we ever find those guys who picked that fight with me? I wouldn't know where to start looking for them or who they were."

"I wouldn't recognize them either, and I never took any notice of them back then. But, maybe Stasiura can remember something? He might have had a word with one of them."

"Lord Almighty – that would surely add fuel to the fire! We'd be closer to having some proof. But who knows if those oil workers would admit to anything! Come, Andrus, let's pay Stasiura a visit!"

Matiy dressed quickly, his movements were livelier now that there was this fresh glimmer of hope, he seemed to have become ten years younger. So deeply rooted was the love he had for the only man he felt close to, that he vehemently wished for the truth about Ivan's mysterious death to see the light of day!

Benedio was left alone in the house after the two brothers left. He sat and thought. It wasn't the court case which preoccupied his thoughts, although, of course, he wished them a good outcome. He was more concerned about Matiy's account of the brawl between the locals and the Jews, and Maksym's calls for the Jews to be driven out of Boryslav. 'Would it really be for the better,' he thought, 'if the Jews were driven out of town? Firstly, where would they be forced to go? To other villages, where the same pattern of exploitation would likely be repeated? And secondly: they wouldn't simply leave, they would take with them the wealth they had amassed from the people. And wherever they went, they would continue with their predatory behaviour. No, this wouldn't do the workers much good!'

Matiy returned home late that night. He was greatly changed – cheerful and talkative. Their hopes regarding Stasiura turned out to be justified. Stasiura knew one of the fellows who had picked the fight with Matiy in the tavern. He was from the same village, although both men had stopped working in Boryslav three years ago and had returned to their farms. Andrus Basarab and Stasiura were ready to testify in court. So Matiy decided so set off for Drohobych the next day to see his lawyer and to consult with him what could be done now.

"Well, now that villain Mortko won't escape justice!" Matiy kept saying. "Now we'll bind his arms and legs with our evidence, and he won't see it coming! Even though the Lord supposedly says not to take vengeance on your fellow man, but in the case of such a thief, it will be no sin to wish him not only hard times, but also misfortune!"

And with such pious thoughts, Matiy fell asleep.

VIII

The workdays in Boryslav dragged on slowly and laboriously, with each day blurring into the next. Benedio toiled away at the factory site from dawn till dusk, drawing up building plans, supervising the labourers, ensuring the punctual arrival of bricks, stones, lime, and various materials. Throughout it all, he treated the workers warmly and genuinely, as if he were consistently reaffirming his status as their equal, just another struggling labourer like themselves. It was almost as if he sought to apologize for unintentionally having assumed a position of authority over them.

After work, in the evenings, he often roamed the muddied streets of Boryslav until the late hours, peering into the squalid dosshouses, cramped shanties, and tiny lodgings where the workers dwelled. He frequently struck up conversations with both the old and the young, inquiring about their lives and struggles. His heart grew heavy as he listened to their stories and witnessed the wretchedness and filth of their existence. But what disheartened him even more was observing the oppressors, who had amassed wealth from this misery and squalor, parading around in luxurious carriages, adorned in extravagant attire, carelessly splashing mud on the ignorant, subjugated masses.

The days dragged on slowly, and with a heavy heart, Benedio observed that life in Boryslav was growing increasingly arduous for the working class. From all directions – mountains and valleys, villages and towns – hundreds of people streamed into Boryslav daily, like bees swarming into a beehive.

'Work! Any kind of work! No matter how strenuous! No matter how meagre the wages! Just to stave off starvation!' This was the collective plea, the lament that hung like a dark cloud over the heads of these thousands of emaciated individuals, their skin tinged blue from cold and hunger. The hopes of these farmers had been crushed alongside the wheat and oats on their parched plots of land, which had turned brick-red due to the drought. Cattle had perished because there was no pasture. The farmers had no choice but to seek employment elsewhere, yet there was no work to be found anywhere in the Carpathian foothills except in Boryslav. And so, the destitute streamed here from all corners, clinging to this as their last glimmer of hope – much like drowning individuals grasping at straws. Heaven and earth seemed firmly locked, and yet the impoverished believed that the wealthy of Boryslav would be more compassionate, opening the gates of their affluence to them.

Indeed, the wealthy residents of Boryslav couldn't have asked for more favourable circumstances. They had long harboured hopes of a significant famine that would greatly increase their profits, and their wishes were fulfilled. Hordes of cheap and compliant labourers arrived, tearfully begging for work, regardless of the pay, which continued to plummet. Meanwhile, the price of bread soared, for it arrived sporadically in Boryslav in limited quantities. Even workers with a few coins in their pockets often succumbed to hunger. Consequently, the newcomers found little improvement in their circumstances, while the long-time residents of Boryslav fared even worse.

Every week the pit owners lowered wages, and those who dared to protest were met with scornful responses: 'If you don't want to accept what's offered, you can go and starve to death. There are a dozen others clamouring for your job, and they'll accept even lower wages!'

Benedio analysed the situation deeply during his walks through Boryslav. He wondered what would happen if all these thousands of people united and decided not to work until their wages were increased? Surely the pit owners wouldn't be able to hold out for long – some had contracts to fulfill, others had promissory notes to settle, which they couldn't do unless they sold their oil and wax. They would have to relent. Honed by the relentless misery he witnessed, his mind clung tenaciously to this idea. However, the more he contemplated this approach, the more challenges and insurmountable obstacles arose.

How could one foster such consensus and solidarity among this vast sea of people, each preoccupied with their own survival? And even if this were possible, the wealthy would not capitulate immediately. Not only would they need to be intimidated, but the threat to abandon all work sites would also need to be carried out. But wouldn't the affluent then enlist workers from other villages, rendering the effort futile? Moreover, how would the thousands of unemployed, starving people in Boryslav subsist while they were not working?

No, he saw no way out at all! There was no glimmer of hope on the horizon. After arriving at these despairing conclusions, Benedio clenched his fists, pressed them to his forehead, and ran through the streets like a man possessed.

At the same time, Benedio eagerly awaited the next meeting of the fraternity, hoping that, with their assistance, he could gain a clearer understanding of the necessary actions given the current situation. During his strolls through Boryslav, he occasionally spotted some of the fraternity members, and he observed that they all appeared disheartened, as if weighed down by an immense burden. Uncertainty and hesitation seemed to gnaw at their core, raising his hopes that one of them might offer a practical solution.

Back at home, Benedio remained silent. Old Matiy was preoccupied with his ongoing court case, and each evening, he engaged in hushed conversations with Andrus, Stasiura, or other oil workers. Eventually, they all departed for Drohobych and were absent for several days, making his solitude even more unbearable. This deep contemplation, to which he was unaccustomed, seemed to induce a feverish state in him and rapidly drained his energy. He grew thin and pale, his already long face becoming even more gaunt, and only his eyes continued to burn with fervour, like two glowing embers. Nevertheless, he did not relinquish his ideas, did not lose hope, and did not cease to empathize deeply with those impoverished souls who stared out, cold and helpless, from every corner, resigned to an untimely demise. Benedio could not conceive of a solution, but he felt profoundly for these people, with all his heart and every fibre in his body. He needed to help them, but the question remained – how? His thoughts repeatedly crashed against this formidable barrier, draining his physical and mental vitality. Yet, he never gave up hope that this obstacle could be overcome.

One evening, Benedio returned home from work later than usual and found Sen Basarab, Andrus' brother, sitting on the porch and calmly puffing on his pipe with that typical unruffled expression on his ruddy face. They exchanged greetings.

"Is Matiy home?"

"No."

"And Andrus?"

"He hasn't come yet either. Nor has Stasiura."

"I heard they'd embarked on something extraordinary in Drohobych."

"We'll see," blurted out Sen, and fell silent. "Did you hear what happened?" he asked a minute later, as he followed Benedio into the house.

"No?"

"It's like a true parable," Sen remarked.

"What kind?"

"What kind? A gentleman has disappeared. You know, the one that our Pryidevolia complained about, that paymaster, remember?"

"Yes, so what's happened to him?"

"What do you think? He wasn't seen for a few days, and today they fished him out of an oil well. A commission has arrived, they're going to cut up the fellow's body, as if it can tell them how it ended up in an oil well and became hooked by the ribs onto a pike pole!"

A cold shiver ran down Benedio's spine at these words. "This is exactly what happened to Matiy's friend, Ivan Pivtorak," he whispered.

"Ah-hah, exactly and yet not exactly," replied Sen. "Ivan was poisoned by the tavern keeper, but this fellow…"

Sen Basarab left the sentence unfinished, but Benedio had no need to inquire further, comprehending the meaning behind his words.

"Well, and…?" he asked after a moment's heavy silence.

"What do you mean? Before, the wolf was the one doing the killing, and now it's the wolf's turn to be killed. There are absolutely no clues."

"And what are people saying?"

"Which people? You mean the commission? The commission will wine and dine its fill, slice and dice the body, and go on its merry way."

"No, I didn't mean the authorities. What are rank-and-file oil workers saying?"

"The oil workers? What are they supposed to say? They gathered around, stared at the remains, shook their heads, and a few muttered quietly: 'He was a thief, may the Lord punish him!' And then they all returned to work."

"That means the deed was for nothing, all that work was wasted," Benedio said through clenched teeth.

"What do you mean, for nothing?" Sen asked, taken aback.

"It certainly won't help anyone else."

"But there's one thief less on this earth."

"Well, never fear, he'll be replaced soon enough by another."

"But at least the fellow will be afraid."

"Of what? If they don't find out who did it, they'll say he slipped and fell accidentally. And if they do find out, they'll take the man responsible and lock him away, so the thief won't be afraid anymore!"

Sen listened and was greatly puzzled. He had expected Benedio to rejoice, but was met with reproaches.

"So what do you expect then?" Sen asked.

"I expect that when something is carried out, especially when such a great sin is taken upon one's conscience, it should benefit not just one person, but everyone. Otherwise, I don't see the point of it."

"Well, well!" Sen shook his head, said goodbye to Benedio, and left.

After his departure, even weightier thoughts occupied Benedio's mind. 'Well, maybe it's true. Perhaps we are better off with one less rogue in this world. But does it improve the lot of the workers? Not at all. Did it make things any better for those oil workers who were celebrating his demise? Once again – no. Another paymaster will replace him, and everything will remain the same, possibly taking a turn for the worse. If only you could eliminate all the evil people in one fell swoop… but then that's impossible. There's no point dwelling on it, it's better to focus on what is right in front of us, something we can act upon!'

The fraternity of oil workers, into which Benedio had been so unexpectedly accepted the day he arrived in Boryslav, had a profound influence on his thoughts and gave them a definite, though initially unclear direction. Even during that first gathering when he was deeply moved by their accounts and their call for action, Benedio had already envisioned a powerful and united fraternity that could bring together all the smaller groups of workers. He believed that their collective strength could protect each worker from poverty and injustice more effectively than they could individually. As the events in Boryslav became increasingly troubling and heart-wrenching, Benedio's idea of such a fraternity grew clearer and more compelling.

He believed that only by coordinating their efforts and providing mutual assistance could the workers bring about positive change. Determined to introduce this idea at the next fraternity meeting, he hoped to steer Andrus Basarab's group away from a path of hatred and vengeance, which, given their small numbers, would only harm them and benefit no one. Instead, he aimed to redirect the fraternity's attention and energies in a broader, less violent, and more productive direction.

The fraternity had planned a meeting for Sunday evening. Earlier that day, Matiy, Andrus, Stasiura, and a few other oil workers had returned from Drohobych. Matiy was particularly cheerful and talkative. However, when Benedio inquired if there was any news and the reason for their prolonged stay in Drohobych, Matiy offered only a vague response, smacking his lips and saying:

"Don't worry, young fellow, all's well!"

It was not quite dark when Matiy lit the mineral wax night lamp just as members of the fraternity began to file into the house. Derkach slithered in before the others like some lizard, greeted Matiy and Benedio, and immediately started poking about in every corner, as was his habit. He was followed by the others. The Basarab brothers were grim and silent as usual. Stasiura shook Benedio's hand with genuine warmth, and everyone else treated him as an equal. Pryidevolia appeared last and seemed visibly tense, his youthful face pale as he surveyed the room discreetly before finding a dark corner to settle in near the entrance The atmosphere was different from previous meetings. There was a palpable sense of heaviness, and conversation was subdued. Everyone felt they were approaching a critical turning point and that open communication was crucial. They sensed that the recent death of the paymaster had signalled a change in the situation, but they were uncertain about the nature of that change and the response it necessitated. Despite this uncertainty, they all recognized the urgency brought about by the growing poverty and unemployment, and the influx of people seeking work. Yet, no one had a clear plan, and they hoped the meeting would provide some guidance.

Only Andrus Basarab seemed unaffected by the unusual atmosphere. He sat by the window, his eyes scanning those assembled.

"Well, here we are," he said. "We can start our business. Derkach, fetch your sticks!"

Always obedient and quick, Derkach began making his way through the crowd toward the middle of the room. However, old Stasiura suddenly stood up and asked if he could speak.

"What's this about?" Andrus asked without much enthusiasm. "Alright, have your say, Stasiura, though I think it would have been better if Derkach had those sticks within reach first. It wouldn't hurt to notch some of the more interesting items onto them."

"What I have to say doesn't need to be notched onto those sticks," Stasiura stated in a firm voice.

"And what then?" asked Andrus, letting his eyes wander over the men again. He noticed that they were all sitting or standing with downcast faces, and although they weren't looking at Stasiura, all seemed eager to hear his words. Andrus guessed that this had been decided in advance.

"It's like this, brother Andrus," the old oil worker began. "It's high time we found something better to do than putting notches in sticks. Do you think we are children? Brother Derkach has bundles of those notched sticks, and what's the good of them? Whom has this helped?"

Andrus looked at the old man with astonishment in his eyes. No one had ever brought this up before, and he himself had often wondered what the use was of these notched sticks. But since he couldn't immediately come up with a sufficiently compelling argument, he decided to stick to his original stance to provoke a more thorough discussion.

"Whom has it helped?" he repeated slowly. "Who were we supposed to help with what we're doing? Have you forgotten that we're doing this for revenge?"

"For revenge, sure! But how are you going to get revenge with those sticks? If we're to have revenge, I think we must use other means, and not waste our time playing childish games. If we want revenge, we must have power, and there's no power in those sticks."

"That's true," Andrus replied, "but when the time came, we wanted to administer justice to those who had wronged us with a clear conscience."

"Our work is futile," Stasiura responded. "We can have a clear conscience even now, for each of us knows all too well how much he is suffering, the reasons, and how he is bearing it. But for vengeance, to overcome evil, apart from a clear conscience, we need power. But where is our power?"

"Hear, hear," the brethren chimed in, "what kind of power have we got? Even if we had three cartloads of notched sticks, it wouldn't give us a thimbleful more power!"

"And how do you propose we acquire more power?" Andrus asked.

"We must allow more people into our fraternity and unite them all by the demonstration of a shared aim," Benedio spoke up.

Everyone looked at him somewhat distrustfully and fearfully, except for Stasiura, who supported him enthusiastically:

"That's what I say, that's what I say too!"

Andrus disagreed. "But for God's sake, brothers, have you considered the potential consequences? Any vagabond could betray us, report us to the authorities, and we would all be shackled and thrown into Sambir jail as criminals!"

These words sent a chill down the spines of the brethren, and they all looked anxiously and expectantly at Benedio, waiting for his response.

"That may be," Benedio said. "But if it is so, what does that imply? It means that we won't be able to publicly declare the aims we've been pursuing until now. To unite people, we must show that there is more to this than revenge, because nobody's belly will be satiated by revenge. We must show them that there will be benefits, assistance, and improvements!"

"He's always going on about assistance!" Sen Basarab's deep voice boomed from the doorway just as Benedio, due to his intense excitement, had found himself out of breath and was compelled to pause. He felt that his blood was beginning to boil and that his thoughts, which until now had stubbornly evaded him, had by some miracle begun to flow freely and took shape in his mind. Sen Basarab's words, brimming with anger and derision, were to Benedio what spurs were to a racehorse.

"Yes, I'm always harping on about assistance, and I won't stop, because it seems to me that only we can help ourselves – no one else will come to our rescue. The pit owners aren't interested in improving workers' conditions. They thrive when workers are desperate and entirely dependent on them. Because when people are starving and vulnerable, they can force them into any job and pay them whatever they please. If we don't want to endure this forever, we need to help ourselves. And think about it, where will revenge take us? Revenge won't make things better, unless we want to start a war throughout the entire country! Punish one bloodsucker, and another will take his place. And you won't even be able to frighten them, because you'll need to act secretly, so that no one will know who was responsible and the reason for an attack. But if they find out, it will be worse still, because they'll throw the person behind bars and leave them there to rot! I believe we need to give this matter careful consideration and explore other avenues."

Benedio fell silent, and all the brethren grew quiet as well. His words had impressed them, but unfortunately, their hope of revenge was taken from them, without being replaced by something else. Sitting in the doorway with a pipe between his teeth, Sen Basarab shook his head dubiously, but said nothing. Even Andrus – although you could see that he found this change in the viewpoint of some of the brethren very unpleasant and undesirable – even his powerful shoulders slumped and his head drooped. Benedio's words forced him to reflect as well.

"Sure it would be good," he said finally, "but how can we do it, how can we help ourselves, when each man can't even help himself?"

"That's the point, that an individual is powerless, but if many people band together, they will have power. You can't lift a large rock on your own, but with the help of several friends you can lift it effortlessly. It's not too hard for an oil worker who is earning an average wage to contribute a shistka in dues every week, but if a hundred of us did this, we would have ten rinskys each week, and then we could help at least a few unfortunates in dire need! Aren't I speaking the truth, brothers?"

"Hm, it's the truth, sure!" voices rang out from all sides.

Pryidevolia sat morosely in the corner by the door, and Sen Basarab grumbled resentfully:

"It's alright for him, a townsman, to talk about dues! Just try and see if you'll find ten such people in the whole of Boryslav who will want to contribute any dues!"

"That's just idle chatter, brother," Benedio replied warmly. "There are twelve of us here and I think that every one of us will gladly agree to contribute something."

"I'm in, I'm in!" some of the brethren cried out.

"Only we'll have to consider what the collection is for and how the money will be used!" Andrus said sedately.

"Of course. We can start considering that right now!" Stasiura backed him.

"No," said Benedio, "let's first decide whether we should contribute dues or not. I see that some of those present aren't too happy about it and would rather that things remained as they were…"

"Don't play with words there," Matiy interrupted him somewhat angrily. Until now he had been sitting silently beside Andrus, as if lost in thought about other matters. However, his interest in the discussion had grown steadily and finally he was listening attentively to every word being said in the room. "Don't ask whether somebody finds it pleasant or unpleasant to listen to. If you know that something is good and wise, and will benefit us all, then out with it, there's no need to beat about the bush. If we see that your ideas are better than other people's, we'll accept them. If they're worse, well, then you can apologise for taking up our time with your foolish nonsense!"

Encouraged by the urgency of the situation, Benedio began to speak directly and without hesitation.

"What if we moved to a system of collecting dues to provide for mutual assistance?" he began. "It will mean significant changes, you know. No more notching, no more avoiding important issues." At these words, it seemed to Benedio that Pryidevolia's intensely burning eyes were piercing into him from the far corner, scorching his face with their critical gaze, making him blush and look down. "We'd also need to communicate with people differently – focusing on support rather than revenge. Of course, we won't tolerate injustice or theft, but we'll call on the workers to unite. Because standing up to the rich and powerful as an individual is almost impossible, but as a united group, it's far easier."

"Can they really do that?" Sen interjected sceptically. "I'd like to know how? Will they pressure the wealthy to raise wages, or what?"

"And why shouldn't they be able to demand higher wages?" Benedio retorted. "What if all the workers united and declared: we won't work until our wages are increased? How would the wealthy respond then?"

"Exactly, that's a valid point! It's a brilliant idea!" the brothers exclaimed in unison. Even Andrus seemed somewhat more hopeful.

"But what if they bring in a bunch of new workers from elsewhere and replace us?" Sen countered.

"And what if we stood our ground and didn't allow newcomers in? Instead, we could ask them to hold off until we had won our battle? Maybe it would be wise, under such circumstances, to send our people to the surrounding villages to spread the word that until a certain time, no one should come to Boryslav, until our conflict was resolved!"

"Hurrah!" the brothers cheered. "That's excellent advice! A battle against the wealthy and the profiteers!"

"Well, I believe such a struggle is better than any other approach," Benedio continued. "Firstly, because it's a peaceful, bloodless struggle, and secondly, because it can be conducted in the open, and no one can take action against us. Anyone can declare: I won't work unless they pay me enough. I'm willing to work, if they pay me this much."

The brothers were overjoyed upon hearing this advice, and Benedio himself was no less thrilled than the others. The idea had come to him unexpectedly during his heated argument with Sen Basarab.

"Well, it's all well and good to say: 'Stop working!' But even if everyone agreed to this, tell me, how would they support themselves while they were unemployed? It's hard to imagine that the rich pit owners would agree voluntarily to raise the wages of the workers on the very first day. It might take a week or even longer. In the meantime, how would you provide for all those people?"

The criticism held weight, and the workers' faces grew long once more. Their newly-kindled hope for a battle and a victory against the rich felt somewhat fragile and uncertain, fading at the first sign of an obstacle.

"That's why we need to collect dues, which would serve us in situations like these. We can't plan anything until we've saved up a substantial amount from those dues, enough to sustain us for a week or two. It's clear that those who refuse to contribute dues and later want to work, will be swiftly escorted out of Boryslav to avoid disrupting our efforts. Our people could also take on other jobs during the work stoppage, such as in forestry or construction, so long as it wasn't in the oil industry. This way, we can effectively challenge the arrogant pit owners and secure better wages."

"That's good advice! Let's do it!" the oil workers enthusiastically agreed. The house filled with lively chatter, and everyone boasted how they would hold the pit owners accountable. Each man offered his own suggestions, not always listening to others, and twisted Benedio's words to his own liking. Sen Basarab sat quietly on his stool, gazing at the animated crowd with a hint of pity.

"What can you do with them," he grumbled, "if they're ready to follow anyone who utters a few powerful words! Let them chase after their dreams. We'll see how much they like it. But I won't stray from my path! And you, brother?" he turned around to Pryidevolia, who remained standing in his dark corner, glancing uncertainly first at Benedio, then at the bustling and animated oil workers.

Pryidevolia gave a start when Sen addressed him and hastily replied:

"Yeah, I'm with you too!"

"Which 'you'?" Sen asked gruffly. "Because, as you can see, we are divided now. Are you with these fellows, or with me and my brother?"

"Of course, I'm with you and your brother! You heard what this guy said? It felt like he stabbed me in the heart with a red-hot poker."

"Well, there's no need to get worked up about it!" Sen reassured him in a hushed tone. "It's not a big deal. After all, that guy probably got what was coming to him. Have you forgotten about your...?"

"No, no, no, I haven't!" Pryidevolia interrupted him. "I'm sure he deserved it, a hundred times over!"

"Well, then why are you getting so upset? Are you afraid of a trial? Don't be, the commission has already left, and they're convinced he fell into the pit accidentally. They might even consider sentencing the Jewish owner for not fencing off the pit!"

"No, no, no," Pryidevolia interjected in a feverish and somewhat agonized voice, "I'm not afraid of the commission! They're nothing to me! However, it seems to me, that if the commission... you know... uncovered the truth, I would feel much better!"

"Oh, God forbid, what are you babbling about?"

"Listen to me, Sen," Pryidevolia whispered, leaning closer to him and convulsively clutching at his shoulder, "it seems to me that... the Jew... you know, the one who died in the pit, he was innocent. And that someone else was responsible for it all."

"What do you mean? Come on! Wasn't he there?"

"Yes, he was there, and he even laughed. But did he deserve to die just for laughing at something? Maybe he didn't do a thing, and it was all the doing of those others?"

"Where are you getting these ideas from, young fellow?" Sen asked, astonished. "If a man falls into a pit, then the devil take him! He's gone, and that's that!"

"But what if he's not guilty? You see, when I cornered him and he realized what was happening, he squealed: 'Let me live, please!' And when I pushed him into... you know... he cried out: 'I'm innocent! It wasn't me!' After that all I heard was blubbering and crashing, and I ran off. But his voice keeps haunting me, it's inside me, I can't stop hearing it! Lord Almighty, what have I done?!"

Poor Pryidevolia wrung his hands, tormented by the belief that the paymaster he had pushed into the pit might have been innocent. Sen's attempts to persuade him otherwise were in vain.

"Well, if he was innocent," Sen said angrily, "then let's send the guilty ones down the same path! So the innocent fellow doesn't repent in vain!"

The words struck Pryidevolia like a hammer. Stunned, he lowered his head and retreated into his corner without saying a word.

Meanwhile, the brethren finished deliberating.

"The main thing now," said Benedio, "is for us to recruit people to our cause. Whoever you work with or meet at the tavern, or strike up a conversation with in the street, immediately steer the discussion in that direction! Explain everything: how miserable the wages are and what can be done to change things. And let's collect dues. I think each one of us should collect among our acquaintances and each evening turn over whatever we collect to the treasurer, whom we'll need to elect tonight."

"Fine, fine, let's elect a treasurer," they all agreed. "Let's see, who would make a good treasurer!"

One after another, people were suggested, but they eventually concluded that Sen Basarab would be the best treasurer.

"Really, do you want me to be your treasurer?" he said with hostility upon hearing this. "Never! From now on I don't want to be associated with you lot at all! Neither me nor my brother."

"You don't want to belong? Why?" everyone exclaimed.

"Because you're straying from the path which you chose after thorough consideration. I won't switch roads!"

"But who's switching?" Andrus asked. "Nothing is changing here!"

"Are you with them too?" Sen asked morosely.

"Yes! I'm with them!"

"Have you forgotten your vow?"

"No, I haven't."

"Well, you're trampling on it, even though you haven't forgotten it."

"Not at all! Hear me out and stop getting hot under the collar!"

Andrus went up to him and began to whisper into his ear. At first, whatever it was he said didn't meet with Sen's approval, but after a while his face began to relax, and finally, he cried out almost joyously:

"Well, if it's like that, then it's alright! I was a fool not to guess! Greetings, brothers, I'll be your treasurer, and I hope that there won't be any complaints!"

"And one more thing," Benedio exclaimed with joyous conviction, his voice filled with newfound confidence as he addressed those assembled. On this remarkable day, he had transitioned from a mere rank-and-file worker to their leader. "My dear comrades, you all know that I'm just a common labourer like each one of you. I grew up in poverty and am nothing more than an assistant mason. I never sought favours or asked for special treatment. Yet for some unexplained reason Hammerschlag appointed me as a Master Mason and has entrusted me with the role of construction manager at the new refinery. I owe him no gratitude, for I never requested such a favour. In fact he is the one who benefits, as he no longer needs to hire a separate building supervisor. He pays me three rinskys a day, a considerable sum for a poor worker like me. I have an ageing mother in Drohobych who relies on my support. I send her two rinskys every week. Another two rinskys I spend on myself. That means there's fourteen rinskys left over every week and I pledge to contribute this into our treasury!"

"Hurrah!" shouted the brethren in unison.

"Long live Benedio! I also pledge one rinsky per week!"

"And I pledge five shistkas!"

"Here are my three shistkas!"

"And mine!"

"Mine, too!"

Benedio's impassioned speech, along with his own generous commitment, had ignited a spark of enthusiasm in all who were present. Sen Basarab promptly began collecting the dues, while Pryidevolia, whom he had enlisted as his assistant, noted down each donation with a carpenter's pencil on the back of a tobacco wrapper.

Filled with hope, the brothers left, their spirits soaring after the discouragement caused by their difficult circumstances. Their renewed sense of purpose and solidarity warmed their earnest hearts, much like the soft, pink rays of dawn casting a warm glow on the rugged peaks of the Beskyd Mountains.

IX

In autumn, when the flowers have withered and the bees have completed their harvest, the beehives come alive with noise and commotion. Just like people, after their arduous labour is finished, bees enjoy socializing. They gather in groups near the openings to the hive, buzzing and stretching their wings. Initially, it is unclear what is happening or where this energy is being directed. Inside the hive, nothing new seems to be taking place. A few diligent worker bees continue to venture into the fields each morning, returning in the evening with meagre pollen loads on their legs. The drones, unaware of what is to come, carry on feasting, arrogantly strolling among the honey-filled combs. They still make their regular midday pilgrimage to the roof of the hive to soak up the sun, savour the fresh air, and stretch their idle wings.

For now, the hive appears peaceful and harmonious. However, an undercurrent of change is emerging. Worker bees exchange secretive whispers, nod their heads secretively, ominously rub their pincers together, and shake their legs. It is unclear what is happening and what might be brewing in the bee kingdom.

This same transformation began to unfold in Boryslav a few days after the meeting described earlier. It was unclear how or from where the new spirit had emerged, but it permeated the town. Typically, fresh currents of change are initially felt in the upper echelons of society, but in this case, the opposite occurred. The populous working-class, at the very bottom of society's ladder, felt it first and was the first to be stirred by it. The exact origin of this movement remained elusive. Out of nowhere, at the hand cranks, the exhaust fans, the wax storage depots, and in the taverns, the oil workers began discussing the harshness of their life, the challenges of working in Boryslav, and how the bosses, without rhyme or reason, kept reducing their wages, mistreating and deceiving workers, and even mocking them.

No one could say who initiated such conversations, as tales of hardship had long been etched into everyone's mind. However, once the discussions began, they did not dissipate and instead spread, growing more fervent and vocal. It was as though the people had suddenly awakened to their dire and hopeless circumstances and could not talk about anything else. Each conversation inevitably ended with the painful and daunting question: 'Lord, must we endure this suffering indefinitely? Is there no way out? Can we do something to remedy this injustice?' While no immediate solutions were proposed, the discussions intensified and became more incisive. Those who initially spoke of their troubles with resignation, as if these were preordained by divine will, eventually came to believe that they were mistaken. They grew impatient and irritable because they did not know how to address their grievances. They walked and talked as if consumed by fever, eagerly grasping at every word that might shed light on their miserable plight.

These conversations penetrated even the smallest huts and the darkest corners, spreading like wildfires. The young boys toiling in the muck, and the girls and women extracting wax from the clay also joined the chorus of complaints about their atrocious conditions. They insisted on discussing the problem and finding ways to help themselves.

"Are you carrying on about this as well?" grinned the older oil workers as they listened to the complaints of the younger fellows.

"Oh, come on, as if it's not as tough for you as for us?" replied the younger fellows. "Of course for us it's even worse! They won't lay you off as easily, and they won't cut your wages as much as ours. And even if they do, your pay is still more than ours. But we need to eat just as much as you!"

"But who put this idea into your heads that you need to change things?"

"And who was meant to teach us? It's not as if people don't know that when you scald yourself, you need to apply something cold to it, right? If only it didn't sting so badly! But, you see, there's hunger back home, we couldn't harvest anything, mum and dad are starving. We thought we might make a little here to feed ourselves and maybe help them as well. But look what's happening! We can't even earn enough in this darned pit to feed ourselves! There's a crowd of people vying for work, wages are low and keep dropping, and now the pit owners have conspired to stop delivering bread here, driving prices sky-high. It's hard to find any bread at all! How can anyone live like this? It's better to die straight away or to find salvation elsewhere!"

Similar conversations were heard everywhere among the oil workers, and the same concerns were being voiced. These words made it clear that each worker bore an immense burden of survival on their shoulders. Personal grievances, individual needs, and the unbearable hardships faced by each worker became part of a collective grievance. It was as if each complaint added one more drop to an overflowing barrel of shared discontent. On the one hand, all of this weighed heavily on people who were unaccustomed to thinking critically, but on the other hand, it stirred their emotions, awakening expectations and hopes. And the greater these were, the more acutely they paid attention to their current situation and every incident that took place, no matter how minor. They reacted more intensely to every new injustice and offence.

Conflicts between workers and overseers became more frequent. Overseers had long regarded workers as mere beasts of burden to be pushed around, kicked, or dismissed at will. The idea that workers had human rights was laughable to them. The workers themselves, often hailing from the poorest of villages, had endured these abuses patiently since childhood. Occasionally, there were individuals, like the Basarab brothers, with strong and upright characters, but they were few and far between and the Boryslav pit owners hated them for being assertive and outspoken.

But suddenly things began to change. Even the humblest of the workers, including the boys and girls who had previously silently endured insults and mistreatment, started reacting forcefully and angrily. What was most remarkable was the birth of a sense of fraternity in the barracks. The idea of 'all for one and one for all' took root. This feeling of unity grew from constant lively exchanges of ideas and a shared understanding of the common hardships faced by everyone. When an overseer unjustly targeted a worker with insults and abuse, the entire barracks would come to the worker's defence, silencing the overseer with curses, taunts, or even threats. During the weekly wage distribution, increasingly heated and menacing protests could be heard. Dozens of comrades would rally behind an aggrieved worker, sometimes even workers from other barracks would join in, crowding the pay office, demanding full payment, and firmly standing their ground.

The overseers initially responded with screams and threats, but then began to relent when they saw that the oil workers stood their ground and became more enraged, rather than becoming frightened. The overseers were not ready to admit that the situation had changed and could turn nasty. The small pit owners and rich industrialists continued to parade haughtily in Boryslav, looking down on the workers and rejoicing at the growing hunger in the villages, as more people arrived in Boryslav each day. They were still focused on their speculative business deals and had no inkling that the workers might disrupt their plans and claim a share of the profits for themselves. They still slept peacefully and remained oblivious to the growing unrest, failing to sense the ominous heaviness in the air that typically preceded a storm.

This significant transformation occurred among the Boryslav workers with unexpected rapidity. Even the brethren themselves, who had initially spurred this transformation, were astonished by how loudly their message resonated throughout Boryslav. Even the most sceptical among them, those who had reservations about the changes made to the fraternity's goals and operations, including the Basarab brothers, observed how eagerly the oil workers embraced their message and began articulating it in their own words. This prompted them to support the new movement with greater gusto. They realized that Benedio and Stasiura had been right to advocate for the expansion of their outreach beyond the tight-knit fraternity and the dissemination of their message and ideas to the widest possible audience. They saw that the groundwork had been well laid among the people for spreading this message and that making it public would not diminish its impact; on the contrary, it would gain strength.

The Basarab brothers and other previously sceptical brethren, while not necessarily in complete agreement with Benedio, recognised that his advice was worth pursuing. They no longer feared that he had led the fraternity astray. On the contrary, they were grateful to him for giving the movement a common cause and assuming leadership in a direction they had hesitated to explore. They worked diligently to implement Benedio's ideas, knowing that if they succeeded in achieving the goals he had articulated, their initial desires would also be fulfilled. If Benedio's ideas did not bear fruit, they believed that at least the attainment of their original goal would become more certain. In this way, Benedio worked on behalf of all workers striving for a common good, regardless of their differences.

Life in the tiny house on the outskirts of Boryslav, where Matiy and Benedio lived, was filled with activity and excitement. Each evening, the brethren would visit, usually in groups of two or three, to provide updates on the progress of their mission. They discussed how the oil workers were receiving their message, seeking advice, and standing up to the pit owners. These conversations often extended late into the night, clarifying the path ahead for our friends.

Initially, when they had decided to broaden their efforts by recruiting a wider spectrum of Boryslav workers into their fraternity, they had spent two whole evenings deliberating on how to achieve their goals discreetly, without drawing the attention of the authorities. The persecution and arrests of Poles who had participated in the 1863 uprising was still fresh in people's minds, and some of the brethren expressed fears that exposure could lead to police crackdowns and charges of rebellion, potentially undermining all their efforts.

Finally, Benedio proposed a new strategy: they would present their ideas as if they had heard them elsewhere by chance. Gradually, in every conversation, they would instill in the workers an awareness of their dire living conditions while highlighting the possibility of future improvement. Benedio believed that this approach would stoke unrest, irritation, and a desire for action among the workers. If handled skilfully, this tension could be harnessed and transformed into powerful action when the time was right. The brethren embraced the strategy and pledged to act on it.

In less than two weeks, it appeared that their objective had been achieved. After finishing their shifts, the workers gathered in large, noisy groups, discussing their situation as they strolled through Boryslav. The taverns gradually emptied as unrest among the people continued to mount. Some of the more impatient brethren began to assert more forcefully that

it was time to take control of the broader labour movement.
However, Benedio, supported by the Basarab brothers, insisted on waiting a bit longer, allowing the workers' anger to continue to grow and become more turbulent. The tide of discontent, fuelled by poverty and oppression, and coaxed along by the candid words of the brethren, continued to surge and grow in intensity.

The common man is not known for prolonged contemplation and deliberation. While he may take his time arriving at a clear and definitive conclusion using his own judgment, once that conclusion is reached and firmly settles in his mind, he abhors indecision and is driven by an intense desire to translate his ideas into action. This often leads to clashes with those who oppose him. Such was the case here. Although it may seem that a person enduring daily poverty and suffering should quickly recognize their plight, it took a long time for the Boryslav workers to come to this realization. Strangely, despite its inherent sadness and helplessness, this awareness stirred unrest and a storm of determination, unity, and defiance against those who were causing them distress.

From words they progressed to actions. The news spread across Boryslav that in one incident, workers had confronted a timekeeper in a narrow alley after he had attempted to collect a timekeeper's fee of four cents for a twelve-hour shift, instead of the usual two cents. The news acted as a catalyst for similar incidents to follow swiftly. With each report of such an event, the oil workers' resolve and courage grew. They started warning timekeepers, foremen, and overseers directly that they would not tolerate further mistreatment. Those who had been exploiting them grew fearful.

One day, a rumour spread through Boryslav that when a foreman had unjustly fined an oil worker and the timekeeper tried to deduct the fine from the worker's wages on payday, the oil workers created a commotion at the pay window, demanding that the foreman be brought there to explain his actions. Unable to locate the foreman, the timekeeper had said facetiously: 'Go and find him, and when you do, bring him here by the ear!' The oil workers scattered in all directions with loud cheers and soon located the foreman. They forcibly dragged him to the pay window by the ears, leaving him bruised, scratched, and with torn earlobes. Several oil workers were arrested and held in the town's jail. This news sent shockwaves through Boryslav and struck fear into the hearts of the Jewish pit owners.

That very evening, a large mob of oil workers, led by the Basarab brothers, marched to the office of the Boryslav mayor and compelled him to release the detained men. Joyful laughter filled the air, and songs and chants echoed through the streets of Boryslav. The freed men were taken from one tavern to another, treated to drinks, and repeatedly made to recount how they had led the foreman to the pay window by the ears.

While the workers revelled in the streets of Boryslav, their spirits intoxicated by happiness, inside Matiy's modest shanty, the brethren had congregated to deliberate on their next course of action. All were agreed that the time had come for action.

"Let's call a meeting!" they all said.

They resolved to organize a gathering of oil workers on the green, near Boryslav, following Sunday mass. Importantly, they decided not to disclose the existence of their secret fraternity. The next day news of this gathering quickly spread like wildfire, passed on from one mouth to another, from pit to pit, from barracks to barracks, and from one oil works to another:

"On Sunday after mass! On the green near Boryslav! Attend a meeting!"

The words buzzed throughout the community. No one knew the nature of this meeting, what it would consider, or who had called it. No one even asked. But there was a general feeling that this event held immense significance. Although their hopes were grand but somewhat nebulous, everyone pinned great expectations on the meeting. The mere utterance of the word acted like a magical incantation, breathing life into withered and weary faces, invigorating calloused hands, and straightening arched spines. 'Meeting! Our meeting!' The message spread, spoken loudly and in hushed whispers, reaching every corner, and thousands of hearts pulsated with impatience, eagerly awaiting Sunday and the forthcoming gathering.

The brethren, particularly Benedio and Andrus Basarab, also awaited the meeting with restless anticipation.

X

A storm was brewing over Boryslav, not in the sky descending to the earth, but rising from the earth toward the heavens.

Menacing clouds gathered on the barren expanse serving as Boryslav's green, where the oil workers were assembling for their momentous workers' meeting. All were stirred by this new and previously unknown phenomenon; all were filled with hope, and yet there was a hidden fear; all were united in their anger and resentment against their oppressors. They arrived in large groups and small, at times raucous and at times silent, from the upper end of town and from the lower end, as well as from the centre. Clad in dark, oil-stained kaftans, vests, and long coats made of coarse homespun wool, belted with leather thongs or rope, their faces pale, tinged with yellow and green hues, hiding under ragged oil-smeared caps, hats, army 'holtzmitzes,' felt or straw hats, they spread across the green like a dense, sooty grey cloud. They pressed together, swaying in waves, the collective sound of their presence resembling an approaching flood.

"What's there to discuss?" one group insisted. "It's crystal clear: the Jewish pit owners have ensnared the land, they won't let us live, they have brought famine upon the people!"

"We must unite and stand our ground!" came shouts from another group.

"It's easy for you to say we should stand firm. But when you're hungry and out of work, you'll put your tail between your legs and agree to anything!"

Hunger was the raw nerve. Like a haunting nightmare, it loomed over every shoulder. Mention hunger, and once-loud and bold voices grew quiet.

"Throw all those who mistreat us into the oil pits!" echoed cries from the far end of the green.

"What good will that do?" old Stasiura tried to calm the crowd. "Firstly, anyone who throws a person into a pit is likely to rot in prison…"

"Hah! Who knows if it will come to that," Matiy lamented sadly. "The thief Mortko threw my dear Ivan in, even stole his money, and yet he still walks the earth to this day, mocking us Christian folk!"

"And secondly," Stasiura continued, "a hundred may cheat us, but there are a thousand skinning us alive within the law, so you can't even rightly call it mistreatment. They are polite and courteous, saying: 'Take what's your just deserts,' although a man knows he is being fleeced. That's our problem!"

"That's true, so true!" the oil workers chorused.

"Who knows, there may be no remedy for that," others chimed in.

"Why not?" Stasiura asked. "There's a medicinal herb for every type of ailment; you just need to find the right one. How can there be no cure for our ills? We must find the right approach. We've gathered here today, a large crowd, thanks be to the Lord, to talk things over. As you know, a crowd wields power. Where a single individual can't make progress, an entire community can soon find a solution."

"May God grant that we reach some agreement today," the oil workers implored. "The time is long overdue, and poverty is gnawing us to the bone."

Similar discussions took place in every corner, among every group. The brethren moved through the crowd, sowing their ideas among the people, instilling confidence in the potential for improvement and reform, and strengthening people's belief in collective intelligence and power. New groups continued to arrive. The sun had climbed high into the sky, beating down relentlessly and creating thick, noxious, suffocating clouds of oil fumes over Boryslav.

"Come on, it's time to get the ball rolling, let's start the meeting – everyone's here!" workers called out from all directions.

"Anyone with something to say, come here to the centre and stand on this rock!" Andrus Basarab proclaimed in his powerful, resonant voice.

"Gather round, make space around the rock," the oil workers shouted, moving toward the centre.

Benedio climbed onto the rock. He wasn't accustomed to speaking before such a large crowd and felt a bit flustered. He twisted his cap in his hands and looked about in all directions.

"Who's this?" the oil workers shouted.

"I'm a working man, a mason," Benedio declared.

"Well, then, say your piece!"

"There's not much to say," Benedio began, gaining confidence. "I simply want to repeat what everyone here knows for a fact, without me needing to say it. We working folks are in dire straits. We work hard, we rarely enjoy a peaceful night's sleep, we find no respite during the day, and our hands bear callouses that never go away. And what do we get in return? They tell us to work diligently so that we can enjoy the sweet fruits of our labour. But how often do we savour that sweetness? We earn our wages through strenuous toil, that's a fact, but our existence is even more strenuous. We suffer from hunger, never enjoying a square meal. But to compound our misery, we must endure being mistreated, badmouthed, and humiliated at every turn! You all know how little respect we receive. They value an animal more than they value a worker!"

"He speaks the truth, it's plain as day! They value their cattle and dogs more than us poor folk! Hey, hey, does the good Lord ever notice this?"

"And what's more," Benedio continued, "who do we work for, and who reaps the benefits of our labour? The wealthy gentlemen! The pit owners! While the impoverished oil worker spends six to eight, sometimes even twelve hours in the foul-smelling, stifling pits, suffering as they hammer away and dig the drifts underground. Other workers stand at the fans, turning the cranks until their minds spin and the last ounce of strength drains from their bodies. Meanwhile, the owners sell the wax and oil, amassing fortunes. They are the masters, building grand stone mansions for themselves, dressing up and riding in carriages, splashing mud on the poor. And not a word of gratitude ever escapes their lips. That's who we toil for, and that's the appreciation we receive!"

"May the Lord punish them for our hard work and poverty!" oil workers cried out from all directions.

"Well, in that regard, yes," Benedio continued after taking a moment to catch his breath. "May the Lord punish them, of course. But who is to know if the Lord will indeed punish them, and even if He does, who's to say it will make our lives any easier? As it stands, it seems as if God prefers to punish us more than them! Consider the present circumstances: He has inflicted famine upon our villages, while here in Boryslav, the pit owners have taken it upon themselves to punish us as well. They're reducing wages week by week, and if anyone dares to protest, they mock him to his face with the words: 'Leave, if you're dissatisfied!' And they add: 'I can easily find a dozen others to take your place at the same pay.' So, consider for yourselves whether relying solely on God's punishment will help us in any way! I believe it's best to follow the wise old proverb: call upon the Lord for help, but also roll up your sleeves. God's punishment is His prerogative, but we must unite and figure out how to overcome our hardships through our own efforts."

"Hah, there's the rub! How can we overcome them when we're poor and can't get help from anywhere?" the workers called out.

"Well, I can't give you a foolproof recipe," Benedio replied, "but if you are willing to listen, I'd like to share my thoughts on the matter."

"Go ahead, we're all ears!" the oil workers buzzed.

"If it's your will, then I'll speak. What you say is true: waiting for help from others is futile because no one will lend a hand to a poor worker today! And even if someone were willing to lend a helping hand, he wouldn't be able to assist everyone, there are simply too many of us. Only through our united efforts can we help ourselves."

"What do you mean by that?" sceptical voices called out.

"It's true," Benedio affirmed, "that at present, we are in no position to help ourselves. What kind of assistance can there be when a man doesn't work for his own benefit, but toils endlessly, while someone else reaps the rewards of his labour? Until our labour starts to benefit us, we won't experience true well-being. However, we can help ourselves to some extent. Consider this: how often does a man find himself out of work? He wanders around as if in a daze, darting here and there in desperation, but failing to find work. When such a man begins to wither from hunger, he'll accept any work, no matter how degrading, simply to avoid starving. But if each of us here were to commit to contributing just a cent from our weekly wages, imagine what we could achieve. With a thousand of us, no one would feel the loss of a single cent from their pockets, yet every week, there would be a substantial sum to help a dozen people in desperate need."

"That's true!" the workers cried.

"It may not be an enormous amount of help," Benedio continued, "but it wouldn't be insignificant either. You see, if a man can be sustained for a while with a rinsky or a rinsky and a half, he won't need to scramble and beg for work at abysmal wages. This way, he won't be compelled to drag down the wages of other workers. Moreover, any amount we provide to him can be gradually repaid when he finds work. In this way our workers' treasury would not become depleted, on the contrary, it would continue to grow."

The oil workers stood in silence, contemplating the words. Initially the proposal appeared promising, and they were ready to agree to it. But then objections began to be heard.

"What good will that do?" some oil workers argued. "Suppose we agree and begin making contributions, who will benefit from them? It might end up like the community fund pools in certain villages, where the wealthy borrow the money and profit from it, while the poorer individuals contribute their meagre amounts without securing any advantage. And then there's this: so we elect a treasurer, an oil worker like the rest of us, say, but where's the guarantee he won't run off with the money?"

Benedio listened attentively to the objections.

"I've considered that as well," he replied calmly, "and this is the conclusion I've reached. Firstly, there's no risk of the wealthy benefiting from our funds, because among us, there are no rich fellows, we're all poor. Secondly, we're not moneylenders; we won't be lending out our funds at interest. We'll provide help only in cases of dire need, illness or unemployment. That means we'll only offer help in situations where it's apparent that help is needed. Those who have the means will return these funds when they're able, and if someone is incapable of doing so, we won't hold it against them. As for selecting a treasurer, here's my suggestion. If lots of us decide to pay dues, let the workers themselves elect a treasurer from each barracks or group of neighbouring barracks, someone who works full-time here in Boryslav and is well-known to all. Such a treasurer would only collect funds from the barracks that elected him. Everyone could easily calculate the amount in the treasury based on the number of workers and the amount of contributions. And if they aren't satisfied with their treasurer, they can always elect another. All the barracks with their own treasurer will be responsible for aiding those in need within their ranks, and they will be the best judges of who requires help and how much."

"Now, that's talking," the workers nodded in agreement. "This way we can always keep an eye on the treasurer. And if there are a lot of them, each will only hold a small sum, thus reducing the temptation for any mischief. And even if the money were lost, it wouldn't be much of a loss. Sure, we can agree to that."

"Allow me, please, that's not all," said Benedio. "Who knows, there may arise a need for help that exceeds the capacity of one barracks' treasury. Something might need to be done for the welfare of all Boryslav workers, which would require more money than any single treasury holds. I suggest we divide all the money being collected in each of these local treasuries into three parts. Two of those parts should remain in the barracks for local help, while the remaining third should be contributed to a main central treasury. Neither the treasurer nor any single barracks would be able to withdraw money from that central treasury, needing a full assembly of workers who contribute to the fund to approve that. We should withdraw only the minimum amount needed and build our funds up for a larger common purpose."

"What sort of purpose could that possibly be?" asked some of the oil workers.

"Here's how I see it," said Benedio. "As you can see, the pit owners have become convinced that there are lots of us, and with famine driving more and more workers into Boryslav, they don't care whether we can manage or not. They keep cutting our wages, and they won't stop until we take action."

"We've tried that already, and what good did it do?"

"Wait, just let me explain how we need to act," Benedio continued. "Talking to them, whether politely or with threats, won't work because they won't listen. What we must do is take action that will hit them so hard they won't know where it came from. Here's what I suggest: one morning, all of us, as many as are assembled here, and even those who aren't present, each at their workplace, stand up and say: 'Enough! We're not going to work for such meagre wages. We'd rather stay home. We won't lift a finger until our wages are increased.' And having said that, everyone goes home!"

The oil workers were stunned by this bold advice.

"But… how can we do that? Just walk away from our jobs?"

"It would only be for a while, until they offered us better pay."

"But that might last a long time."

"Well, it can't last too long. You see, the pit owners have contracts with various merchants to deliver specific amounts of wax and oil by certain dates. If they fail to deliver on time, they stand to lose much more than the increase in wages we are after. Rest assured, they won't go down into the wells themselves. They might be able to hold out for a few days, but eventually they'll have to accede to our demands."

"But they'll bring in other workers from outside!" someone piped up.

"We'll need to make sure they don't," Benedio replied confidently. "We need to send out men to all the villages in the region and announce that during such-and-such a period, no one should come to Boryslav because something important is taking place there."

"And if they bring in the Masurians[15]?"

"We must not let them in! Whether we do it with words or by force, we must not let them in."

"Hm, it could be done. But how are we supposed to live while we're unemployed?"

"That's why I think we should build up that main treasury," Benedio responded.

....

[15] An ethnic group originating from the region of Masuria in Poland.

"But surely the pit owners will conspire to stop bread being delivered. They'll try to starve us."

"But we wouldn't be buying bread from them anyway. When we have our own money, we can bring it in ourselves for even less!"

"Do you think it will work, will they raise our wages?"

"I think they must, so long as we stand firm."

"But it will take a tremendous sum of money to feed such a crowd of people!"

"During the time when there's no work, we can send some of the people to the villages or the towns, to other factories, to lighten the load," Benedio explained. "And we shouldn't rush into such a significant action until we have enough money to sustain us for at least a week. And before we begin, we'll have to prepare well, send our people off to the villages to stock up on bread and other supplies. But there will be plenty of time to discuss these details later. For now, we need to decide whether you agree to the idea of having treasuries: both local ones and a main one."

"Agreed! Agreed!" the workers called out enthusiastically.

"And do you agree that two-thirds of the funds should remain in the local treasuries and one-third should go to the main treasury?"

"No, let two-thirds go to the main treasury! We would be willing to pay two cents in dues, if only it meant quicker improvements for all of us!"

"I suggest we elect a three-member executive to oversee the main treasury. It's crucial that the treasury be in the hands of someone who has property here."

"But where will we find such a person, since we're all poor and from out of town?" a worker called out.

"I know such a man, old Matiy. He has a house of his own here. In my opinion, it would be best to keep the treasury in his place. It should be maintained in a way that allows every local treasurer to visit at any time, count the money, and report back to their people. The other two executive members would be responsible for visiting the barracks every week to collect money. This way there would be a greater guarantee that no one is cheating anyone or pocketing any of the funds. Do you agree?"

"We agree! We agree!" the workers responded enthusiastically.

"Where's this Matiy? We want to see him!" shouted some of those who didn't know Matiy. Matiy climbed up onto the rock and bowed before the crowd.

"Who are you?" some men shouted.

"I'm an oil worker, good people."

"Do you have a house of your own?"

"It's mine and not mine, but more mine than not. It belongs to my daughter-in-law, but she's away in service and doesn't live here."

"Do you agree to keep the treasury there and to be responsible for it?"

"I'll be as responsible to you as I am to God and to my conscience. If it's your will, I'm ready to serve the community. And anyway, almost half of you know me."

"Yes, we know him!" many voices rang out. "You can depend on him!"

"Whom do we elect as the other two treasurers?" some of the oil workers asked.

"Choose people you know," said Benedio, "and they should also be the kind who can get around."

"How about you?"

"No, I can't," Benedio declined. "I'm not well, as you can see, and I'm too busy at work. I wouldn't be able to move around much. I'll do what I can to help without being elected."

And at this point Benedio thanked the crowd for listening to him and stepped down from the rock. The oil-workers crowded around him to express their gratitude, shaking his hand and thanking him for his valuable advice with loud and sincere words.

The workers quickly agreed to elect Pryidevolia and Sen Basarab as the other two executive members of the treasury.

"Thank you for your confidence!" Sen Basarab addressed the crowd. "We will do our best to serve our common cause well! And now, whoever is able, please throw in a cent or two apiece, so that our treasury won't be empty!"

"Hurrah! A cent apiece into the treasury!" the workers shouted enthusiastically.

"Let's all put in one cent each," Matiy announced. "That way, when we count the money, we'll know how many of us there are here!"

Everyone agreed and when the money was collected and counted, they had thirty-five rinskys.

"There are three and a half thousand of us assembled here!" exclaimed Sen Basarab. "We have thirty-five rinskys in the treasury! See, it wasn't so hard for us to collect such a healthy sum!"

The oil workers marvelled at the power of a crowd, repeating to each other: "Someone put it very succinctly: if everyone in a community were to spit at once, they could drown a person!"

The despair and fear which had pervaded the atmosphere shifted to one of joy and hope. The workers now felt the promise of a brighter future and the strength of their unity.

XI

Leon Hammerschlag was on cloud nine, consumed by pride and joy. His business dealings were going well, and even though this was only the start of his main enterprise, it already boded well for the deal. Leon had received good news from the Wax Association in Russia: 'Supply the ceresin wax, if possible, prior to the terms set out in the contract. The Association is happy to report that by applying well-known local methods we were able to sign a contract with the holy synod for the supply of ceresin wax to Orthodox churches. A deposit of 100,000 has been made. Request you notify us when the first shipment will be ready for dispatch.'

After reading this news, Leon was overjoyed. So, the deal was set in concrete. Straight after this he set off for Boryslav, to see how the construction of the factory was proceeding. He sorely regretted that the building would only be ready in a week and that it would not be possible to start manufacturing the wax the very next day. Leon chose not to dwell on the fact that the factory was a fraudulent enterprise. His sense of justice was practically non-existent at the best of times, and he cared little about adherence to laws and government regulations, as was generally the case among the local pit owners.

Because he had been managing his ongoing business affairs in Drohobych, particularly overseeing the procurement of raw earth wax from the various small pit owners, Leon had not visited Boryslav in over a week and had no idea of the current situation there. He had placed complete trust in Benedio, firmly believing in his competence and diligence.

To Leon's astonishment, upon his arrival in Boryslav, he found that there were no labourers at the construction site, save for a few individuals who were finishing off the roof.

Benedio appeared and confidently declared that the work had been successfully concluded and that the building was ready. All that remained was for Leon to personally inspect everything before releasing Benedio from his duties. Leon was left speechless. If Benedio had been a building supervisor, rather than an ordinary labourer and a lowly mason's assistant, Leon might have embraced him and expressed his appreciation on the spot.

This showed that good fortune was forever on his side! It eavesdropped on his innermost thoughts and desires and ran ahead of him like a mistress to fulfill them in the blink of an eye! Joy spread across Leon's face. He began to thank Benedio and went off with him to inspect the building. It stood before him in all its grandeur: extremely long, low, with small doors and windows, which seemed to peer at him thievishly. Two extremely tall chimneys rose high into the sky. Around the building there was a spacious yard, surrounded by a very high fence with a wide entrance gate and a narrow door beside it. The yard was smoothed out, the lime pits filled in, there was even an extensive dormitory for the workers and a warehouse for the fabricated wax stood ready. The walls, neither white-washed nor plastered, blushed a pale red. In short, everything was as it should be and it made Leon's heart jump for joy. He didn't even venture inside to examine it. "For that," he said, "I need to bring along my specialist, he will know, if everything has been built properly." The pipes and boilers, and all the equipment ordered in Vienna had already arrived and stood in the yard in large containers. Leon didn't give himself or the horses a chance to rest, and immediately rushed off to Drohobych to fetch Scheffel. Meanwhile Benedio was to assemble the workers, who under Scheffel's guidance would install and cement in place the boilers and machines that same day.

Scheffel arrived and after examining the insides of the factory and measuring everything up, he spoke highly of the structure. Leon followed him about, smacking his lips, and kept rolling up his sleeves. Meanwhile Benedio toiled away with the hired workers in the yard, unpacking the machines. They broke open the wooden containers and packages, unwinding canvas belts and ropes, set up wooden rollers and skids, so that everything could be moved inside the factory.

The hammering and rattling continued late into the night as the machines were being installed. In some places a bigger hole needed to be made in the brick walls for a pipe, in other places a boiler needed to be bricked into position – Scheffel measured things up and issued orders, while Benedio and the workers carried them out. Finally, as twilight fell, everything was ready.

Leon and Scheffel remained inside the factory. The light from the small wax nightlights flickered away, reflecting with hundreds of sparks from the shiny big-bellied boilers made of polished copper. Large columns of darkness seemed to rise from the corners, becoming suspended from the bare wooden ceiling, threatening to smother these faint glimmering specks of light.

"So will you be able to begin tomorrow?" Leon asked, his eyes wandering over the nest in which his golden dreams were to be incubated and hatched.

"We sure will," Scheffel replied. "Are the workers ready?"

"Ah, sure, the workers," said Leon. "Yes, they will be. There's enough of them in Boryslav now."

"There's just one thing, you know," Scheffel said. "What we're doing is not exactly kosher. You will need to hire at least three workers, who can be completely relied on. Fellows who won't go about blabbing what's happening here. They'll need to be working in the main section of the distillery, in the chemical room, where, you know, the ceresin wax is produced. The rest of the workers will be under the impression that it's ordinary paraffin wax. Please try to ensure this!"

'Hm,' Leon thought, 'three workers on whom I can fully rely! It's true, I'll need to find them. But it won't be easy to find such workers among this rabble!'

Meanwhile the workers gathered around Benedio in the yard of the new factory. They were waiting to thank Leon for having employed them and to receive the rest of the wages they were owed. The moon rose in the serene sky, while here and there golden stars peeped dreamily through wisps of white, semi-transparent cloud. The workers sat down on rocks and off-cuts of wooden beams and talked among themselves. The dull echo of their conversation reached the fields and became intermingled with the silvery whispers of a brook babbling over stones. The talk, naturally, was of one thing – the recent workers' meeting, the collection of dues and people's expectations.

"To tell you the truth," Benedio said, "a miracle has happened to the people here. When I came to Boryslav a little more than a month ago and began to inquire whether they had ever tried to help themselves, everyone would either shake his head or laugh at me. But today you yourselves see how all of them, old and young alike, are rushing to pay their dues. Why, we already have 150 rinskys in the main treasury alone!"

"One hundred and fifty rinskys," repeated one of the workmen, "and what of it? It would really be something for one man, but what does it mean for so many thousands of people?"

"That's true, it doesn't mean much," said Benedio, "but don't forget that it's been less than a week since we started collecting. In a month's time we should have at least five hundred."

"And can we start what you've planned with five hundred?"

"Hm, we'll need to estimate the number of people and the money required," said Benedio. "If you figure just a rinsky and a half to sustain a man for a week, and that people will be without work for a week, then even if we only need to feed a thousand men during that time, we'll need at least fifteen hundred rinskys in the treasury. I say 'at least' because apart from feeding the people, there'll be other expenses."

"Fifteen hundred rinskys!" the workers cried out together. "Merciful God, when will we be able collect such a sum! By that time half of us will have starved to death, and tens of thousands of new folk will have drifted in from the villages!"

"What can we do?" Benedio said sadly. "We can't ask for higher dues because the bosses are cutting the pay at every step as it is, and when they learn of our collection, they'll cut it further still. We must stick to it, collect and suffer, even if it takes three months!"

"Three months! Who knows what can happen in three months!"

The workers grew silent and sadness descended on the small talkative group of men. Benedio lowered his head dejectedly. He truly sensed that the matter was urgent, that the greatest strength of these people lay in their sudden awakening and to not take advantage of this awareness meant to lose the initiative. But what could be done? There wasn't enough money to call a strike. They really needed to be patient.

"There's another thing," Benedio said, awakening from his daydreams, "I'm going to have to return to Drohobych."

"To Drohobych? Why?" exclaimed the workers.

"What do you mean, why? Because my work here has finished."

"Then find another job."

"Why, can't you do without me here? Although it is a pity to leave such a thing unfinished, after having worked so hard starting it up…"

"So don't go then!"

"Sure, I shouldn't be leaving. If only there was a way to remain."

The workers sensed this keenly, and even Benedio occasionally thought that without him, the whole thing might easily have gone the wrong way and might have fallen through. He felt that in any community formed for new and unusual purposes, very much depended on the leader, on his personal influence and advice. However, at times he felt all too well the weakness of his own opinions and was convinced that had he not come across the brotherhood in Boryslav and such sound-thinking people as Matiy and Stasiura, he might not have reached the point where he was now. The cooperation of all those here was very strong and pronounced, but Benedio realized that breaking out of that circle of co-operation would mean harming each of the individual parts and everyone in general. Nevertheless, what could he do in Boryslav if there was no work for him? But fate had a surprise in store for him from a direction he never expected.

Leon emerged from the factory in the company of Scheffel. Both men approached the workers, who rose to their feet.

"Well, men," Leon said in a loud voice, "your work is done here and you did well. Thank you for your effort!"

"And we are grateful to you, sir, for the work!" shouted the workers. "May the Lord grant you good fortune!"

"Thank you, thank you," Leon said cheerfully. "And now let me know how much I owe each of you, so that we can part with a clear conscience."

The workers were issued their wages. Benedio stood to one side. After they had finished, Leon came up to him.

"And you, master builder, I thank you from the depths of my heart for your work and for finishing everything so quickly! I would very much like for us not to part our ways… But now, for the joy you have brought me today, please accept this keepsake from me!" And he pressed ten rinskys in silver wrapped in paper into Benedio's hand.

'Our kitty will now have an additional 160 rinskys,' Benedio thought to himself, gratefully accepting Leon's gift. "And I would also ask," Leon said in addition, "that you step into my office, as I have some things to discuss."

With these words Leon and Scheffel left, followed by the workers. Benedio stayed behind to lock all the doors and gates, and then hobbled along behind Leon, trying to guess what he might be wanting to discuss with him. Along the way he dropped into his lodgings, found Matiy there and handed him the ten silver rinskys which Leon had given him, to put into the workers' kitty

"Here's what I wanted to say," Leon said to him, when Benedio arrived at his office. "I can see that you are an honest and decent worker, and I really wouldn't want us to part ways. Right now I need several honest and trusted people to work in my new refinery to do some not so difficult work. So this is what I wanted to say: would you mind, unless you've grown sick and tired of working for me, to remain in my employ?"

"But what would I do? I mean, hasn't all the masonry work been completed?"

"No, it's nothing to do with masonry, but rather the manufacture of wax," Leon said.

"But will I be able to manage that kind of work, if I've never tried my hand at it and have no idea what it involves?" asked Benedio.

"Eh, there's nothing to it!" said Leon. "You think an ordinary lad is any more experienced than you? There's nothing to know here: the director will show you what needs to be done. I'm telling you, this has nothing to do with experience, but requires someone who is honest and conscientious, and who will..."

Leon stopped in mid-sentence, as if hesitant about something.

"Who will not go round blabbing how things are being done in the factory," he finished after a pause. "Because you see, there's a little secret involved here… My director has dreamed up a new way to manufacture the wax, and I wouldn't want it to become common knowledge."

"Sure…" answered Benedio, not knowing what else to say.

"Because, you see," Leon continued, "people can't be trusted here. They'll quickly copy the new process and profit from it, and I'll lose out. Which is why I wanted to…"

"But that will be hard. I mean, let's say I don't tell anyone, but apart from me, there'll be lots of other workers in the factory."

"Well, not everyone will need to see and know everything. Throughout the factory everything will be done as in other factories, and there will only be one closed room, where things will be done a little differently. There'll be a director in charge of the process, and he'll need several workers to help him. So, can I rely on you?"

"Of course," said Benedio, barely able to conceal his joy. "I'm easy. So long as I can handle the work. Masonry jobs are hard to come by these days so it will be good to have some experience in wax manufacturing. And as for your secret not being revealed, you can count on me."

"Well," Leon said with a smile, "I know that I can trust you. But you know, if you could find a few other people, say two or three like yourself! You've worked on the site here, so you've gotten to know the workers, and maybe you could choose a few trusted fellows from among them? I'll reward you for your efforts. And one more thing! The most important thing, of course, is the pay. You know yourself, this isn't masonry work, so I can't pay the wages you've been getting so far…"

"Well that's understood!" said Benedio. "The work of a bootmaker and tailor is measured with different rulers."

"Exactly! And you can see the situation here now. The place is inundated with workers, wages are being cut everywhere, so understandably, why should I pay higher wages, when I can have the same worker for less pay? But with you, it's different, you follow me? So I'll pay you and the others working with you in that room one rinsky per day, and I promise not to lower your wages, and you won't need to pay the paymaster any fees. Do you agree to this?"

Benedio stood and thought.

"Yes, but I would rather that you yourself choose the other people to work in the separate room with me!" he said after a short while. "Because, if I pick them and something happens… One can always be wrong about people, and the responsibility will be all mine then! As for the work and the pay, there's no problem, I agree."

"No, no," Leon insisted, "I want you to pick the people! Anyone will do for the other factory, but here I need trusted people. You will know much better than me or the director who can be trusted."

"As you please," said Benedio, "let it be so. I'll try to find three people who can be trusted. When do we start work?"

"Tomorrow morning. And the work needs to proceed as quickly as possible. The wax has already been ordered. You'll be forming it into blocks and packing it in a separate room."

'What's all this about?' Benedio thought to himself as he walked home in the twilight. 'He says he's invented a new way of manufacturing wax and is afraid the workers may blab about it to others! As if the workers understand anything? Anyway, we'll see what happens! As it is, this has been quite fortuitous! From out of nowhere I have work, and the pay is good, so I'll be able to remain in Boryslav, and I'll be able to top up the kitty each week with at least four rinskys. As for those other three workers, who should I choose?'

Benedio thought for a long time about which three to choose, but somehow couldn't make up his mind. He decided to discuss this with Matiy. Benedio would have liked to choose all three of the brethren, but Matiy advised against it, fearing that, in case of anything, it might arouse suspicion.

"The pit owners are now worried about our meeting," Matiy said. "I'm sure there will some workers who let them know what we advised the people to do. If that's the case, they'll soon begin to spy on us, and so with such a large group of brethren working together in the one place they might catch on."

Benedio replied that it was a possibility that the pit owners would begin to spy on them, but he couldn't see any reason to fear that they might uncover the activities of the fraternity, even if several of the brethren worked together. For they needn't talk openly about their business among strangers.

"Besides," Benedio added, "it's not important who we choose, but rather that we choose those who are unemployed right now."

And two such fellows were Derkach and Pryidevolia. And so Benedio dashed off to find them, to invite them to work in Hammerschlag's factory. He also chose another honest oil worker, who although not a member of their fraternity, had taken an active interest in the newly-floated idea of workers' treasuries and whom the brethren had in jest nicknamed Trotter on account of his tireless activity and readiness to dash from pit to pit, whether to collect dues or simply to attract new people to the workers' movement.

After Leon Hammerschlag had sorted things out with Benedio, he put on a light coat and went out into the street to take a walk and chat with some of the other pit owners who, as usual at this time, were strolling along the street. A group of pit owners soon surrounded him, shaking hands and wishing him good fortune with the newly-built factory. Then the conversation turned to various business matters, which interested them more than anything else. Some asked Leon about the current exchange rates, whether he needed any more wax, and how much paraffin he intended to produce each week in his new factory. Only after their curiosity was satisfied, did the conversation turn to local matters.

"*Oh-oh-oh, Gott über die Welt!*" said Itsyk Bauch, sighing heavily. He was a short and very rotund fellow who owned several pits. "The things that are happening here, it frightens me just to talk about them! Haven't you heard, Mr. Hammerschlag? Oh-oh-oh, we have a rebellion on our hands, that's what! Haven't I been saying for a long time that we shouldn't be paying those rascals, those rebels, such high wages, because once they figure it out for themselves, they'll think – oh-oh-oh – that they are entitled to more! And now you can see for yourself, that my words were prophetic!"

"What are you talking about? What rebellion?" Leon asked incredulously.

"Oh-oh-oh, God in heaven above!" Itsyk Bauch continued. "All honest businessmen will soon have to flee Boryslav! The workers are rebelling, they are becoming more and more hostile toward us, and last Sunday – 'Oh-oh-oh,' – we thought it would be our last day, that they were about to start slaughtering us! They assembled on the green like crows on garbage. We all nearly died of fright. Nobody, of course, dared to venture near them, because they would have torn us to shreds – it was such a savage crowd! Oh-oh-oh, we don't know what they were saying among themselves, and there's no way to find out. I asked the Baniuses who work for me, and they only replied: 'We were just performing ancient spring rites!' The lying hounds! We watched them from our roof; one of them got up on a rock and spoke for a long time, and they listened and listened, and then they started shouting: 'Vivat!' Oh-oh-oh, such terrible things!"

"But I can't see anything terrible in all of this," Leon said, smiling proudly. "Maybe they really were just performing their spring rites."

"Oh, no-no-no," Itsyk Bauch would not relent. "I know for a fact that's not the case. And they returned from there all cheerful, singing songs, and now they are conspiring, holding secret meetings. Mark my words, trouble is brewing!"

"I still can't see…" Leon began once more, but the other Jews interrupted him, supporting Itsyk Bauch and recounting numerous additional details. It must be said of the good name of the Boryslav workers that they immediately understood their cause well, and back then not one of them betrayed to the Jewish businessmen what the aim of their meeting had been and what had been decided there. However, it might well have been that not even most of the workers had heard and understood everything that had been discussed: those who understood did not pass it on to the Jewish pit owners, and those who did not hear, could not tell them much of interest. They were only able to learn that a collection of some kind was taken up among the workers so that they could support one another and that the instigator of this was the mason Benedio Synytsia.

"Benedio! The one who built my new factory?" Leon exclaimed in astonishment.

"That same one."

"Collection? To support one another? Hm, I never thought that Benedio was so smart. He's just a mason's assistant, born and bred in Drohobych – where could he have come up with such ideas?"

"Eh, the devil knows, but come up with them he did!" Itsyk Bauch grumbled. "But how dare he incite the people to rebellion? They need to send gendarmes to Drohobych, to chain him up and drive him out of here!"

"Please, gentlemen," Leon said, pausing, "I don't understand why you're so worried. What's so terrible here? I've been in Germany and there the workers assemble everywhere, consulting and cooperating as they please, and no one stops them, it doesn't scare anyone. On the contrary, smart capitalists even encourage them. Every capitalist there, when he speaks to his workers, keeps harking on the word 'self-reliance,' it's always on the tip of their tongue. 'Help yourselves, because any outside help is useless!' And do you think anything bad comes out of that? On the contrary! When workers help themselves, it means the capitalist no longer needs to help them. If someone is injured or grows old at the factory, you have self-reliance! They can take collections and help themselves, so long as we don't need to help them! And we'll make sure their wages don't rise too high. As soon as they start strutting about too much, we'll lower their pay, just as we please!"

Leon uttered these words with such enthusiasm and inner conviction that he managed to reassure and please his listeners. Only the obese, red-nosed Itsyk Bauch shook his head sceptically, and when Leon finished, he piped up, gasping heavily:

"Oh-oh-oh! If only it were like you said, Mr. Hammerschlag! But I fear it won't be like that. How can you expect our wild, uneducated worker to undertake sensible 'self-reliance'? Oh-oh-oh, God in heaven! And what if he understood 'self-reliance' as meaning that he should grab knives and start butchering the Jews? Hah?"

All those present, including Leon himself, were startled by such ominous words, and a shiver ran down their spines. Just then, a group of oil workers passed by, and towering over everyone else was the gloomy Sen Basarab. He cast a threatening glance at the Jews, especially at Bauch, his employer. Sen's gaze filled Bauch with unease and he fell silent until the group had passed.

"Take a look at them," he said, once the oil workers had disappeared into a dark alley. "Savages, that's what they are! That tall one among them – he works for me – isn't he just like a wild bear? Mention 'self-reliance' to him, and he'll grab a knife and come at you!"

However, Leon, followed by many of the other Jews, began to contradict Bauch. The more frightened they were, the more vehemently they argued. By trying to convince him that there was no danger at all, they tried to persuade themselves of that fact.

"It's not as bad as you're making it out to be," they reassured Bauch. "The locals, although perhaps a little uncouth and not the most cordial of folks, are not as wicked and bloodthirsty as you make them out to be. Instances of proper, honourable associations are not unheard of in this area, and the locals are familiar with them. If any 'disorder' was meant to happen, it would have already occurred after that initial gathering. Besides, Benedio is a man of frail health and a gentle disposition. And anyway, Leon will speak with him tomorrow and get all the details. To some extent Benedio will be compelled to tell him the truth because he relies on Leon. We can then be certain there's no danger to anyone."

"Oh-oh-oh, the more words there are, the more confusion there is!" said the implacable Bauch. "But I advise you, don't trust those bandits; stop their collections and make sure to lower their wages so that they have barely enough to subsist on – then they'll stop wanting to set up any kind of collection!"

"Ye-es, we'll see if they stop wanting!" growled Sen Basarab through clenched teeth. He had crept up to the spot where the conversation was taking place and, hiding behind a fence, had overheard everything, understanding their dialect perfectly. "Hey there, my friend, we'll see if they stop or not!" he muttered, rising to his feet after the Jewish pit owners had moved on. "Let's hope you don't lose your taste for something else!"

And giving his feet free reign, Sen hurried off to Matiy's house to tell the brethren what the Jewish pit owners had been saying about their meeting and what they knew about it.

Early the following morning before work Leon bumped into Benedio in the factory. Benedio introduced him to Derkach, Pryidevolia and Trotter, as those he had chosen to work in the separate room. Leon now regretted somewhat that he had so hastily given Benedio the undertaking the day before, as he was convinced that Benedio had chosen some like-minded associates! He even began to fear that Benedio might suspect something untoward about his dealings with the ceresin wax and ordered Scheffel to tread carefully with these selected workers. It was too late now to go back on his word, so Leon, though with some unease, decided that what would be, would be. He just needed to question Benedio about this meeting.

After a few words of encouragement to his new workers, he asked Benedio to come with him into a separate storeroom and asked point-blank what the workers' meeting had been about and what Benedio had said to the workers. He thought to himself that if Benedio was up to no good, such a direct question would stun and confuse him. But Benedio had been well-briefed, and without showing the slightest confusion, replied that since some of the workers had floated the idea of helping one another by raising money, he had advised them to create a treasury, something akin to the ones guild crafts-men had in the towns. And that equal numbers of oil workers and pit owners should oversee it. After hearing out Benedio, Leon was even more amazed, for he had taken the fellow to be a simple worker who thought little about anything.

"Where did you get such ideas from?" Leon asked.

"It's really nothing much," replied Benedio, "that's what they all do back home, so I advised them to do the same. These aren't my ideas, I'm not that smart!"

Leon praised Benedio for the advice he had given the workers and added that for the management of such a fund, they should select one of the literate pit owners who could keep accounts. He also mentioned that they needed to draft the statutes of such a fund and submit them for approval to the local authorities. Leon even offered to take care of doing this himself, for which Benedio thanked him. After this, they went their separate ways. Benedio felt guilty about lying to Leon, but he saw no alternative, given the circumstances.

Meanwhile, Leon walked away feeling satisfied, considering himself a progressive individual who was encouraging workers to embrace unity and self-reliance. He saw himself as superior to those fellow pit owners who regarded self-reliance for workers as rebellion and subterfuge, and were ready to seek refuge like frightened baby chicks under the protective wings of the gendarmes and police. In Leon's view, it was high time for Boryslav to have its own labour movement, one that was legal, peaceful, and intelligently managed. He even daydreamed about a distant future when 'the reconciliation of capital and labour' would commence right here in Boryslav, and his conversation with Benedio and support for the emerging workers' movement would act as a catalyst.

'Yes, yes,' Leon confidently concluded as he was lulled to sleep in his light carriage, 'my business affairs are proceeding very well!'

XII

Oh, Gottlieb, Gottlieb! Did you know, did you even think of the trouble your letter and your reckless act would stir up in your mother's mind!

Rifka was weak, but it wasn't physical weakness, for her body remained healthy and strong. It was a strange spiritual distress, an overwhelming tension followed by waves of indifference and utter apathy. She moved about the rooms of the house as if in a daze, failing to notice anything and caring only about her son. He was injured, he was unwell! Was he in danger? Was he alone? Was he suffering or maybe dying? And meanwhile, she, his mother, for whom there was nothing dearer than him in this world, didn't even know where he was or how he was. But he had chosen not to let her know! What was he planning to do? How long would he continue to wander among strangers, like an orphan, in those wretched old clothes?

She wept, grew angry, tore at whatever came to hand, unable to find answers to these questions. At times she was ready to tell Hermann everything and to rush off to search for Gottlieb all over Drohobych. But then a crazy stubbornness would take control of her, her imagination would paint images of Gottlieb's terrible suffering and his demise, and tears would stream from her eyes. Her fists clenched spasmodically as she stood outside the door to her husband's office, and her lips whispered: "May he perish, may he die, just to spite this inhuman tyrant!" And she forgot that this inhuman tyrant was completely unaware of what was taking place and had seen none of it. The lifeless, impassive expression on his face infuriated Rifka immensely, and she tried to avoid appearing before him as much as possible.

She mostly sat locked inside her bedroom, reading Gottlieb's letters a hundred times over, but even this could not allay her disquiet and anxiety. Everything had become unbearable. For hours on end she stared out of the window into the orchard, or onto the street, hoping the chimney sweep might appear with a letter. But the chimney sweep never appeared, and Rifka became consumed with anguish, torn apart by conflicting emotions, unable to decide what course of action to take. After a week of such restlessness, she started to become genuinely ill.

"What's wrong with you, Rifka?" Hermann once asked her over lunch. "Are you sick?"

"Yes!" she answered, without looking at him.

"That's exactly it. I can see that you're sick. We need to send for a doctor."

"There's no need!"

"What do you mean? Why not?"

"A doctor won't be able to help me!"

"Really?" Hermann asked in amazement. "Who can help then?"

"Give me back my son!" Rifka snapped back. "That is all that can help me!"

Hermann shrugged his shoulders and left the table. Obviously, he did not send for a doctor. After ten long days, Rifka finally received news from her son. The chimney sweep had paced up and down the street until she leaned out of the window: he tossed Gottlieb's postcard into the house. This was what Gottlieb had written:

'She must become mine! I'm telling you once and for all – she must. Whether she wants to or not. And anyway, why would she not want to: after all, I am wealthy, she couldn't find a wealthier suitor in the entire country. And I feel that I can't survive without her. In my dreams and in real life, she continues to appear before me, and I don't even know her name. But who cares, if I've fallen for her! Where could she be? If I knew where she had gone, I would set off after her right away. Oh, I forgot to mention that I feel well now, at least well enough to walk. I spend the whole day sitting across the street from her house, but I haven't yet dared ask anyone whose house it is and who she is. Tomorrow morning, my messenger will pay you a visit: pass on some money for me.'

Rifka didn't have much money. The chimney sweep did turn up the next day, and at a time when Hermann was not at home. She began questioning him about her son, but the chimney sweep knew nothing and only said that he was instructed to bring back some money, and nothing more. Rifka gave him ten rinskys, the last ten rinskys that she had, and remained alone in the room, cursing the chimney sweep for failing to allay her curiosity.

The news that Gottlieb was healthy and could walk again pleased her. However, his excessive and blind love began to trouble her. She suddenly thought: 'What if Gottlieb's love interest is a Christian girl? What then, if she absolutely refused to marry a Jew? Who knows what Gottlieb might do to himself if he can't have her.' This suspicion settled in her restless mind and gave her no peace. Once more she began to suffer and worry, unable to sleep at night, cursing the whole world, including her husband and herself. For some reason, she wished that Gottlieb would marry a poor, working-class Jewish girl from Lahn, someone exactly like herself. The idea of Gottlieb marrying into a wealthy family filled her with loathing and dread.

But the money caused Rifka the most anguish. A few days later, when Hermann was away again, the chimney sweep returned with a card. The card bore the following brief text:

'I need money, lots of money. I need to dress decently. She's coming tomorrow. I need to talk to her. I know which family she's from. Can you pass on at least a hundred rinskys, please.'

Upon reading these words, Rifka began to shake. Her son knew who the girl was but wouldn't tell his own mother! Did he have a heart, not telling her? And he was asking for a hundred rinskys – where would she find such money? These past few days Hermann hadn't given her any money at all, and didn't leave any lying around, as he usually did. All the money was locked inside a large iron safe with three keys, and he took the keys with him. Rifka had failed to notice this until this very moment. But now that her son demanded such a large sum from her, she grew terribly angry. She rushed from room to room, from one drawer to another, but couldn't find even a cent anywhere. She loudly cursed her husband, but the curses had no effect, and with a heavy heart, she had to send the chimney sweep on his way empty-handed and to come back the next day. The chimney sweep shook his head and departed. After this, Rifka ran through the rooms as if she were insane, pushing furniture about and filling the house with curses and swearing. Hermann found her in this state when he returned home.

"What's the matter?" he exclaimed, stopping in the doorway. "Have you gone mad?"

"Yes!" yelled Rifka.

"What do you want? Why are you dashing about?"

"I need money."

"Money? Why do you need money?"

"I need it, that's all."

"How much?"

"Lots. Two hundred rinskys!"

Hermann smiled.

"What's the matter, preparing to pack your bags and leave?" he said.

"Don't ask, just hand over the money!"

"Bah-bah-bah, where's this strict order coming from? I don't have any money to hand out," Hermann replied.

"No money!" yelled Rifka and glared at him. "Who are you talking to like that? Give it to me now, or there will be trouble!" She approached him with raised fists. Hermann shrugged his shoulders and took a step back.

"You've gone insane!" he growled in a low voice. "Give her money, but she won't say why. You think," he said to her in a calm, persuasive voice, "that I have money lying around? My money is invested in business."

"But I need it right now!" Rifka said adamantly.

"Why? If you need to buy something, tell me, I can get it on credit, because I have no money on hand."

"I don't need any of your credit, just cash! Do you hear!"

"Give me a break," replied Hermann and, without engaging in any further conversation, slowly made his way to his office, constantly looking back in case Rifka decided to run after him. When he reached his office, he initially considered locking the door, but then changed his mind, knowing Rifka's nature. With a light, secretive smile, he sat down at his desk and began writing.

'I knew it would come to this,' he thought, still smiling mysteriously. 'But that's alright! I won't give in to her. We'll see who is stronger!'

Rifka entered a moment later, breathing heavily. Her face kept changing, turning red as a beet, then pale as a sheet. Her eyes burned feverishly as she sat down.

"Tell me, for god's sake, what you want from me?" Hermann asked her, trying to remain calm.

"Money," replied Rifka with the obsessiveness of a madwoman.

"What for?"

"For our son," she said assertively.

"Which son?"

"Gottlieb."

"Gottlieb? But Gottlieb is no longer among the living," said Hermann, feigning astonishment.

"I'd rather you were no longer among the living!"

"So he's alive then! Do you know where he is? Can you tell me? Why doesn't he come home?"

"No, I won't tell you."

"Why's that? After all, I'm his father, I won't eat him alive."

"He's afraid of you and doesn't want to be with you."

"But he wants my money, yes?" Hermann said, wonder-struck. Rifka did not answer.

"Know what," Hermann said decisively. "If you know where he is, tell him to come home. Enough of this foolish comedy. Until he returns, he won't get a cent either from me or from you!"

"But he's ready to do himself in!" exclaimed Rifka in a desperate voice.

"Don't worry! It'll be a repeat of his drowning in Lviv. He thinks he can break me with his threats. No! I gave in once, that's enough."

"But he's ready to run away, ready to do something terrible to himself."

"Hah-hah-hah," Hermann said derisively, "he won't be going anywhere without money, but wait… Listen, Rifka, so that you don't feel bad about having told me about him. I know that he made you promise not to tell me, and I never put pressure on you. But I've known for a while where he lives and what he does, I know everything. And he should consider himself lucky that I know this, or the gendarmes would have tossed him into the clink long ago and taken him off to Lviv. Understand? Luckily for him the Jewish coalman, with whom he came here from Lviv and with whom he now lives, told me everything as soon as I returned. And now listen! I won't go poking my nose into his business, or try to catch him, because basically he's already in my hands. Tell him to return home, that everything will be fine. And if he doesn't want to, tell him he must. The gendarmes are watching him and they won't let him leave Drohobych. And he won't get any money, pass that on to him through that thief of a chimney sweep who brings you letters from him. I've had my eye on the fellow for a while, let him know that too. And that's that!"

Hermann got up from his armchair. Rifka remained seated, dumbfounded by her husband's words. She was shaking all over, and barely able to breathe. Just as Hermann was leaving, she suddenly exploded with frightening spasmodic guffaws, which echoed throughout the large empty rooms like thunderclaps. A moment later the laughter suddenly broke off, and Rifka fell out of her armchair and began to thrash about on the floor in terrible convulsions.

"Lord Almighty, release me from her!" growled Hermann and hurried off to the kitchen to summon the servants to rub her down. He did not return to the room. Grabbing his coat and hat, he left for the city on business. With his grand new plans coming closer to fruition, now was not the time to be dealing with domestic problems. Van Hecht had written to him from Vienna that the equipment for producing ceresin was ready and the manufacturer was awaiting news where and when it should be sent. Hermann was not keen on building a new factory to produce ceresin and preferred to use a part of his old extensive oil refinery near Drohobych for the manufacture of this new product. He had examined the building to see if the layout corresponded to the plans drawn up by Van Hecht – some sections needed to be demolished or modified, new walls had to be erected. Hermann insisted on closely supervising the work himself. Finally, after everything was ready, he wrote to Van Hecht asking him to dispatch the equipment as quickly as possible and to come himself.

Hermann was also involved in a flurry of activities related to the significant contract he had signed with the Association for the Extraction of Earth Wax in Vienna. The contract involved the delivery of a substantial quantity of raw earth wax. While the Association had not provided Hermann with an advance payment against the contract, they were supposed to pay him in full upon the delivery of the wax. Nonetheless, the Association had already issued numerous shares based on this contract and attempted to boost their market value through advertising. The shares sold remarkably well, and in the middle of summer, the Association decided that something needed to be done in Boryslav.

They decided to establish a sizeable office in Drohobych, where the Association's representatives could oversee contracts, make payments, and explore new contacts and revenue streams. Naturally, the establishment of the office, the salaries paid to employees and fees to various government officials ended up costing at least three times more than what would have been necessary with prudent business practices. However, such concerns were of little consequence to them. The Association began to massively promote its transactions, portraying them as extraordinary accomplishments. Once again, the value of the Association's shares surged.

Hermann was deeply involved with the Association and closely monitored the actions of its representatives. In private he often shook his head in disbelief as he observed their operations. "No, no," he muttered to himself, "they can't last long with such practices! Regardless of how well their shares are performing, I won't be investing in them, nor do I want any association with them. It was foolish of me to enter into such a massive contract without requesting an advance. Although, even if this large bubble bursts before the contract is fulfilled, I won't suffer any losses because the wax will remain mine. Nonetheless, it would be much better if they paid me before facing financial ruin. When the time comes, I must insist on receiving payment in cash rather than in shares!"

While Hermann was aware that the Association was headed for insolvency and was, in fact, a fraudulent operation, it couldn't be said that he deliberately intended to defraud the company. His contract was entirely legitimate and realistic. Since returning from Vienna, he had worked diligently to supply the massive quantity of wax as swiftly as possible, within the terms of the contract. He was concerned that the company might face bankruptcy due to the ignorance and activities of its founders and authorized representatives. Hermann hired nearly three times more workers to service his pits and reopened eighty others that had stood idle for years due to various soil-related issues, all of which justified his earlier expectations.

The work progressed rapidly, and labour costs were significantly lower than in previous years because dire circumstances had driven more people to Boryslav, compelling them to work for less money. Hermann continuously reduced wages without regard for the indignation, tears, and curses of the workers. His warehouses soon filled with large blocks of wax, and he eagerly awaited the accumulation of the required quantity as stipulated in the contract. Once that happened, the Association would have no choice but to accept the wax immediately and pay him in full on the spot. 'After that,' Hermann thought, 'they can go to hell, for all I care!'

While Hermann was busy with his plans to produce ceresin and the servants were rubbing down Rifka, who thrashed about on the floor in terrible convulsions, Gottlieb, dressed in a dirty coalman's shirt and covered in grime up to his ears, waited patiently in the small dirty coalman's quarters for the chimney sweep to return with his money. Gottlieb had made friends with the chimney sweep, who lived next door, and had paid the fellow handsomely to be a messenger between himself and his mother. At last the fellow entered the house and Gottlieb hastily turned to face him.

"Well?" he asked.

"Nuthin'," replied the chimney sweep.

"What do you mean, nuthin'? Didn't she give you the money?"

"Nope, she said to come tomorrow."

"Damn tomorrow!" growled Gottlieb angrily. "I need it today!"

"What can you do? She said there was none today."

With this the chimney sweep left. As if possessed, Gottlieb began to dash about the house, waving his arms about and growling to himself:

"I'm meeting her tomorrow, I badly need to see her, but what do we have here! No money! How dare she! Is my mother against me as well, refusing to give me money? In that case, in that case…" and he threateningly shook his clenched fists at the door. His passion, blind and turbulent, just like his nature, suddenly and unexpectedly flared up, and overwhelmed by it, he was ready to follow the first thought that entered his head.

'What if,' he continued to think, 'he has found out? Maybe this is his doing… He's intentionally not giving mother any money, so that she can't pass it on to me? Oh, this may very well be… I know how tight he is with his money! But no, no, it can't be! He thinks that I've died, otherwise he'd be trying his hardest now to make me return home like some lost calf! But you can keep waiting there! I'll return when I'm good and ready, and meanwhile you can suffer a little!'

Poor Gottlieb! He really thought that Hermann was suffering terribly because of his absence!

But Gottlieb's tantrums and threats unfortunately were unable to fill his pockets with money. His thoughts, willingly or unwillingly, needed to calm down and focus on other subjects, specifically – the subject of his love. The day before he had learned from a servant in the employ of her father, whom he had spied in a nearby tavern and whose acquaintance he had made over a glass of vodka, that her father was a really big fish, one of the wealthiest men in Boryslav and Drohobych, and that he had arrived here two years earlier from Vienna, and was building a large sumptuous house, and that his name was Leon Hammerschlag, a widower, and that he had an only daughter, Fanny. The daughter had gone off on a trip to Lviv for some reason, but was meant to return the following day. She was a very nice girl, gentle and agreeable, and her father was also an upstanding gentleman.

Gottlieb found this account highly pleasing. 'That means she is my equal and can be mine – must be mine!' This was the only thought that occupied his mind, but it was enough to make him ecstatic. He waited impatiently for the next day, so that he could see her. Initially, he considered buying some clothes befitting his status, so that he could present himself in the best possible light. However, he was thwarted by an unexpected obstacle – his mother had been unable to provide him with any money. Thus, he had no choice but to approach her in his coalman's attire, which he now despised more than ever.

At the break of day, Gottlieb tucked some bread into his pocket and hurried off to the outskirts of the city, well beyond the suburb of Zadvirne, along the Stryj highway – the route Fanny would be taking, for there was no railroad in those days. He squatted by the side of the road in the shade of a bushy rowan tree, his gaze fixed on the dusty road that stretched far into the distance in a straight grey streak, before disappearing into a small grove on a hillside. Covered wagons with woven reed bonnets crowded with passengers, peasant carts, and herds of cattle en route to the Stryj market all stirred up little clouds of dust as they passed by. However, there was no sign of the shiny carriage drawn by a pair of fiery bay horses that would have been carrying Fanny.

Gottlieb sat beneath the rowan tree with the determination of a tormented American Indian, his eyes locked onto the highway. The sun had ascended high into the sky, its slanting rays mercilessly burning his face and arms, but he remained impervious to the pain. People passed by him on the wide highway, talking, shouting, laughing, and throwing sidelong glances at the young coalman, who stared fixedly at a single point like some madman. A gendarme, rifle topped with a gleaming bayonet, drenched in sweat and dust, his coat rolled into a tube on his shoulders, trudged past, leading a half-naked, bloodied man in chains. He scrutinized Gottlieb, shrugged his shoulders, spat on the ground, and continued on his way. However, Gottlieb noticed none of this.

At last, a large carriage emerged like a black arrow from the distant grove and sped along the highway toward Drohobych. The closer it drew, the brighter Gottlieb's face became. Yes, he had recognized her! It was Fanny! He jumped to his feet and stepped onto the highway, ready to run alongside the carriage toward town, to be with her. When he could clearly see Fanny in the carriage, his whole face flushed with blood, and his heart began to beat so wildly that he stopped breathing.

But having spotted him, Fanny must have remembered that same young coalman who had so recklessly run up to her carriage and given her such a fright. Reckless bravery, blind ardour at times – or maybe always – appealed to women, leading them to think of boundless devotion and dedication.

And while previously Fanny couldn't understand the reason for the reckless behaviour of the grimy young coalman, this time, upon seeing that he was waiting for her on the outskirts of town in the heat and dust, and noticing how impassioned he became upon seeing her, how courteously and anxiously he bowed before her, as if seeking forgiveness for his past recklessness, it suddenly occurred to her: 'Who knows, maybe this halfwit has fallen in love with me?' She had specifically used the word 'halfwit' because why would a bedraggled young coalman in his right mind think of falling in love with the only daughter of a rich man, throwing himself at her carriage and injuring himself, and now waiting by the side of the road for her to come along? But all the same, she was not displeased with his display of insanely passionate love. Although she was far from having romantic feelings for him, she felt a certain sympathy toward him, akin to the affection one might have for a small puppy.

'Alright,' she thought, 'let me talk to him, to find out what he wants. It's still a fair distance to town, the highway is empty, no one will see me.' And she instructed the cabby to slow down. Upon hearing her request, Gottlieb began to shake all over; he felt that this was a significant moment for him and quickly caught up with the carriage. When Fanny saw him, she slid open the small window and leaned out.

"What do you want?" she asked timidly, seeing that Gottlieb had taken off his hat once more and dumbstruck, made his way toward her. She spoke in Polish, thinking that he was a Christian.

"I wanted to take a look at you!" Gottlieb replied boldly in Yiddish.

"And who told you that I'm Jewish?" Fanny asked with a smile, also in Yiddish.

"I know that for a fact."

"So maybe you know who I am?"

"I do."

"Then you must know, that it won't augur you well to look at me too much," she said haughtily.

"Why don't you first ask me who I am?" Gottlieb asked proudly.

"Come on, there's no need to ask, your clothes give you away."

"No, they don't! The clothes lie! Go on, ask me!"

"Alright, who are you?"

"Someone, who will not be hurt by laying his eyes on you."

"I'd like to believe that, but I find it hard to do so."

"I'll prove it to you. Where can I meet you?"

"If you know who I am, then you must know where I live. We can meet at my place."

And at this she slid the window closed, gave the cabby a sign, and the horses raced off toward the town's outskirts. A dusty mist obscured her miraculous appearance from Gottlieb's eyes.

'Strange lad,' thought Fanny, 'a real halfwit, a proper halfwit! But what did he mean by the words: the clothes lie? Wasn't he a young coalman? Well, but if not, who was he then? Just a halfwit, and nothing more!'

'A wonderful girl,' Gottlieb thought to himself, 'how beautiful she is, and how courteous! She even stopped to speak to a simple coalman! But what did she mean by the words: 'we can meet at my place'? Was that an invitation to come? Eh, if only I could dress in something decent! Well, I'll have to try!'

With such thoughts swirling about in his head, Gottlieb trudged off to his coalman's lodgings.

XIII

A few weeks passed, and an unexpected silence settled over Boryslav. The Jewish community, quite frightened by the recent ominous workers' rally, was now utterly perplexed, not knowing which way to turn or what to think. Of course, there were those among them who dismissed the entire movement and its audacious silence, claiming it was all in the past, that goys were like idle wind, making lots of noise and fuss but unable to bring about change. They argued that now, after the goys had again become more docile and compliant, it was time to assert authority over them, to quash any desire for rebellion.

"Goys are only good when they're roasted!" they declared. "Give them an easy time of it, and they'll start thinking it's their due, and keep grabbing more, like a cat on a grill. Only when they are constantly pressured, fearing consequences, will they grow accustomed to obedience, submission, vigilance, and precision. Only then will they, as Leon Hammerschlag likes to say, become 'individuals inclined toward high culture.'"

The Boryslav pit owners concurred that, now that the turbulent waves of the labour movement had suddenly subsided, it was imperative to exert even greater pressure on the rebellious workers. They all shared the belief that the recent storm had passed and tranquillity had returned to stay.

However, there were dissenting voices, particularly that of Itsyk Bauch. He stubbornly argued that this newfound calm was merely a deceptive superficial calm, the calm before a terrible storm. He insisted that they should be wary of this silence and apparent submission, as it indicated that the workers' rebellion, in one way or another, was well-organized and coordinated. Without a doubt, the workers were arming themselves, and their secrecy and quietude in their actions were evidence that they had sinister intentions and were carrying out their plans systematically, thoroughly, and incessantly.

Every time the pit owners gathered, whether by chance in the street or in someone's living room for a meeting, Itsyk Bauch tirelessly sounded the alarm about the looming danger. He never stopped trying to convince his comrades to visit the district administration in Drohobych and request an urgent investigation or, at the very least, the dispatch of a strong detachment of gendarmes to maintain law and order in Boryslav.

While, in principle, no one had any objections to this, and likely welcomed the presence of the gendarmes to protect them from their own workers, they couldn't seem to muster the collective effort needed to make the request. Perhaps the times were too turbulent and draining, or it was the usual lack of initiative when it came to public affairs among our people, be they Jewish or Christian, matters that extended beyond individual private interests. Or perhaps it was the vehement conviction, as expressed by Leon, that the government was responsible for the safety of the pit owners in Boryslav, for that was its primary role. In any case, the Jewish community in Boryslav somehow failed to approach the authorities or even inform them of the burgeoning labour movement.

Furthermore, seeing as the labour movement had suddenly calmed down, they felt they no longer had a reason to take such a step. What was there to report to the authorities? What should the authorities be vigilant about? Those alarming pronouncements made by the emerging labour movement several weeks earlier had quickly dissipated. Why hadn't there been a timely report back then? Thus, the entire issue remained concealed until this unexpected and somewhat clandestine incident had jolted the Jewish community from their complacency, like a sudden clap of thunder from a small dark cloud.

It went without saying that the abrupt shift from turmoil to silence and submission was orchestrated by our brethren with the specific intention of alleviating suspicion and apprehension from the Jewish community. Itsyk Bauch's arguments, overheard by Sen Basarab, had convinced the brothers that the Jewish pit owners could pose a significant threat to them and disrupt their plans if they continued to agitate publicly. So they began persuading everyone to remain silent for a while, to exercise restraint, and to suppress the tumultuous feelings of anger and joy until the right time arrived. It required a great deal of effort for the brothers to artificially calm the storm and to hold it in check, preventing it from erupting prematurely. The daunting task kept them in constant fear that something might happen at any moment that could endanger their aims and scatter the workers.

The only way to pacify the workers was by making promises that the 'right time' for action would come soon. However, the brothers knew how risky and ambiguous such promises could be. They understood that by making these promises, they might inadvertently set the stage for the failure of their plan. The main challenge was finding the finances needed to initiate a strike in the near future, as the workers were eager for it. So far, over eight hundred rinskys had been collected in the main treasury, but they couldn't rely solely on dues, as the Jewish employers were now putting more pressure than ever on the workers. It was expected that the flow of dues would soon decrease, and a significant portion of the money would be needed to help the needy, the sick, and the unemployed. At this rate, it would take several more months to collect the required funds. If this were the case, the planned struggle could not begin promptly, leading to workers doubting their own power and losing their enthusiasm. On the other hand, if the frustrated workers exploded prematurely without order or purpose, their energy would be wasted, and the intended goal would not be achieved.

Such thoughts likely tormented Benedio more than anyone else. After all, this was his life's work, earned through a thousand trials and tribulations, bathed in brilliant rays of hope. He keenly felt that he had invested his soul and strength, his entire life in this endeavour. He thought of nothing else and cared about nothing else, and the prospect of failure seemed equivalent to his own demise. It was no wonder that as he worked toward his goal, facing an ever-increasing array of challenges, Benedio spent entire days and nights consumed by thoughts of how to surmount them. He had become as thin as a rake, often wandering the streets of Boryslav at night like a sleep-walker, his demeanour sad, dejected, taciturn, and occasionally punctuated by deep sighs, as he gazed at the dark, unwelcoming sky. The challenges continued to mount, and Benedio felt he had no strength left, that his head had been struck by a sledgehammer, his mind becoming lifeless, no longer capable of functioning with its former vitality, unable to discover a favourable solution.

Benedio waited until the evening when the brethren gathered in Matiy's house. What should they do? The people were becoming restless. Why hadn't the signal been given? Why hadn't something happened? Why was nothing being done? The people were starting to lose hope. The dues were dwindling, and the pit owners kept reducing people's wages. While the hunger in the villages had lessened somewhat, the harvest had been so poor that even in the leanest years, people had never seen such scarcity. Few would have enough to feed themselves until Great Lent, and less than half would barely make it to the Feast of Intercession.[16] People would soon begin converging on Boryslav in greater numbers than ever before. If something were to be started, now was the best time because it was easier to prevent people in the villages from coming to Boryslav. They could even send a larger portion of the Boryslav workforce to the villages for two to three weeks, where they might have a better chance of survival when they weren't working. But the problem was a lack of money – that was the issue! When the brothers agreed that this was the stumbling block, everyone grew solemn, heads hanging low, not knowing how to overcome the problem. A heavy silence descended upon the house, broken only by the irregular, anxious breathing of twelve people reverberating within the low, uneven walls of the small dwelling. The silence lasted a long time.

"May God's will be done!" Sen Basarab suddenly exclaimed. "Don't worry, I'll fix this!"

Sen Basarab's bold, resolute voice shattered the prevailing despondent silence and startled the brethren. It was as if a gunshot had pierced the stillness. All heads turned toward Sen, who sat in his customary spot on the stool near the doorway, his pipe in his mouth.

"You'll fix this?" they all asked in unison.

"Yes."

"But how?"

"That's my business. Don't ask, just leave now. Be here tomorrow at this time and you will see!"

He said nothing more, and no one asked any questions, although everyone, and especially Benedio, was seized with anxiety. A cold pain filled their hearts. The brethren silently dispersed.

....

[16]   Great Lent begins seven weeks before Easter. The Feast of the Intercession of the Blessed Virgin Mary is a Christian holiday celebrated in those times on 1 October.

When they stepped outside, Sen Basarab grabbed Pryidevolia by the arm and whispered:

"Come with me."

"Sure," said the lad, even though his hand began to shake for some reason.

"Will you do what I tell you?"

"Sure," repeated the lad, but with an uncertain, almost involuntary voice.

"Don't be afraid," Sen reassured them, "there's nothing to fear. If we act boldly and swiftly, everything will turn out fine!"

"Stop jabbering and tell me what to do," Pryidevolia interrupted him. "You know that it's all the same to me!"

Sen and Pryidevolia walked in silence in the darkness. Except for the taverns, the lights were out in practically every house. Sen carefully observed the houses they passed, many of which were adorned with shutters, brass door latches, and small flower gardens. These were the homes of the town's wealthy industrialists. The grandest house belonged to Hermann Goldkrämer, covered in tin and now often empty, as Hermann rarely stayed overnight in Boryslav. Nearby was Itsyk Bauch's less impressive house, with a light still burning in his office window, indicating that Itsyk was still awake and working.

Sen Basarab knew this house. He had worked in Itsyk's pits for a long time and came here more than once to collect his wages. He knew that apart from an old Jewish maid, and Itsyk himself, there was no one else in the house and that the maid was most likely already asleep in the kitchen. This was exactly what he needed. He pulled Pryidevolia along with him, and by the nearest pit, both smeared their faces with black crude so that no one would be able to recognise them.

"Follow me and don't utter a word, just do what I tell you," Sen whispered. And off they went. They tried several doors, but these were locked. Sen then turned his attention to the windows. Pryidevolia let out a quiet whimper to signal that he had found a window that wasn't secured. Sen opened it, and they entered the kitchen. It was eerily quiet, except for the sleepy mutterings of the maid coming from behind the oven. The kitchen door was unlocked, and they entered the hallway. Sen found the door to Itsyk's office and tried to look through the keyhole, but there was a key there. He tried to turn the handle quietly but found that the door was locked from the inside. But even here, Sen did not hesitate for long. He whispered a few words to Pryidevolia, softly rattled the latch, and then squeaked in a hoarse, elderly voice, similar to that of the old maid:

"*Herr, Herr, öffnen Sie!*"

"*Wus is?*"[17] Itsyk's harsh voice could be heard from inside, followed by the heavy sound of boots scraping on the floor and the jingle of the key as it unlocked the spring lock. The door opened quietly, and a stream of light spilled from the office into the dark hallway. In that moment, two figures, as black as devils, lunged at Itsyk and covered his mouth before he could scream. However, who knows if this was even necessary. The unexpected attack shocked Itsyk so much that he just stood there with his arms outstretched and a bewildered expression on his face, almost as if he had turned to stone. Only the blinking of his bulging grey eyes indicated that he was no lifeless lump of meat and fat, but a living creature.

"*Wie geht's, Herr, wie geht's?*"[18] Sen continued in a voice imitating the old servant. "Don't be afraid, dearie. We don't want to harm you, no! We're not devils coming for your soul. We've just come to borrow a little money from you!"

Itsyk didn't resist, cry out, or groan. He continued to stand there without moving, unresponsive, his mouth gagged,

....

[17] "Sir, sir, open up!"; "What is it?" (German)

[18] "How are you, sir, how are you?" (German)

breathing heavily through his nostrils. His attackers took him by the shoulders and led him to a chair where they sat him down.

"Hold him well and make sure he doesn't scream!" squeaked Sen to Pryidevolia. "And if he tries anything, strangle him! Let me search the office!"

But there was no need for Sen's threat. Itsyk didn't move, and, like a lifeless body, allowed Pryidevolia to tie his hands with a scarf. Meanwhile, Sen, keeping an eye on Itsyk, quickly reached for the small metal safe box on the desk and began to remove the neatly bundled banknotes. At that moment, a deep, muffled sound, resembling the final moan of a slaughtered ox, emerged from Itsyk's chest for the first time.

"Keep quiet!" squeaked Sen and continued to remove bundles of banknotes from the safe box. He did this calmly and, in a whisper, counted the banknotes bound with narrow strips of paper, as he slid them down his shirt front. The banknotes were in nominations of one rinsky and from the thickness of each bundle Sen guessed there had to be a hundred notes. He had already counted thirty bundles.

"That's enough, time to leave!" he whispered to Pryidevolia. Both men glanced at Itsyk. He was still breathing through his nose, but his fat, bloated face had turned terribly red and his bulging eyes had a kind of foolish, inquisitive expression.

"If you make a noise, it'll be the death of you!" Sen whispered into Itsyk's ear, after Pryidevolia had untied his hands. The hands were cold and hung limply by his side; Pryidevolia lifted them and rested them on the desk. Sen whispered to Pryidevolia:

"I'll leave first, and when you hear me whistle in the street, take the rag out of his mouth and clear out of here!"

Sen cautiously made his way outside. Pryidevolia thought Itsyk would begin to struggle and shout, and was ready to throttle him as a last resort. He stood behind Itsyk, pale and trembling, shaken to the core, but Itsyk seemed oblivious to his presence, not understanding a thing, sitting in his armchair with bulging eyes, the air whistling as it passed through his nostrils. He no longer blinked.

At last there came a muffled whistle from outside. With a shaking hand Pryidevolia removed the rag from Itsyk's mouth, certain that at that moment a terrible cry would be heard, waking up the whole of Boryslav, certain that crowds of people would come barging into this peaceful house, grabbing him, tying him up, beating him and parading him through the streets, before throwing him into some godforsaken underground cell, and that this was the final moment of his freedom. But no, Itsyk didn't blink an eyelid. He began to breathe more freely, but gradually the breaths grew slower.

Pryidevolia stood for a moment longer behind him, unable to comprehend what was happening, and if it wasn't for the distinct loud wheezing, he would have thought that Itsyk was dead. But when he heard the second whistle outside, he left Itsyk and quietly slipped out of the room. 'Wait,' he thought, 'I need to turn off the light!' and he returned once more, closed the safe box, from which Sen had taken the money, grabbed the rag with which they had gagged Itsyk, turned off the light and, as he left, locked the door, closed the kitchen window through which he had crawled outside, and whistled softly to Sen.

"Well?" asked Sen.

"Nothing," replied Pryidevolia. "He's just sitting there, not moving."

"Think he might have suffocated?"

"No, he's still breathing."

"Hm, must have really taken fright. I don't care, they can bring him to his senses tomorrow! Meanwhile it's time for us to hit the sack. We have thirty bundles of notes, that'll do us! We need to wash our faces with soap and hot water so that there won't be a sign left. Well, what will Itsyk say tomorrow, when he sobers up? This time he'll surely rush off to fetch the gendarmes!"

But Itsyk was in no condition to fetch any gendarmes. A dark gloom and a deathly silence surrounded him in his office. He remained seated in his armchair, his hands propped up against the desk, his eyes open wide, but the heavy breathing had long since stopped. That was how the morning sun found him when it rose over the black roofs of Boryslav and peered through the window into his lifeless glassy eyes. This was how the maid found him, and this was how the barber found him, together with his other friends, who came running when they heard the maid's screams – none of them had any idea what had happened to Itsyk. The barber said that the devil had taken Itsyk, for there wasn't the slightest trace of violence on his body, his clothes were unruffled and nothing suggested that he might have been attacked.

True, his maid had mentioned something about hearing rustling and footsteps at night, and that she had heard Itsyk unlock his office door, but she said this with little certainty or clarity, not sure whether it had been in her dreams or had actually happened. Next the government authorities turned up, the entire house and everything around it was inspected, but nothing suspicious was found. The safe box was opened: it contained money and securities. True, when the accounts, over which the deceased was still sitting, were tallied up, it appeared that there were three thousand rinskys less in the safe box. But here, too, there was a hitch. The accounts had not been finalized, obviously, the final amount was only partly recorded: it was possible that the deceased had spent the money on something. And secondly, if it had been a robbery, the robbers would have surely taken the rest of the cash, of which there was more than two thousand rinskys. Besides, his watch and his wallet with small change were still in his pockets, so there was no reason to believe it was robbery and murder. Only two or three spots of crude oil on the face and white shirt of the deceased left everyone with a faint suspicion, which, however, no one could clarify.

There was a rumour among the pit owners that perhaps the oil workers, who had a strong dislike for Itsyk, were behind this. Such rumours certainly caused more than one entrepreneur to tremble with fear, but publicly, everyone denied this, especially since an autopsy of the body had confirmed that Itsyk had indeed died of apoplexy, to which he had been predisposed for quite some time.

A sense of dread overwhelmed Benedio and the other brothers when they learned of Itsyk's sudden death the following day. They had no doubt that his abrupt demise was directly linked to Sen Basarab's conversation the day before. When they gathered once more at Matiy's house that evening, a heavy silence hung over them for a long while, as if they felt guilt for their involvement in a vile act. Sen Basarab was the first to break the silence:

"Well, why are you all sitting there, like you've lost your tongues?" he said angrily. "Saying prayers for Itsyk's soul, are you? Do I need to swear in front of you that I did nothing bad to him, and that when the devil took him, it was of his own free will! And even if this wasn't the case, so what? What I did, I did off my own bat. Here, take my dues and do your thing. There's three thousand rinskys here! That the devil took Itsyk is even better for us, because he won't go about blabbing, and others won't be any the wiser, because I left the rest of the money behind on purpose and didn't pocket any! What's the problem here? There's now one less bloodsucker on this earth! When wood is being chopped, splinters fly! After all, you're not going to throw away the money just because we didn't get it through honest toil! Don't worry, Itsyk never earned it through hard work; it's our blood and sweat, and God won't punish us if we make use of it. Besides, it's not like we took the money for our personal use. No, it's for the cause! Take it!"

No one responded to Sen's speech, but Benedio, as if under the pressure of some heavy hand, sighed and said:

"Clean work requires clean hands!"

"Of course," Andrus Basarab was quick to reply, "but having clean hands won't get you far because, in addition to that, you need financial backing to get the cause off the ground! It's like when you need to lift a heavy beam, you require heavy lifting equipment, and it makes no difference if it's clean or dirty!"

"Manure is cleaned out with pitchforks, not silk rags!" Pryidevolia added from his corner, and Benedio had to reluctantly yield. There really was no other way out!

After this exchange, the brethren visibly came to life. It was as if a weight had been lifted from everyone's shoulders, and they felt a sense of relief. They began to plan their next steps. It was clear that there was no time to convene a general workers' meeting, as this would alert the pit owners. They needed to act suddenly, without warning, to shock and confuse the pit owners. This was the only way to achieve victory. Therefore, they decided to discreetly pass on information to the workers through special couriers and the local treasurers. They would consult with the treasurers about bringing in food supplies to Boryslav and decide which workers could voluntarily leave the town for the duration of the struggle. Those who agreed to leave would be provided with something for their journey. The workers would depart gradually, in small groups, under various pretexts.

It was also decided to rent grain storage bins in nearby villages like Popeli, Banya, Hubychi, and Tustanovychi to store food. A workers' guard would be placed to watch over these storage sites. Twenty men would be dispatched immediately to the surrounding villages to inform the residents to avoid coming into Boryslav for several weeks until the workers had achieved better wages for themselves and others.

Matiy and Sen Basarab were tasked with going to Drohobych as soon as possible, perhaps even the next day, to purchase bread. Matiy knew a baker in Drohobych, and they hoped to place a discreet order for a large supply of bread without arousing suspicion. They would transport most of these supplies during the week leading up to the strike in casks and cases used for transporting wax and oil. This would allow them to prepare quickly and without drawing attention, which was crucial for the success of their plan. The pit owners would then be convinced of the workers' power and the effectiveness of their organisation, while the workers, shielded from hunger, would gain confidence and boldness.

Andrus Basarab and Derkach would also visit the neighbouring villages to see the farmers they knew. The Basarab brothers hailed from Banya, the closest village to Boryslav, and they also had connections with many farmers in the surrounding areas. Their purpose was to rent suitable storage buildings in these villages. The rest of the brotherhood members were to remain in Boryslav and ensure that everything went smoothly without the pit owners learning too soon of the workers' intentions.

As it was a Sunday and the meeting had ended relatively early, the brethren dispersed to contact the local treasurers and notify them of the plan. Matiy's shanty remained busy until late at night, with yellowish ruddy faces moving about in the poorly-lit windows. It was only long after midnight that everyone finally went home. Boryslav was fast asleep under the cover of darkness, with only the distant sounds of a group of labourers singing in a tavern somewhere beyond Novy Svit:

Because I'm drinking, my darling, don't cry,
There'll be time enough for weeping when I die!

XIV

Calm prevailed in Boryslav for another week. During this time, the pit owners walked the streets without a worry, conducting their business as usual. They made deals, bargained, engaged in deception, accepted money, and paid it out. The workers, too, continued with their daily routines. They worked in the pits, their clothes tattered, their bodies covered in oil, and they crawled down into the mines as they had before. They turned the cranks, ate stale bread and onions, and rarely had the luxury of warm meals, drinking more vodka instead.

Although the raucous, senseless drinking bouts that were common before had ceased, and crowds of people were no longer spending hours in the taverns, the tavernkeepers, who were often also the owners of oil wells, didn't complain too much. The hot weather had accelerated work to fulfill wax orders pouring in from all directions, and sober workers were always more reliable and productive than intoxicated ones.

Life flowed like a shallow, muddy stream, and it seemed it would flow this way forever. And yet this was the final week before a great change would occur!

And in Matiy's house, which had become the true centre of the workers' movement, workers from all over Boryslav gathered for meetings, regardless of the weather, making their way through rain or shine, along various paths, to attend discussions, review the treasury, contribute their dues, or simply engage in conversation and camaraderie. It was always bustling.

Benedio continued working for Leon in his new ceresin factory, and Matiy, after spending two days in Drohobych with Sen Basarab, returned and informed the brethren what they had arranged. He then resumed work in one of Leon's pits. The old man seemed rejuvenated. Benedio had never seen him so eager, cheerful, and joyous. He cared about everything, inquired about everything, and it was evident that he put all his energy into contributing to the success of the burgeoning movement.

Benedio, although occupied with other tasks, couldn't help but notice this change and secretly felt pleased. One day, as he struck up a conversation with Matiy and jokingly asked him about the reason for his transformation, Matiy's face at once took on a very dignified expression.

"I have news, I've good news!" he said mysteriously.

"About what?" asked Benedio.

"About my case."

"Well, and what's the news?"

"Everything is going well. The Sambir Court will soon issue a warrant for Mortko's arrest."

"That's not bad," said Benedio, though he felt a sense of ambivalence in his heart. He almost pitied Matiy for finding joy in such seemingly insignificant matters at such a crucial time for the workers. However, his practical mindset quickly took over. He considered the possibility of giving this case maximum exposure, of piquing the interest of the entire workers' community in this intriguing trial where a humble oil worker was standing up to a powerful gentleman (for it was evident to him, and likely to most others, that Hermann was behind Mortko). If, during their struggle, the gendarmes were to arrive and arrest Mortko, throw him onto a cart and parade him through Boryslav, it could serve as a source of inspiration for the oil workers. Such a spectacle could rejuvenate their spirits and hopes, demonstrating that they too could achieve success when truth was on their side!

He shared his thoughts with Matiy, who eagerly embraced the idea. Indeed, within a few days, through Derkach and Trotter, through the Basarab brothers, and even through Benedio himself, practically every worker in Boryslav knew about Matiy's court case. People in all the barracks were discussing it, speculating how it would end. They were generally amazed at Matiy's courage in deciding to reopen the case, even though the prosecutor had withdrawn from it, and this greatly heightened their interest. True, new and more significant events soon captured the attention of the workers, but nevertheless, from this seed sown, something had sprouted and would eventually mature with time.

Preparations for the workers' struggle were quickly being completed. The Basarab brothers supervised the transportation of bread, millet meal and other food they had bought in Drohobych to secret warehouses in Hubychi, Banya and Tustanovychi, and farmers had also been hired to deliver food to Boryslav. Three large boilers had already been purchased to cook porridge for the workers. The brethren also had not forgotten to obtain canvas for tents to house the homeless in case any of the workers were evicted from their lodgings. By Saturday everything was ready and a joyous and equally disturbing whisper passed through the barracks:

"The time has come! It's time! It's time!"

It was like a gentle summer breeze moving across a field of ripe grain. The silent, bowed stalks bent lower still, then straightened, then bent again, waving in unison, their full spikes whispering softly at first and then more assertively: 'It's time! It's time! It's time!' And the wind roamed further and further afield, stirring up new waves, running in wider circles – bringing with it the ever louder blessed whisper: 'It's time! It's time! It's time!'

The envoys of the workers spread out along dozens of roads leading out of Boryslav to all the towns and villages, bringing tidings of the impending strike. They were seen in

Urovy and Pidbuzh, in Hayi and Dobrivliany, in Stryj and Medenychi, in Sambir and Turka, in Stara Sil and Dzvyniach, in Dobrohostiv and in Korchyn. The poor received their message with joy, the rich with jeers and scepticism. In some places they were wined and dined, and in others they were asked to show their passports and threatened with arrest, but they were not stopped and went further afield, without missing a single settlement, begging and arguing that no one venture into Boryslav for the next few weeks to seek work, until their struggle was over.

Throughout the villages, countless rumours circulated about the impending strike, often fuelled by fear and uncertainty. Some claimed that the Boryslav workers intended to kill all the Jews, while others believed they aimed to drive the pit owners out of Boryslav. These rumours came to the attention of the gendarmes, who began to investigate, at times threatening and at times reassuring the people, in an effort to eradicate the rumours. The authorities in Drohobych received two dozen similar reports, but before any official action could be taken, the oil workers were already back in Boryslav after spreading their message. For a long time after this, the gendarmes continued to roam the villages, detaining students on their holidays and itinerant workers from the city, unaware that the agents they sought often passed right by them, dressed in simple, oil-stained shirts.

At last the preparations were finished and the strike began on the Sunday, with several crucial steps having been taken to ensure its success. One of the primary actions was the immediate departure of a significant portion of the workers, including the timid, the sickly, the women and young people from Boryslav. Initially, the plan was for this departure to occur quietly, without drawing attention, with small groups leaving gradually to avoid alerting the employers too soon about the intentions of the workers. Benedio had supported this approach initially. However, after much contemplation, he changed his mind. He believed that if this was to be a genuine struggle, it should be conducted openly and boldly from the outset. He wanted the first stage of the strike, the mass departure of people from Boryslav, to be done in broad daylight, openly, with flair. In his view, this would instil fear in the pit owners and undermine their resolve from the very start. Since the 'holiday' was set to begin the next day, there was no harm in letting the bosses know ahead of time which way the wind was blowing.

After church service on Sunday the streets of Boryslav began to fill in an unusual way with working men and women. The din was akin to market day, as more and more workers assembled. Half of them had sacks over their shoulders, parcels in their arms and all their clothes on their backs.

"What's going on? Where are you headed?" the Jewish pit owners asked some of the oil workers.

"Back home to the village," was the usual reply.

"Why?"

"Need to! There's still work to be done in the fields, besides there's no money to be made here."

"What do you mean? You're earning money now."

"Eh, call this money! It's hardly enough to live on, let alone provide help for the farm. Enough! Someone else can earn that kind of money!"

The people flowed like a river down the streets, quiet and somewhat melancholy. On the outskirts of Boryslav, on the green, other groups were already waiting for them. They began to bid each other farewell.

"Farewell, comrades! May God grant you success! Let us know what happens here!"

"Goodbye! We'll soon meet again in happier circumstances!"

Slowly the mass of workers split up and wound their way in all directions, to the mountains and the valleys, to the forests and the plains, looking back from time to time at the town they were leaving behind. Meanwhile Boryslav basked peacefully in the sun, much like a contented cat, stretching and purring, oblivious to the iron trap that was about to snap shut and seize it with its iron jaws, wrenching ribs and limbs apart.

True, the Jewish businessmen of Boryslav were not at all like that cat. The mass departure of the workers greatly unsettled them. They couldn't understand what was happening and what it was the workers wanted. Toward the end of the day they calmed down somewhat, reasoning that even though half the workforce had left, the other half remained, and if that proved insufficient, new workers would surely arrive from the villages. With such thoughts in mind, they slept peacefully that night. However, their expectations, while quite reasonable, did not materialize on this occasion.

Early the next morning, a considerable number of work barracks stood completely empty. Well, not quite. The overseers arrived, unlocked the gates, and were puzzled when the workers failed to show up. Some grew agitated and unleashed a barrage of curses, while others, of a more stoic disposition, settled onto benches near the entrance, vowing to thrash the lazy bastards for their unprecedented tardiness. Yet neither approach yielded any results.

The sun had already climbed high in the sky and still the workers did not make an appearance. The overseers might have continued to wait, increasingly bored and irritable, if it weren't for the shouts and curses coming from neighbouring work places. These cries and the commotion hinted that, although workers had swarmed to these locations like hornets to a hive, something unusual, something unsettling and inconceivable, was taking place. But in fact it was all quite straightforward.

The workers had congregated en masse at these work sites, standing silently by the gates. When the overseers arrived and unlocked the gates, the workers did not budge, refusing to enter.

"Get to work!" the overseer would shout.

"Oh, we have plenty of time for that," one or other of the oil workers would reply calmly.

"What do you mean, you've plenty of time?" the overseer would retort. "I don't have time to waste!"

"Then crawl into the pit and do the work yourself, if you're in such a hurry," the workers would respond mirthfully.

The overseer's face would turn red with anger and he'd clench his fists, ready to punch the nearest worker.

"No need to get angry, Shloma," the workers would try to placate him. "We're just here to let you know that we don't care to work anymore!"

"You won't work?" the stunned overseer would mutter. "And why not?"

"Firstly, because we don't want a lowlife like you for our overseer, and secondly, because your master doesn't pay us enough. Farewell! And tell your master that if he gives us a better overseer and pays us twelve shistkas a day, then we'll return to work."

And this occurred simultaneously, with unanimous resolve, at all the barracks throughout Boryslav! A tremendous cry of amazement, anger, and helplessness erupted from the mouths of the Jewish pit owners and reverberated from one end of town to the other.

Some of the overseers stood like pillars of salt, their mouths agape, shocked by such unheard-of, impious words. Others exploded in boundless anger, falling into a rage, attacking the workers with their fists, threatening to force them to work with punches and blows. Others still merely smiled sceptically, accepting it all as a big joke. When the workers finally dispersed, they waved dismissively, grumbling: "Phew, what strange people, carrying on like that! You'd think there's no one else in Boryslav besides them. Don't worry, my friend, we'll find people besides you to work for us, better ones, more obedient, and willing to work for lower wages!"

Meanwhile, other overseers, stunned, rushed off to their employers, explaining the situation and seeking further instructions on how to handle this unexpected turn of events. However, this unforeseen blow had caught their employers equally off guard. By midday on Monday, they weren't entirely sure whether the strike had truly occurred in all the pits, barracks, and oil refineries. They scurried through the streets like hounds, grabbing any worker they could find by the shoulder with trembling hands. Although their fingers were ready to dig into the worker's flesh with the tenacity of iron hooks, they struggled to restrain themselves and asked with a blend of sweetness and urgency:

"Eh, Hryts, why aren't you coming to work?"

"Because there's no work to be had."

"Why do you say that? I have work."

"How much will you pay me?"

"Stop asking questions, come and work. I pay the same as everyone else."

"But that's not enough."

"You won't come, eh? So what will you do then?"

"That's my business. There's no need to ask!"

The Jewish pit owners frantically rushed through the streets in search of workers. However, they quickly realized that their efforts were in vain, and that the workers had clearly conspired. True, some among them refused to acknowledge that this might be the case, while others, though they believed it, were so stunned by the unprecedented event that they didn't know how to react. They helplessly scurried about, lamenting their potential losses, angered by the audacity of the workers to stall business in Boryslav. But it never occurred to any of them to consider offering some assistance, apart from calling in the gendarmes. They never even attempted to discover what the workers were demanding.

The first day of the conflict passed relatively peacefully. Both opposing sides, shaken and alarmed by this unexpected turn of events, attempted to calm down, collect their thoughts, and reassess the situation. The jubilant workers moved hesitantly through the streets, avoiding large crowds, and instead gathered in small groups in quiet corners to discuss their next steps. Only on the outskirts of Boryslav, on the common, was there a large gathering. There, they cooked porridge and distributed it to the needy, mostly those from the barracks. This area also served as the centre of activity for the workers' council, attended by all the brethren and Benedio.

Benedio remained outwardly calm, speaking with a steady, resonant voice. However, his unusually bright eyes, pale face, and the deep wrinkles on his forehead bore witness to the intensity of his thoughts. The council discussed the demands they should present to the pit owners in the event of negotiations. Most advised requesting a modest increase in wages to increase the likelihood of acceptance. In response, Benedio said:

"You're right. In many cases, those who ask for less often receive more. However, in our situation, it would be unwise to request too little. We initiated this strike with the aim of achieving tangible gains. I think it is important to formulate demands that not only improve our daily lives but also empower us as a force and strengthen our resilience. It's possible that the pit owners may agree to any terms now, especially when they see that we're not only refusing to work ourselves but are also preventing others from working. Nevertheless, once we accept their promises and end this conflict, they might go back on their commitments and treat us even worse than before. Therefore, my proposal is to establish demands that secure our position, ensuring that we have the strength to restart our struggle if need be."

Everyone agreed that this was a fair and reasonable approach. Benedio continued:

"So far, we've all seen that our strength lies in our unity. While we each cared only about ourselves, there could never have been talk of help. But now, as you can see, through our collective efforts, we've been able to start this significant undertaking – a struggle against the wealthy. I believe that if we stick together, the rich won't be able to prevail. Therefore, we need to present demands that will not only keep our community intact, but also make it stronger. We want our workers' treasury to continue to grow. For as the saying goes, things that are good for the community, are good for grandma too. If our collective power continues to grow and develop, then everyone will benefit because the community will be able to support them in times of need. The pit owners will need to fear us and dare not break their word, treating workers like human beings rather than livestock or worse."

"Yes, yes!" the workers echoed. "But what specific demands should we make?"

"I propose the following: first and foremost, naturally, they should increase our wages. Those working in the pits should earn no less than twelve shistkas, and those above ground, at least eight shistkas. Secondly, no paymaster should be allowed to charge a fee; thirdly, the owners should contribute to the workers' assistance fund, each of them giving at least one rinsky per month. Furthermore, in the event of an accident resulting in injury or death, they must cover hospital and medical expenses and provide support to orphaned families of workers for at least six months. I don't think such demands are excessive, and they would greatly benefit us."

"Yes, yes," the workers exclaimed in unison. "Let's make these demands! And once we have our own treasury, we can negotiate even better terms in the future."

The Jewish pit owners were unaware of the meeting. As night fell, their fear of the workers grew. They locked themselves in their homes and rarely ventured into the streets. There were only muffled conversations, whispers, and a pervasive anxiety which swept across Boryslav like a plague, infecting thousands of people. It was like a howling autumn wind passing through a forest.

XV

Fanny, Leon's only daughter, sat deep in thought, alone on a soft sofa in her sumptuous room. From time to time she glanced at the clock ticking away under a glass dome next to her on the marble side table.

"Three o'clock," she said in a bored voice. "How slowly time passes! Father will be returning after five, and meanwhile you, Fanny, must sit here all alone!"

How many hours, how many days had she sat like this on the soft sofa beside the marble side-table with the glass dome clock! How many times had she complained about the slow passage of time! She had nothing to do to keep her hands busy, and felt she wasn't needed by anyone and was of no use to anyone. She couldn't even find a book to entertain herself. This unbearable boredom, this solitude pressed down on her, oozing into every pore of her body. Her lively, full-blooded nature languished in this cold idle solitude. Young blood boiled in her veins, her passionate imagination added more fire, and she felt imprisoned. She wanted love – exciting, romantic adventures, the passionate embrace of a dashing hero, loyalty until death, and boundless commitment. Meanwhile Drohobych society, especially the circle of Drohobych's 'emancipated gentlemen,' those stupid and arrogant young sons of the rich industrialists, had the same effect on her as water had on fire. She hated them for their continual compliments gleaned from books, their simian kowtowing, which blatantly revealed that they had more respect for her father's wealth than her attributes.

'How slowly time passes!' she repeated in her mind, somehow in a gentler, more timid tone, and looked out the window into the street. Was she expecting someone? Yes, she was – she was expecting *him*, her hero, that amazing young man, who several weeks ago had appeared like a bright meteor on her horizon – so unexpectedly and so mysteriously. And he had appeared in accordance with her romantic daydreams: a prince in pauper's clothing! A poor young coalman, whose large black eyes simply devoured her. He had terrified her immensely when he had clung to her carriage. And after falling off, his passionate declaration of love had taken her by surprise. She was even more astonished when he later appeared at her home, donned in elegant attire, with a transformed and refined demeanour. He spoke with such candour, his words imbued with passion and energy. He was utterly undeterred by barriers – truly resembling a powerful prince! He was nothing like those pale, measly, timid and ridiculous suitors, whom she had seen until now! How much power there was in his muscles, how much fire in his gaze, how much smouldering passion in his heart! And how he loved her! But who was he? He had mentioned that his name was Gottlieb, but what was his surname? Could he become hers?

These thoughts coursed through lonely Fanny's head like golden-pink strands, and she looked at the clock with growing impatience.

"He promised to come after three," she whispered, "so why isn't he here yet? The secret is to be revealed today, but why has he not yet appeared? Unless all this is merely a dream, and he is a figment of my frustrated imagination? But no, he held my hand in his, he kissed my lips, oh, how hot they were, how passionate! Surely, he must appear!"

"And he has finally appeared!" announced Gottlieb, entering quietly and bowing.

"Oh, it's you!" Fanny said softly, blushing. "I was actually thinking about you."

“I've never stopped thinking about you, not ever since I saw you.”

“Really?”

The conversation continued wordlessly, but was clearly understood by both. Finally Fanny whispered:

“You promised to reveal the secret of your identity today.”

“And you still haven't guessed? You still haven't figured it out, haven't any of your servants told you?”

“No, I haven't spoken to anyone about you.”

“I'm the son of Hermann Goldkrämer. Do you know him?”

“What? You're Hermann's son, the same one father tried to marry me off to?”

“What? Your father offered that I marry you? When was this?”

“Just recently, two months ago. I was so scared, not having ever seen you!”

“But what did my parents say?”

“I don't know. It seemed your father didn't mind, but that your mother was very much against it. I guess she must have badly offended my father in some way, because he returned from your place awfully upset and angry, cursing your mother.”

“What are you saying!” exclaimed Gottlieb. “My mother was opposed to this? Although,” he added after a moment, “it's possible, it's in her nature. But she must right this wrong herself, she must ask for your father's forgiveness, this very day!”

Gottlieb's face burned with wild determination.

“When is your father returning?”

“At five.”

“Then farewell! I'm leaving and I'll send my mother here to settle this matter. She must do this for our happiness. Farewell, my love!”

And he left.

“What strength, what decisiveness, what passionate words!” Fanny whispered as if intoxicated. “No, no, he is nothing like those other insipid, pathetic suitors. My God, how I love him, how much I love him!"

Meanwhile Gottlieb hastily made his way home. He had already been informed that his father knew that he was in Drohobych. His mother had told him everything when she handed him the required money. Gottlieb remained silent upon hearing the news; his newfound, fervent love for Fanny had melted away his resentment toward his father. He would have gladly forgiven his father and returned home, if only Hermann had been ready to reconcile.

But no, Hermann said nothing, pretending as if he didn't care one bit about his son, obviously waiting for Gottlieb to repent first and reconcile with his father. Gottlieb, on the other hand, was against this. Several times they passed each other in the street, but Hermann pretended not to notice the young, decked-out gentleman, and Gottlieb was not about to be the first to back down. Gottlieb rarely dropped by to see his mother, and then always when his father was not at home. But now the matter was urgent, and he entered the house even though the maid informed him that her ladyship was in her room, and the master was in his office. That didn't concern him, for he had nothing to discuss with his father.

Rifka sat in her bedroom, her eyes fixed on the ceiling. The unfortunate ruination of her spirit was coming to an end, it had now reached the point where after great irritation comes numbness, a mindless heaviness, and sulking melancholy. She remained sitting in the same place for days on end, said little and even then, spoke in a weak, broken voice. It was evident that the recent imperceptibly strong energy of her willpower had now completely disappeared, shattering into tiny shards.

When she was in this mesmerised state, one could do whatever one wanted with her. There was only one lively feeling left inside her – her love for her son and her hatred toward her husband. Hermann fretted because of this change, in which he saw the signs of some serious illness, but the doctors assured him, that these were merely signs of excessive irritation and nervous exhaustion, and if she rested in peace, all would be fine. And Rifka surely had enough peace and quiet – all day long no one troubled her, except perhaps for the servants who summoned her to eat or helped her into bed. But it was also evident, that this deadening, empty, destructive stillness did not help her one bit!

Engrossed in his own love, Gottlieb took no notice of her condition, and upon entering her bedroom immediately declared the reason for his visit.

"Mama!" he said, coming closer and sitting next to her. A spark of life appeared in her extinguished blurry eyes.

"Yes, my son?"

"Did Leon Hammerschlag want to marry off his daughter to me?"

"Leon? Yes, it's true, that heathen did try."

"And what did you say to him?"

"Me? That I would rather die alone than have his daughter become a part of our family!"

Gottlieb looked at her angrily, almost furiously.

"You're a fool, Mama!"

"Why, my dear Gottlieb?"

"Because it is Leon's daughter whom I love and would rather die, if she were not to become mine."

Rifka jumped to her feet. Gottlieb's words were like a strong, awakening blow.

"Never!" she said firmly.

"No, it must be!" Gottlieb said emphatically.

"But how can you be in love with her?"

"But how can you hate her so much?"

"Oh, I hate them all, I hate them to death: that Leon, and your father, and her, and all those who for the sake of money are ready to renounce life and conscience, and ready to drag others into that damned quicksand of gold!"

"But how has she wronged you? By the way, Mama, do you love me, your only child?"

"How can you even ask such a question?"

"And do you wish me happiness?"

"More than I wish it for myself."

"Then, please, do as I ask of you."

"What should I do, my dearest?"

The momentary explosion of her former energy quickly subsided in Rifka's heart, and she sat down once more, powerless and inert, as she had been only a moment earlier.

"Go to Leon, talk with him, patch things up with him and arrange, so that we can become engaged as soon as possible. Arrange for my future happiness!"

"Your happiness, my dearest? Alright, alright!" Rifka said, understanding little of what he had said.

"Yes, Mama, my happiness! Get up, pull yourself together, and off you go!"

"Where to, my dearest?"

"I told you, to see Leon."

"To see Leon? No, never!"

Unable to understand his mother's ailing state, Gottlieb went into a rage, threatening to kill himself, which frightened Rifka to the core.

"Alright then, my dear, alright! I'll go with you wherever you want, just don't do anything to yourself! I beg you, stay calm! I'll do anything you ask, as long as you stay calm."

And with trembling hands she began to dress, but quite ineffectually, taking forever to try on and take off clothes. In his impatience Gottlieb had to call the maid to help her dress. At last they both left the house.

Leon Hammerschlag was sitting at his desk in his office in a very good mood. The new factory was operating very well, and the first lot of ceresin wax would be ready for shipment abroad in a week at the latest. Then there would be money, allowing the factory to keep operating, and he would be able to continue building his house, which had been stopped during this busy time. Good fortune was smiling on Leon, never had he felt so powerful and proud. There was a knock at the door and Rifka entered – pale, with lifeless, motionless eyes, and a slow, almost sleepy gait. Leon had never seen her like this. Her unusual appearance amazed him, and gradually he became rather perplexed.

"Sit down, please," he said in answer to her greeting, uttered in a dull whisper. Rifka sat down and said nothing for a while. Leon remained silent too.

"I've come to you about a matter," Rifka said slowly, "which doesn't concern me, but all the same…"

"I will be very pleased to hear you out," replied Leon.

"Are you angry with me, Mr. Leon?" she suddenly asked.

"But… but, my dear lady… How can you think such things…"

"No, no, I just asked in case you were, and thus refused to help me with the matter, I dare say, I dare say, with this very important matter, even though it doesn't concern me…"

"Oh, please, please!" Leon blurted out.

"It's like this, Mr. Leon. Have you abandoned your former idea of marrying off our two children?"

"Well, what was I to do, I was forced to abandon it, despite my regrets, but what was I to do when your son seemed to have disappeared!"

"And if he were to reappear?"

Leon looked at her intently and noticed the obvious anxiety expressed on her face.

'Aha,' he thought to himself, 'so that's where this is headed. Things must have turned sour for them, and now they're trying to seek my favour. But just you wait, I'll pay you back for what happened!' And he added out loud:

"Unfortunately, at the present time I cannot be of assistance… I have other plans for my daughter."

"Well, if that's the case, then, sure… I merely thought… I mean, I wasn't asking for myself…"

Rifka could barely string her words together. Obviously, Leon's refusal was a painful blow to her.

"But what if… if your daughter was in love with my son?"

"My daughter… in love with your son? Impossible!"

"No, no, I'm not saying that it is the case, but what if it happened, that it was?"

"Eh, tall tales and fantasy! I have other plans and please don't waste my time with such nonsense!"

Leon turned away, glad that he was able to pay back Rifka an eye for an eye, never even entertaining the possibility of what she had hinted at.

At that moment the heavy clatter of footsteps sounded in the hallway and Leon's cashier from Boryslav burst into the office, short of breath, covered in dust and dripping with sweat. On seeing him, Leon jumped to his feet.

"What's this? Why have you come running here?"

"Sir, there's been a misfortune!"

"What's happened?"

"The workers have banded together and refuse to work."

"They refuse to work? Why?"

"They claim we don't pay them enough."

"That can't be. Are you drunk!"

"No, sir, it's the truth! I've come to you for advice. What should we do?"

"Have they only stopped working in the pits, or in the factory itself?"

"In both places."

"*Gott über die Welt!*[19] What a misfortune! What can we do? Work must proceed in the factory, of course! Listen, Schlomo, go into the city, round up some workers and take them back with you to Boryslav. I'll come along and help you."

....

[19] "God in heaven!" (German).

And the two men ran out, taking no notice of Rifka. She heard the news and smiled upon their departure.

"Hah, good, that's good news!" she whispered. "Serves you right! If they aren't fools, they'll rebel and toss every one of you lot into those pits! Just look at him now! He's no longer interested, he refuses! My poor Gottlieb! What will he say when he hears this? He may be ready to harm himself. But serves him right, he shouldn't have taken up with a girl like that, he should have found himself some poor kind girl… But what will I tell him now? He's so unstable, like a spark! No, I won't tell him the truth, come what may!"

And she stepped out into the street, where Gottlieb was impatiently waiting for her.

"Well?" he asked, looking into her eyes.

"It's fine, my dear, everything's fine."

"Did he accept?"

"Of course, of course! The engagement will be in a month."

"In a month? Why so late?"

"It can't be arranged any sooner. And why be in a hurry? After all, she'll have time enough to poison your young life!"

And she began to sob like a child.

"Mama, please don't say such things, you don't know her!" Gottlieb exclaimed angrily.

"Alright, my dear, I won't say a word!"

But for some reason the news did not comfort Gottlieb. Maybe it was because he needed to wait so long for that happy moment, or because his mother had announced the news in such a cold, ominous, unpleasant tone. Suffice to say that Gottlieb did not feel the joy he would have liked to feel. He walked in silence alongside his mother the whole way home. Here they parted ways: Rifka went to her room and Gottlieb to the hotel where he was staying.

By the time Rifka had returned home, Hermann had already left. The news about the workers had also reached him about the same time as Leon had heard about it, and he immediately ordered a horse be harnessed and, together with Mortko, who had brought him the sad news about the workers' rebellion, they set off for Boryslav. After all that had transpired, Rifka threw herself fully-clothed onto the soft armchair and drifted off into thoughtless melancholia.

Meanwhile Gottlieb paced about his room in the hotel, pondering his happiness and trying hard to feel happy. Only poor Fanny, who had overheard the conversation between Rifka and Leon through a door in the wall, threw herself onto her sofa and wept bitterly, covering her face with a kerchief.

XVI

For the first time that day Hermann Goldkrämer was not sure what to do. This new, hitherto unheard-of thing in Boryslav, where the workers had conspired to stop work, puzzled him. Having arrived in Boryslav the night before, he was unable to fall asleep long into the night, mulling over what he had seen and heard. How much Boryslav had changed since he had left here last! It was as if some magician had turned everything upside down. Whereas before the Jewish pit owners strolled proudly in small groups through the streets and looked down on the workers, now there was not a Jewish person to be seen in the streets, but on the other hand there were heaps of workers everywhere, like swarms of hornets, talking loudly, roaring with laughter, threatening passers-by or singing. Whereas before, wherever you looked, there were winches spinning above the pits, and hundreds of pairs of hands were busy working – now the pits were dead quiet and the work-ers' barracks empty, derricks stood like dirty skeletons from which the flesh had fallen away, and the fans peered with their dark maws into the pits, as if asking if anyone there desired some fresh air.

But on the common, on the other hand, on the outskirts of Boryslav, it was lively and bustling now! From his window Hermann could see the smoke rising from the fire burning beneath a huge cauldron in which the workers were cooking porridge. He could hear the din of the meetings taking place, the shouts of the guards set out on every road, guarding every path leading to Boryslav. 'The devil take them! What were they up to?' Hermann thought, and he impatiently waited for eight o'clock to come around, when the other pit owners would be assembling at his place for a meeting.

'No, this needs to stop!' he thought to himself, as he paced about the lounge room. 'We must break their resistance. I badly need workers, lots of workers, this very week. I urgently need to supply fifty thousand hundredweight of wax to the Association for the Extraction of Earth Wax by the end of this week and receive their money. The devil take me, I can't delay a single day! While the Association is on the verge of going belly up, these cursed robbers are threatening to perform their dastardly deeds. I was a fool to risk all this! I need to extract another two thousand hundredweight, and I can pass the wax onto those gentlemen from the Association right here and now, and they can do as they please with it, so long as I get my money. Just as well that I divided the contracted amount of wax into two parts – a few more days and the first shipment will be ready for delivery. Whether there will be a need to supply the second part, only the good Lord knows, but all the better for me if they still want it.'

These were Hermann's thoughts as he paced about the lounge room, and all his thoughts rested on the fact that everything would be fine, if only the workers stopped rebelling and returned to work.

'But they must! It can't be otherwise!' he continued. 'Even if I need to pay them more, all the same it won't be any more than my profits!'

Only then did he recall that the day before he had sent Mortko off to Drohobych to round up all the rabble, every unemployed Jew and Christian, every water carter, rubbish collector and claypit labourer, promising them a good wage and to direct all of them to Boryslav. Hermann knew full well, that there would be little productive work from this rabble, but he wanted to use this as a mechanism to break the resistance of the Boryslav workers. 'This is the best medicine for their ailment,' he thought, rubbing his hands with glee. 'When they see that I can make do without them, that I have my own workers, then they'll come begging me to take them on. Let's see, who gets the upper hand!'

A strange kind of hubbub that competed more and more with the noise coming from the common, drew Hermann to the window. But he couldn't see a thing, apart from a large group of frightened Jews hurrying along the street toward his house.

"What's going on there?" Hermann asked them from the window.

"Some kind of fight! They're fighting!" the Jews replied in unison.

"Who's fighting whom?"

"The local workers are fighting, but it's hard to say with whom. A crowd of guys have come from Hubychi, but they won't let them into Boryslav, so a fight has erupted."

The hubbub lasted for a short while and then began to fade away.

"Hurrah! Hurrah!" shouts filled the air. All the Jews, Hermann being no exception, turned pale for some reason and began to tremble, but they didn't utter a word. In anxious silence they continued to listen.

"Hurrah! Hurrah!" joyous shouts continued to pervade the air, but it was impossible to understand what was happening.

"Please, gentlemen, step inside and let's talk," Hermann said after a long silence.

No sooner had all the Jewish pit owners entered and the sounds of greeting had died down, when the door burst open and a pale frightened Leon Hammerschlag rushed inside. His clothes were covered in dust, and in places they were in tatters. Breathing heavily, he dashed across the room and threw himself into an armchair, seeking to catch his breath for a long time. The others surrounded him and watched him with an expression of utter trepidation, as if he were the harbinger of their certain death.

"What happened, Lord Almighty, what happened?" they kept asking, but it took Leon quite a while before he was able to speak.

"*Gott soll sie strafen!*"[20] he finally exclaimed, getting up from the armchair. "They want to butcher us all, that's what! The robbers have conspired to have our souls!"

"How? What? Can this be true? Who said this? How do you know?" the men buzzed, trembling with fear.

"No one needed to say anything!" replied Leon. "I saw it with my own eyes. See what they did to me! Did you hear the yelling? It's all their doing! Oh, what will become of us, what will become of us!"

"I said a long time ago that we need to send for the gendarmes. They'll drive them to work with clubs!" yelled one of the Jewish pit owners.

"What good are gendarmes?" another objected. "What good would gendarmes do here? We need a whole company of soldiers to shoot half of them dead!"

"Tell us what happened?" the Jews asked Leon. "Tell us what took place there!"

"Things are bad, very bad. Early in the morning I went out onto the common to wait for those workers, whom I had asked to be hired in Drohobych. The fellows there on the common were like clouds of rooks gathered for breakfast! Where the hell do they get all that flour and porridge from? There are several thousand people there, and they're cooking away all day long, everyone is eating and eating! Someone must be helping them!"

Leon grew silent for a moment, to give greater weight to his last words, and, after looking about the room, he rested

....

[20] "God must punish them" (German).

his gaze on Hermann, who was standing by the window, lost in thought, drumming his fingers against the windowpane. Many of those in the room looked in that direction as well, while others let out a gasp, as if enlightened by a sudden revelation.

"No! It can't be!"

"As if I know," replied Leon, feigning indifference and shrugging his shoulders. "I have no proof, and am merely saying what's on my mind." His bad conscience prompted him to see in Hermann his arch enemy, and he was satisfied now, that he had ignited a spark of suspicion in the minds of his audience, that this workers' rebellion was all Hermann's doing, initiated with the aim of putting pressure on the small pit owners and even Leon himself.

"But listen to what happened next. I was walking along the highway, when a whole crowd of these ragamuffins comes toward me. 'Where you headed?' they asked. I summoned my courage: 'And what's it to you?' I replied. 'It's our business to know!' they replied. 'Can't you see that we're on guard here, making sure no one leaves Boryslav!' 'Stop that foolish talk,' I exclaimed, 'and leave people in peace. I'm not doing anything to you. Leave me alone!' 'Well, then leave us in peace too,' they answered, 'and head back to your Boryslav!' And without further ado, they grabbed me by the shoulders and pushed me back. I tried to push my way through, started shouting, but they only burst out laughing. They grabbed firm hold of me and dragged me through the streets. 'Oh, woe is me,' I thought to myself, completely exhausted and barely breathing.

"I stopped and looked back, when I caught sight of my workers from Drohobych coming along the road. 'Glory be to God!' I thought. 'Here come my saviours! They're not letting anyone out of Boryslav, but surely, they'll let these men into Boryslav.' And I set off toward them, overjoyed that there were so many of them, more than a hundred men! But before I had gone too far, I heard the damned guards call out to them: 'Stop! Who goes there?' 'Good people, workers,' the fellows replied. 'Where you headed?' 'We've come to work in Boryslav.' 'That's not allowed!' 'What do you mean, it's not allowed?' 'You can't work. Didn't you hear our request? We sent our people everywhere and asked that no one come here to work for the next couple of days, until we've won better wages for everyone?' 'No, we haven't heard that,' said the Drohobych workers. 'Then hear our request now, and we ask you nicely to turn back to where you've come from!'

"The workers began to hesitate, some were obviously keen to turn back and began to exchange whispers with the thieves, others who may not have been convinced by the talk, were afraid of the large crowd that had assembled to stop them. Enough said, the new arrivals stood there, not sure what to do next. I lost my patience at this point, rushed into their midst and called out: 'Don't listen to them, good people! They're bandits, lazybones! They'll be put behind bars! Come to work, take no notice of them! I'm paying eight shistkas a day to each man – what more do you need!' My words seemed to stun everyone a little. The new arrivals began to make their way forward. But those guards stood their ground. 'Stop there! We're not letting anyone pass!' I yelled once more: 'Follow me!' A ruckus erupted, fists started flying, there was pushing and shoving, and then rocks began to sail through the air. Lots of people came running and an almighty melee ensued. I can't remember what happened to me. A few fists struck my face, ears and the back of my head, between my shoulders. Before I knew it, I was in the very thick of it, and from there I was thrown out onto Boryslav Street once more. When I looked back, the fighting had finished, the new arrivals had all scattered and were heading off to Hubychi. There was shouting, and the howls of: 'Hurrah! Hurrah!' were deafening. Seeing that I could do nothing more, I returned here. That's what happened!"

Having finished his account, Leon spat on the ground and once more cursed 'those robbers,' who had caused nothing but turmoil and were ready to cause even more trouble. The industrialists grew silent for a moment, pondering what they had just heard. None of them were able to come up with a better solution than summoning the gendarmes or the army. Until now Hermann had not taken part in the conversation and remained standing by the window. From his wrinkled forehead and fixed gaze it was obvious that he was deep in thought. Obviously, the matter required great prudence, a decisive moment was approaching, when it would not be possible to vouch for what was to come the next day, and thus required serious concentration to navigate the twists and turns of a hostile future.

"And the damned fellows also made fun of me," exclaimed Leon, his face ruddy from exertion, "when they saw how my clothes were in complete disarray. But don't worry, we'll see who has the last laugh here, us or them!"

'You mean us or you,' thought Hermann, 'or more exactly: me or you! Hah, what a thought!' and he waved his hand about, as if trying to catch some fortuitous thought, which at that moment had flashed through his head. 'Yes, this way, this is the right way to go, this is what must be done! Success can be easy, and if it works out, then there will be no question as to which of us will be laughing, me or your lot!'

Hermann quickly figured out a plan of attack and promptly moved to the middle of the room, asking those assembled for a moment of their attention.

"Gentlemen, I've listened to your advice and it surprises me," he began in a voice unlike his usual harsh tone. "Gendarmes! Do you think the gendarmes will force the workers to get into the pits and start working? No, they'll simply arrest some, and drive the rest away, which won't make things any the better for us, because we don't need public order, we need workers, cheap labour! Is that not so?"

"Of course it is!" shouted the pit owners.

"And soldiers," Hermann continued, "will give us the same result as the gendarmes, except that we'll have to feed them, with no useful outcome. I think both these approaches are of no use to us."

"But what can we do? What can we do?"

"That's exactly the question: what can we do? In my opinion this rebellion is some kind of contagious weakness for which a general recipe has not yet been invented, and maybe there isn't one. But sometimes one thing will help, other times – another thing, depending on the circumstances. One needs to ascertain, what gave rise to this ailment and how it manifests itself, and only after that seek a cure. In our case here, it's obvious that up until now we haven't been paying the workers enough, given the bad harvests this year."

"What do you mean, not enough?" those assembled started to shout.

"Enough!" Leon called out derisively. "Mr. Goldkrämer wants to play the advocate of these thieves and will probably advise us to give in to all their demands and hand them everything we have!"

"I have no intention of being anyone's advocate," Hermann replied sharply, but calmly. "I don't even wish to play the liberal here, like Mr. Hammerschlag did yesterday, and won't go praising those thieves for their 'self-reliance,' I'll only speak here as a businessman, *als ein praktischer Geschäftsmann*,[21] and nothing more."

Leon pressed his lips together at these words – Hermann's biting attack had hurt him deeply, but he sensed that he could say nothing in reply, and remained silent.

"I'll repeat what I said," Hermann stressed, "they weren't being paid enough! We are behind closed doors, gentlemen,

....

[21] As a practical businessman (German).

so we can admit that to one another, and it will help us understand the reason for this rebellion. Oxen don't bellow when their mangers are full! Of course, it's one thing to admit to this in our closed circle, and quite another to admit to this in front of the workers! That would be the end of us!"

"Oh, for sure!" exclaimed the businessmen, glad of the turn Hermann's speech had taken.

"The reason I'm raising this," Hermann continued, "is to convince you that no one is instigating this rebellion from the outside and that it's a very serious and important matter, which must be resolved as soon as possible, before it gives birth to an even greater misfortune."

"What has now befallen us is bad enough!"

"Eh, this is still small potatoes," Hermann replied, "far worse may yet come, if we don't quell the storm quickly."

"But how can we do that?"

"There are two ways, as I see it. It is obvious that they are prepared for this conspiracy of theirs, and well prepared at that. Just look what's happened! More than half the workers have left Boryslav, throughout the villages their messengers have persuaded the people not to come looking for work here, and they've organized supplies of food – in short, they are well prepared. But, dear gentlemen, please consider that all this requires money, lots of money. And where have they been able to get it? True, we've heard they collect dues, but how much could they have collected? Obviously, not that much. In that case, I might advise that we sit tight, take no notice of them, stop worrying about them, and wait until their reserves are exhausted. Then they will surely come to us and be ready to work for whatever wage we offer them."

At these words Hermann studied the faces of those surrounding him, to try to understand what effect his speech was having on them. The effect must not have been a very good one, for many of the faces were contorted, as if the men had bitten into something bitter.

"It would be fine to wait," Leon said in finishing, "if we knew that their supplies will finish sometime soon. But what if they are prepared to wait a week or even longer?"

"Where could they have gotten all that money from?" asked Hermann.

"Who knows?" replied some of the men, after exchanging glances with Leon.

"And we can't wait that long," Leon continued. "You yourselves know, that we have contracts to fill, deadlines are drawing to a close, the work must be finished as soon as possible, there's no time to lose! And if that's the case, then only the second approach is viable: to agree to their demands."

"Their demands!" exclaimed the Jewish businessmen in a chorus.

"No, never! Better to call in the army and the gendarmes!"

"But, gentlemen," Hermann tried to placate them, "you are afraid of those demands, as if they were the devil knows what. Please inform me then, which of you know what their demands are?"

The pit owners stood flabbergasted. It was true, they had not stopped to consider this question. Until now they had always viewed the workers as the enemy, which needed to be defeated at any cost. The idea of negotiating with the workers, attempting to understand their demands, had never occurred to them. Leon was the first to speak:

"Of course we know! They are demanding one thing: higher wages!"

"Well, but who knows how much they are after," Hermann answered. "Do they want their wages to increase by five cents, or do they want double what they were being paid before. If they in general want 'more,' that's nothing to fear, obviously we can negotiate with them. But what I'm saying is, let's first find out in detail what their demands are. Maybe they want something quite different, or maybe apart from higher wages, they want other things? After all, no one has yet talked to them about it!"

"You're right, we need to ask them what they are after!" the assembled men agreed.

"But who will we send to talk with them?" asked Hermann.

"Let someone else go, I refuse," said Leon. "They're thieves, ready to tear a man apart at a moment's notice."

"If it be your will, I can take this task upon myself," Hermann said. "I will gladly accept this mission."

"Agreed, agreed!" voices filled the room.

"If that's the case, then hear me out. Another thing occurred to me that might make them more amenable to reach an agreement. As we can see, they are well prepared for everything, they've bought food and set up guard posts – but they probably haven't considered accommodation. After all, they all live in your dwellings! What if we were to throw them out of their lodgings this very day, right now. The weather is cold enough now, an icy wind has picked up, people will be forced to freeze in the open, and they will immediately realise that there is no sense in waging a war against us."

"That is true," some of the Jews said timidly, "but who knows, if they will be willing to concede? It might upset them even more?"

"We'll see," said Hermann, "but I think we should give it a try! It's no big deal? Everyone has the right to ask tenants to leave whenever they wish."

"Alright, let's try," said the Jews.

"If that's the case, then let's go! I'll visit them and hear out their demands. And at about three in the afternoon I invite all of you back here, to learn where we stand and we'll be able to decide how we should act!"

After this, the Jewish pit owners all left.

XVII

Putting on his hat and grabbing his cane, Hermann made his way down onto the common, where the workers were assembled. He walked along, pretending to be oblivious to everything, until he reached the workers' guards assembled on the highway.

"Hey," the guards called out to him, "where are you headed?"

"Me? To see you!" replied Hermann.

"What do you want?"

"I'd like to talk with you peaceably."

"About what?"

"That perhaps it's time that you resumed work, instead of wasting your time here, standing on guard and achieving nothing."

"We are well aware of that ourselves," replied some of the guards, "but what can we do, when there's no other way to come to an agreement with you lot."

"Come, come, who knows if there's no other way. You don't know us. You think that if someone's Jewish, they're not a person. We're people too and we know who deserves what. What's the point of this banter, I'll put it to you simply, after all you know who I am!"

"Of course we know who you are!"

"Then I'll put it to you simply, that the local pit owners, seeing that they can't remedy the situation using force, have sent me to try and reach an agreement, and have asked me to find out first and foremost what it is that you desire? What are your demands?"

"Well, that's another matter, sure, we understand!" the workers rejoiced. "Go to that house over there, please, our council will be assembling there and you'll be able to talk to them."

One of the guards escorted Hermann to Matiy's house, a second raced off to summon the brethren and other workers to come and try to reach a solution. Hermann didn't have long to wait. The brethren came, together with a whole crowd of workers, who not only piled into Matiy's tiny house, but also crowded around outside, curious to learn what kind of agreement could be reached.

In the house Hermann was asked to sit on the wooden bench, while the brethren and some of the older workers sat around the table, on the bed and the hearth of the oven. Stasiura, being the oldest present, sat at the head of the table, while Sen Basarab sat in his usual spot near the doorway.

"Mr. Goldkrämer, can you please tell all of those assembled, why you have come here?" Stasiura asked respectfully.

"Well, why have I come?" repeated Hermann. He stood up and ran his eyes over the workers. "I've been sent by the Jewish pit owners. They want to know why you refuse to work yourselves, and prevent others from working?"

"It's impossible, with the wages you are offering, Mr. Goldkrämer," replied Stasiura. "You don't pay us enough. People are dying of hunger."

"We pay what we can!" replied Hermann. "How can we pay you more, if we are not able to do so? Business is bad, where can we find the money? We'll be destitute ourselves soon."

"There's no need for that! And anyway, Mr. Goldkrämer, tell us honestly, why should we care if business is bad, to use your words? Just because you charge only forty-nine rinskys instead of fifty for each hundredweight of wax, so I'm meant to die of hunger? If you can't make ends meet in this business, then maybe you should drop it and someone else will come in your place who can make ends meet. And if not, then it will be evident that the whole business is not profitable in these parts and needs to be abandoned, and one needs to embark on another enterprise. But that's for you to decide! That's not the worry of the worker. Tell him to plough ice, if you like – that's up to you, but pay him so that he can lead a normal life!"

"Your words are good and wise," replied Hermann. "Let it be your way. We won't go into that. The Jews themselves can see that things can't go on like this much longer, that each person needs to earn enough to live on, we are people too! Tell me, what your demands are, so that you can return to work."

"We are people too, Mr. Goldkrämer," replied Stasiura. "We're not thieves, as it might appear to you. We are not rebelling to strip you of your wealth, but because things have become so bad for us, that it is impossible to bear any longer. Thus our demands are not great. So, Mr. Goldkrämer, this is what we want. Firstly, that wages be increased: those who go down into the pits get twelve shistkas a day, and those who work on the surface – one rinsky, and children – eight shistkas a day."

"Well," said Hermann, "that can be agreed to. And what else?"

"Secondly, that the paymasters levy no charges on the workers."

"That's no big thing either, the paymasters can be informed and they'll stop taking a cut."

"Thirdly, in the event that a worker suffers an accident at work, resulting in death, injury or similar, that the pit owner be obliged to pay hospital and medical expenses, and financially assist the family of a deceased person for at least six months."

"Hm, I think this could be arranged as well. So, is that all?"

"Just about, but not quite," said Stasiura. "In fact, the most important thing remains: that we have a guarantee from you that if we reach an agreement, you will not break it the next day.”

“A guarantee?” Hermann repeated in astonishment. “What sort of a guarantee do you want from us?”

“This too is less frightening than it sounds. We want to set up a treasury, which would assist us in the event of something happening. So, our desire is that before we return to work, every pit owner pay ten rinskys from every barracks into the treasury, and thereafter to promise to pay one rinsky each week for every barracks they have. And that’s it.”

Hermann stood, eyes agog, unable to see anything. This last demand had struck him like a sledgehammer. Up until now, listening to the modest and minimal demands of the workers, in his heart he had begun to scoff at them for ever having begun a strike because of such petty things. But now he saw things a little more clearly. He immediately realised, what their demands were leading to.

“How can this be a guarantee to you?” he asked, pretending not to understand the whole import of the workers’ demand.

“That’s our business,” replied Stasiura. “In any case, as you can see for yourself, it’s no major guarantee, but what else can we do, such is our miserable fate that we are unable to obtain anything better.”

‘And the bastard is sneering at us!’ Hermann thought to himself, not sure what to do with these demands: whether to negotiate, or to refuse them outright. But both courses of action seemed to him equally dangerous. He quickly made up his mind.

“No, that’s not on,” he said decisively, “don’t even propose such a demand, because you’ll never get it! Think of some other guarantee!”

“Which one? This one is enough for us. If you think this is impossible, then suggest an alternative, but something which will truly satisfy us.”

"I would have thought, that our honest word would suffice."

"Yes, honest word! We know your honest words! No, honest words will be for another time, but right now please do as we ask. And you can give your honest word on top of that."

"But, my good people," Hermann tried to change their minds, "who do you think you are, putting forward such demands? Are you kings or autocrats? Don't make me laugh! You want too much and you'll get nothing. You'll become the laughing stock of Boryslav!"

"The laughing stock of Boryslav? And who comprises that Boryslav? We, sir, are Boryslav! And the time has come for us to laugh at you! Whether we achieve anything or not, time will tell, but we won't back down from our demands, no matter what!"

"As you please," said Hermann. "I'll pass on your demands to the pit owners and return with an answer. Goodbye!"

He nodded haughtily and left.

"You saw for yourself," Benedio said after the fellow had left, "that we did well by asking the Jewish pit owners to donate toward our treasury. They'll accede to all our demands now, once we put pressure on them, but they'll find this one the hardest to do. And we should learn from this, knowing that this is exactly what we need to stand firm on. No matter what, they can resist for only so long. We just need to stand our ground! They know only too well, that if they give us a tenner for each barracks, we can organize a similar strike right under their noses a week later!"

Meanwhile Hermann was making his way along Boryslav Street, deep in thought. 'Has some devil given those people advice? What has happened here? After all, if we fill their coffers with that much money, and it will amount to several thousand, then at any moment they can stage an even greater concert. And it won't be possible to fool them into abandoning this demand. The devil take them!'

After returning home, Hermann spent a long time thinking over the matter, but was unable to reach a good resolution. Noon had passed, and soon the clock struck three. The Jewish businessmen arrived in a large crowd to Hermann's house, to hear about the demands of the workers. But once they heard them, they became quite upset.

"No, we can't do that!" they exclaimed in unison. "It will destroy us, we'll be forced to go begging in the streets!"

"Well, then we have only one alternative: to wait until their resources run dry."

"We can't do that either!"

"Really, you're like small children," Hermann yelled angrily. "Don't leave me behind at home, and don't take me with you into the fields! So what do we do then? Let me know if you come up with a better idea."

A hush descended on the men.

"Maybe we could bargain with them?"

"No, that's out of the question. I've already tried, don't even go down that path."

"Hah, then the devil take them all, if that's the case!" the Jewish businessmen exclaimed.

"I agree with you," added Hermann, "but it's of little help to us."

A moment later, having remained silent during this argument, Leon sidled up to Hermann and whispered something into his ear. Hermann shuddered and gave him a look bordering on joy and derision.

"Just don't come back at me again about my liberalism of the past," he whispered, smiling. "*Not bricht Eisen*,[22] and liberalism is not iron!"

'You're all such liberals, when the price is cheap!' Hermann thought to himself, but instead replied:

....

[22] "Necessity can break iron" (German).

"Well, your advice has merit! We now have only one aim in mind and that is to break their resistance, and this is sure to cool them down somewhat. If only it will work."

"Why shouldn't it? It must work. It merely has to be done properly."

"What's this, what are you on about?" the others asked.

Leon whispered his idea into several ears, and a moment later the word had spread in a rustle throughout the room. No one dared speak out loud, even though they all knew that everyone present was from their inner circle.

"Hurrah, what a good idea!" everyone exclaimed joyously. "Now we'll show them who'll be laughing at whom! We'll take them for a ride! Like a baby kitten!"

"So everyone's agreed then?" asked Hermann, after the laughter had subsided.

"We agree, we agree, of course."

"If that's the case, then let's all set off to see them. All the money they want must be handed over today, straight away, so that they can start work tomorrow!"

The pit owners filed out of Hermann's lounge room, talking loudly among themselves. Hermann stayed behind for a moment longer, called over Mortko and discussed something with him for a long time. Mortko's face, pockmarked and ugly, lit up with a thievish smile.

"Alright, sir, I'll do this for you, but I will seek your help with that other matter. Bad news is beginning to reach me..."

"Don't worry, I'll look after it. I'll do everything in my power to help you."

After this both men joined the group of pit owners in the street outside. But their conversations were no longer so carefree and joyous. The cold wind outside had somewhat dampened their high spirits.

"Who knows, if it will work? It's a risk, a risk!" the men exchanged words.

"Yes, but what else can we do?" said Hermann. "It surely is a risk, but for our people every step is a risk, so let's take this risk right now. If it succeeds, all good and well, and if it doesn't – it still won't be the end of the world, and we'll still have them in our grasp."

The group of men proceeded slowly down the street, as if in a procession. Hermann went on ahead to Matiy's house, to be the first to bring the workers the good news. Rumours of the Jewish procession had already spread across Boryslav, and a crowd of workers was following the Jews, while another crowd was already assembling across the road from Matiy's house. But no one yet knew, what all this meant.

"Well, then?" asked Hermann, after the workers in the house assumed their usual places. "Have you reflected?"

"And what were we meant to reflect on?" replied Stasiura. "We have only one thing on our minds. Perhaps the good Lord has endowed your soul with a different mind."

"It's bad that you're so stubborn," said Hermann. "But what can be done? That's the lot of us poor Jews. When someone can't reach agreement with us through reason, they use force against us, because they know we can't resist force. We have the same thing here now. You refuse to go back on your word – and so we must concede. If the mountain won't come to the prophet, then the prophet must go to the mountain."

"So, you agree to our demands?" asked Stasiura.

"Of course, what else can we do, we accept! And you need to thank me for this, do you hear? There were those among us, who advised that we send in the gendarmes and the army, but I said: 'Take it easy there!' and in the end they saw that I was right and acquiesced to your demands."

"All of them?"

"Of course, all of them. You don't buy a horse without a tail. They are all making their way here, to hand over the money into your treasury. The only question we have now is, since we are paying into this treasury, we need to have some supervision over it as well."

"And why is that?"

"What do you mean, why? We are paying. What if someone steals the money?"

"Well, there'll be a council overseeing the money, we've still to decide on that."

"Let that be so," Hermann said good-heartedly, "we must leave it to you, because… well, because we must! But we need to know at least one thing: how much money will flow into the treasury today and where the safe box will be kept."

Stasiura wasn't sure what to answer. He got up from the table and began to exchange whispers with Sen Basarab, Matiy and Benedio. They all had no idea how to react to this brazen request from the Jewish businessmen. Sen Basarab immediately declared, that he was afraid there were ill intentions behind all this. But sincere and good-natured Benedio allayed any suspicions they might have had. In any case, the thing being requested did not seem suspicious. If the Jews had been looking for ways to avoid keeping their promises, that would be another thing, but they were keen to donate money, and there was nothing false about money: you took it into your hands, locked it away in a safe box, and it would be safe there. The brothers agreed to these arguments and decided that justice demanded that the Jews should also know, how much of their money had flowed into the treasury and where the safe box was being kept.

"Let it be as you wish," said Stasiura. "Select two men from among yourselves, who will be present at the lodgement of the dues: the money will be placed into the safe box in their presence, together with a list of donated amounts, and then the safe box will be locked, and this will take place each week, until we can come up with a better idea of how to do things."

An unconcealed ray of joy passed across Hermann's face upon hearing these words. The clamour outside the house indicated that the Jewish businessmen had arrived. They filed into the house, touching their hats and greeting the workers with a brief 'God bless.' Hermann explained to them in Yiddish the agreement that had been reached, and they quickly agreed that Hermann and Leon should represent them during the collection of dues. And so the collection began. Pryidevolia recorded how much each person was donating. The first ones to step up were the small pit owners, who paid with a sour expression on their faces, with loud sighs, some even tried to bargain, others simply gave a rinsky or two less. The wealthier pit owners uttered barbed jokes when they paid, some gave eleven or even twelve rinskys. In the end Leon gave twenty, and Hermann – fifty. The workers merely exchanged glances, and outside joyful cries were heard from time to time – the workers were celebrating their first victory in the hard battle for the improvement of their conditions. Their first and, for now, their final victory!

The payment of dues was completed, and the money counted – it amounted to just over three thousand. From the doorway, Sen Basarab announced the sum loudly for all the workers to hear. Everyone was thrilled. They were prepared to carry out Hermann and Leon in their arms – the men only smiled, their faces flushed and sweaty from the stifling air in the cramped, overcrowded hut. The money was secured in a small, iron-bound chest, which was to be kept at Matiy's house. The Jewish pit owners departed amidst widespread boisterous celebration.

"Hurrah! We've won! Hurrah!" the workers continued shouting for quite some time, walking in crowds about Boryslav. Joyous songs resounded from one end of town to the other.

"But it's off to work tomorrow," some said, sighing heavily.

"And so what! We can't sit around forever. We've celebrated for three days as if it were Easter, isn't that enough? This has been a true Resurrection!"

Bubbling over with joy, others said to Matiy and Sen: "Watch over our treasury there, guard it like the apple of your eye. Three thousand in silver, that's a pretty sum!"

"Hey, gentlemen, who wants to start work now?" the overseers yelled in the streets. "Into the pits before evening! Come on, come on!"

A crowd of workers followed them.

In Leon's factory, from the very first moment that the agreement was struck, work was in full swing. Leon was acting hastily. He wanted to finish an entire order of ceresin wax by the next day, have it packed by the end of the week, and shipped off to Russia. He was burning with impatience during the time the workers had stopped working, and Scheffel was a little worried as well. No sooner was the agreement in force, he immediately called on Benedio and the others, who had previously worked in his factory, to resume work.

Benedio returned home late at night. There was no one there. Matiy was out working as well – Hermann had personally asked him to come and work in his pit, promising him fifteen shistkas a day, and old Matiy set off gladly. The pit was deep, but the greater part of it was sealed, since there was no oil. But some 140 feet down there was gallery, and 35 feet below this ran a second gallery, and below this was a third, which was now being worked. The pit was productive, the galleries producing some ten hundredweight of wax each day – and Hermann had over eighty such pits.

Matiy returned from work late at night as well, exhausted and barely breathing, and as soon as he entered the house, he collapsed on his bed and fell asleep like a log. He hadn't even noticed that Mortko was following him on tiptoe through the streets, and after Matiy entered the house, without locking the door, the fellow snuck into the anteroom, and hid in a dark corner. After Matiy locked the door, undressed and fell asleep, Mortko quietly slunk into the room, pulled out the safe box filled with money from under the oven, placed it under his arm and crept out of the house. No one saw him, except perhaps for the pale-faced moon, which peered timidly from behind the clouds from time to time. And no one heard the scrape of the wooden lock in the door to the anteroom, the creak of the door as it opened, or Mortko's stealthy steps down the street. No one heard, except perhaps for the biting cold wind blowing from the east toward Boryslav, moaning and howling among the steep banks of the nearby river.

The following morning there was shouting and clamour in Matiy's house – the small chest, the workers' safe box, had disappeared without trace!

On the second day all the workers learned that they had laughed too soon! The Jews openly derided them, and even treated them to insults and threats. The wages were immediately cut to below what they had been before, and they laughed at the curses and threats of the deceived workers.

"That'll teach you to fight us, you stupid goys! And where's your treasury, huh? You thought we would fund it just like that? Take a break there, sneeze as much as you want! We are Boryslav, and now it's our turn to have the last laugh!"

XVIII

Van Hecht left Vienna for Galicia with a sense of foreboding. It was as if something intimated that in the unfamiliar new world he would be beset by numerous challenges and adventures, and should brace himself for his fair share of conflict and unpleasantness. However, rational thinking and a legally binding contract assured him that property and prosperity awaited him in this new land, and there was no reason to disregard this second, more pragmatic intuition.

Embarking on this lengthy and uncertain journey, he realized he could use an assistant and immediately thought of Scheffel. Where was he, what had happened to him? He rushed to the police, where he received the address of his former assistant. However, Van Hecht did not find his assistant at home, as he had left several months earlier. Where to? No one knew for sure, only that he had gone somewhere *nach Polen.*[23] Although Van Hecht was not a suspicious fellow, he couldn't help but wonder where in Poland Scheffel might have gone. 'It's a shame that he has left,' he thought, 'he could have made a good amount of money by coming along with me!'

Just before his departure from Vienna, Van Hecht received a letter from Russia from a distinguished individual of high standing – possibly a member of the Holy Synod, or

....

[23] *Nach Polen* – for Poland (German). Referring here to Galicia, located in the western (German) provinces of Austria.

someone similar. The distinguished individual inquired about the status of his project to supply ceresin wax, and why his intentions might have changed. Had he sold his patent to the Association for the Extraction of Earth Wax, which had already signed a contract with the Holy Synod concerning such a delivery, had paid a deposit of 100,000 roubles, and would soon be supplying the first shipment of 50,000 hundredweight?

A bolt from the blue would not have alarmed poor Van Hecht as much as this seemingly innocuous letter. "What's all this?" he exclaimed. "Where did this curse from heaven appear from? Who has dared, who could have done this?" As if scalded, he dashed about in every direction, not knowing what to do. He telegraphed the distinguished gentleman, kindly asking him to inform him with whom the Association for the Extraction of Earth Wax had signed the contract and from where they were expecting the shipment of ceresin. Still, the distinguished individual did not reply, possibly because he didn't know himself. Then Van Hecht rushed with the letter from the esteemed correspondent and his patent to the state prosecutor's office, notifying them of the intended fraud against him. At the prosecutor's office he was told: 'Fine, find the fraudster, and you can rest assured that he will be punished.' Bah, find the fraudster! If only he knew who it was and where to find him? As if consumed by fever, Van Hecht ran to the government clerk and obtained an order which declared that due to justifiable suspicion of fraud, all parcels of earth wax coming from Galicia to Russia and Romania were subject to detailed examination. If any ceresin wax was found, it should be detained and sent to the state prosecutor's office as material evidence. At his own expense, without waiting for the wheels of bureaucracy to turn, Van Hecht telegraphed the order to every border warehouse, adding the promise of a generous reward from himself to any official who discovered such a parcel. Having arranged all this, Van Hecht finally exhaled a sigh of relief and, quickly gathering his things, set off.

Deeply disturbed, he couldn't stop mulling over one question: who could have done this to him? It was evident that there were only two possibilities: either someone, unaware of his patent, had accidentally discovered ceresin wax independently from him; or Scheffel, who was aware of his secret, had betrayed him. And whereas the first possibility seemed less and less likely the more he thought about it, his suspicion regarding Scheffel grew stronger and seemed more plausible. Supporting his suspicion was the rumour that Scheffel had departed 'for Poland.' Van Hecht resolved that as soon as he arrived in Drohobych, he would start making discreet inquiries to see if he could learn anything about Scheffel.

Luck was indeed on Van Hecht's side. Having arrived in Drohobych, he did not find Hermann at home. There was only a message from him, requesting him to kindly make his way to the factory and inspect the ceresin wax section, built according to his plans. He went off to the factory. There he came across the building supervisor, who had just finished installing the boiler. After inspecting the ceresin wax section, Van Hecht told the building supervisor that he was completely satisfied with the work, and since the building supervisor, having completed his work, was about to return to Drohobych, Van Hecht invited him into the carriage in which he had arrived. Along the way, they began talking. The building supervisor told Van Hecht about Boryslav and the fact that disturbances had erupted there the day before, about which nothing definite was yet known. 'Probably plain old peasant disobedience, nothing more!' he added haughtily. After that the conversation turned to other Boryslav matters, the state of wax production and the wax market. From the conversation, it appeared that the building supervisor knew nothing about the new ceresin wax, and Van Hecht began to think that it was unlikely that he would learn anything of interest to him from this fellow. But the building supervisor was a talkative chap and babbled on about anything that came to mind.

"I'm telling you, all this won't last too long," he continued, "the day will come when everything will turn to ashes, and everyone will go bankrupt. The small pit owners are holding on by a thread, and all it takes is a minor incident, and they'll all be out on the streets begging. And as for the bigger pit owners, apart from Hermann Goldkrämer, of course, there isn't a single solid businessman among them. They're all swindlers and charlatans! For example, one of the wealthiest among them recently built a new factory, something very modern. He told me that it was to be a steam mill; handed me the plans, having already forgotten who drew them up. Fine, I looked at them and could see straight away that it was no mill, just a refinery. But I'm thinking: 'If you wish it to be a mill, then let it be a mill.' And he, the fool, no sooner had the foundations begun to be laid, spilled the beans, and compromised me to boot! Tell me, how can one do business with such people?"

Van Hecht was not particularly interested in the story. But, so as not to appear impolite and to somehow keep the conversation flowing, he asked the building supervisor:

"So you say it's some newfangled factory? Can you tell me what's so newfangled about it?"

"I can't tell you that, because as I said, I didn't supervise its construction. But since you are familiar with such matters, I can explain the system according to which the factory operates. Just a second, I recall now, the factory plans were drawn by a fellow named Scheffel. You must be acquainted with his system of production?"

Van Hecht jumped up from his seat, as if struck by a sudden electric current.

"Scheffel, you say?! And has the factory already been built?"

"Oh, a long time ago. They say it's working day and night."

"And what's the factory owner's name…?"

"Leon Hammerschlag."

Van Hecht entered the name into his notebook.

"Can you tell me, by any chance, and my apologies for being such a boor, where this factory is located?"

"On the outskirts of Boryslav. If you go along this road down the hill and along the river through a village called Hubychi, then before you reach Boryslav, it will be on the left by the river."

"Thank you. I'm very much interested in that new system of production. I must go there today to see this factory. Farewell!"

The coach stopped in front of the building supervisor's house, who shook Van Hecht's hand with the composure of an old elegant nobleman. Hopping out of the coach, the fellow disappeared into his house.

For a long moment, Van Hecht considered what he should do, but finally told the driver to take him to Hermann's house for lunch.

'Let it be so,' he thought to himself along the way, 'now that I have him in my hands, he won't get away from me!'

XIX

Happy, delighted, and dressed in his Sunday best, Gottlieb entered the room where Fanny was sitting. This was the first time he was seeing her since the successful resolution of the matter between his mother and her father. He walked without feeling the ground under his feet. His head was full of images of a happy future, his heart was brimming with inexpressible yearning and unquenchable passion. How would he find her? He imagined her loving smile as they met, her wonderful blush as she fell into his embrace, resting her beautiful head onto his shoulder; he would kiss, caress, and cherish her! All this stirred his imagination like rosy, fragrant lightning bolts, and he seemed to be walking on thin air, eager to see her.

But what was this? There she was, standing by the window, her back to the door, her head pressed against the windowpane. Had she not heard him enter, didn't she want to turn around. She was wearing a dress made of grey silk, which although expensive, still somehow looked very mundane; nothing indicated that she was expecting something good, joyous, festive. Quietly, he approached her, took her by the shoulder and leaned in to kiss her face, but suddenly recoiled, seeing the abundant tears flowing from her eyes and hearing her muffled words, interrupted by sobs:

"Go away!"

"What's wrong? Fanny, what's happened? Fanny, my darling, why are you crying?"

"Go away, don't talk to me!"

"What do you mean? What's all this about? Do you really hate me that much, am I so repulsive, that you don't even want to look at me, Fanny?"

And he rested his hands on her shoulders once more, squeezing them lightly. Fanny began to cry even harder, but did not turn around.

"Go away! Don't you know that we are to be parted, that we are not to be together?"

"We? Parted? What are you saying, Fanny? Are you ill, what's wrong? We are not to be together? Who dares say such things?"

"My father."

"Your father? When was this? Because the day before yesterday he gave his consent to my mother. Could he really have gone back on his word?"

Fanny turned around involuntarily, unable to understand what he was saying.

"On the contrary, Gottlieb, my father told your mother that he would not give my hand in marriage to you, that he had other plans for me."

"But my mother told me the exact opposite!"

"I'm telling you the truth, I overheard everything!"

"So my mother has lied to me?"

"Maybe she just… so that you wouldn't be upset…"

"Lord Almighty, so what you're saying is true? No, this can't be! What have I done to your father, what have you done to him, Fanny, that he wants to bury us both alive?"

"I don't know, Gottlieb!"

"But no, no, no, this can't be!" and he stamped his foot angrily. "I won't let him play with me, as if I were a kitten. I'm no baby kitten, Fanny. I'm a wolf, I know how to bite!"

He turned red as a beet, his eyes began to bulge, rage took his breath away. Fanny looked at him, as if he were a saint. He had never seemed so handsome and alluring to her as at this moment of wild fury. After a moment, Gottlieb continued to speak in a gentler tone:

"For God's sake, Fanny, tell me why your father doesn't want me to marry you?"

"I don't know," Fanny replied. "It seems he is angry at your parents about something."

"And you, Fanny, what about you?" and with wild passion he stared into her eyes. "Would you… marry someone else, if your father ordered you to?"

"Gottlieb, how can you ask me such a question? You know that I would weep my eyes dry, crying out of longing for you, and I would die soon after, but I could not go against my father's will."

"Do you love me, then?"

"Gottlieb!" and she fell into his embrace. Sorrow and their threatened parting added urgency to their caresses, tears added passion to their kisses.

"But what plans could your father have for you, Fanny?"

"As if I know! Father is a rich man, he has connections with various merchants and bankers, maybe he wants to marry me off to one of them!"

"Damned wealth!" hissed Gottlieb through his teeth.

"I would rather that my father was poor," Fanny said sorrowfully, "then he would need the favours of your father and would happily give me away in marriage to you."

Gottlieb's eyes lit up at Fanny's words. He firmly squeezed her hand, making her let out a squeal.

"Well said, Fanny," he declared, "I agree! Farewell!"

"Where are you off to?"

"Don't ask! I'll try to remove all the obstacles in the way of our happiness! You must become mine, no matter what…"

She did not hear the rest of his words. He raced out of Leon's house like a storm cloud, and poor Fanny's heart missed a beat.

"What does he intend to do?" she whispered. "He is so impulsive and passionate, he loves me so fervently and blindly, that he is ready to do something drastic. May the Lord, protect him!"

Dashing out into the street, Gottlieb paused for a moment, as if deliberating where to go. Then he shook his head and hurried off home.

"Mama!" he exclaimed, rushing into her bedroom. "Why did you deceive me?"

"How, when?"

"Why did you say that Leon promised his daughter's hand in marriage to me?"

"Why, doesn't he want to anymore?"

"Didn't he tell you to your face, that he didn't want to?"

"Yes, he did. He's a mean bastard, I told you long ago not to have anything to do with them!" Rifka spoke as if she was half asleep, as if trying to recall something from the dim past. But this only made Gottlieb lose his patience. He stamped his foot, making the windows rattle, and yelled:

"Mama! Haven't I told you, talk sense to me! I've told you that I love Leon's daughter and that I want her to become mine, so I don't want to hear anything said against her! Do you understand?"

Rifka was trembling all over from these threatening words, the meaning of which she only half understood, and peeled her eyes to his face, as if enchanted.

"Alright, my darling, alright, but what do you want from me?"

"I want Fanny to become mine."

"But what can we do, if that bastard doesn't want you to marry her."

"He must, Mama!"

"Must? How can you make him?"

"That's where I wanted to ask your advice, Mama."

"My advice? What advice can I give you? You have a much better mind than mine, seek your own advice!"

"Ah, so you get Leon all upset, you push him away, and then you tell me, 'seek your own advice'! Yes, I can see how much you love me!"

Rifka began to sob like a small child.

"My darling Gottlieb, don't say that! You can say whatever you like, just never say that I don't love you."

"How can I not, when you are completely to blame for my misfortune, and now you can't even offer me any advice on how I can disentangle myself from all of this."

Poor Rifka thrashed about, like a fish caught in a net. She so much wanted to think of a very, very wise solution for her son, but her feeble, dismembered and delusional thoughts failed to coalesce – she thought of thousands of ways out of this predicament, but was unable to utter any of them, realizing that all her advice was foolish and would come to nothing.

"Go to him, Gottlieb, go and ask him… or no, better still, get some oil workers to give him a good hiding… or no, the best thing would be to push that bastard from a bridge into the… or no… Oh, what was it that I wanted to say…?"

"You're a fool, Mama!"

Rifka was delighted with the word, because it removed from her the heavy burden of thinking.

"You see, my dear, I told you that I couldn't come up with any sensible advice, because I'm stupid, dumb as a doornail, dumber than a box of rocks! Oh, my poor stupid head!" and Rifka began to sob uncontrollably, for no apparent reason.

Suddenly she sat upright, and a lively spark glistened in her eye.

"Listen, Gottlieb, I have an idea!"

"Yes?"

"He said he had other plans for his daughter – probably wants to marry her off to some wealthy fellow."

"Sure."

"But if he were poor, he would be happy for you to marry her."

"Sure."

"Well, is it such a big deal to turn a rich man into a poor man?"

"Not really."

"I think so too. Go at night and set fire to his damned factory. All his wealth will go up in smoke in an hour – and his daughter will be yours!"

Gottlieb's eyes blazed with determination.

"Well said, Mama! My thoughts exactly. Thank you!"

And he dashed out of the room, leaving Rifka alone with her thoughts. At first, she sat limply, smiling, the strenuous thinking having left her exhausted. She was happy that she had given her son such wise advice. At that moment her face bore the expression of an idiot roaring with laughter after having beheaded his beloved pet cat. But that idiotic calm did not last long. From out of nowhere, it suddenly dawned on Rifka that she had pushed her son into a bottomless abyss. She imagined him creeping up with a burning wisp to some tall, dark building, setting fire to it and running off, being caught, getting beaten up, placed in chains, thrown into some damp underground cell, and in terrible desperation she grabbed hold of her head with both hands and, tearing out her hair, exclaimed:

"My son! My son! Come back!"

But Gottlieb was already far away.

<h1 style="text-align:center">XX</h1>

Once again, the brothers assembled for a meeting in Matiy's house. As they gathered, they looked as if they had been taken down from the cross, as if they had been battered and broken. Seated on the benches, they kept their eyes cast downward, avoiding one another's gaze, as though they held themselves responsible for the calamity that had befallen the workers' community. Benedio appeared the most shattered among them. His sunken, clouded eyes, his pallid, almost sickly-green complexion, his dejected posture, and lifeless arms hanging limply at his sides revealed the extent to which his vitality had been sapped. His once-vibrant lips seemed destined never to smile again. He appeared to be living as if on borrowed time, as if the tragedy that had befallen the workers had crushed his very spirit.

The agony he had endured these past two days was etched across his features. He had painfully extracted one golden hope after another from his heart. The initial shock, when he and Matiy discovered the unlocked door and their heartbreaking realization that the safe box was missing – that first moment had likely been the most challenging and terrifying of his life. His strength had left him, his entire body had frozen, his memory had gone blank, and he had stood like a statue, unable to move.

Gradually, his memory returned, only to intensify his anguish. What would the workers say? And the brothers? Would their first thoughts not be, that the two of them, bribed by the Jewish pit owners, had handed them the safe box? This terrible thought burned into his heart like a red-hot poker. 'And it might well be true,' a malevolent, persistent voice kept whispering in his ear, insinuating that it was inconceivable for the box to have vanished without their complicity, especially considering the absence of any signs of forced entry and that the two of them were present. The implication was clear: one of them had betrayed the cause. The very thought that Benedio, who had devoted his entire life and soul to this mission, could be implicated in its downfall, bordered on madness.

Even though Mortko had confessed, while laughing raucously, that same day to Matiy and the other workers that he had pilfered the safe box and stashed it away in a much more secure location, Benedio found no solace in this revelation. Hermann, too, had boldly asserted that anyone contemplating a complaint against him could go to hell, warning them that they would end up in jail for their illicit contributions. But these developments did nothing to alleviate Benedio's anguish. He was haunted by new distressing thoughts, exacerbating his already grievous wounds. Those who had seen him during the workers' rebellion – enthusiastic, tireless, joyful, always brimming with plans and offering counsel and encouragement to others – would scarcely recognize him now. He appeared utterly desolate and disheartened. People might have believed he was a different person or that he was severely afflicted by illness. Benedio was indeed suffering from a grave ailment, one for which in his mind there was no remedy.

The others, especially Matiy and Stasiura, had not fared much better. Only the Basarab brothers seemed unaffected, displaying something akin to secretive joy on their faces, as if their expectations had finally been realized.

"Well, brothers," said Andrus after a prolonged silence, "our beautiful dream has come to an end and we have been awakened!"

There was no reaction to his words.

"There's no use crying over spilt milk, comrades," Andrus continued, his voice growing softer. "Sorrow won't serve us any longer. What's done is done, and believe me, it was destined to be this way! I've been saying from the outset that we can't deal with these Jewish pit owners in the way we thought possible. They're not the kind of people you can reach an agreement with easily! And just as well that we have been able to demonstrate this in the past couple of days. Whether this happened today or on Thursday, their actions would have been the same. Continuing to engage with them as we have until now is pointless!"

"So what do we do then?" Benedio practically shrieked. "Do we completely surrender and rely on their mercy?"

"No, and no again!" Andrus quickly responded. "No, brothers, our struggle with the Jewish pit owners may have just begun, but it's still far from over. Until now it may have seemed like a joke, but now we're ready for a proper intense battle!"

Andrus' words carried so much power, so much passion and zeal, that everyone involuntarily turned to face him.

"Yes, now we need to show that the Jewish pit owners are needlessly making fun of us, that Boryslav is in fact us, the working people! Now that we have seen that we cannot deal with them in a friendly manner, we need to take a different approach!"

"Andrus, up until now we haven't exactly been upfront with them ourselves. They've merely paid us back an eye for an eye," said Benedio.

Those painful words bore such a sharp, profound rebuke that Sen Basarab, who was sitting in the doorway, puffing on his pipe, sprang to his feet and took several steps toward Benedio.

"Don't you go recalling the past, Benedio!" he said forcefully. "Because you know only too well that without that dirty money your virtuous struggle could not have begun."

"I'm not here to be reminding anyone of anything," replied Benedio meekly. "I am fully aware that it had to come to this. Unfortunately for us we needed to extricate ourselves from deceit with even more deceit. But, brothers, trust me, the less deceit we employ, the more assured our path will become, and the sooner we will defeat our enemies!"

"If only our enemies shared the same views and treated us justly, then indeed we could face them on equal terms, and perhaps even outdo them!" said Andrus. "But now, with truth entangled and falsehood in their grasp, I fear that until we can properly unravel the truth, falsehood may entirely suffocate it. But this is not what we came here to discuss today, brethren, but rather – where to from here? I think we have only one alternative left – but before I have my say, who knows, maybe one of you can come up with something different, or better... less harsh. Because my words will be abrasive, brethren! So, please, if anyone has anything to say, please take the floor. You, Benedio?"

"I have nothing to say. I have no idea, what to do now! Except perhaps to start from scratch."

"Yes, yes, it's a long road, and all the bridges have been burnt. No, we need to think of something different now!"

Benedio was silent. What could he say?

"What about you others?" asked Andrus. "Does anyone want the floor!"

Silence fell over the assembly. All sat with heads bowed, with a foreboding that something ominous was approaching, a looming catastrophe. At the same time they felt powerless to prevent it.

"Alright then, if no one wants to speak, let me have my say. There's only one alternative left to us – to set fire to this damned nest of snakes. That's how I see it."

Benedio flinched.

"Don't worry, the innocent will not suffer because of the guilty, because they're all guilty."

There was silence in the room. No one contradicted Andrus, although they weren't keen to support him either.

"Why are you all sitting there like stunned mullets?" Andrus exclaimed. "Don't tell me you're afraid of a good fight? Remember the intentions with which you joined the brotherhood. We still have those notched sticks – and there isn't a single pit owner in Boryslav who has no notches against him. You kept asking me when the day of reckoning would come. Today is that day, and not long ago, another new notch was added, the deepest one of them all: they deceived and plundered the entire workers' community, making it abundantly clear that they intend to keep us in perpetual servitude. What more evidence do you need? I believe that this fact alone carries more weight than all the others!"

"But what will the reckoning amount to? You'll set fire to a few houses, a few shops, and then either they'll catch you and toss you in jail, and if not, the pit owners will declare once more that it was an accident!"

"Oh, no, it won't be anything like that. If we do battle with them, then everyone will join in this time," Andrus said calmly.

"How can you manage that? Even if there's one fellow among the workers who snitches, we'll all be arrested."

"That won't happen either. Each of us who agrees to take part will select a dozen or so trusted friends. Without saying anything to them, he will instruct them to assemble at an assigned time and place. Only then will he tell them what needs to be done. And if anything should surface, then I'll take full responsibility for everything."

"But the workers are angry now, they're annoyed with the pit owners, another misfortune can easily happen, and I fear there could be bloodshed," Benedio continued, trying to come up with any, even the weakest, reason to dissuade them from this terrifying certainty.

"That's all the better for us, all the better!" Andrus exclaimed. "Now my struggle will be far more effective, after yours has gotten the people riled up. You have been a great help, for which I thank you heartily!"

"You're terrible, Andrus!" shrieked Benedio, covering his face with his hands.

"I am the person life has made me and they are my sworn enemies! Listen, Benedio, and you listen too, my brothers, to my account, so that you know, what made me set up this brotherhood to wreak vengeance on the Jewish pit owners. Our father was the wealthiest farmer in all Banya. After serfdom was abolished, my dad obtained a tavern licence from the landlord, to stop Jews opening one in the village. There wasn't much profit from the tavern, but all the same he upset the Jews from the surrounding areas, who had it out for him. My dad was an honest tavern keeper, he never watered down the vodka, and people came to him from all the nearby villages.

"That really upset the Jews. They began to cast aspersions on father. However, the landlord knew my father well and refused to believe them. Since they couldn't achieve anything this way, the Jews resorted to other methods. They persuaded some thieves – at that time there were plenty in the villages – to give father a hard time. They took a couple of horses from the stable, drained a vat of vodka, and even broke into the storehouse. But even by that means, they couldn't stop father. The thieves were caught, and those who had emptied the vat turned themselves in and had to pay compensation.

"Then the Jews decided to burn our place down. We barely managed to escape with the shirts on our backs – everything went up in flames. Our father was a strong, resilient man, and this misfortune failed to break him. He went here and there, to the landlord, to our neighbours – and they helped him to get back on his feet. Then the Jews persuaded several drunkards, former lackeys of the landlord, to kill my father. They ambushed him at night in the middle of the road, but father managed to overpower them and dragged one of them back home, barely alive. The man admitted to everything, revealed who had put them up to it, and what they had been paid. Father took the case to court, and two Jews ended up in jail.

"Then another group decided to do father in. They invited him as if to reconcile their differences and gave him something to drink. When he returned home, he collapsed into bed, as if struck down, and within a week he was dead. The landlord, who liked my father very much, organized a commission that found that father had been poisoned. But there was no one to insist on justice, and the case was hushed up. And then the Jews threatened my mother, warning her that if she opened her mouth, there would be trouble. Mother got scared and decided to keep quiet.

"But the Jews did not leave us in peace for long. It seemed they had decided to completely ruin us. Mother died during a cholera outbreak, leaving Sen and me orphaned. A Jewish man took over father's tavern licence and began to wrangle his way into our confidence. Somehow, he became our guardian and was able to use our land, while taking us under his wing. By then, there were already quite a few Jews in Banya, so it was no surprise that a Jew was taking care of Christian orphans. However, bit by bit we experienced the true nature of his 'care.' Things were fine at first, he seemed heaven-sent; he tried to please us, didn't make us work, and plied us with vodka. But as time passed, he tightened his grip, and in the end, he turned us into hired labour. We began to ask for our land back, but in the meantime, he had manipulated the nobles and local authorities so effectively that the court completely deprived us of our land.

"And yet the fellow still felt ill at ease and tried to do away with us completely. He began persuading soldiers on leave to attack us, and then he bribed the bailiff to get the recruitment committee to conscript us into the army. But we survived, served our time in the army and returned to the village.

"The Jew trembled; he knew we wouldn't forgive him the wrongs he'd done to us, so he tried to forestall us. He invited us over for dinner, and wanted to poison us, just as he'd done with our father. But this time he didn't succeed. We realized what he was up to and force-fed the fellow the food he had prepared for us. Within a week he was dead. Then we left our village and came here, and along the way swore that we would wreak vengeance on people like him until the day we died. We decided to give them back their own medicine: to turn as many people as possible against them, to create problems for them wherever we could, and to do this so discreetly that they wouldn't understand where the misfortune was coming from. Ten years have passed since then. I won't recount how we've been fulfilling our oath until now. But our greatest revenge is now approaching, and anyone who wants to be our brother, our true friend, anyone who wants to avenge both their personal and public wrongs, can join us in this endeavour!"

Andrus spoke these last words in a passionate, almost imploring tone. His account, dry and fragmented, as if reluctantly shared, but precisely matching the sombre mood of those present, made a profound impact on everyone. Pryidevolia was the first to rise from his seat and extend his hand to the Basarab brothers.

"Here is my hand," he said, "I'm with you, even if it's to the grave! I don't care what happens, I'll do whatever you ask of me. Vengeance is all I seek!"

"And will you be thumbing your nose at old man Derkach," a voice sounded from the corner of the room and Andrus' face lit up with a smile.

"We won't refuse anyone, brother, no one!" Andrus told him.

After Derkach, the other brothers raised their hands one by one, except for Matiy, Stasiura and Benedio. Andrus was pleased and made light-hearted remarks:

"Well, those two old men, they wouldn't have been of much use anyway. And you, Benedio? Still dreaming of your 'clean hands'?"

"What I dream about is my own business. But I can see that we are parting our ways today. Brothers, allow me to have my say, before we all leave."

"What's the point of listening to him!" grunted Sen Basarab and spat on the ground.

"No, go on, speak!" said Andrus, who now once more felt he was in control of these people, who were devoted to him with heart and soul. This feeling gave him confidence and determination, something which had somewhat waned during Benedio's brief leadership. "Speak, Benedio, you were an honourable brother and sincerely wished everyone well. We believe you still want the same. Since our paths are now diverging, it's not because we are wilfully turning away from your counsel, but because inevitability is pushing us toward a place where you cannot or have no wish to go."

"Thank you, Andrus, for your trust in me. What you are saying about the inevitability that supposedly compels you to commit evil – because even you acknowledge that the act you are considering is not virtuous – I somehow find hard to believe. What inevitability is there? Yes, the Jewish pit owners have deceived and stolen from us, they have bound our hands and temporarily obstructed our path to salvation. But does it necessarily imply that we must forsake our clear conscience and resort to arson? No, my brothers, we do not need to tread down that path. Let's bear this misfortune. Time will mend our wounds, soothe our rage, and eventually, we will rediscover the strength within us to resume our work and, in time, restore it to the level it once was. Once bitten, twice shy. This time we will exercise more caution.

What will you accomplish by setting fire to the pits, whom will you help?"

"We will hurt them, and that will be enough for us!" exclaimed Sen.

"Oh, it's not sufficient, brother Sen, it's not sufficient! It might be enough for you, for a handful of you, because you are committed to this cause. But what about the others? The remainder of the workers? Will their situation improve if the pit owners become impoverished? No, they will have to continue working as they did before and accept even lower wages, because when pressured, a wealthy person can afford to pay more than a poor one. And God forbid if the authorities discover your actions, then who knows how many of you will end up languishing in prison, or perhaps even worse! No, brothers, I beseech you, heed my words, forsake your heinous intentions and let's persevere in our efforts together and leave retribution to the Lord, who balances truth against deceit and rewards each according to his deeds."

"Oh, come on there, it's beginning to sound like a priest's sermon," Sen said in a derisive tone. "We can't wait for that heavenly court, about which we still know nothing. In my opinion, those with strong fists can weigh up the truth for themselves. And this is the only way to act. God helps those who help themselves!"

"Brother Benedio," Andrus said, adopting a more pacifying tone, "we can't backtrack now. Once we've swung our axe, we must follow through with the chop, even if it rebounds in our faces. If you choose not to remain part of our brotherhood, no one is making you stay. But we trust you won't betray us."

"Ah, if there is no other way," Benedio said, "then let it be so, I'll stay with you to the bitter end. Just don't expect me to go lighting fires with you. Maybe I can help with something else or provide advice – it would be a sin to run away at such a critical time to save my skin."

"I'm with you!" exclaimed Stasiura and Matiy. "In happier times we all stood shoulder to shoulder, so we must stick together now."

"Yes, brothers! Thank you for that," said Andrus, shaking each of their hands in turn. "Now I feel empowered and confident, now our adversaries can quake with fear, for the moment of retribution is nearing. Whatever seed destiny hands us, we will sow. But what comes up, and who will reap its fruits, is not our concern, for we may not live to see that day. We only need to plan in detail when and how this will take place."

All the brothers, except for Benedio, Matiy, and Stasiura, crowded around Andrus and in hushed voices began an animated discussion. Matiy sat on the hearth, absentmindedly holding his long-since extinguished pipe in his teeth. Stasiura tapped the ground with his stick, while Benedio sat on the bench, his head hung low, and after some time rose to his feet, wiped away two burning tears with his sleeve, which were on the verge of splashing from his eyes, and stepped outside to bid farewell to his golden dreams…

XXI

Mortko, Hermann's faithful lapdog, had a very troubled sleep that night. Nightmares spurred him on and gripped his heart with a sickening dread. At one point, he dreamt he was plummeting headfirst from a towering cliff and saw sharp, jagged rocks below; then again, it seemed to him that his house was ablaze, and that amid choking smoke and blinding flames, he was lying bound to the bed, a massive millstone weighing down on his chest, unable to move, or scream, or even think coherently. And when he woke in the middle of this dream, his heart pounding wildly, his body quivering and drenched in sweat, even then his head was still reeling, and every conceivable horrific thought flooded into his mind – he was incapable of escaping his own demons. For some reason, he kept recalling Ivan Pivtorak, whom he had plied with alcohol, whose money he had stolen, and whom he had dumped into a deep oil pit. The memory of it took his breath away, as if someone was gripping his throat with an icy hand and pressing their knee against his chest. Mortko's attempts at spitting and pinching himself on the calf, as he whispered Jewish incantations, were all in vain – nothing could dissipate the darkness that encroached on his heart.

Without waiting for daybreak, he leapt out of bed, dressed quickly, and dashed off to the pits. Ever since wax extraction had become the primary source of income in Boryslav, and the rapid expansion of the industry promised heightened profits, a night shift was introduced in the pits in addition to the day shift. The workers rotated: one group worked the 'day pit,' which meant twelve hours, and a second group worked through the night. The day shift had its own paymaster, and there was a separate paymaster for the night shift. Mortko was the paymaster for the day shift, but he was responsible for overseeing all the work in the pits. Being obliging and devoted to his master, from whom he received a generous salary for his efforts, he would arrive at the barracks before the start of the day shift so he could also supervise the work of the night shift as much as possible.

And especially now, his oversight was crucial. The large quantity of earth wax which Hermann had committed to deliver to the Association for the Extraction of Earth Wax, needed to be topped up that morning because by noon that day, Hermann was supposed to hand over all the wax to representatives of the Association, after which he would receive his payment from them. Hermann was not contractually obliged to deliver the wax to the processing location, regardless of where that was. Which is why Mortko had to constantly hustle, shout, and grow angry, because sometimes the workers did not follow instructions, or they dragged their feet when they needed to hurry. At times the fan would break down, or the key to the warehouse would go missing – in short, everything seemed to be conspiring against poor Mortko, who was left hoarse from shouting and soaked in sweat from running around trying to maintain order.

Finally, it appeared that everything was done: the last block of wax needed to fulfill the contract was remelted, shaped, weighed, and labelled. Three vast warehouses, the largest in all Boryslav, were piled high with wax. Two luxurious carriages rolled in from Drohobych: in one sat Hermann with Van Hecht, and in the other, the two plenipotentiaries from the Association for the Extraction of Earth Wax. Hermann sat in his carriage on a soft cushion, anxious to relinquish these enormous treasures as soon as possible, which now represented the greater part of his fortune. Since the inception of mining and extraction in Boryslav, people had never witnessed such a massive stockpile of wax in one place. The Jewish industrialists of Boryslav frequently visited these enormous warehouses and gazed enviously at the treasures stacked inside, but Hermann had never seemed satisfied with the towering pyramids of wax blocks. But now, for the first time, he surveyed them with delight, knowing that in a moment, all this mass of wax would be transformed into a bundle of banknotes, which would be safely stored away in his heavy iron Wertheim safe.

* * *

ABOUT THE AUTHOR

Ivan Franko (1856–1916) was a prominent Ukrainian poet, writer, journalist, and social activist. Born in a small village in Galicia, then part of the Austro-Hungarian Empire and now Ukraine, Franko emerged as a leading figure in Ukrainian literature and cultural revival during the late nineteenth and early twentieth centuries.

Franko's literary career began with poetry, where he expressed his deep love for his homeland and its people. His works often touched on themes of social justice and the plight of the Ukrainian peasantry. He also contributed significantly to the development of modern Ukrainian literature, introducing innovative literary forms and styles.

Beyond his literary pursuits, Franko actively engaged in political and social activism, fighting for the recognition of the Ukrainian language, culture, and education. He co-founded and edited several Ukrainian newspapers and journals, using them as platforms to promote his ideas.

Franko's contributions extended beyond literature and politics. He was an accomplished translator, bringing the works of many Western European authors to Ukrainian readers. Additionally, his plays and novels, such as *Zahar Berkut* and "Stolen Happiness" remain staples of Ukrainian literature.

ABOUT THE TRANSLATOR

Born in Melbourne, Australia in 1954 and educated as an engineer, Yuri Tkacz left the profession to translate a broad range of works from Ukrainian by such authors as Kaczurowskyj, Honchar, Dimarov, Valeriy Shevchuk, Kariuk, Vynnychenko, Yanovsky and Antonenko-Davydovych. He lived and worked in Canada in the 1980s and in Ukraine in the 1990s. His translations of *Hardly Ever Otherwise* by Matios, *Hard Times* by Vyshnia, *The Lawyer from Lychakiv Street* by Kokotiukha and *Precursor* by Vasyl Shevchuk have been published by Glagoslav Publications.

Glagoslav Publications Catalogue

- *The Time of Women* by Elena Chizhova
- *Andrei Tarkovsky: A Life on the Cross* by Lyudmila Boyadzhieva
- *Sin* by Zakhar Prilepin
- *Hardly Ever Otherwise* by Maria Matios
- *Khatyn* by Ales Adamovich
- *The Lost Button* by Irene Rozdobudko
- *Christened with Crosses* by Eduard Kochergin
- *The Vital Needs of the Dead* by Igor Sakhnovsky
- *The Sarabande of Sara's Band* by Larysa Denysenko
- *A Poet and Bin Laden* by Hamid Ismailov
- *Zo Gaat Dat in Rusland* (Dutch Edition) by Maria Konjoekova
- *Kobzar* by Taras Shevchenko
- *The Stone Bridge* by Alexander Terekhov
- *Moryak* by Lee Mandel
- *King Stakh's Wild Hunt* by Uladzimir Karatkevich
- *The Hawks of Peace* by Dmitry Rogozin
- *Harlequin's Costume* by Leonid Yuzefovich
- *Depeche Mode* by Serhii Zhadan
- *Groot Slem en Andere Verhalen* (Dutch Edition) by Leonid Andrejev
- *METRO 2033* (Dutch Edition) by Dmitry Glukhovsky
- *METRO 2034* (Dutch Edition) by Dmitry Glukhovsky
- *A Russian Story* by Eugenia Kononenko
- *Herstories, An Anthology of New Ukrainian Women Prose Writers*
- *The Battle of the Sexes Russian Style* by Nadezhda Ptushkina
- *A Book Without Photographs* by Sergey Shargunov
- *Down Among The Fishes* by Natalka Babina
- *disUNITY* by Anatoly Kudryavitsky
- *Sankya* by Zakhar Prilepin
- *Wolf Messing* by Tatiana Lungin
- *Good Stalin* by Victor Erofeyev
- *Solar Plexus* by Rustam Ibragimbekov
- *Don't Call me a Victim!* by Dina Yafasova
- *Poetin* (Dutch Edition) by Chris Hutchins and Alexander Korobko

- *A History of Belarus* by Lubov Bazan
- *Children's Fashion of the Russian Empire* by Alexander Vasiliev
- *Empire of Corruption: The Russian National Pastime* by Vladimir Soloviev
- *Heroes of the 90s: People and Money. The Modern History of Russian Capitalism* by Alexander Solovev, Vladislav Dorofeev and Valeria Bashkirova
- *Fifty Highlights from the Russian Literature* (Dutch Edition) by Maarten Tengbergen
- *Bajesvolk* (Dutch Edition) by Michail Chodorkovsky
- *Dagboek van Keizerin Alexandra* (Dutch Edition)
- *Myths about Russia* by Vladimir Medinskiy
- *Boris Yeltsin: The Decade that Shook the World* by Boris Minaev
- *A Man Of Change: A study of the political life of Boris Yeltsin*
- *Sberbank: The Rebirth of Russia's Financial Giant* by Evgeny Karasyuk
- *To Get Ukraine* by Oleksandr Shyshko
- *Asystole* by Oleg Pavlov
- *Gnedich* by Maria Rybakova
- *Marina Tsvetaeva: The Essential Poetry*
- *Multiple Personalities* by Tatyana Shcherbina
- *The Investigator* by Margarita Khemlin
- *The Exile* by Zinaida Tulub
- *Leo Tolstoy: Flight from Paradise* by Pavel Basinsky
- *Moscow in the 1930* by Natalia Gromova
- *Laurus* (Dutch edition) by Evgenij Vodolazkin
- *Prisoner* by Anna Nemzer
- *The Crime of Chernobyl: The Nuclear Goulag* by Wladimir Tchertkoff
- *Alpine Ballad* by Vasil Bykau
- *The Complete Correspondence of Hryhory Skovoroda*
- *The Tale of Aypi* by Ak Welsapar
- *Selected Poems* by Lydia Grigorieva
- *The Fantastic Worlds of Yuri Vynnychuk*
- *The Garden of Divine Songs and Collected Poetry of Hryhory Skovoroda*
- *Adventures in the Slavic Kitchen: A Book of Essays with Recipes* by Igor Klekh
- *Seven Signs of the Lion* by Michael M. Naydan

- *Forefathers' Eve* by Adam Mickiewicz
- *One-Two* by Igor Eliseev
- *Girls, be Good* by Bojan Babić
- *Time of the Octopus* by Anatoly Kucherena
- *The Grand Harmony* by Bohdan Ihor Antonych
- *The Selected Lyric Poetry Of Maksym Rylsky*
- *The Shining Light* by Galymkair Mutanov
- *The Frontier: 28 Contemporary Ukrainian Poets - An Anthology*
- *Acropolis: The Wawel Plays* by Stanisław Wyspiański
- *Contours of the City* by Attyla Mohylny
- *Conversations Before Silence: The Selected Poetry of Oles Ilchenko*
- *The Secret History of my Sojourn in Russia* by Jaroslav Hašek
- *Mirror Sand: An Anthology of Russian Short Poems*
- *Maybe We're Leaving* by Jan Balaban
- *Death of the Snake Catcher* by Ak Welsapar
- *A Brown Man in Russia* by Vijay Menon
- *Hard Times* by Ostap Vyshnia
- *The Flying Dutchman* by Anatoly Kudryavitsky
- *Nikolai Gumilev's Africa* by Nikolai Gumilev
- *Combustions* by Srđan Srdić
- *The Sonnets* by Adam Mickiewicz
- *Dramatic Works* by Zygmunt Krasiński
- *Four Plays* by Juliusz Słowacki
- *Little Zinnobers* by Elena Chizhova
- *We Are Building Capitalism! Moscow in Transition 1992-1997* by Robert Stephenson
- *The Nuremberg Trials* by Alexander Zvyagintsev
- *The Hemingway Game* by Evgeni Grishkovets
- *A Flame Out at Sea* by Dmitry Novikov
- *Jesus' Cat* by Grig
- *Want a Baby and Other Plays* by Sergei Tretyakov
- *Mikhail Bulgakov: The Life and Times* by Marietta Chudakova
- *Leonardo's Handwriting* by Dina Rubina
- *A Burglar of the Better Sort* by Tytus Czyżewski
- *The Mouseiad and other Mock Epics* by Ignacy Krasicki

- *Ravens before Noah* by Susanna Harutyunyan
- *An English Queen and Stalingrad* by Natalia Kulishenko
- *Point Zero* by Narek Malian
- *Absolute Zero* by Artem Chekh
- *Olanda* by Rafał Wojasiński
- *Robinsons* by Aram Pachyan
- *The Monastery* by Zakhar Prilepin
- *The Selected Poetry of Bohdan Rubchak: Songs of Love, Songs of Death, Songs of the Moon*
- *Mebet* by Alexander Grigorenko
- *The Orchestra* by Vladimir Gonik
- *Everyday Stories* by Mima Mihajlović
- *Slavdom* by Ľudovít Štúr
- *The Code of Civilization* by Vyacheslav Nikonov
- *Where Was the Angel Going?* by Jan Balaban
- *De Zwarte Kip* (Dutch Edition) by Antoni Pogorelski
- *Głosy / Voices* by Jan Polkowski
- *Sergei Tretyakov: A Revolutionary Writer in Stalin's Russia* by Robert Leach
- *Opstand* (Dutch Edition) by Władysław Reymont
- *Dramatic Works* by Cyprian Kamil Norwid
- *Children's First Book of Chess* by Natalie Shevando and Matthew McMillion
- *Precursor* by Vasyl Shevchuk
- *The Vow: A Requiem for the Fifties* by Jiří Kratochvil
- *De Bibliothecaris* (Dutch edition) by Mikhail Jelizarov
- *Subterranean Fire* by Natalka Bilotserkivets
- *Vladimir Vysotsky: Selected Works*
- *Behind the Silk Curtain* by Gulistan Khamzayeva
- *The Village Teacher and Other Stories* by Theodore Odrach
- *Duel* by Borys Antonenko-Davydovych
- *War Poems* by Alexander Korotko
- *Ballads and Romances* by Adam Mickiewicz
- *The Revolt of the Animals* by Wladyslaw Reymont
- *Poems about my Psychiatrist* by Andrzej Kotański
- *Someone Else's Life* by Elena Dolgopyat
- *Selected Works: Poetry, Drama, Prose* by Jan Kochanowski

- *The Riven Heart of Moscow (Sivtsev Vrazhek)* by Mikhail Osorgin
- *Bera and Cucumber* by Alexander Korotko
- *The Big Fellow* by Anastasiia Marsiz
- *Boryslav in Flames* by Ivan Franko
- *The Witch of Konotop* by Hryhoriy Kvitka-Osnovyanenko
- *De afdeling* (Dutch edition) by Aleksej Salnikov
- *The Food Block* by Alexey Ivanov
- *Ilget* by Alexander Grigorenko
- *Tefil* by Rafał Wojasiński
- *A Dream of Annapurna* by Igor Zavilinsky
- *Down and Out in Drohobych* by Ivan Franko
- The World of Koliada
- *Letter Z* by Oleksandr Sambrus
- *Liza's Waterfall: The Hidden Story of a Russian Feminist* by Pavel Basinsky
- *Biography of Sergei Prokofiev* by Igor Vishnevetsky
- *The Food Block* by Alexey Ivanov
- *A City Drawn from Memory* by Elena Chizhova
- *Guide to M. Bulgakov's The Master and Margarita* by Ksenia Atarova and Georgy Lesskis

And more forthcoming . . .